Valley of my Heart

Judy Yoder

Christian Light Publications, Inc.
Harrisonburg, Virginia 22801

VALLEY OF MY HEART

Christian Light Publications, Inc., Harrisonburg, Virginia 22801
©1999 by Christian Light Publications, Inc.
 Published 1999
Printed in the United States of America

09 08 07 06 05 04 03 02 01 00   6 5 4 3 2

Cover by David Miller

ISBN 0-87813-580-4

Dedication and Acknowledgments

I dedicate this book to my husband,
   the knight of my spiritual pilgrimage;
To my four sons,
   from which I fashioned Ellen's family,
   and who have given their support
   and the joy of their growing up years
   to my memories...
And to little Robin Marie,
   who joined our family after this manuscript
   was already completed—a delightful reminder
   of the goodness of God.

I wish to give grateful recognition to Leon Yoder. Without his review and helpful advice, I would never have been brave enough to place this effort into a publisher's hands.

A special thanks to my uncle, Robert Yoder; a true saint, who helped with the German wording and translation, and whose faithful service to God through years of suffering, has become to me, my Wilhelm Gochenour.

Contents

Publisher's Note

This historical fiction is set in the Civil War, first in Staunton, Virginia, then among the Mennonites in the Weyers Cave area. Carefully researched, it accurately portrays the suffering and testimony of Mennonites during the Civil War. Many of the events and incidents in this book are based on fact.

Although the Shull family never really existed, the times in which they lived and the struggles they faced were stark reality for many people during the Civil War. In the South it became a matter of survival, of finding enough food and clothing, and hoping foraging soldiers would not confiscate what little there was.

In addition to the turmoil of war, seekers such as David and Ellen struggled with troubling questions about patriotism and nonresistance. They, with other peace-loving Christians, suffered scornful opposition.

In that darkness of hatred and evil, Christ-like love and forgiveness shone as a powerful testimony. David and Ellen's difficult pilgrimage toward the light is typical of those caught between conflicting loyalties.

Only God knows what Christians of our time may need to face. It is our prayer that this book will strengthen faith and conviction in its readers.

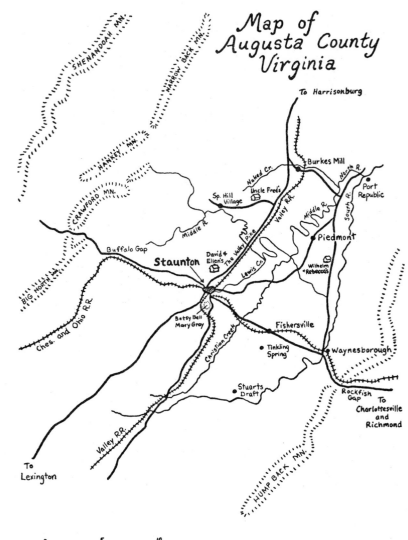

Map of Augusta County Virginia

To Harrisonburg

SHENANDOAH MTN.

NARROW BACK MTN.

HANKEY MTN.

CRAWFORD MTN.

Burkes Mill

North R.

Naked Cr.

Uncle Fred's

Sp. Hill Village

Valley R.R.

Middle R.

Middle R.

South R.

Port Republic

Buffalo Gap

BIG NORTH MTN.

David & Ellen's

The Valley Pike

Lewis Cr.

Staunton

Piedmont

Wilhelm & Rebecca's

Ches. and Ohio R.R.

Betsy Bell Mary Gray

Christian Creek

Fishersville

Waynesborough

Tinkling Spring

Stuarts Draft

Rockfish Gap

To Charlottesville and Richmond

Valley R.R.

To Lexington

HUMP BACK MTN.

0   5   10

Scale of Miles

Chapter I

"A ndy!"

Even as I screamed, I could tell he was oblivious to all but the splendor of prancing horses, the roar of the crowd, and the pounding of marching feet.

As the lead horse reared skyward, I flung myself into its path and grabbed my youngest son by the shoulders, shoving him blindly away from the flailing hooves.

On the wooden sidewalk again with one hand clutching Andy's arm, I felt the color rising in my face, conscious of many eyes upon me, and heads wagging in disapproval.

Then the parade was marching past, and all attention was focused on what was happening before us. I lifted my head, searching—searching for the only face that mattered. *Oh, David . . . David. Do you have to go?*

"Victory! Victory!" The whole town seemed to have gone wild. The cry was picked up on both sides of the street, and the chant grew and swelled around me. Bands played, handkerchiefs waved frantically from the cheering crowd; little boys raced alongside the columns of marching feet. These were local men, Staunton's own flesh and blood!

I swallowed hard. Was everyone naive? Didn't they know many of these soldiers, polished though they were, would probably never see their families again?

And then I saw him . . . how I wanted to run to him. But I dared not waver. We had already said our good-byes. He must remember me as I now tried to appear—smiling and strong, as convinced as everyone else that with men of this caliber, a speedy victory was certain.

For months trainloads of men had been arriving from all over the South. The lights from their camp-fires on the surrounding hills had given a glow to hot summer nights, and by day their white tents could be seen scattered thickly over the countryside.

Our town of Staunton had become a hub of sorts—a gathering place for men preparing for an invasion.[1] Not an invasion by a foreign nation determined to bring us to our knees, but an invasion from within, from our own countrymen.

I kept smiling blindly, waving until the last of the column had turned the corner and the spectators were surging into the street behind them. Then I turned the opposite way toward home.

A Negro pushing a cart and two men in a farm wagon approached us. I stopped to let them pass, reaching out a steadying hand as the panting boys caught up with me.

"Mommy, didn't Papa look splendid?" Davie's head, thrown back, was flushed and laughing, his dark hair damp with sweat.

Andy pulled his chubby fingers from his brother's grasp and tugged at my skirt. His eyes sparkled. "Didn't he, Mommy?"

I forced a smile. "Yes, boys, he did." I turned my eyes from their eager gaze, letting my bonnet slide back along my neck. The slight breeze felt good against my throbbing forehead.

Splendid? Yes, everyone would have pronounced him a handsome sight—crisp, new uniform, boots polished to a shine, new musket held stiffly erect as he marched past. Yet in my heart, I knew otherwise. He looked worn and grim, his eyes haggard, not the clear gray I knew.

The heat had left the hair on my forehead limp and disordered, and I shoved it roughly back. Squinting against the bright September sun, I quickened my step, pulling Andy along. I had to get away—away from the frantic, milling crowds that had thronged Staunton's dusty streets the entire afternoon. I needed to be alone.

In the growing shadows of evening, a killdeer burst into flight, skimming low overhead, its plaintive call trailing after it. The boys stopped kicking up dust to watch. "Let's catch it!" Davie bounded forward. "Look, it's landed already."

The bird poised in mid-step, its colors blending

with the shriveled grasses of the field, then a sudden thrust of wings lifted it again. It caught Davie off guard, and he craned his neck to watch it wheel gracefully against the brilliant blue overhead.

I waited a bit impatiently. The smell of fall was unmistakable, the scent of tangy goldenrod and aster came to me from the roadside along with the sharp muskiness of tangled sumac thickets. Greenbrier stems, with leaves turned red, ran helter-skelter like streaks of blood across the grass. I shuddered and began walking again. Why must I think of blood just now?

The killdeer called once more, and was joined by a second bird, then a third. The boys stood hand-in-hand, watching as the birds rose higher, higher, then dipped out of sight in the direction of the creek.

The clatter of horses' hooves pulled their attention back to the road, and they crowded together, waving, as a stream of buggies swept by. The loud laughter and talking could be heard even from a distance.

"Come, boys, the parade must be over. We need to hurry now." I took them by the hand and set a quick pace along the pike.

Ten minutes of brisk walking took us past my parents' farm and within sight of home. Set on a slight rise of ground on the west side of the thoroughfare, the small frame dwelling was dwarfed by several large maples in the front lawn. A split rail fence, aged to a mellow gray, ran up the field's edge and out of sight to the woods. The barn stood on its stone foundation to one side in the back. A small blacksmith shop had been erected next to it.

The silence of the house reached out to us,

4

causing the boys' lively chatter to falter.

"Mommy, when will Papa come home?"

"I don't know, Davie. We hope it won't be long."

We stepped onto the lean-to porch. Reaching over the jumble of garden tools, I lifted a basket off its nail. "We didn't gather the eggs before we left this morning. Would you and Andy like to do that? John and Peter will be here before long to start chores."

I followed them to the porch edge and lifted my face toward the mountains thrusting their multicolor ridges into the glow of evening. My lips trembled. What had that stubble-faced man, forced against me in the press of the crowd muttered to himself under cover of the noise and confusion?

"Food for gun powder, that's what they are!" he had spat disgustedly, tobacco juice dribbling off his chin and splattering the back of my dress.

I sank down on the step, shuddering as I pulled the folds of my skirt around to brush again at the stain. It seemed I could still feel David's last deep look . . . the quick kiss . . . the touch of his hand.

"You know I don't want to go, Ellen." His face had been hollow-eyed, his hand firm on my shoulder. "If there were any other choice, I wouldn't be doing this to you. If I return, we'll never separate again." His grip had tightened until it hurt.

He turned away, and his voice had become husky. "Maybe Bernice will be kinder to you if I'm gone. At least my going will keep from disgracing your family name."

There was a trace of bitterness in his words, and I flinched.

"I'm sorry, Ellen. I didn't mean to hurt you. I've caused you enough pain already."

5

"To break away from Mother's rigid hand? No, David, that was not pain!" I had whispered fiercely. "I found freedom. Mother is bringing pain upon herself—on herself and Father.

"We will manage—the boys and I—with the help of Providence. But you . . ." I had turned blindly to the window, my tears mirrored in the rain beating against the darkened glass.

I shook myself. Reliving the past would change nothing. I stood and moved into the house. Reaching onto a shelf, I pulled down a big wooden bowl and quickly began to mix up a batch of corncakes.

"Mother, we're home." Peter's cheerful voice came from the front door.

I turned to greet them. "Good. Is town clearing out?"

"Yes. I've never seen so many people!" Peter whistled. "Those soldiers sure looked fine." There was a trace of envy in his voice.

I turned back to the fireplace and desperately began laying strips of salt pork in the griddle. I could see reality had not yet hit Peter. The meat sizzled and popped, its edges curling from the heat.

Peter sniffed the air appreciatively. "I'm starved. Our picnic lunch disappeared hours ago." He came closer, and leaned over the table's edge. "Didn't you like the band that played? I liked the drummer boy best of all. I'm just as big as he is. Don't you think so?"

Only John stood silent. I looked up from flipping the strips of meat, and caught the look of understanding in his eyes. It reminded me so much of his father it made me catch my breath.

"Tell the little boys to come wash up. We will be

ready to eat." My voice was unsteady. I opened the bake kettle to lift out the corncakes, steaming and golden brown.

We had barely started eating when there came a tap on the door

"Good evening, Sis. May I come in?"

Davie jumped up. "It's Uncle James!"

My half-brother hesitated in the doorway. "Am I coming at a bad time?"

"Come right in and join us." I spoke brightly. "You know we're always glad to see you. Have you had supper?"

"Uh, not yet . . . But say, that was quite a show this afternoon. Our men were the most handsome bunch of soldiers I've seen so far.[2] Aren't you proud David could be part of them?"

He slapped his fist onto his open palm. "I wish I . . ." He stopped short as he caught my warning glance, and sat down, tilting the back of his chair against the wall. The boys' eyes turned expectantly toward him, waiting for him to continue.

Peter set his glass down and wiped his mouth on the back of his sleeve. "Wish what?"

James laughed self-consciously. "Oh, lots of things I suppose. Mother said . . ." He caught himself again and changed the subject. "Are your chores done yet? I'll be glad to help." He waved his hand. "But take your time. While you eat, I'll tell you what happened to some children I saw today."

He launched into a lively tale about two boys that took the chance to jump on a cavalryman's horse while he was strutting about trying to impress the ladies.

My heart was warmed by his light-hearted impulsiveness. He had been only a toddler when I left home. Now suddenly he was a young man, a handsome one at that, and already taller than I.

Never would I forget the astonishment I'd felt at his addition to our family. I had been alone so long. My older brothers were usually off at boarding school, or working alongside the slave hands in the fields. Father was a strong believer in hard work.

My real mother had died when I was ten. A thin, brown-haired woman, she had been immaculate and poised in every way. Though I admired her deeply, I had never quite felt free to approach her with trivial things.

It was strange. As particular as the folks had been about choosing the best of schooling for me and taking me to the fanciest church in town, they had never talked to me about the most important things of life—understanding myself . . . and God, the reason for living, why some people could freely accumulate possessions and enjoy the finer things of life while others were bound to serve every whim of someone said to be their master. My feelings about such things were absorbed mostly from a scattering of other people.

Mother's frequent spells of sickness and headaches sometimes kept me from seeing her for days at a time. But I hadn't really minded. I hadn't known anything different.

Others filled the role of mothering in my life. There was Tansy, the tall, sturdy cook with skin the color of sourwood honey. Another was Aunt Dorella, Father's youngest sister, who helped out at times. She was now married and lived in New York. And then there was Silas, the old black caretaker.

8

Silas . . . just the thought of him brought back a flood of memories. The summer I turned ten, Mother, Silas, and I spent the summer at Liberty Springs, the famous mineral water resort twenty miles down the Valley. Father had entrusted Silas to take her there in an effort to stabilize Mother's weakening condition. And I, timid as I was, had been sent along. "To keep her company," Father had said.

Those days were relaxing, but one morning Mother could not get out of bed without my help. From that day on, I could no longer deny what I saw happening. Her death soon afterwards was traumatic for us all. Father had been devastated.

Five long years later, he had come home from a business trip with a new bride. Bernice took over the household with an iron hand. I had never felt more alone. But then David had come and changed all that.

The boys left the house, and I stood up from the table. Lifting the teakettle off the stove, I emptied it into the dishpan, swishing the shavings of soap around to raise the suds.

There was a crash of wood being dropped into the woodbox, and I jumped. I turned with dripping hands on both hips. "James Ellis Palmer! What's the idea, scaring me so?"

He chuckled, running his fingers through his tawny brown hair. Stepping closer, he leaned onto the table, his voice low. "I had to find a chance to talk with you before the boys come in. You're not thrilled about David going off as an honorable soldier? Everyone else is excited, yet you've been fighting tears all evening."

He stopped at my look of surprise. "I could tell, Sis."

I leaned heavily against the wall. Outside the sun had slipped below the peaks, and darkness was bringing damper air. Before I could answer, there was a stomping of shoes on the steps, and I whispered hoarsely, "Later, please . . ."

John set the pail of milk on the floor and rubbed his hands together. "It's getting a little chilly outside."

The other boys came in and crowded around the fireplace, holding their hands out to the low flicker of light. James gave me a knowing look, then turned abruptly and began to stir up the fire. The flames leaped higher, playing shadows across the rough-hewn oak walls.

"Well, I suppose I should be getting on home. Mother will be worried about me."

"Stay! Stay and play us a game, Uncle James, please do." Davie pulled on the older boy's pants leg.

"No, tell story." Andy smiled confidently into his face.

James grinned, hesitating a bit. "Well . . . I guess I have time for that."

As the boys settled down in a circle on the rug, James gave me a wink. I smiled and turned again to the dishpan, carrying it to the door and giving the dirty water a fling out onto the grass. The grimness of the night reached chilly fingers under the porch roof. I shivered. Somewhere out in that darkness David was bedding down.

I latched the door carefully, then joined the others. The wicker rocking chair in the corner stood empty, and I sank into its familiar comfort.

"Mommy, James says you aren't afraid of the dark. Is that so?" Davie moved closer, propping his elbow on my knee.

I smiled. "What made him say that?"

"Because one time you rode a long trip in the dark to save his life. Did you?"

I stroked his hair absentmindedly. "It was only several miles. Haven't I ever told you that story?"

Andy climbed onto my lap, shaking his head vigorously. He patted my cheek. "Tell it, Mommy."

I began rocking back and forth. "Yes, Mother and I were very worried about little James that evening. Let's see, how old would you have been—less than three?"

Andy whirled around. "Like me?" He looked at his uncle sprawled out on the rug in disbelief.

"A little younger than you even. That seems strange, doesn't it? He would have been just a little tousle-headed fellow, for I was not quite eighteen."

"That's been sixteen years ago." Peter whistled.

"Has it been that long?" I shook my head. "Then James would have been a mere baby.

"It happened the last winter we still lived in Bridgewater. A sudden snowstorm came up, with winds so fierce drifts were piled high as the fence posts.[3] James had a bad case of whooping cough. Mother had fixed a tent over his bed and kept steaming pans of water under it all the time."

Andy tugged at my sleeve. "Why, Mommy? Was he cold?"

"No, son. His throat was swollen so tight he could

11

breathe only in little gasping breaths.

"I was scared. Father was gone for a week on business, and my older brothers had left for a horse auction the day before. We didn't expect them back for another day or more.

"The only one left who could go after the doctor was our old caretaker, Silas. Mother sent me to get him."

I glanced over at James. "You don't remember him, do you?"

He shook his head. "Silas was Tansy's pa?" He grinned. "She and I get along just fine. She says I'll be the death of her yet."

I felt amusement pushing up inside. I could well imagine! "I wish you boys could have known Silas. He had the blackest skin you ever saw, and his heart was as good as gold. Father bought him and Tansy before I was born. He had quite the story to tell about his younger days in the deep South, if you could pry it out of him.

"Father could trust him with anything. This may sound strange, but he was my closest friend after my own mother died."

I stopped rocking and looked into the fire, remembering. The night had been bitter cold and still spitting snow. When I had stepped out the front door, the wind had nearly taken my breath away. I had to hold the lantern close to keep it from blowing out.

Davie shook my arm. "Go on, Mommy."

"Well, son, when I reached his cabin, all was dark except one candle flickering in the back window. I pushed open the door and stumbled in.

"Silas was sitting in the corner by the fireplace

with his leg propped on a chunk of wood. Even through the ragged strips of cloth, I could see it was swollen. My heart just sank."

"What happened, Mommy?"

I hugged Davie's head with my hand. "I can still hear his gruff voice. 'De new horse kicked me, Miss Ellen, when I was a brushin' it dis eve-nun,' " I imitated.

Andy giggled and snuggled up tighter.

"I scolded him. 'Why didn't you call Tansy?' 'Cause she be sick wid de flu. I dasn't ax her.'

"Somehow in my urgency, I'd forgotten. I grabbed a shirt lying on the end of his bed and dipped it in the kettle of water hanging over the fire. I could hardly bring myself to wash the wound. A large knot oozed blood. Despite his dark skin, I could tell his leg was badly bruised.

"I told him, 'You need a doctor, Silas. I'm afraid the bone might be broken.'

" 'Don't reckon ders any doc-tahs out tonight, missy. I reckons I can make it till day. God bless your soul, Miss Ellen.' And he thanked me over and over.

" 'I'll send young Willie out to stay with you,' I told him desperately. Then I picked up my lantern and slipped out into the storm.

"I struggled back to the house. I was running out of time! Stumbling into the kitchen, I shook Willie, lying on a mat on the floor. He was to tend the fires through the night.

" 'Willie,' I hissed, 'you've got to help me saddle Lucy! James is sick and needs a doctor. Hurry now!'

"When he went out, I slipped into the pantry and pulled on all my brothers' wraps I could manage."

"You wore boy clothes?" Davie wrinkled his nose

13

in disbelief. John and Peter grinned.

I buried my face in Andy's hair to hide my smile. If they could have seen . . . ! I had been so large, I could hardly walk.

"I'm afraid I did. And Willie, too timid to protest, helped me mount. After I told him how to care for Silas, I was off.

"It was hard going. By the time we had gone the mile and a half to the doctor's house on the other side of town, Lucy was blowing, and I was miserably cold. The doctor's wife finally heard my knocking and opened the door just a crack. She told me the doctor had left several hours ago to help a woman having a baby.

" 'You best just come in and wait for his return, sir,' she called out through the crack.

"I wasn't about to let her see I was only a young girl, so I replied, 'I've got to find him, ma'am. The child may die before morning.'

"She directed me to a place three miles away. I have never been so cold in all my life!" I shivered, remembering.

James grinned and shook his head sorrowfully. "I didn't mean to cause you all that trouble."

I laughed. "Oh, it was worth all the trouble. No apology is needed." I leaned back against the chair and stared into the fire. "I don't remember much about the ride after that. My whole body felt numb, and I hardly knew where I was—or even why I was going.

"It had begun snowing heavily again. Finally I saw a faint light up ahead. I forced Lucy up the driveway toward a lantern bobbing from the barn to the house.

"There was a shout, and a man hurried up. 'Looking for the doctor?' My mind was too foggy to answer. My legs refused to cooperate. I slid over the side, and the man caught me before I hit the ground.

"After I was inside and thawed a bit, I was able to gasp out my message, and the doctor hurried off to try to save James' life."

Andy sat up, clenching his fists in excitement. "Did he, Mommy?"

There was a snicker of laughter, and he frowned, looking from one brother to another. "Don't laugh!" he said. Then his glance took in his uncle still chuckling on the floor beside him. He leaned back, giggling. "Sure 'nuff, he did."

I scooted him off onto the floor. "And now, it's time for little fellows to go to bed. Come, let me help you wash up. John, I'll let you fix the fire for the night."

James followed me to the door, his voice low. "I may be back."

I turned in surprise. "Why, James, whatever for?"

"Ah, come on, Sis, you're not as brave as you try to let on."

My shoulders sagged. "You're a dear brother, but I think we can manage. I have to get used to it sometime."

James thrust his hands deep into his pockets and leaned back against the door. "Don't turn me down, Ellen. There's more to your story that you didn't tell. And there are a few other things I'd like you to . . ."

He stopped in mid-sentence as Davie and Andy bounded between us.

"Mommy! Andy said he's got my rabbit skin!" Davie came after him with fists flailing.

I caught the oil lamp out of danger, and grabbed Davie's arm. "Hush, boys. James, I won't turn you out, but I'm afraid of what Mother will say. You know . . ." My voice trailed off helplessly.

He nodded and slipped out the door.

"Know what, Mommy?" Davie tugged at my skirt as he trailed along up the steps. "What were you talking about?"

I shook my head. "Something little heads need not worry about. Did Andy give your rabbit skin back?"

"I don't have it, Mommy. I hided it under Davie's pillow."

I turned the lamp low. "Good, then it's in a safe place." There was a trickle of water as I filled the wash basin and began scrubbing their faces. "Hold still, Andy. It isn't as bad as all that."

When I finished, I sat on the cot beside them, the faint smell of soap still fresh on their faces. "Ready to go to sleep?"

"No . . . I'm scared, Mommy."

"Why, you shouldn't be, Davie. John and Peter will be up in a minute."

"I wish Papa was home."

Andy's chin began to quiver.

I swallowed hard. "We must be brave for Papa. Before long we can send a letter to him. It will make him happy to hear you are acting like little men."

Davie wrapped his arms around his knees. "Why does he have to fight, Mommy? Will he kill people?"

"I . . . I hope not, son. Maybe they will get things settled, and he can come home soon." I pushed myself to my feet.

My words did not sound reassuring, even to my

16

own ears. Already the armies had clashed in a number of battles during the past months and staggered from the blows. This would be no summer picnic as some had bragged.

"You see, boys, some people feel it's wrong to have slaves. They want to force the slave holders to change their way of life."

"Is slaves bad, Mommy? You said Silas was your friend. He wasn't naughty, was he?" Davie's dark eyes were intense.

"*Having* slaves, son. Buying and selling them. Your grandfather is respectful to the few he has. They are human beings just as we are. But sad to say, many people don't treat them as humans. Any slave can be bought or sold at any time. Like . . . like Papa's horse, or your chickens. Like the rag doll I had when I was a girl. I loved it, for Tansy had made it for me. But if I decided to throw it into the stove, I could— because I owned it."

I leaned over to kiss them goodnight. "But don't think about those things. Here come the big boys.

"And look—the same moon that is shining in our window, is shining down on Papa, wherever he is."

The gentle chime striking the hour startled me as I sank back into the rocking chair. Picking up a sock from the darning basket, I focused my eyes on the small wooden clock on the mantelpiece. With its glass face ringed with a miniature oval of pink painted roses, it was one of my most prized possessions.

It had been a wedding gift from David's parents in

17

Pennsylvania. It seemed only yesterday we had boarded the train after the wedding ceremony. I could still remember the rumbling wheels; the wailing whistle as the train headed north; the cold dampness of the cars; the large fluffy snowflakes that swept by the dingy, dust-streaked windows; and above all, the nervous fluttering in my stomach that grew as the snorting engine ate up the miles. What would David's folks think of this southern girl he had taken as his bride?

It had been after midnight when we finally reached the station where we were to board the next train. The other passengers had scattered to find lodging. Unable to afford a hotel, we had huddled together, shivering on one of the backless benches, our small bit of luggage heaped beside us. Despite my embarrassment, David had insisted on draping his overcoat over us both.

Through the small open window, the bespeckled ticket agent glanced up from his work, eyeing us curiously. He pushed his cap back on his head and clucked disapprovingly. "No night to be out in this kind of weather."

"No, sir. This is quite a storm."

The bald-headed man grunted. "Don't 'sir' me. Just call me Hiram. Everyone does. Yep, this one will beat 'em all, I'd say. Hotel's right up the street. Why don't you turn in? Next train's not due till six."

"I guess we'll just wait. We don't want to take the chance of missing it."

"Well, if ya do, you can just catch the next one at ten."

"Thanks just the same. I guess we'll wait. My parents are expecting me . . . us," David quickly corrected himself.

The old man gazed in my direction. "I take it this is your wife. Must be so new you ain't got used to it yet. How long?"

The color heightened in David's face. "Three days."

"Three days! Land sakes! Well, come along. We can't let a new bride freeze."

He fixed us up in the ticket cubicle, stoking up the fire and banking it for the few hours till morning. "I reckon that will hold you till the next feller comes. You best be up and perk'en by then, or you'll scare him out of a day's growth of whiskers."

I smiled, now, recalling it all. There had been no need to worry. David's people had taken me in, accepting me as having a rightful place in the Shull family. That had been a precious two weeks, an oasis of spring in the middle of winter.

Muffled footsteps coming across the porch brought me up short. "Yes?"

"It's me. You're still up?"

"Yes, come in, James. I thought maybe you had changed your mind."

"No, I just had to wait until it was more convenient."

"Mother said you could come?"

"Mother said I most certainly did *not* need to come, and I went upstairs as a very obedient son."

"Why . . . !"

"Don't fuss, Ellen. I merely waited till their bedroom light went out, then slipped out the window." He grinned down at my look of dismay. "Yes, I know Mother would be angry if she knew, but she doesn't need to find out. This isn't the first time I've needed to alter her instructions a little. I'm not a little boy anymore, you know."

I focused on the sock I held in my lap. If only he knew how aware I had become of that tonight.

James squirmed uncomfortably in the silence. "Don't make me feel too guilty, Sis. You know Mother is impossible to please. I'm pretty sure you were getting close to a confession of your own in your story tonight." He sprawled out on the rug, and after casting a glance my way, turned and stared into the fire.

When I spoke, my voice was troubled. "I wish it wouldn't have needed to have been that way, James. Sometimes I've wondered if I did the right thing, yet when I weigh the happiness David and I have had, against the alternative . . ."

I shook my head. "We've made special effort to be respectful to her and Father. Perhaps it helped a little. Father invited us to move into the tenant house two years ago. But Mother seems as cold as ever."

James shifted position. "Aw, don't let her get under your skin. She's always been this way, I suppose, and always will be."

"Somehow you've been able to take it, James. It hasn't caused you to lose your cheerfulness."

"I just let her fuss, then go on the way I think I should." He gave a careless toss of his head.

I picked up my needle once more. "I'm not sure I agree with you. But I must admit, you're not struggling with bitterness as I did. David helped me so much. Mother gave me such a tongue lashing the night we moved down, I thought I couldn't bear it. I guess I had been expecting too much. After my sobs subsided, David said something I've never forgotten.

" 'Ellen, we can't change your mother, but we can

keep ourselves from becoming like her. Don't let it make you bitter. It will sap all the joy out of living and make you her slave. Just let it go, and pity her. You'll find freedom to live above it.' "

"David rescued you the night of your ride, didn't he?"

I nodded. "He had come down from Pennsylvania the summer before to work on his Uncle Fred's farm."

"What did Mother say about it?"

"I didn't tell her much. David brought me home the next morning in his uncle's sleigh. I had doctor's orders to rest for a week.

"It wasn't long afterwards that Mother persuaded Father to move here. She said a bigger town like Staunton would be a better place for his business."

James stretched his legs and rolled over onto his back. "So, how did you ever get together again?"

I smiled. "We happened to meet at the vegetable display table at the fair the next summer."

"Why was Mother so set against him?"

I felt a wave of shame. "He wasn't good enough for me. He had no means to flaunt about."

"Why, Ellen, David isn't low class!"

"Of course not. His family is very respectable and hard-working, worthy in every way. But bloodlines and ancestry mean everything to Mother, and when we went ahead with plans to get married, she sent me away with nothing but the clothes on my back."

He sat up sharply. "How could she do that? Why didn't Father stand up against it?"

"Oh, I knew beforehand what would happen. She had held that over my head for a long time. And I don't believe Father really believed I would go against her when she was that angry. I had been a rather shy, even timid, girl up to that time. It was a bitter blow to her pride when I chose to leave.

"Things were pretty tight for us, but Uncle Freds let us stay there in a one-room shanty until we could afford something better. David gradually took over the blacksmith shop and worked it up to a profitable business. From then on, things got a little easier.

"And then Father offered us this house to live in, in trade for shoeing his horses and doing business here."

James began pacing back and forth. "Father respects him—I can tell that. I've never seen a man who can calm a horse like he can. Too bad he couldn't take Ginger along to war with him. He could have joined the cavalry. That's what I'm going to do."

I stood up, my scissors making a clatter as they hit the floor. "Don't you go making such plans, James Ellis Palmer! I hope they get this war settled and everyone home before Christmas."

James stretched and made his way to the door. "Then you and I have different opinions on that. I better head home again. Good night, Sis."

I watched the door close behind him. Had I said too much? I dropped my unfinished mending back into the basket and climbed the stairs, slipping through the little boys' room to the tiny cubicle David had partitioned off for us along the east side of the eaves. I dropped onto the bed, too tired to undress.

I lay in the dark a long time. Thinking of David, I smiled. He always teased me about falling into his arms that snowy night.

So much of that night always remained hazy to

me. I could faintly remember David almost carrying me to the house and laying me on the settee inside the front door. Then he had called the maid, "Help this fellow out of his wraps. I'm afraid his feet are frostbitten."

The next hour had been filled with the anguish of thawing out—ebbing in and out of consciousness, waves of pain washing over me, and trying to muffle my groans in the cushions. Then the dark form of the doctor leaned over me, the faint smell of ether clinging to his rumpled clothes. I had gasped out my message. His gruff voice mingled bewilderingly with the sharp new cry of a baby from somewhere.

I remembered David's incredulous voice from the next room, "But no girl could have ridden that far in the storm tonight."

ᘓᕹ Chapter II ᕹᘓ

S leep was a long time coming. I fitfully tossed and turned. My mind could not stop going over every detail leading to David's decision to join the army. He had had many animated discussions with those bringing their horses to be shod. No one seemed able to understand David's reluctance to become a part of the political fervor and the righteous indignation.

It was strange. People at first had felt strongly the country should stay united. Only last November a county meeting had been called to discuss what course was necessary "for the preservation of the Union in this present alarming condition of our country."[1]

David had gone. He came home and reported a committee of thirteen had been appointed to form a set of resolutions for the people of Augusta to follow.

A week later, a second meeting was so packed he had not been able to get inside. I had waited anxiously at home, and it was late before he returned. I could tell it had gone well by the spring in his step as he entered the door.

"Good news, Ellen. We're sticking with the Union by an overwhelming vote."

I felt a great weight lift from my shoulders. "What did they say?"

He ran his hand through his hair and laughed. "In their words, 'We are to bend all our energies to keep Virginia to her moorings as a flag ship of the Union.' And not only that . . ." He reached for my hand. "We're to do all we can to encourage other states to stay in the Union."

I let my head drop against his shoulder. "Oh, David! I was so worried."

He squeezed my hand, then stepped back and looked me in the face. "So was I. But this looks better than I had hoped. They did say they were against any measure of force by the government to stop any state from experimenting with secession if they so desired. And although they hold to peace, they will reserve the right to determine on which side we should fight, if it should come to that."

"Let us pray it doesn't."

His face turned grim. "I couldn't agree more."

All that winter people were tense and watching. When the President appointed a day of fasting on January 4, 1861, the whole town took it seriously. Stores were closed and churches open for preaching and earnest prayer.

The rest of the winter, the State Convention worked to prevent disunion, hoping to bridge the widening gap between the two factions. At the same time, unrest continued to ferment and grow in the far southern states.

After President Lincoln's inauguration, people were repulsed by his proclamation asking for seventy thousand troops to put down the "Rebellion." Our own state, which had worked so hard for peace, was asked to furnish her quota.

From that moment, the tide of feeling turned. Virginia would side with secession, and soon, anything less than full-fledged support for the southern cause was disdained.

The first shots, fired at Fort Sumter, South Carolina, seemed unreal and far away, but by midsummer the war had come to Virginia.

But David was not a Virginian. We owned no slaves and felt no need to defend slavery. How could David fight against his own people? We were caught in a grip of circumstances tightening like a noose around us.

We discussed all the angles of what we saw happening before us, going over and over the same arguments until I wasn't sure if there was a right or wrong to anything any more.

Everyone had been ecstatic when the telegraph chattered out news of the first victory. By mere chance, I was in town with David that day. What stood out in my memory was not the jubilation, but the shrieks of the widowed bakery lady who stepped out into the street as we walked by. She had also received a telegram.

"Nay, not my lad, my only laddie!" Overcome with grief, she threw her apron over her head, and before anyone could reach her, collapsed in a heap in the dust. Her wails followed us down the street, haunting me for days afterwards.

The South had won the battle. It was loudly acclaimed an omen of God's blessing. But victory still spelled death. Where was the glory in taking away the joy in a woman's life?

In the last hours before dawn, sleep finally came. When I awoke, I crept out of bed and hobbled, shivering, to the window. The gray mists of morning shrouded the surrounding hills and muffled the outline of woods at the back side of the pasture.

Shaken down by the wind during the night, maple leaves were strewn across the lane and onto the roof of the now empty blacksmith shop. I drew a sharp breath, then turned to slip into a fresh dress. After tiptoeing down the darkened stairs, I knelt to rake out the ashes from the hearth.

I jumped as I felt a hand on my shoulder. "John! I didn't hear you coming."

"I heard you stirring around."

I held the kindling against the wood until it lit, then straightened. "You must have been sleeping with one ear open." I smiled at him. "Let me go with you to do the milking.

"What time is it?"

"Six o'clock. The sun rises in half an hour." I reached for my shawl.

He opened his mouth, then thought better of it and nodded, opening the door.

The dew was heavy on the grass and soaked through my shoes, numbing my feet. I lifted my skirts against its dragging weight.

"They're moving already this morning."

"Moving what?"

"The wagons. Out on the pike." John pointed to the dim outline of objects coming toward us through the mist.

"What a long line of them!" I strained my eyes to see. "Do you suppose they could be hauling supplies for the men who left yesterday?"

"It's hard to say. Someone in town told me they take loads out to army camps one hundred miles around. Railroad cars were being unloaded yesterday even during the parade. I saw it."[2]

I frowned. "It seems impossible. There are thousands of men in camps in the area! The fall rains will soon make the roads almost impassable, and in winter . . ." I fingered the latch on the barn gate.

"What if they come after our wagon?"

"If they come after it, we have no choice."

"It seems every wagon in town is being pressed into use. If they are grabbing wagons, they'll soon be taking horses. The government's supply of horses can't keep up with all of this."

He cleared his throat. "What about Ginger, Mother?"

I paused in the doorway of the barn and looked at

him, biting my finger. The sun's disk was just appearing above the mountains, coating the thread-like clouds along the sky's rim with gauzy streaks of pink, lavender, and rose. The shrill whistle of the Valley Express rang out clearly in the morning air. The train's black smoke boiled up on the far side of town.

"Your father and I talked about that possibility. We feel she is safe, at least for the time being. Later . . . ?" I pinched my lips together.

He glanced sideways at me as if hesitant to continue. "I heard rumors yesterday that the Fifty-second is being sent to hold off the enemy coming south through the Alleghenies. One of the porters at the railroad station said four hundred of General Lee's men were killed in battles near Huntersville."

Fear forced out the words before I could stop them. "That's near Greenbrier River, isn't it. That's part of those counties that just pulled aside?"

"I think so. They call it Kanawha."

"That would mean your father would be in enemy territory from the start."

John didn't look my way. He was shading his eyes toward the west. "It may just be a rumor. I've heard other stories that weren't true."

I found no solace in his reply.

For the first month, though there was news of other detachments, we heard nothing of David, rumor or otherwise. Only a week after the Fifty-second pulled out, the remnants of the Twentieth Regiment arrived back in Staunton with only a third of its men. Of the ninety who left in high spirits only a few months before, more than half were dead from combat or disease. Many others had been taken prisoner.

The few fortunate ones who returned were almost all admitted to the hospital on the other side of town. For many of them, war had become a slow and inglorious death.

Reality was also setting in on the home front, even for the most patriotic. Food prices had begun to climb. Salt especially jumped to ten dollars, and now eighteen dollars a sack. There was talk of rationing food—when any was available.

James told us the new Confederate money was rapidly losing value. David had expected as much before he left.

"A house divided against itself cannot hope to stand, Ellen. Someday it must go down in defeat, and when it does, its money will be useless."

"Oh, David! You feel you will be fighting a losing battle?"

He had stared moodily out the window. "Yes, Ellen, I guess that's how I feel. It doesn't make sense, does it?"

"Then it is all useless . . . senseless!" I had flung the words out angrily. David had pressed his finger over my lips.

"You are forgetting the boys are already asleep."

I pulled his hand aside, my voice dropping to an angry whisper, "Is that actually how it is? Thousands of dollars, destruction of life and limb, hours and days of sacrifice away from family, all wasted? All to no purpose?" I burst into tears, and nothing he could say would comfort me.

One morning in November I had the boys draw an extra tub of water, and after breakfast I filled the pot over the fireplace to heat for washing clothes.

Moist clouds of steam rose as John and I carried the tub to the back porch. Since the clothes were already on piles, I dumped in the closest one and rapidly stirred the sudsy collection.

When I stopped to rest, the sun's rays were beginning to reach under the slanting roof. The air gradually warmed until it was almost pleasant. I took a deep breath, enjoying the smell of fallen leaves and the whiff of smoke in the air.

As I watched, John led Ginger, saddled and bridled, out of the barn. Lifting a hand in my direction, he mounted easily, and rode off toward the back field. David had given him the responsibility of giving her daily exercise, and I was glad to see he took it seriously.

I thought back to the first time we saw Ginger. It had been a fall morning such as this when a stranger had driven in with a gleaming green sulky. His two chestnut mares had shone like satin in the sun. The boys had clustered around, in awe of the man's drooping mustache and long blacksnake whip.

Ginger's bucking had nearly broken the carriage shafts. It had taken both men to unhitch her and lead her to the shoeing block. Her eyes rolled, and she was snorting wildly. The man's efforts to quiet her with repeated lashes of his whip only increased her terror. I could see the anger mounting in David's eyes.

He placed a hand on the man's elbow, and his voice had been quiet but cold. "I'd be obliged if you'd step around the corner until I finish with that loose shoe. And then I have an offer to make you on this mare."

The man had looked at David so angrily I had been afraid he would bring the whip down on David's back. "Worthless bit of mincemeat! Paid a pretty price for her. Had nothing but trouble ever since." He turned away, still fuming. But when he left an hour later, Ginger was ours.

I had swallowed hard when David said how much he paid for her. "She'll prove her worth," he had reassured me, "just wait and see. All she needs is someone who can show her who is boss—in the right way."

And his prediction had proven true, for Ginger had become a horse even I could handle.

I stood now, watching until John had ridden out of sight. Sounds of boyish laughter came faintly from inside the barn. Davie's head appeared in the doorway.

"Are you finished helping Peter clean out the stalls?" I asked.

"Yes."

"Then you may play awhile." I waited until his head disappeared, then bent back over my laundry, rubbing each garment vigorously over the washboard before plunging it into the rinse water.

When my basket was full, I carried it to the side

yard. Picking out a pair of trousers, I gave it a hard flap. Then I spread it over the fence and reached for another.

Suddenly I stopped, listening hard. There were rapid hoofbeats coming our way. Hurrying to where I could see, I stepped out into the lane just as Father's carriage came at a fast trot around the side of the house.

"Whoa. Whoa there!"

"Father! What's wrong?" Self-consciously I tucked back the strands of dark hair slipping out from my bun and put one hand to the near horse's sweating neck.

Father jumped down and paced back and forth. "I'm on my way home for lunch and thought I should stop by. There's been trouble . . ."

My heart leaped. "David! It's something about David."

"No . . . no, I've heard nothing of him." He stopped pacing and pulled at his beard. "Were any of the boys in town this morning? The Virginia Hotel stables just burned down, and most of the horses were lost.[3] I had eight of mine there to rent. Didn't save a one."

I stepped back. "Oh, Father, I am so sorry. No, we've been here all morning."

"I just wondered. I thought I saw David's mare tied up at the stables when I stopped by."

I remembered the stormy night lightning struck our barn in Bridgewater. I had been only five, but I never forgot huddling under the cedar tree, watching my father and older brothers work frantically to lead the horses to safety. I could still see the terrified horses, their rolling eyes, neighing screams, and lathered sides.

34

I fumbled with the carriage straps. "How dreadful, Father. How could it have started?"

He shook his head. "There is some talk that one of the stable hands was smoking. No smokers are supposed to be working there. Two workers got badly burned trying to rescue the animals.

"But it's hard to tell. There's certainly no way of proving anything. But that's a lot of money lost. Eight of mine—gone in a day." He turned on his heel and climbed into the carriage. He reached for the reins then stopped suddenly. "Oh, yes, I was at the post office and happened to see this." He tossed a letter into my hands.

I held it against me. "Thank you, Father! I'm very sorry about the horses." I stepped back out of the way. "You were considerate to stop by."

I watched him urge the horses into a trot as the buggy started out the lane. There was a tug on my skirt, and Davie dropped panting onto the stone step by the well. "What did Grandfather want?"

Andy reached for the bucket to get a drink. "Here, let me help you." I held the dripping bucket down where he could reach it. "Grandfather says there's been a fire in town, at the stables where some of his renting horses were."

I sat down and pulled them close. "He lost eight horses, a dreadful loss." I drew the letter out of my pocket and held it up. "But look what he brought us."

"A letter from Papa? Open it, Mommy! Open it quick."

I laughed shakily. "I don't know whether to laugh or cry. Let's go inside."

When John returned I read it out loud.

My dear family,

I haven't had a spare moment to start a letter until today. We have been pushing hard, marching northwest for over a week through very mountainous country. My legs are trying to adjust to walking fifteen or more miles a day. We have wagons to help haul luggage, for which I am thankful.

How is my family? I miss you so very much, but I'm sure you are standing by Mother and doing your best.

Davie, you would enjoy trying out your fishing pole. These mountain streams are full of trout, and the men have been catching some. They are delicious.

The Alleghenies are beautiful. Leaves are dropping fast. I got to try out my gun on a flock of wild turkeys. This is very untamed country with mountain ridges as far as you can see in all directions. Makes you feel miles from anywhere.

Saturday we got caught in a terrible storm. All of us were soaked to the skin, so we stopped to set up camp on a level field close to an old deserted mill. In the middle of the night, the river overflowed the dam and washed a lot of bedding and equipment away. Everything we could grab had to be moved to the nearest hillside, and there we huddled together till morning. I wished for home that night.

We expect a call any day to move further north. I suppose before long we will

have to set up winter camp somewhere.
I don't know when I can write again.

        All my love to each of you,
        Papa

The room was silent for a few moments, then Peter spoke. "Fifteen miles a day! Where did he say he is now?"

"He didn't actually say, only west of here, somewhere in the Alleghenies. It sounds like they were still on the move."[4] I reached for the envelope. Some faint writing on the inside flap caught my eye. *A message for me*, I thought and dropped it quickly into my pocket.

The boys spent the afternoon replenishing the woodpile. I could hear the sharp crack of the ax as I took the dry clothes off the fence, holding them close and breathing deeply. They smelled of fresh air and sunshine.

Supper came and went, and the boys were already upstairs when there came a quiet tapping on the door. I hurried to unbolt it.

"Why, James! I wondered if it might be you. Come in."

He nodded briefly, slipping inside to look around before he whispered, "The boys in bed?"

"Yes. Why?"

"Then I'll go ahead and warn you, Ellen. I heard Mother talking to Father this evening. She is very upset about losing the horses and is trying to convince Father to go along with a scheme of hers."

"Whatever could that be?"

"I didn't hear her say, but I can guess. She wants Father to buy Ginger."

"Buy Ginger? They know we wouldn't want to get rid of her. Are good horses that hard to come by?"

"It seems so." He knelt to stir up the dying bed of coals. "You ought to keep a better lock on those barn doors, Ellen."

"James Palmer! You aren't saying Mother would steal?"

"Perhaps not steal." He glanced up quickly. "Mother has her ways. If David isn't here to shoe horses for Father, and you aren't paying rent . . ."

"Father assured me we did not have to worry about that."

"Father did, but that wasn't Mother's word." James stood up. "But aside from that, there are plenty of less scrupulous people who would be glad to make off with a horse of that quality. I don't have any answers. I just wanted you to know the facts." He placed his hand on the door, and his lips tightened. "Did you hear the results of last Thursday's election?"

"I'm afraid I . . ."

He brushed my words aside. "There was no opposition to President Jefferson Davis, which didn't surprise us. The folks are pleased. But their man was not chosen for Congress, and you can imagine how they feel about *that*. Baldwin was not their choice at all.[5]

"And to top it all, with the horses killed in the fire . . . Well, I'm just saying, keep your ears open. You know how Mother is when she gets 'peppered up' as Tansy would say."

His eyes held mine for a long moment, then he turned away. "I must hurry back before they find out I'm gone."

After James disappeared, I bolted the door again and stood by the fireplace deep in thought. At length

I stirred the embers, waiting till the flames leaped up and cast shadows across the scarred wooden floor.

I reached for David's letter once more. Slipping a hairpin from my hair, I carefully slit the envelope along the seams. The writing was faint and cramped, and I knelt down, holding it to the light to read.

My dearest wife,

I couldn't send this off without a little note for you alone. I long to ask you how things are going, and I would need to look deep into your eyes to know whether you spoke the truth. Letters can be deceiving.

Are your mother and father looking out for you since I'm gone, or do they turn their backs as usual? I am torn between two: hoping that my absence will prompt a little more kindness on their part; and jealousy, that they may be doing a better job of caring for you than I ever could!

It makes a strange combination of emotions for a man to harbor. There is no one here really to talk to. My tent mates and I are getting to be pretty good friends. We have interesting conversations, some fairly serious ones, but I don't feel free to talk about things of home as some of them do.

Many of them are itching for action. I hope we can bypass it till spring.

Take care, my dearest. Surely God will see fit for us to be together again. We have so much living yet to do.

Your husband,
David

I slumped back against the wall and stared unseeing into the darkness. *Oh, David . . . David! How I need you! There are so many decisions to make. The future looks so long and dark.*

How long I sat there I do not know. I must have dozed off, for when I awoke, the fire had gone out, and there was a hint of dawn along the horizon.

❧ Chapter III ❧

With James' forewarning, Bernice's visit several days later did not come completely by surprise. The rigid figure beside the slouch-shouldered Negro driver sent tremors through my body. I set the egg basket heavily on the ground, waiting.

It was still early morning, and the heavy frost from the night before had not yet melted. By the pump, the hackberry tree with its warty bark was completely bare now, its leaves lying crumpled and brown where they had fallen.

As the open buggy came to a stop, the gray mare tossed her head and snorted, her breath cloudy puffs in the chilly air.

I reached out a hand in greeting. "Good morning, Mother . . . and Willie." My voice sounded too loud in my own ears. Clearing my throat, I began again, this time more softly. "Won't you come in where it is warm? Patty can be taken to the barn for a spell."

"I don't aim to stay long." Bernice adjusted her shawl and brushed impatiently at her lap robe. "I am correct that David left his mare here when he enlisted?" Her eyes were as cold as the sky overhead.

I nodded but said nothing.

She leaned over the buggy's side. "Good. Then you'll be glad to hear what I have to offer." She stopped as the boys came racing out of the barn to stand beside me.

Nodding curtly in their direction, she turned back again. "Bernard and I have talked it over. We are willing to pay a good price for Ginger. You need the money, and we need a mare. We could even throw in enough cornmeal to last you quite a while. You aren't earning anything right now, you know."

She waited for a reply, her mouth working. When none came, she hurried on. "You just say when it will suit, and Bernard and I will come down and settle it business fashion."

She leaned back with a satisfied air and surveyed us with upraised eyebrows. Willie rolled his eyes in embarrassment, giving his hemp-rope belt a hitch.

The boys turned to me with wide eyes. "What does she mean? She doesn't mean Ginger, does she? Ginger's not for sale!"

My look silenced the words they were begging to say. Steeling myself against the sensation in my stomach, I laid one hand on the buggy step. "Mother,

I appreciate your offer, but Ginger is not for sale, not at any price."

Mother sat up straighter, adjusting her gray felt hat indignantly. The feather sewed in its band quivered. Her blue eyes snapped. "I'm afraid you don't understand. We need good mares to restart our horse stock, and the way food prices are, you'll need all the income you can get. I don't believe you have much choice in the matter."

"Perhaps I don't, but surely David does. I will write him immediately. I will do nothing without his consent."

"You're a fool, Ellen! You'll change your mind before long!"

The crack of her pearl-handled whip startled the mare. She took off with a jerk, and Willie, caught off-guard, grabbed for the reins, losing his hat in the process. Mother reached up quickly to steady her own, and the buggy rattled rapidly out the lane.

Suddenly I felt weak and leaned against the rock wall enclosing the well.

"Mommy, you won't let her get Ginger, will you? Why did she act so mad at us?"

Andy studied my face, and his little hand crept into mine. "Grandma wasn't bery nice!"

I gave his hand a squeeze and picked up the egg basket once more. "Come, let's go inside. We can talk about this where it's warm."

The crisp beauty of the morning had faded, and a low layer of dark clouds was sliding past the mountain range to the west. If only David were here, he would know how to be respectful, yet firm enough that his answer would be accepted.

Once inside, I gathered the boys around me.

"Maybe it's time I explained a few things to you. You know your grandparents don't care to spend much time with us. In the two years we have been here Grandmother has only been in our home once, and that was right after we moved."

"Why, Mommy?" Andy leaned against my shoulder, his face puzzled. "Don't they like us?"

I sighed and pulled him onto my lap. How do you explain the cruelties of life to a small child?

"I'm not sure I can say it so you can understand. It's . . . it's not that we've done anything we should be ashamed of. We have always tried to treat my parents with kindness and respect. It's just that . . . well, Grandmother has always been this way. She's used to having things happen the way she thinks best and gets very upset if they don't."

"But, Mommy," Davie frowned, "why do they think they need Ginger?"

"Because the fire has left your grandfather without many mares. He needs more to raise horses to sell. Ginger is a good horse, and he knows it."

I bent over my paper, turning the oil lamp low as I poised the pen over the paper.

Dear David,

We need you tonight. Something has happened, and I wish you could be in charge again. We both know that is impossible, so I will try to be brave. Right now I'm not brave—only lonely and afraid.

A fire in the Virginia Hotel Stables killed most of the horses. Father lost eight. Understandably, he is pretty upset. So is Mother.

Mother came by today with an offer for Ginger to help replace some of the lost mares. She was very upset when I told her Ginger was not for sale at any price.

We need your advice. I told her we will do nothing until we hear from you. I'm not sure what she will scheme up. I have never known her to wait for what she wants.

We are making out well except for missing you dreadfully. The boys are being little men.

I stand by the window every night and look out over the mountains that tower between us, praying you will always remember my love for you.

As always,
Your wife, Ellen

I creased the letter carefully and laid it on the shelf, then impulsively grabbed my shawl and stepped into the night. I made my way to the barn, huddling in the doorway until I heard the reassuring rhythm of Ginger's breathing. James had said there were people who would steal her if they could. Would they? Even a stabled animal?

If only we could lock her up, hide her—do *something*. Hide her? My mind scoured the farm, then stopped guiltily. How dare I think so. It seemed so contriving, so like the ways of my stepmother.

Yet I couldn't sit back and do nothing, could I? A howl set my heart beating faster. A wolf? I wished my imagination was less vivid. I turned back to the house, shivering.

I lay awake for long hours, wrestling between conscience and desperation. Suddenly the large outcropping of granite boulders beyond the creek came to my mind.

David had been out hunting one evening several winters ago when a sudden snowstorm had forced him to look for cover. He had ended up spending the whole night in this shelter. We had taken picnics there several times since.

It was a place hidden by dense mountain laurel thickets and close-growing pine and hemlock. The rock formed an overhang high enough for a person to stand in if they bent over, and an adjoining boulder partially shielded the entrance.

Could we move Ginger there? It would place her out of Mother's reach. And if she did come by, I could honestly say the barn was empty. But would she be satisfied with such an answer? It was unlikely, but what else could I do?

The next several days I found myself looking out the windows, starting at every sound. Finally I could stand it no longer. I approached John with my idea. Then without explaining anything to the younger boys, I announced a picnic.

The next morning I gathered a few things together, and we started out. When we reached the creek, I let them run on ahead. Lifting my woolen skirts with one hand, I balanced the milk pail in the other and stepped over a rotten log onto a long flat boulder jutting into the creek. The water that sucked at my shoes was dark and cold. I stopped for a moment to watch it swirling, finding passages between the jumbled rocks at my feet.

Downstream, the creek widened into a quiet pool, reflecting the bare, spreading branches of elm and maple.

There was a slurping sound as John caught up with me and let Ginger stop for a drink. I glanced quickly over my shoulder toward the barn. Ginger lifted her head, water dripping from her nostrils, and snorted.

John tugged at the reins. "Come along, girl. We've got to get you settled. Have the boys gone ahead?"

I jerked my eyes away. "They thought they couldn't wait on you. Was there anyone around when you left?"

The mare stopped to bite off a clump of grass, and John jiggled again at her picket line. "Not that I could see. I circled around a different way, then came along the fence row toward the creek."

Up ahead came the sounds of boyish laughter. Ginger's ears pricked forward. She took another step forward and gave a low whinny, tossing her head restlessly.

"Whoa, girl, whoa . . . we're almost there." John ran a gentle hand down her neck. "Why don't you go ahead, Mother, and tell the boys to keep it quiet. I think she's nervous."

I nodded and slipped past him. The pines grew thickly here, and the land's gradual slope grew into a series of low-lying hills that repeated themselves until they rose to meet the leafless mountains in the distance. But a tightness in my chest kept me from feeling my usual thrill from an outing like this.

It had been spring when we had last been here. The trillium and bloodroot had been in bloom. But that had been for a far nobler reason. I gulped. *May God forgive me if I'm doing wrong!* I thought. A bramble slapped against my coat. I pulled roughly away.

The last time we were here, David had drawn a small book of poetry from his pocket and placed it in my hands. "A gift for your birthday," he had smiled at my look of delight. We had sat together as I browsed through its cream-colored pages.

I had read through it often, and even now certain phrases came easily to mind. *Is it not better, then, to be alone and love earth only for its earthly sake . . .*[1]

Right now I almost agreed with Lord Byron, the English poet. Nature is usually a neutral friend who allows you to live at peace with yourself. Fear of people often causes us to do things we wouldn't do otherwise.

The boys were already scrambling up onto the rocks and dangling their feet over the edge.

"Look, Mommy. My whistle! It's still where I left it." Davie picked up the piece of hickory he had worked on last spring.

"Where's John?"

"He will be here shortly." I shoved the milk pail up to them, then carefully picked my way along a wide crack to the top of the boulder. It was comfortable here. A thick stand of trees sheltered us from the wind, and the rocks which had soaked up the pale sunshine warmed the place where we sat.

"I'm hungry. When can we eat?" Andy's eyes were pleading.

I felt pain at his eagerness. There wasn't much to

48

offer them. A hard-boiled egg for each from the precious supply in the wire basket, bread toasted by the fireplace this morning, and a few apples from the nearly empty barrel in the corner of the attic. The Macintosh tree had dropped several bushels this fall, and we had all worked together to carefully peel and slice them to dry.

Hidden in the bottom of the lunch pail was my special surprise, a bit of paper with four pieces of horehound candy that Mrs. Waller, the mercantile lady, had given.

"We ain't got much," her husband had said, pointing to the dusty shelves. "And it's terr-bul high, what we got. This here war's gonna make it right hard for awhile." He had worked up a mouthful of tobacco juice and skillfully spit in the direction of the potbellied stove in the corner. The juice hissed and sizzled as it boiled away.

" 'Pears to me, we ought to just run them Yankees back where they come from. We didn' ask 'em to come down here a'telling us what to do. I was born a free man, and I aim to stay that'a way." He snapped his suspenders and turned to spit once more.

I hadn't answered him, but as I stepped out the door, Mrs. Waller slipped the bit of paper into my hand. "It's fer the children. I've been saving it back fer special. I don't mind the scrimp'en and making do—it's the children suff'rin that I can't abide. Tears a body up." And her work-worn fingers had dabbed at the dampness in her eyes.

There was a snapping in the underbrush. Andy's eyes grew large as he crawled closer, fumbling to grasp my coat. "What is it?"

Peter jumped up to see. "It's John. Why, he has Ginger! You said he had chores to finish. Whatever does . . ." The puzzled frown that crossed his face turned to a look of understanding. "We're going to hide her."

"Hide her? Why?" Davie tried to peer over his brother's shoulder.

"To keep her safe, of course. Don't you remember how Grandmother wants to get her?" explained Peter.

I took a breath and stood, brushing the leaves from my coat. "More than that, Peter. James says there are lots of horses being taken from people in this community. More than I realized. Ginger isn't safe in the barn anymore."

"Who's taking horses?"

"The army, to pull wagons and cannons." Peter dusted his hands against his pants leg. "Droves of horses are getting worn out. They need new ones. I heard Uncle James tell Mother so."

There was a swaying in the branches, then John's head appeared, followed by the bulk of Ginger's body. She jerked her head sideways, and her nostrils flared, as she took in her new surroundings.

We sat there, watching her as we ate our lunch. Afterwards we scraped out and enlarged a little basin for Ginger to drink from where water seeped down the front of the overhanging rock. The boys scattered to pull dried grass from the meadow to lay thickly across the dirt floor.

For awhile we stood huddled around the entrance, watching Ginger explore every cranny and corner, snuffing at its strangeness and lipping up wisps of the dry grass from around her feet. John fastened the picket rope around a large root, then stepped back.

"Well, children, we must go," I forced out the words reluctantly. Hazy clouds were pushing their way across the sun. The wind had picked up, swaying the hemlock boughs above our heads.

"I don't wanna leave her here all by herselfs." Tears welled up in Andy's eyes.

"I know, son." I hugged his shivering body against me. "I hope it won't be long. And please don't talk about it to anyone. It will be better for us all if you just truthfully say she is not with us right now." I lifted the branches for them to go ahead. Ginger's whinny followed us, and Peter pivoted to look back. "Are you sure she'll be okay?"

"We'll check on her every day. And maybe this war will soon be over. Let us pray that it is."

On the outside of the thicket, we stopped to catch our breath. "Wouldn't it be wonderful if everyone had the kind of love old Silas had?" I reached to help Andy over a stump. "Then there wouldn't even be a need for war, or hiding, or holding people at bay. That man loved everyone alike, and he worshiped a God who did the same.

"I've never forgotten the day a neighbor man treated him roughly. I cried. But he just set me on his knee and said, 'Now, Miss Ellen, I's don' need to fight fo mysef. I's got somebody inside dat's much stronger den dey. I jus' luv folks and let Him worry 'bout de punish'en. Maybe dey see ole Silas act'en calm an co'lected, maybe dat get undah deh skin.' "

I felt a sense of wonder, thinking back. How far

out of reach that kind of love seemed to be! What had he found that no one else had? I wished I could bring him back to ask. It would be so good to sit on his knee again like a child. Funny. I felt the need for it now more than in any of my younger years.

As we stepped out into the field's edge, Davie looked up and held out his hand. "Mommy, look . . . !"

A faint scattering of white whirled high above the treetops and floated down toward us.

"Snow? Why, the ground isn't even frozen yet!"

We were hurrying now. The flakes soon filled the air, blowing before the wind, sifting their way inside collars, stiffening fingers and ears.

A letter was wedged into the crack of the door when we stumbled onto the porch. I held it against my cheek as we pushed inside and crowded around the fireplace. The boys were panting.

"Whew! I never knew a storm to come up so soon!" John beat his hands together and grabbed up the tongs to rake the small pieces of half-burned wood together and lay another piece on top. The fire spit and popped.

My fingers fumbled, and I lit the lamp, turning up the wick as the flame brightened. Eagerly I held the letter close to the light. Words were scrawled on the outside. I read them out loud.

Wherever could you be? Dropped this off on the way home from town. Sorry I missed you. James

Quickly I opened the letter. The boys crowded around eagerly.

Dear family,

A long time has passed since I've had a chance to send word your way. I have only heard from you once—soon after we arrived in camp. Is everything going well? I am lonely tonight.

We have been very busy for several weeks building log cabins for the winter ahead. It looks like this will be home for us till spring.

I finished chinking our cabin yesterday, and it's none too soon. The wind is whistling over this mountaintop like greased lightning, and a cabin furnishes a lot more protection than a tent.

There are over sixty cabins being built with about twelve men in each. We have finally been issued blankets. Their delivery was delayed because our wagons were being used to haul logs for building.

John and Peter, I would enjoy showing you around here. Mountains rise in all directions. We have cut off, I would guess, over one hundred acres of timber to set up camp, and we can see across to Cheat Mountain where the Yankees' tents are perched. Sometimes I can see their fires at night. It's probably seventeen miles away. I wish to God we would never get any closer.

I drew an overcoat yesterday, and by

using my blanket and two coats, I can sleep fairly well.

The food isn't bad. We get plenty of meat, also sugar, rice, and coffee. There isn't much flour, but we can make out.

Many are sick with typhoid, mumps, and measles, and everyone has their rounds with dysentery. We call it the "Virginia quick-step." It's nothing pleasant.

Standing guard duty is hard on a man. I have a bad cold but am hoping to avoid the other illnesses. A vain hope, I imagine.[2]

I helped build a hospital, and it is already full. We have also been digging trenches around the camp. It is hard work with all the rain and snow.

Colonel Baldwin has been sick with typhoid for some time. When his wife came to see him last week, she had us load him up to take along back home. It pulled mighty hard to see that wagon heading out your way and not be allowed to go along.

The new leader, Colonel Johnson, feels it important to hold our position. If my being here will help keep the Yankees from advancing any closer to my dear family, then all these months away from home will seem more worthwhile. I wish something could be worked out and peace made before spring.

Boys, take care of Mother and please write when you can. The fire is getting

low, and I'm pretty stiff with cold. Guess
I'll crawl in.

Miss you as much as ever,
David

PS: One of the boys in our cabin, with the
memorable name of Newton Hogshead,
died of fever two days ago. Poor boy—
he was only seventeen.

A week went by. Ginger seemed to be adjusting
well to her strange surroundings and I found myself
beginning to relax. Then one morning John brought
bad news. I looked up sharply as he told what he had
found.

"Are you sure?"

John shrugged off his coat and held his hands out
to the blaze in the fireplace. "I'm afraid so. Her foot
is swollen and hot to the touch. I first noticed it when
she wouldn't put her weight on it."

I took a deep breath. "Have you tried to do
anything with it?"

He nodded. "I cleaned it out, but she flinches
terribly."

I closed my eyes and pressed my hands to my
forehead. It had been almost two weeks since we
moved Ginger to her hiding place. It was taking
more work than I had thought to keep her fed, and
now this.

I turned toward the window. "There's no medi-
cine left in Papa's shop, is there?"

He shook his head.

I sighed. "Let me think a bit, son. She needs help, I feel sure. But I'm not sure what to do."

John picked up the ax leaning against the corner. "The other boys are still out pulling grass. I'm going to the woodpile."

I watched his arms swing and heard the ax strike, but my mind was elsewhere. Who could we trust for help? Should I have let Mother go ahead with her plans? But how could I without David's knowledge?

I reached for the broom and began sweeping vigorously. Then I remembered Jimmy Two Lane, the old Indian half-breed who lived in a mud-daubed shack almost a mile off the pike. Could we dare ask him for help?

He was a mysterious man, an eccentric everyone recognized but knew little about. It was undisputed that he had ways with animals beyond any white man.

His thin gray hair hung long over his lanky shoulders; and his back, held erect despite a crippled hip, made him appear taller than his short frame. Jimmy Two Lane lived in a house perched against the base of a ridge with a sharp drop-off not ten feet in front of it. No one could approach without being seen for 250 yards, either on the trail running along the ledge, or by the path picking its way down the ridge's steep slope.

No one knew how he came to make his home in our area. Some said he had come up from the Smokies when the Cherokees were forced from their homes almost thirty years before. Other people were sure he was the son of a white trader who had lived with an Indian girl, leaving her when Jimmy was born. David had pointed him out to me once, walking beside the pike with a sack thrown over his shoulder.

Jimmy Two Lane was our only chance. Would David think it was worth the risk? He had sought the old man's help a couple times, the first time for a gelding with a split hoof.

"You *aren't* going there, are you, David?" I had shrunk back in dismay at the thought.

"I'm willing to take the chance." He stopped by the door. "I can't afford to lose this client's mount if there's any way to save it. This is none other than Attorney William Baylor's personal carriage horse. I can't shoe the horse until I get that swelling cleared up. And nothing I've tried seems to help."

I had said no more, but waited anxiously for him to return. And when he did, he wouldn't satisfy my curiosity except to say, "You wouldn't care to go there, Ellen. One visit is enough for me. I'm positive I saw two women there, carrying around his children. I've heard tales. It's a strange place."

David had held out a dirty, canvas-wrapped bit of pottery. "I had to pay dearly, but I aim to try the foul-smelling stuff."

"Pay dearly, David?"

"Yes. He didn't care to do business with me until I showed him the newest, polished bridle I had."

It had rankled at the time not to be told more. The gelding soon recovered and was returned to its owner, and the incident was forgotten. Not every case had been so phenomenally successful, but for serious problems, David always used Jimmy Two Lane's paste.

I called John inside. "I've thought of something, but I'm not sure if it's wise."

He listened carefully as I shared my idea, then nodded slowly. "It may work. It's surely worth a try."

"You think she needs help today?"

He ran his fingers through his hair. "The sooner the better. But I can go by myself. From what you've told me, I'm sure I could find the place. If I tell him I'm blacksmith Shull's son, he will surely feel friendly toward me."

My brow furrowed. "No, I think I should go along. We'll leave the boys at the rock with Ginger while we go. If we hurry, we ought to be back within an hour, surely not more than that."

Midday found the two of us going at a fast walk single file up the creek, further than I had ever been before. We came to where it divided into several branches, and the water flow dwindled down to a width easy to step across. From there we headed due west. There was no time for talk. I had to lengthen my steps to keep up with John. A gully ran off to our left, broadening to a width of ten feet or more. It lay thick with broken branches and brambles. Somewhere below I could hear the trickle of water. A log bridge crossed it. I paused to gather courage.

John glanced back. "Here, Mother, reach for my hand."

I took a deep breath and started out at almost a crouch, not daring to look down till I felt his hand firm on my arm. He led me to a rock and sat down beside me till I caught my breath and the dizziness passed.

"I'm sorry. I didn't realize it would affect you so."

I managed a smile. "I never learned to enjoy heights, son. I'll be all right now. Let's go before I lose my courage."

Looking back, I wondered that I had gone as far as I had. When the dark-skinned man stepped suddenly into our path from some hidden crevice, only John's hand tightening on my shoulder kept me from sinking to my knees.

The narrow face with protruding cheekbones was creased by wind and weather, and the thin lips showed no emotion. His eyes, set deep in their sockets, were penetrating, measuring us as though determining our reason for being there. I found myself unable to pull my eyes away.

His gaze did not waver through John's repeated explanations of who we were, what we needed, and our promise of payment for his services. I was caught off guard by the swiftness of his answer.

"I be there. At sundown." He held up one hand and turned on his heel to leave.

John reached after him. "Wait, I haven't told you where to find the mare."

He turned for a brief moment, his gray hair blowing back from his face. His hand swept along the horizon in one quick motion. "I know."

"But, sir . . ."

This time he did not turn back.

Ginger responded well to Jimmy Two Lane's treatment. After the first visit, the only certain proof we had of his repeated visits was Ginger's continued improvement. In their daily trips with grass and whatever else they could find for feed, the boys never caught sight of the man, and the forest floor around the thicket was always carefully brushed smooth.

As the last days of November came and went, the streets of town became crowded again with soldiers. James burst through the door one evening just as we sat down around the supper table.

"Oh, I'm sorry I scared you. I should have knocked." He was breathing hard, his face red from running.

I pulled another chair close. "You know you are family, James. I suppose you haven't eaten. Come and share our humble fare."

He looked at the bowl of stewed turnips and the two small pie tins on the table. "Ah . . . no thanks. What kind of pie? Chicken?"

"No." I smiled. "This is Peter's doings. He took along a handful of corn and some string when they went to cut firewood today. He figured out some kind of trap and caught two partridges. I laid the meat across the crust and filled it with lots of good gravy. Try some."

He shook his head. "It smells delicious but . . . no thanks. I'm not hungry." He turned and busied himself stirring up the fire. "I'm on my way home from the first day on my job."

"Job! How did this come about? I'm surprised . . ."

"Surprised that the folks would let me go?" He grinned, sitting back on his heels and watching us. Then his face sobered. "I know it's getting hard for you, Ellen. It's even getting a little tight for us, food-wise. They reluctantly agreed to let me work several days a week, helping rebuild the burned stables. I can trade in part of my hours for food."

Then his face brightened. "Town sure was full

today. The streets were lousy with men. There's talk that a large part of the army stationed in the mountains is moving out."

He leaned over the table. "I met a fellow who says he just came in from Greenbrier Mountain."

The effect was electrical. I started, my serving spoon held aloft. "Greenbrier? That's where David is. Is . . . is . . ."

James grinned. "I was standing on a street corner gawking, I guess, when an older fellow came up behind me. He looked hungry as all get out. That's how all of them looked—dirty, and hungry enough to eat their hats. They were knocking on doors up and down the street, asking for bread."

"You didn't see David?"

He shook his head. "From what I could learn, none of the Fifty-second were among them. But this fellow said he was stationed only eight miles away from Camp Baldwin."

"Where were all the soldiers going?" John's quiet voice broke the silence.

"I heard snatches they are being moved either east to Manassas or north to Winchester. They all seemed worn out. Mountain life must be pretty hard . . ." He stopped. "Sorry, Sis, I shouldn't be saying this."

"That's okay, James. David wrote of the hardships of camp in his letters. And I've been told the hospital in town is overflowing with the sick—750 already squeezed in. They are preparing for 500 more, and that was several weeks ago."

Davie stopped eating, lowering his spoon to his plate. I quickly changed the subject. "But let's talk about pleasant things. Are things going well on the farm?"

James straightened up in his chair. "This should make you happy. Father bought two mares yesterday."

I felt as though a big weight had lifted from my shoulders.

John leaned forward. "From where?"

"The stationmaster out near Betsy Bell has some good horses. He was willing to sell a couple. He said it's better to be sure and get his money than lose horses to the armed men who pass his place."

James caught the look of relief on the boys' faces. "By the way, where is Ginger? I noticed she was gone already the last time I was here."

They glanced quickly at each other but said nothing. I answered simply, "She's safe." Then turning back to the table I added, "Betsy Bell . . . That reminds me of the legend about those two hills. You can see them from the railroad station, just south of town."

"I think I've heard some story about how those hills got their names. But I never knew if it was true." James reached for a scrap of meat pie, winking at Andy as he did so.

"They say it's so." I stood to clear the table. "Mother let me go with some of my girlfriends once to pick huckleberries there. About halfway up the slope, in a clump of pine and cedar, we found a tiny graveyard enclosed by a low rock wall. In the center was one gravestone, leaning sideways. When we pushed back the briar and honeysuckle, we found traces of two names carved there—Betsy Bell and Mary Gray. The story is that over two hundred years ago, these two Scottish girls went out to live on those round hills to escape the plague."

"What'sa plague?" Andy's eyes were wide.

62

"A terrible sickness, son, that can be passed from one person to the next. They lived there for some time, even had their food brought to them. But eventually they caught the sickness from a young man who brought them their food. They both died and were buried there, with only a heap of stones left to remember them by. Many years later, a landowner cleared away the rubble and built the little cemetery we had found."

"Do you think it's still there?" James stood up and stretched.

I gave the table another swipe with my rag. "I have no idea. Perhaps."

When James pulled on his coat to leave, I followed him to the door. "Thank you for checking on us. How is it going at home? I haven't seen the folks for a while."

"They're okay. Say, was Mother upset when she found out Ginger was gone. Where'd you put her?"

"I'd rather not say. Not that I don't trust you, but so that Mother can know you had nothing to do with it. And please forgive me if it seemed underhanded. It's a great relief to hear they found another mare."

"I suppose Ginger's safe for now—at least if none of those roaming bandits find her. Just don't think Mother has forgotten what you've done. She doesn't easily overlook resistance to what she wants."

After the other boys had gone up to bed, John came and stood behind me as I banked the fire for the night.

"I didn't get to tell you yet, but I saw him today."

I straightened up. "Jimmy Two Lane?"

He nodded. "He says she should be moved. 'This too close to creek. Someone find.' "

"Move her! Where?"

"He offered to take her to his home."

"Oh, John." The thought filled me with apprehension. "Did you tell him how pleased we were with her progress?"

"Yes. That seemed to please him. I offered him money for what he's done, but he just grunted and shook his head. I thought he hadn't understood, but then he actually smiled and asked if we had a good saddle. I told him Papa had one hanging in the barn.

" 'I take that,' he grunted, and he was satisfied."

"I'm afraid, son. I'm not sure I really trust him. Not that far anyway? Do you think we can?"

John watched the flames dying into coals. "For some reason, Mother, I feel we can."

"I don't know what to say," I said. "Let me think it over till morning."

All the next day my thoughts centered around Ginger. I needed to make a decision. Today.

We had not gotten a letter from David for so long, and I didn't want to go ahead on my own. I found myself letting the brown beans cook dry, then adding so much salt to the corncake batter that I had to dump it out and start over again.

But all that was forgotten when the older boys came in from cutting firewood. Even as they

64

stepped in the door I could tell something was wrong—terribly wrong. Peter was struggling to control himself, and John's face was white and silent.

"Boys, what's the matter?"

There was no answer. I gave Peter a shake. "What happened? John, are you hurt?"

He shook his head.

"Peter, are you?"

"It's . . . it's Ginger."

"Ginger?"

"She's gone!"

"Gone? No!"

Angry tears came to Peter's eyes. "We couldn't stop them. Those men wouldn't even listen to us! We begged, but they wouldn't listen."

I slumped into a chair. "Start from the beginning."

John swallowed hard. "We were coming back across the creek when we heard them. There were five of them—watering their horses. We hid behind some bushes."

He blinked rapidly. "Their uniforms were dirty, and they had guns strapped to their sides. Just as they were leaving, one of their horses nickered. Ginger must have heard, because she answered. It didn't take them long to find her."

Peter stared at me, the wild look in his eyes frightening me with its intensity. "We ran out and begged them not to, but they waved their guns at us and told us to *get*." His hands trembled.

I felt as if I were choking. I forced myself to take several deep breaths before answering. Even so, I couldn't hold back the tears that trickled down my cheeks. "I suppose they are taking all the horses they can get their hands on. All we can do is tell Papa we did the best we could." I stood up, pulling Peter against me. I could feel him shivering through his coat. "Papa won't blame either of you. You couldn't have tried harder."

I turned suddenly away. All those night hours of worrying and planning, the time spent gathering feed, all the effort put into her infected foot—all snatched away by strangers in a moment. If we had only agreed to let Mother take her. I felt sick on my stomach. My appetite for supper had disappeared.

↬ Chapter IV ↫

Dear David,

I will sit close to the fire and write this tonight to save lamp oil. The boys are asleep, and James just left. He stops by frequently and helps out with heavy work when he can. He has a regular job now, helping rebuild the hotel stables.

Oh, David, I can hardly bring myself to write this to you. Ginger has been taken. Strangers discovered her hiding place by the creek and made off with her this evening about nightfall. The boys are heartbroken. I am torn to pieces inside, for I feel responsible for her being there. Did I do the right thing by trying to keep her for you?

If I would have allowed my folks to take her, at least we would have had hopes for her safety. But how could I have known this would happen?

If I was unwise, please forgive me this wrong. All I can say is I tried to please you.

I need you to tell me again there is Someone who hears when we pray; who knows how terrible war is and cares for those who suffer. My whole world has fallen apart.

This evening I dug out your Bible and paged through looking for—I don't know what—but something that would help.

I'm afraid to think too much for fear I will miss you too dearly, yet I can't turn off my mind, especially at night when I am alone.

Are you reading from your Testament? Somehow I couldn't bring myself to hold your Bible before this. It was too painful.

Oh, David, the first verse that met my eyes was this, "Oh that I had wings like a dove! for then would I fly away, and be at rest." Yes, I long for wings to catch us all up to soar above the hatred and blood-shed, and find a place of rest.

I caught the sob rising in my throat. David had said for me to be honest, and yet . . . I shouldn't be sharing my doubts like this. Perhaps I should copy it over. I sat for a time, my head buried in my hands. At last I picked up my pen once more.

James handed me an envelope from Mother before he left. She has become very involved in a women's civic group in town which makes things to send to men in the winter camps.

I haven't gone at all before this. Her note sounded just like herself:

"You are expected to attend the Auxiliary Women's Gathering, Tues. afternoon (Dec. 12), at the Stuart residence (164 Church St.) to help knit stockings for the brave and loyal men of the Confederacy. The meeting begins at 2:00."

I fear to go, yet I am more afraid not to. I must be brave for your sake.

I whisper your name every night, praying Providence will grant you protection.

Your wife,
Ellen

A lethargy seemed to have taken hold of us, and it took all my effort during the next days to appear cheerful. With Ginger taken, it was as if the one tie to David's existence had been snatched from our grasp. The boys would not talk about her in their conversations with me or each other.

The morning of the auxiliary meeting I awoke with a feeling of dread. I resisted the urge to pull the covers up over my head and forced my feet onto the floor, dressing quickly.

The face that stared back at me in the mirror startled me with its grimness. I pinned back my hair with flying fingers, all the while trying to muster up a warm expression. My efforts were so absurd I turned away in defeat. Forced smiles could not mask the dark circles under my eyes, or the emptiness I felt inside. But surely there were others who had also felt the blows of misfortune. Surely not all could put on a pretense of gaiety.

When it was time to leave, I wrapped my coat around me and picked up my basket of knitting supplies.

"Are you boys ready?" I stepped into their bedroom. Davie was pulling on his shoes. John glanced up from helping Andy button his coat.

"Just about."

"I don't think I'll ever be ready." Peter's voice was gruff, and he turned away from my surprised look.

"What's wrong, son?"

"Oh, nothing . . . It's just that . . ."

"That what?" I ran my eyes down over his clothes. Even though I had carefully washed and pressed his only set of going-away clothes, no amount of care could hide the shiny knees and the too-short sleeves. "You don't look any worse than the rest of us." I tried to smile.

"It's not these." He looked embarrassed. "It's my coat." He jerked it off the hook and turned his back to shrug it on.

It wasn't like him to complain. I pulled him around and then I saw. A big rip ran down the coat's front from the shoulder to the pocket. The padded lining gapped widely.

"Peter! When did this happen?"

He glanced at John guiltily. "Yesterday, while we were cutting firewood."

John spoke quickly. "It was my fault, Mother. We were sawing down an oak close to the creek, and halfway down it got caught in the limbs of a dead tree. Peter was trying to get the pinched saw out. All of a sudden the dead tree broke and the oak fell . . ."

He swallowed hard. "The . . . the butt of the oak side-swiped Peter and knocked him over. If he had been over another step . . ." He swallowed again. "We didn't want to tell you."

We all stood transfixed. Finally I found my voice. "Are you sure you're all right? Here, let me take a look."

My fingers fumbled as I opened his shirt buttons. Quickly I scanned his chest. A faint bruise and a red scrape showed up clearly on his white skin. I prodded gently along his ribs.

"Nothing broken?"

He flinched slightly as my fingers pressed against the scrape. "No. It's just sore, that's all. And it was my fault, not John's. I knew better than to be that close."

I dropped weakly onto the bed, and though he was obviously safe, I burst into tears.

The boys stood awkwardly around the bed, not knowing what to say. Finally John patted me on the shoulder, pulling his handkerchief out of his pocket and pushing it into my hands. I took it gratefully and dabbed at my eyes.

Andy leaned onto my lap, peering anxiously into my face. "It's a' wight, Mommy. I'm wight here."

I laughed shakily, hugging him to me. "I'm sorry, boys. I don't know what came over me." I stood up, reaching my arms to encircle them all. "All's well that

ends well, as they say. We still have each other—
that's the wonderful part. That's worth more than all
the coats in the world."

I thought of how I had fingered David's Bible
only a few moments before, wondering whether any
comfort could be found in its pages. Religion had
always been a private thing for my husband, not
something to flaunt openly.

I felt reassured. I smiled as I continued confidently, "I was beginning to doubt whether there really was a God who looks down and 'luvs all His
blessed chilluns' as old Silas used to say. But after
this, how could I question it?"

The road was a maze of icy ruts, and I picked my
way carefully. The boys, tiring of my slow pace, had
already gone ahead.

I had hurriedly pinned together Peter's coat as
best I could, but it was impossible to hide the jagged
edges. What a sight he would make going into the
meeting! But for some reason, I didn't care.
Compared to losing a son, a torn coat, or even a
stolen horse for that matter, seemed trivial.

With a shout, James came trotting out of his lane.
The boys gave an answering whoop and broke into a
run. All four of them gathered around him talking
excitedly.

"These fellows say you all are headed into town."
James flashed a wide smile as I caught up, looking
me up and down approvingly. "Dressed up fine,
aren't you? And such shoes for this kind of walking!"

I blushed, glancing down at the patent leather slippers peeping from beneath my skirts. Desperate for something suitable to wear, I had brought the dress and shoes carefully out from the chest. Though not the latest style, and slightly worn around the sleeves, it was the best I could do. I tried again to smooth out the remaining creases.

Self-consciously, I shook my head at his teasing look. "These were my wedding shoes. I know they're impractical, a woman's vanity I suppose. Where are you hurrying off to?"

"To work. I caught a ride home over dinner." His eyes took in Peter's coat, and he gave a low whistle. "Something must have lit into you. What was it, a panther?"

Peter grinned sheepishly and shook his head. "A tree caught me while we were cutting firewood yesterday. Mother didn't have time to mend it."

James was rubbing his hands together to keep warm. "Looks pretty tight on you. Mending won't change that." He glanced back and forth, sizing up the two boys, then nodded. "All of you come with me for just a minute. I've got a coat stuffed in the back of my closet Mother hasn't had a chance to get rid of yet."

"But James . . ."

He smiled reassuringly. "Don't worry. The folks have already left for town."

It was useless to protest. We followed him up the lane. As in a dream I walked across the spacious lawn under the large oaks, past the one with the familiar scar on the side where lightning had struck soon after we had moved here so long ago. There were the familiar flagstone walks leading from the carriage house and hitching post and the brick-encircled flowerbeds with spring bulbs now hidden under their cover of leaf mulch and snow.

The house looked just as I remembered it: tall imposing windows, the boxwoods along the front trimmed to a perfect roundness, the rose bush garden along the rock wall. This was my first close look since the morning David had picked me up on our wedding day. I felt my throat tighten.

We stepped between the tall white columns onto the front porch. The pompous brass knocker still hung in its place on the wooden double doors. Funny how something that small could evoke so many memories.

It had been a warm, humid evening when I answered the hesitant knock on the door to find David standing there, hat in hand. The chance encounter at the fair a month earlier was the only time we had seen each other since the family's move to Staunton. I had shrunk back in the doorway, too surprised to speak.

Finally I found my voice, "How did you find . . ."

"Aren't you glad to see me, Ellen?" He had looked a little hurt.

"Why, no. I mean yes . . . yes, I am. It's only that . . ."

And then Bernice's sharp voice had called from the parlor. "Who's there, Ellen? Don't just stand there with the door open." She had come into the hall, hands on hips, and upon seeing David, had raised her eyebrows suspiciously.

"Good evening, Mrs. Palmer." David had seemed taken aback by her coldness, but not afraid. "I came to ask your permission to talk with . . ."

Bernice had cut him off abruptly. "Ellen is much too busy this evening to be talking with a stranger! If you want to see Mr. Palmer, he's out in the stable. Come along, Ellen."

I had only time to send a pleading look for understanding before the door was shut firmly in his face. To think of it brought back a sharp pain, even after all these years.

I stood nervously in the front hallway, even now fearing sharp footsteps might come suddenly around the corner and find me there.

The boys stood close together, their whispers filled with awe at the richness of the room before them. A plush slate-blue rug covered the floor, with gray paneled walls on both sides. A large chandelier hung from the high ceiling. Against the right wall, a wide imposing stairway led up to a narrow landing.

Through the doorway at the far end of the hall, a dining table with elaborately curved legs could be seen. A white lace tablecloth lay across its top. The quiet, steady ticking of a clock came from a room close by. I could immediately picture the gleaming maple grandfather clock with the little glass drawer at the bottom. I used to hide pieces of candy there from my older brothers.

James came bounding down the stairs, grinning at the wonder on the boys' faces. "A little different for you?" He held out the coat.

"Don't let all this fool you." His face sobered. "When food gets scarce, it doesn't matter how fine your house may be. It just makes it harder to accept, that's all.

"Here, see if John can wear this. Peter can take John's old one. I wish Mother hadn't taken Tansy along to help in the kitchen. How she would love to see you!"

The cold air caught in my throat, and I could no longer feel my toes by the time we passed the stage-coach stop at the edge of town. A row of wagons, empty except for large, folded green tarps lying in the back, was lined up along the street. The teams of horses stood with heads down, waiting out the cold.

"Where are those headed to?" Peter's voice chattered in spite of himself.

Although James' ears and nose were red, he grinned cheerfully. "The wind shouldn't be so bad here in town." Then nodding toward the men coming out from the tavern next door he continued, "They say they're sending out wagons to gather up army supplies left at places like Highland County, where they are no longer needed."[1]

"That far?!"

He nodded. "It's expensive business too. I heard they hired five teams last week for eleven days at $250."

I was repulsed. "But how could their *loads* even be worth that much?!"

He shrugged. "You're asking the wrong person. War must cost a fortune. I'm glad I don't have to fork out the money." His teeth flashed white against his reddened face.

The street was ugly with wheel ruts and hoof prints. Just ahead was the Courthouse, standing tall and solemn on the corner. Smaller law offices squat-

76

ted on either side. The steps of the Courthouse were empty except for two businessmen in tall black hats conversing earnestly halfway up.

"You turn west here." James stopped short at the corner. "Three blocks on Johnson Street, then south two blocks. Think you can find it?"

I nodded uncertainly. "It's on Church Street?"

"Yes. Can't miss it," James said. "The Stuart residence is right beside Mr. Stuart's law office. It has four large pillars in the front and an upstairs balcony.

"And would it be all right if John and Peter come with me? They can help carry lumber for the men. We'll have a place to get warm."

I glanced down the street toward the three-story American Hotel with its stuccoed white walls and rows of windows. Sounds of hammering could be heard even from where we stood.

"Well . . . I guess so . . . if you are sure it's okay."

"Of course it is. I'll take good care of them. I'll bring them by in a couple of hours." He stepped closer, and his lips brushed my cheek. "And don't let Mother worry you. Keep your chin up. You have nothing to be ashamed of."

He was a dear! I watched them jog south along the edge of the street then turned away. Andy thrust his cold hand into mine. "We 'bout deh, Mommy?"

"You poor boys." I shifted my knitting basket onto my arm and reached for Davie's arm. "Your hands feel like little snowmen! Here, let me help you."

We moved along more rapidly, skirting the occasional buggy pulled up beside the large brick warehouses beside us. Squeezed in between was a small gray building with a large sign nailed to the front, SAMSON EAGON, WAGON MAKER.

"You know what these bad roads make me remember, boys? There was a middle-aged bachelor who owned a liquor store a couple blocks north of here. I can still see him walking down the street with a handful of wood chips to throw down to walk on. He kept his shoes polished no matter how muddy the roads were."[2]

"A lick-er store? Like the horses lick where the flies bite dem?"

I felt a trace of amusement in spite of my mounting nervousness. "No, Andy. That would be better than what it *really* is. Liquor is a drink that makes people shaky on their feet, and their minds get all confused."

I hurried them across the street just as three wagons rumbled by, heading toward the railroad station. Davie shouted to make himself heard. "Why do they do it?"

My eyes were taking in the houses beside me, looking for pillars and an upstairs balcony. "Some people don't want to remember painful things in their lives, son. It's a shameful practice."

Although we were numb with cold, our destination came into sight all too quickly. I had hardly raised my hand to knock, when the door opened and a lady dressed in a lilac gown with ruffles that swept the floor ushered us inside. A gathered collar edged with eyelet lace matched the pin at her neck. She looked at me questioningly. "Your name, please?"

"Ellen Shull, and these are two of my sons, Davie and Andy. I received an invitation from my stepmother, Mrs. Palmer."

She nodded briefly, leading the way down the wide hallway toward the sound of voices and clicking knitting needles.

I paused on the threshold, my eyes taking in the large crowd of women, many of whom I had never seen before. My smile felt plastered on my face. These women were the elite of Staunton!

"Just find yourself a seat. Someone beside you can explain the sock pattern we are working on. There are three different sizes."

She gave a quick smile and was gone. My eyes swept the room anxiously. Some of the women were looking at me curiously. Then a friendly face from the back caught my eye, and I began walking woodenly in that direction. I sat down in an empty corner, grateful to melt into the crowd.

"There are some children playing in the library. Would your boys like to join them?" the young woman sitting beside me asked.

"Oh, thank you. You are so kind." I turned to Davie and Andy. "Shall we go see what they are doing?"

"I'll show you where it is. You would enjoy yourself a whole lot more than sitting here. I think they were playing 'I Spy.'" She smiled encouragingly. I caught a scent of lavender as she leaned closer.

"You come too, Mommy." Andy had a tight hold on my skirt.

After seeing them to the next room, we returned to our places.

"Wouldn't it be nice if grown-ups could accept each other as freely and without pretense as children do?" My new friend handed over two skeins of soft gray yarn. "This is what we are to use. I'm just beginning the toe of my second one. Watch me, and I'll show you how to get started."

We chatted pleasantly for awhile, then I gathered up my courage. "I'm Ellen Shull. My husband is part of Colonel Johnson's command, wintering in the Alleghenies. Do you have someone in the army?"

The younger woman bent her head over her knitting without answering, and I berated myself for being so bold.

"Yes, my husband and I were married only a month before the war broke out. He's . . . he's on the list of missing." Her voice faltered, and she turned her face toward the window. "It's a cruel world."

The pain on her face reflected the winter cold, then her expression softened. "But I didn't tell you my name. I'm Agnes Wittington. I've moved back in with my mother. We live on the corner of Lewis and Johnson Streets above our hatmaker's shop. It's two doors down from Dr. Hites, you know, that 'shaman' that claims to cure everything from gangrene to frostbite with his wonderful 'Pain Cure.' "[3]

Her lips curved slightly, then she laughed. "But who am I to dispute his wonderful success stories. McHone's Millinery benefits from having such a well-known resident next door."

I leaned forward. "Is that the shop with the rainbow-colored woolen shawl in the window?"

She nodded, smiling. "You like that one? Mother brought it back on her last trip North." She dropped to a whisper. "We may be planning a run again soon. Our supplies are very low."

My mouth opened then closed. "You mean—run the blockade? You must be very brave!"[4]

Agnes passed it off without comment, and I, after waiting a bit, went back to my knitting. Neither of us talked much after that. It was interesting enough to listen to the conversations on either side. News of the war and bits of family gossip were flowing freely when there came a clapping of hands, and the loud murmur died into silence.

The lady who had met us at the door, I presumed Mrs. Stuart, was standing at the end of the room. While she waited for everyone's attention, she fingered her large silver brooch.

"Ladies . . ." She smiled rigidly. "Ladies of our prosperous town of Staunton, we are privileged to have each of you here today. Our president has some things to share with us. We shall give her our careful attention at this time." She smiled again and turned behind her. "Mrs. Palmer . . ."

There was a rustle of skirts, and my stepmother stepped forward. Mrs. Stuart bobbed her head and made her way to an empty chair.

Bernice's hands fluttered at her throat. "We have met today to fulfill our duty to husbands, fathers, and sons participating in the fight for Southern integrity and independence." Her sharp eyes scanned her audience before continuing.

"We cannot stand by them to ease the weight of their load or help bear their pain and loneliness. But we can gladly give of our time and means to send comfort their way, making the goal they pursue a little easier to achieve.

"As you know, a large quantity of supplies have already been sent out. Many of you may have seen the trains of empty wagons which left over the last few days to help move army supplies from Highland County. When these wagons return, the clothing we are getting together will be taken to our own troops at Greenbrier Mountain.

"There are some . . ." she paused significantly, "who would shrink from helping the Confederate cause. This is . . ." her fists tightened, "treachery! The Northern despotism must be thwarted. Our allegiance to our beloved South and to our fellow Virginians should move us to be the first to give." Her chest rose and fell rapidly. "My two sons volunteered at the first sign of need. It should have been that way for all of us."

There was a stir in the crowd. I could hear murmurs of assent.

Dropping her hands from her hips, Mother picked up a cloth bag from a nearby table and held it up for all to see. "We are hoping to send 150 pairs of socks along with other articles of clothing to our men of the Fifty-second Infantry, and also to our local cannon group, General Imboden's Artillery. If you wish to direct your contribution to a specific person, pick up one of these bags. These should be turned in one week from today."

The murmur of voices that slowly rose around me seemed small protection from the redness I felt creeping up my neck. I bent my head, concentrating on picking up a loose stitch.

"You know her?" There was pity in Agnes' words.

"She's my stepmother."

"Oh. Then her sons . . . ?"

"Stepsons. My two older brothers, William and Henry. They are married and live in Bridgewater."

Agnes carefully steered the conversation in another direction and after a time she said, "They are setting out tea and cookies. Your boys will be glad for that, I feel sure."

Soon everyone was putting on their coats to leave.

Agnes followed me into the hallway. "Here, Ellen, take these home for your older boys." She held out a bag. "We can't let them be left out. It's been good to meet you today. I feel like I've found a special friend." She smiled warmly.

"Thank you, Agnes." I fumbled with the bag, reaching to clasp her hands in mine. "If you ever have a chance, come out to see me. We live a mile out of town, just past the Palmer farm on the left. The blacksmith shop sets next to the house. You can't miss it."

We were standing on the steps.

"I may just do that. And Ellen . . ." Her voice dropped confidentially, "I think this war is wrong too."

I was startled. "What did I say . . . ?"

"You didn't say anything; I just knew. Why, the cost alone is outrageous. But more than that is the hatred and hostility. And we're supposed to all be noble Americans?" She shuddered.

I could see James with John and Peter turning the corner. Davie and Andy pushed past me and ran to meet them. I stepped closer to Agnes.

"My husband is from the North. My boys have uncles and grandparents in Pennsylvania. How can you fight against your own people?"

She shook her head. Our fingertips touched, and then she was gone.

"Mommy! I beat the race!"

"I did almost. Almost I beat-ed all of them." Andy grabbed my hand and swung it, laughing.

There were some indignant stares as the boys jostled for position. "Careful, boys. You are bumping into people." I prodded them in the right direction.

"Come, let us go home. I have some cookies for Peter and John."

Two days later we heard the startling news of a battle fought in the Alleghenies. Not until David's next letter arrived did the paralyzing fear that gripped my heart begin to ease.

Dear Ellen,

I know you are anxious to hear from me since I'm sure you received word of our first skirmish with the Union forces. I am fine and missed out on the worst of the action.

I was on picket duty on the other side of camp when they sneaked in after midnight Thursday night. They flanked our men in the darkness and attacked about daylight.[5]

It was their 4,000 against our 1,300. The fight lasted seven hours. I was back from the front, but could see the bursts of smoke and fire from both sides.

Seven Yankees were taken prisoner. I was on guard duty today and talked with them awhile. I ended up more torn than before. I feel duty bound to protect my family and home, and yet, in so doing, I bring suffering and death to fellow Americans fighting for the same "just cause." It is very confusing.

After the battle I was given burial duty. To see that, takes all the "glory" out of war. These men had family just as dear to them as I. One fellow had his fiancee's tintype in his overcoat pocket. Another had a locket with a picture of his wife and baby son hung about his neck. What if it had been one of my brothers?

I haven't slept well since. Some men have gotten whiskey and drink quite freely.

Reinforcements have been sent in since our victory. The men all call Johnson "Allegheny" now. He has been promoted to General.

We are kept busy trimming and burning brush, blockading roads, and extending our trenches.

Share whatever you think appropriate with the boys. I miss holding little Andy on my knees, and tousling Davie's curly hair.

Tell Peter I'm glad he learned to milk before I left so John doesn't have the whole load on himself. Thank God for John's quiet and steady ways! His shoulders must carry a lot of responsibility for a fourteen-year-old.

I cannot reprimand you for hiding Ginger. Saving her would have been a miracle.

Christmas is almost here, and I long to be there with you. If I could hold all of you for just a moment and soak in your closeness—that would be the best gift I could ask. Though it may be far off, my fervent hope and prayer is that someday it may be granted.

All my love,
David

Christmas came and went. The bag with David's name on it had joined the many others loaded onto wagons heading for camp. I had cut out the bottom of David's worn-out blacksmith apron to make gloves for him, lining them carefully with soft, brown rabbit fur from a rabbit Peter had caught in a trap.

John spent many hours carving a hand-size image of Ginger out of red ash, and we had all been pleased with how realistic it had turned out. The younger boys filled several evenings cracking hickory nuts to send along.

We wrote all the news we could, making a fat letter. Late one night I added a few more lines.

... and David, I keep searching for answers. I read in your Bible every night when I am alone. So much is hard to understand, and yet some hunger drives me on.

I finally decided to start at the beginning of the New Testament and read all the way through. The words are strange, they talk about a new kingdom beginning to dawn where love for all men is the moving force, and the attitude of the heart counts more than the outward action.

It is an awful thing to say, but I see no

evidence of this kind of love in Staunton, even among church-goers, although they would claim otherwise.

I took the boys to the First Presbyterian Church last Sunday. The sermon was on the right of our state to protect itself from the tyranny of the North. I wish I had someone to talk to about it, but I dare not expose my doubts.

The streets are full of war slogans and patriotism. It is held as righteousness and justice, but boils down to nothing more than hate, pride, and selfishness.

Does no one live by the New Testament—pure and simple as it is? They say it is outdated for modern times. I could accept that if it weren't for the memories of old Silas. He had something that enabled him to love everyone, no matter what their skin color or creed.

We are making out well. The boys make the trip back into the woods every day to cut wood. Wood cutting and chores fill most of their waking hours.

They have tried their hand at trapping. Their rare catches make welcome additions to our meals.

Take care—for your sake, and mine.

My heart was with you every moment of Christmas Day. Thank God He has spared you thus far.

Your wife,
Ellen

❧ Chapter V ❧

The first weeks of the new year started out bitterly cold. I opened up the chest by our bed and lifted out clothes, each carrying a faint smell of cedar. We pulled them on—old worn sweaters, handed-down shirts and trousers—one on top of another, and wore them night and day.

One evening John helped me tack a heavy tarp over the stairway. It took too much wood to heat the entire house. The scarcity of food was beginning to take its toll, bringing a weariness that never seemed to leave.

The warm and bountiful days of summer seemed far away. James said shops in town were beginning to close their doors. The frozen, muddied streets held only hollow-eyed townsfolk, heads bent, hurrying to get out of the cold.

I doled out the wrinkled potatoes and few remaining turnips in the barrel. As the bag of cornmeal and flour dwindled, I longed for spring.

One afternoon I was patching the knees on a pair of Peter's trousers when the two youngest boys rushed into the house, colliding with each other in their excitement. "We caught one! We caught one!"

"Caught what?" I laid my mending on the table and helped shove the door shut behind them.

"A squirrel." Davie kicked his boots off and hobbled over to the fireplace. "John put some grains of corn in the trap yesterday, and now we caught a squirrel to eat!" He grimaced, rubbing his feet. "When's supper ready? I'm hungry already."

"Me too." Andy's words were cut short by a coughing spell. I pinched my lips tight as I helped him out of his wraps. Most of the afternoon they had been helping pull the wooden platform loaded with wood. Although getting a supply of fuel ahead was important, I dared not let them help again soon, not in their condition.

Thin gruel with a bit of milk does not give much stamina to growing boys. That, and their worsening coughs, had started keeping me awake at night, worrying. The cornmeal was getting very low. I knew I could only stretch it out so far. To be able to add squirrel meat to our evening meal was wonderful.

But even with occasional wild game, one morning I used the last cup of cornmeal to make breakfast. And there was only one person healthy enough to go after more. I looked anxiously around the table.

"Boys, we have run out of cornmeal. Do you think you could manage if I try to find more?"

John's voice rasped as he spoke, "Let me go, Mother."

"I'm afraid the best place for boys with coughs as bad as all of you have is inside by the fire. You are still reaping from your time spent feeding Ginger and the constant wood cutting."

Peter's eyes flashed. "And now look. It wasn't worth feeding Ginger! I'd like to ki . . ."

"No, son!" I cut in before he could finish the ugly words. "We don't talk that way. If we do, we're no better than those who rob, plunder, and kill. Hatred degrades a man."

His eyes narrowed at my outburst, and I softened. "I didn't mean to sound so sharp. I'm just so tired of war I could . . ."

His grin was lopsided. "Sorry. I won't say it if you don't want me to. I just thought a good solid kick might be all right!"

I couldn't help it, laughter welled up in me, forcing its way to the surface. Not seeing the humor, Andy took hold of my shaking shoulders and pulled hard. "Mommy, Mommy! Watz' so funny? Mommy!" He started giggling, and the snickers from the others increased his perplexity. He pounded on the back of my chair. "Mommy, you jus' too silly."

I wiped my eyes. "I know it, Andy. I shouldn't be laughing. Mommy's not acting very sophisticated right now."

"What's 'fist katydid'? Dehs no katydid bugs in the winter."

We all started laughing again, and he gave up in disgust. He hopped off his chair, his mouth pulled down at the corners. I grabbed him as he went by. "Don't you worry your little head about katydids or fists or anything else, son. Mommy just needed something to take the load off her shoulders." I kissed him hard—once, twice—and set him down.

He looked bewildered, and his mouth opened, then thinking better of it, he closed it again.

I stood. "Could you take care of yourselves if I left you alone for awhile this morning?"

"Sure. We're not babies anymore."

I looked at them thoughtfully. "I want you to bar the doors when I go out." I held up my hand at the protest in their eyes. "No questions, please. I'll feel safer that way, and so will you."

An hour later, I came downstairs buttoning my coat with gloved hands. A pair of David's old boots covered my shoes. Wrapping the fringed ends of my muffler tighter about my neck, I reached for the door. "Why don't you get out your slates and let John be your teacher. Work on your grammar, or . . . or your times tables. It's been several days since we've done anything like that."

I took a deep breath and straightened my shoulders. "If I have good success, we will make cornbread for dinner. I saved up enough cream to make a dab of butter."

I hugged them close with my smile, riveting their faces in my mind. Andy looked a bit frightened. If anything should happen while I was gone . . .!

I stepped out onto the porch, waiting until I

heard the bolt slide into place.

The reflection of sunlight on the snowdrifts was startling. The sky hung over me like an icy blue dome with merely a scattering of wispy clouds painted along the edges. It reminded me of the porcelain cup Mother had kept on the what-not shelf at home.

The pike was a rutted mass of crisscrossing wagon tracks with mud and snow mixed into an icy quagmire. I picked my way carefully along its edge, trying to hold my heavy skirts out of the roadside drifts.

I was glad for David's boots. They brought a warmth inside me, even though their stiffness made it hard to walk. I had stuffed the toes with rags to make them fit.

The road was strangely empty this morning. I heard nothing but my steady clumping footsteps and the cawing of a dozen crows behind the large corn-crib at the far end of Father's hay barn. Stopping to catch my breath, I watched them rise in an angry mass then settle out of sight again, their racket undiminished. The outburst sounded like a bunch of squabbling children on a playground.

I held my gloves over my mouth, warming my hands. The cawing changed into a cackling sound. As I started walking again, I became aware of a horse and rider coming up behind me.

"Howdy!"

A slouch-backed man pulled his horse to a stop and leered down into my face. "What's a lady like you doin' out on a cold day like this?" He fingered a bulge pushing against the form of his coat, and his eyes traveled up and down, as if measuring my worth.

"I . . . I . . ."

He caught my hurried glance in both directions and grinned. "Not a body in sight, ma'am." His voice lowered. "You got any money?"

I didn't answer.

"Those boots of yours, they don't belong to you. They ain't no lady boots." He reached out a greedy hand. I could see the dirt under his nails. "Take 'em off and be quick about it."

My hands felt like ice. I fumbled in my efforts, my heart pounding in my ears. *O God, don't let him get my money!* I stood and handed over David's boots.

"There . . . !" He kicked off his own ragged shoes and bent over in the saddle to pull on David's. "What in the . . ." He uttered an oath, running his hand inside to jerk out the wad of rags, tossing them furiously into the snow.

"Perfect fit. Now . . . about that money . . ." His voice was shrewd. "I could use a little of that too. Ah perdy little woman like you don't have no business carrying sech stuff around." He drew his foot out of the stirrup, ready to swing it over the side. "Your neck is pumping like a hammer. I won't hert you, jest hand it over."

My throat was dry; my lips felt like paper. I held my hands behind my back to hide their trembling. "I don't have any to give you."

There was a rattle of wagon wheels coming toward us. The man's eyes grew hard. "If it weren't for that wagon, I'd . . ." He cursed. Wheeling his horse around he set off at a gallop.

Suddenly I was weak and shaking all over. My heart pounded as I stepped blindly off the road to let the horses pull past. The snow came over my shoes and dragged at my skirts.

"Hello!" said someone in surprise. I looked up and saw James leap off the end of the wagon and come running toward me.

"Ellen! What are you doing out here? Are you all right?"

"Oh, James, I'm so glad to see you!" I unfolded the sack from my arm. "We are out of cornmeal. I . . . I've just been robbed."

His face darkened with anger as he followed the direction of my finger. "Let me hail that wagon again. Just wait till I catch up with him, the rascal!" He turned to sprint after the retreating wagon. I grabbed his coat.

"No, James. Let him go. I was foolish to come out here by myself. I didn't realize the danger. The boys are half sick. I . . . he only took my boots, that is, David's actually. Thank God you came."

I felt for the small wad of bills tucked into the lining of my sleeve.

He scowled, eyebrows raised. "She's on the road alone with boots which plainly say she's trying to do a man's job and carrying a sack which means she must have money somewhere!" He shook his head in mock wonder. "You're lucky that's all you lost, Sis.

"Look, I'll *give* you some cornmeal if you'll help me out." He cleared his throat nervously. "I need a doctor, Ellen. Mother's been sick for two days. Tansy sent me out to look for a doctor, and I've been trying to track one down for the last three hours. They are either out of town, or somewhere on call. I don't know anything about doctoring. Would *you* come?"

My eyes widened. "Mother wouldn't want to see me, James. You know that."

"Just to take a look at her? Please, Sis, for my sake?"

I stood rooted to the spot. "I . . . I don't have the courage."

He caught my arm. "You can't go the rest of the way into town in those shoes, and you can't go home without food. Be brave . . . for me, Ellen."

I found myself walking woodenly after him, feeling numb. Why didn't I turn and run for home?

James took me to the back entrance. I knocked the snow off my shoes then straightened, feeling tense.

"Let me get Tansy. She's around here somewhere." A grin flashed over his face, but disappeared when he looked me in the eyes. "Don't be nervous. Look, I can wrap you up so Mother wouldn't even know you, if you would feel any better. Just think how glad Tansy will be to see you. Come on."

He led me by the elbow into the kitchen and through the back hall to the rear stairway. The muffled sounds of a rich contralto voice came filtering down from overhead.

Oh, where shall we go w'en de great day come,
Wid de blowin' ob de trumpets
An' de bangin' ob de drums . . .[1]

The song broke into humming as the woolly-headed cook, with an armload of towels, started down the stairs. "James! Dat you? Who dat wid you? It be de doctah, I's hopin'."

Suddenly both hands shot up in surprise, the towels sailing where they would, and she flew down the remaining stairs. "Missy Ellen!" She flung her arms around me, almost crushing me in her fervor. "My deah chile, you a sight fo sore eyes, you is! It's been a long, long time! Why, you is plum shivered out. Take off dat puny coat, an' let ole Tansy warm

96

you up."

I couldn't help laughing, tears coming to my eyes. "Tansy, you haven't changed a mite. James met me on the pike."

Her weary eyes widened in alarm. "Lan' sakes, boy. You mean you coulden' fin' no doctah?" Her arms were akimbo, the furrows on her brown face knit together. "Miz Bernice, she gettin' de-leh-re-us by now. I's been runnin' de cold towels 'cross her head somp'pin fe-ro-shus. She be mighty upset if I don' bring de doctah."

James' grin vanished. "There's no doctor available, Tansy. I tried all morning. Can Ellen take a look at her?"

"I neber seed de laks ob it all!" Tansy filled a basin with water and handed it to me, then gathered up the fresh towels lying across the chair by the doorway. "Hard tellin' what de sickness be—but I hab my specs' 'bout it."

We started up the stairs. As we entered Mother's room, my hands were trembling so I was afraid the water would spill onto the bed. Mother's flushed face brightened, and she reached out a grasping hand. I bent closer, feeling the heat of her body. Her shoulders shook with a hacking cough, and she sank back gasping.

"Nurse, just take me to the Springs again. Let me ease down softly . . . softly . . . The water is so hot . . . so hot . . ." Her voice cracked.

"She think'en 'bout dose Raw-ley Springs she go to in de summah times." Tansy's whisper came from behind me. "She been telling me to get de hosses hooked up and de luggage packed. I's can't get huh to lissen to reason."

I wrung out fresh towels, replacing those on Mother's face and arms. The wheezing breath, the tell-tale spots creeping up her neck, the white-coated tongue . . . Suddenly it all came together, and I stepped back involuntarily. "Scarlet fever . . . !"

James caught his breath. "No! Ellen, are you sure?"

"Not positive, but it looks very suspicious. Her breathing . . . was she out in the weather a lot lately? Where would she have gotten this?"

Tansy snorted. "She's eveh mo' goin' to dose meet'ens in town 'bout de war. Can't stay home one blessed day. She took to de bed yes-te-dey, and I's been runnin' eveh since."

Already the restless arms had pushed aside the wet towels and were fumbling at the covers. "Oh, nurse, you never take me to the right place. This pool's too hot. Take me to a cooler one." Even in her feverish state, her voice was sharp, her eyes wild and staring. It was distressing to see her like this.

James leaned forward. "Here, Mother, take a drink." He held a cup to her lips.

After the first sip she turned away. "Hurts . . . the sun beats down so hard . . . so hard . . ."

James put the towels in place again. "This is James, Mother. I'll stay right here with you. You'll feel better soon."

Her restless movements gradually quieted, and she turned her face to the wall. We slipped into the hall.

"Don' you min' her fuss-en, Miss Ellen. She been call-en out at any ob us all mahn'en. Don' know what she say'en."

I clenched my hands together. "What are we to do for her?"

98

"Don' you worry your perdy head 'bout it. I spected sumthin' like dis." She cupped one hand to her ear. "James! Run down an' see. I thinks Mr. Palmer's drive'n in right this very minute. He'll fin' help sho' nuff."

She changed the subject abruptly. "How's all de chilluns?"

"They're okay, Tansy. Things are not the best, but we're making out. I need to hurry back now. I hope you don't catch this."

"Lan' sakes, chile. I had dis when I be a little tike still liven' wid Pappy. I 'member, 'cause we had it de same time."

There was a catch in my throat. "I still miss him, Tansy. I often think of him and wish I could sneak into his lap like I used to do evenings, and listen to his stories and advice."

"Yes-um. I reckon he luved one same as all. Dis here war . . ." She sniffed. "Dey say it's to free de black folks. Pap could'n wait. He dun' foun' his freedom."

She wiped her eyes on the corner of her apron. "Nothin' 'pares wid dat. Pap saw de angels comin' 'fore he died. I saw de glory on his face."

She turned suddenly, pulling me after her. "O . . . bless my soul! I's just recollect'en. I hab sumthin' to deck out dat po thin frame ob yours. Come 'long . . ."

She crouched and gave the small attic door a yank, grunting as she reached inside. Pulling out a large carton, she pulled off the top blanket and gave it a vigorous shake.

I gasped. I recognized the dress lying on top.

Tansy's teeth shone as she chuckled her pleasure. "W'en Miz Bernice sen' you 'way, I says to mysef,

'Some glad day mebbe I get de chance to gib dese perdy dresses back to you.' "

The tears were running down my face. I hugged her hard, dusty dresses and all. "Oh, how I can use them! Tansy, you are the sweetest thing."

A cold wind had sprung up, skimming the tops of the drifts, swirling the dry snow into the air against our faces. Holding my bundles high, I squinted ahead, measuring the distance between us and home. A dozen yards would bring us to the tall pines where walking would be easier.

We trekked across the fields in silence, James tramping ahead, his back bent under the weight of a bulging feedbag. He had said this would be safer than going by the road, and had insisted on carrying it for me.

It was a relief to finally step out of the wind onto the back porch. I draped my load over the empty wash tub and fumbled with the veil over my face. My fingers were stiff with cold.

James let the sack of cornmeal slide off onto the floor with a thud and straightened his shoulders carefully. "Whew! It's a good thing it wasn't any further."

I kicked off the cast-off boots he had loaned me and took hold of both his arms. "James, I . . . How can I ever thank you for all of this?"

His face reddened, and he patted my head. "Aw, glad to do it. And don't worry about Mother. Father was hitching up to go for the doctor when we left."

100

"Did you . . . I mean, did he see what you were up to?"

"He didn't ask any questions, and I didn't volunteer any information. But he had an idea. I think he purposely kept his back turned."

He pulled his collar up around his ears and grinned. "I must go now. So long!"

I followed him with grateful eyes. His bounding figure skirted the snowdrifts until another leap took him out of sight beyond the scattered pine saplings and cedar.

Dear family,

I must sit down and write you a good letter again. Things have been pretty dull since the last time I sent something your way. I was very glad to get your letter and gifts soon after Christmas. I was very sick, but I am feeling much better now, though still weak and unable to shake a bad cough.

Many men are sick. So far thirty have lost the fight with fever, three in my own company. I wonder which battle is the hardest: guns and Yankees, or typhoid and other diseases that stalk the camps? Picket duty and rough weather make unhealthy companions.

The General has started a number of things just the last couple days to liven up the place. We are to have spelling schools three times a week, as well as prayer meetings. Davie, we even have our own chorus with men singing and playing whatever instruments they can come up with.

One of my cabin mates, Adam Kersh, told the others I like to play the harmonica, and they asked me to play once, since I'm feeling better.

Tell Andy I played "When This Cruel War Is O'er"[2] and told the men it was especially for my baby boy back home. There were a lot of wet eyes, for many of them have little ones.

We have a local post office now—moved up from Greenbrier River—so mail should come more regularly. Boys, letters are my most treasured possession; that, and your mother's picture.

Peter, I keep your letter and sketch of home in my wallet. I have gotten it out so often it is starting to come apart at the folds.

We have had quite a bit of snow, and the fierce wind blows it through our clapboard roofs, sifting it over us. The cabins stay damp all the time. I try to stay bundled up close to the fire. My bunk-mate, Joseph Ebby, who is just a young fellow of maybe fifteen or sixteen, faithfully fixes me what we call hot tea. Though a poor substitute, it feels good all the way down.

I am weary of winter and long for warmer days, yet dread spring's appearance, for I know not what will happen when we move on.

John, is my blacksmith shop still waiting for me? I wish I could have brought Ginger with me, but it probably wouldn't have saved her any longer than at home. You wouldn't believe how many horses we must keep on hand in order to have enough useable ones. Winter is as hard on animals as men, maybe more so.[3]

We have some hated little enemies around here called lice, and a lot of joshing goes on about them. Though not as bad as some, they have infested our cabin also.

A few men are gambling on lice. Each player takes his tin dinner plate and places one of these little rascals on it. The first louse to jump off causes his owner to be the winner.

Samuel Whitman told me he learned if he heats his plate first, he remains unbeaten. I suppose the other boys will catch on after awhile!

Please write,

Love,
David

PS: My turmoil is as wretched as yours, dear wife, but please be careful.
  Letters are subject to censorship.

It was Saturday afternoon when I first noticed the fever. By evening I felt awful. Only by sheer determination did I manage to get supper on the table. I sat down, hanging tightly onto my chair.

"Mommy, you look so white."

"Do I? I . . . I feel a little dizzy, that's all. I'll be okay. I think I'll wait to eat till later."

John looked at me. He knew I had been exposed to scarlet fever. "You're going to bed. Right now." Ignoring my feeble protests, he put both hands under my arms and almost lifted me from my chair. I leaned heavily against him.

The wind outside whined and tugged at the house like an angry beast, and the room seemed to sway and tremble with each blast. I felt as though I were swaying along with it. The signs—what were the signs? My mind refused to focus. Mother . . . the spots . . . the swollen tongue . . .

John eased me down onto my mat in the corner. I collapsed, exhausted and my eyelids closed. My mouth felt caked and dry. I ran my tongue over my lips.

"Can I bring you a drink?" There was alarm in John's words, and I forced my eyes open. All four boys were leaning over me.

They're afraid, poor lambs . . . I should tell them it'll be okay; we'll be okay . . . I opened my mouth to speak, but no words came.

The appearance of the dreaded red spots the next morning left no doubt about my illness. Although I tried to keep them from getting too near, one after another, the boys joined me on their blankets, their bodies broken out, their tongues parched and swollen.

The days and nights slipped into a maze of fever and chills, moaning for water, and crying out in our sleep. Once I opened my bloodshot eyes to see Tansy's black face bending over me. I tried to speak, but my peeling lips refused to move.

"Lie down, honey. James fetched me down heah to take care ob all you po chilluns. Take a sip ob dis. Dat's fine . . . dat's plenty fine. Now, jus' lie down and shut yer weary eyes."

A great weight lifted from my mind, and I let myself go, sinking into the first relaxed sleep in three days.

Tansy stayed all that day and the next; "freshnun" up our covers, as she called it, giving out sips of mint tea and gum water, and doling out the bitter laudanum and pepper potion she had brought with her. She shook with laughter at the boys' faces.

"I know dis stuff burns lak de kitchen stove a flamen'. Miz Bernice, she make it pow-ful hahd fer me to git it into huh. I almos' had to hold huh nose shut. But don' you try to trick me and spit id out agin, 'cause dat won' work." She wiped the tears from her eyes. "I believes big folk is wuss than little ones. Swaller id on down. Id be dat strong, you know it mus' work."

The afternoon of the third day she left, promising that James would bring her over as often as we needed her. He had slipped in and out countless times a day ever since he had found us helpless in our misery. And for almost a week he brought over warm, nourishing liquids which eased our swollen throats and slowly brought strength to our arms and legs.

He told us we were not the only ones suffering from scarlet fever. Tansy had been on the go, called out night or day for over a fortnight, tending the sick.

One morning several days later, we were awakened by hoofbeats on the lane. There were rough voices outside the window, horses snorting and blowing, and the creak of saddle leather. A rifle butt hammered against the door. "Open up!"

I shrank back against the wall. Who could it be? The boys crouched under their covers, startled beyond moving.

"Open up, I say! We want some food."

John glanced my way, dismay in his eyes.

"Can you manage, John?" My mouth felt like paper. My voice was scarcely a whisper.

John pulled open the door. The hungry men crowded into the doorway, peering into the dimness. "Where's your ma, boy?"

John motioned across the room where I sat on a pile of covers.

The leader strode over and stood stiffly, scowling down at me. "This is no time of day to be sleeping, ma'am. We need a meal, and we're in a mighty big hurry."

The dirty, sweaty smell that clung to him sent a wave of nausea over me. I pushed myself up onto an elbow. "I . . . I'm sick."

"You'll be sicker still if you don't get up directly. Where's some food around here?" His eyes darted about the room, catching sight of the three younger boys huddled in the corner.

He took a step backward, pulling at his drooping mustache. "What's going on here?" He turned toward John who had sunk down onto a chair by the fireplace.

"We . . . we have scarlet fever."

The man's mouth twisted in anger. "Crazy youngster!" He swore, backing hastily into the doorway. "Why didn't you say so?"

He wiped his hands nervously on the back of his pants. "We'll just see what we can find outside."

John eased the door shut again, his face white. "That's one of the men who came to the woods!"

"Son! Are you sure?"

"I'm sure." He stumbled to the window, hoping to catch a glimpse of Ginger's familiar form among the milling horses. Ginger was not there.

Crashing sounds were heard.

"They're breaking down the door to the barn!"

Fear and anger churned in my stomach. I pulled myself up, swaying dizzily, my hands gripping the window ledge. A few minutes later the men emerged, holding our last few hens, their necks dangling, dripping blood.

The days were growing warmer. The evening sun clung a bit longer each evening to the western mountain peaks before sinking out of sight. The hardened

107

ice and snow softened, and over the weeks, spots of brown grew larger, until at last the whole valley lay open to the sun.

I could feel my body gaining strength. Though still weak, we all were getting around again.

One afternoon we gathered up the blankets and old covers, opened up the stairway, and made up our own beds again. The next day we ventured outside, scouring the fields and creek bottom for spring greens. Though there was no salt to cook with them, they would give us strength.

"Look, Mommy!" Davie's pale face shone as he knelt beside the patch of mottled green leaves pushing their stiff points through the soil.

"Skunk cabbage, Davie. And over here by the creek . . . see the moss? It looks like a tiny bed of emeralds!" I rubbed my fingers over its soft stubble. "And here are fiddleheads." I pulled back the brown shriveled fronds huddling beside a rotten log and gently uncovered the tightly rolled velvet spirals. "They'll be waking up and stretching soon. Some people like to eat them."

"Eat *them!*" David plucked off a nubbin and nibbled it thoughtfully. "Ugh! I'd have to be really hungry to try something that strange."

I couldn't help laughing. "I'm sure they cooked them in a special way. I used to play they were poor cringing servant ladies, held by cruel winter until one day the sun shone warm and set them free. Then they awoke, yawned and stretched, and gradually, gracefully uncurled themselves. They were so surprised to find themselves in lovely gowns of shimmering green and gold."

As I spoke, Peter came up behind us, his hands

108

dripping and his pants legs muddy from the knees down. "Ladies or no ladies, I think I'd rather eat something else. Come. John's found something special."

"You look like Blossom after she's stood in the muddy creek on a hot day." Davie laughed. " 'Member how the tip of her tail would hang in the water, and whenever she'd swat horse flies, it would splatter water over us?"

The marshy ground oozed water over the soles of our shoes. Water was everywhere, seeping up through matted leaves, gathering in little rivulets, trickling into crevices in the ground, gaining momentum as it made its way to the creek. All of last year's grasses and vegetation had been steeped in moisture until the creek flowed with meadow tea.

"Where are you taking us?" I was almost panting, and Andy pulled to a stop to rest. "I've never been to this part of the stream before."

Peter grinned, waiting good-naturedly till we caught our breath. "It's just around that huge poplar tree."

Here the creek had swollen to twice its former self and created a dark pool where the water moved at only a slow gurgle. John was standing knee deep, bent over carefully, gathering handfuls of something into his basket. He looked up as we came into view.

"Cress! Watercress. However did you find it, John? I never knew there was any on the place!"

"I just followed the creek, looking for dandelion shoots and whatever else. I saw this green shine from under a matted bunch of tree branches and leaf rubbish." He looked very pleased. "I think I've gathered enough for now."

I inspected his supply, breaking off a sprig and chewing it hungrily. "It's delicious. Yes, we'd best leave the rest to grow out fresh. Come, boys, let's hurry home. We have enough variety to have a hot cooked dish and a sweet watercress salad besides."

That evening a shrill song rose falteringly, faint from the distant marsh. I threw open the door. "Come here, boys. The spring peepers are awake!"

We gathered on the porch to pay tribute to their courage. The tiny voices joined together, swelling until the night air was filled with their reedy trilling.

With the advance of spring also came news of the armies stirring to life. A new leader, General McClellan, nicknamed "the young Napoleon" by northern newspapers, was beginning to advance up the York River with a large group of Federal troops toward Richmond. At the same time another group was crossing at Harpers Ferry, pushing Confederates under Stonewall Jackson south toward Winchester.

Fearful rumors began filtering into town. James kept us informed. "You can be sure they're heading our way. There's enough army supplies in this town to make a rich haul for the blood-thirsty rascals."

"James!"

"Well, it's true. But we're as eager to beat them as they us. There's been a call for all able-bodied men to report for duty immediately. They'll not find us unprepared." He spat at a honey bee buzzing clumsily near a quince blossom. It dodged disgustedly, then droned out of sight around the corner of the barn.

During the next few days we watched a steady trickle of men march past, heading up the pike toward Winchester. A battle close at hand seemed imminent.

One afternoon James found me working behind the house. He sat down on a pile of old boards and stretched his legs.

"Tired, James?"

"Slightly. What are you doing, digging around in the dirt?"

I leaned against the shovel handle to hide my weakness. "I'm determined to have a bit of garden, even if we have to turn all this ground by hand. We desperately need the food."

"Why, that's impossible!"

"Do you have any better suggestions?"

He frowned. "Where are the boys?"

"I gave them a break." I colored slightly. "Actually, they are going after the cow. We thought we would try hooking her up to the plow."

He raised his eyebrows.

"I know it sounds silly, but don't laugh at me, James."

He swallowed his grin. "All right. But perhaps I can bring Pet down. I'll figure out something. You're too thin and washed out to be doing such things."

"You don't look too chipper yourself."

"Yes? I guess we're all tired. And if our men don't get to the Potomac in time to hold back those Yanks, we'll end up worse than tired." He kicked at a clod of dirt. "We need more men! I wish my birthday was now instead of this fall. I'd enlist right now!"

He looked up suddenly. "You know what I saw yesterday? Seventy men brought into town and locked up in the courthouse."[4]

"Seventy men?"

He nodded. "They were kind of queer-looking people with black hats and plain-looking clothes. What did someone say they were? Menn . . . Mennites or something like that."

"Mennonites?"

"They were trying to escape to Union territory. They don't believe in fighting."

I turned away. Mennonites . . . I remembered them faintly. I had bought milk and garden things from a family close to Rawley Springs where my mother and I had stayed the summer before she died.

I hadn't known what they believed. I had only sensed they were gentle and hardworking. Yes, refusing to fight would fit with their way of life.

I forced my mind back to the present. James was talking again. "Why anyone would want to try and sneak off is beyond my comprehension. Father says they ought to be whipped and sent to the front lines."

I didn't answer.

He stood up abruptly, looking at me quizzically. "You're mighty quiet."

I tried to smile. "I guess I was just thinking how peaceful it would be if everyone believed like they do."

He shook his head. "You're letting your emotions get away with you, Ellen. You know that isn't practical—isn't *possible*. Any feelings like that better be kept under cover. We're into this war now. The only way to bring it to a close is to go forward." He started to walk away.

I hesitated. "What . . . what are they going to do with them?"

He looked back. "They were sent off this morning to Richmond. They'll be secure enough, imprisoned there."

✦ Chapter VI ✦

IARY—3/26/62

    I want to record the events of the spring campaign for my family's sake as well as my own.

The days of March are fast coming to a close. News is beginning to trickle through camp that we are to pull out. Joseph Ebby died last night. Poor boy, struggling for breath, burning with fever. A young life wasted, for what? The pride and selfish ambitions of men!

DIARY—3/30/62

We are packing up to leave. Pandemonium! Men are glad to see an end to the stagnancy of winter. Adam Kersh says we are to light up the place as we leave. All those hundreds of hours of work going up in smoke!

Stonewall Jackson (Old Bluelight, the men call him) met with defeat at Kernstown. I suppose we are to move closer as reinforcements. Will Providence protect me now?

The waiting of winter was over. Pressured by impatient countrymen, the Federal army crossed the Potomac River only to be ordered east to join the larger Union army for an advance on Richmond. Jackson's men hurried to intercept them. They met at the Battle of Kernstown.

It wasn't long until we saw the results. Wagons and ambulances with wounded began rolling past our lane on their way to the hospital on the southern end of town. Worried families began throwing together a few belongings to flee south.

DIARY—4/2/62

We pulled out yesterday. What a roaring, crackling fire! The boys say it's the first time they've been warm enough all winter. Smoldering ashes and smoke—a forsaken-looking place. Spring is trying to show her face. I saw ferns uncurling on our march, and a patch of sweet arbutus in a dip between the hills.

116

DIARY—4/5/62

Am sitting on a rail fence writing on my knee with smoke from the campfire in my eyes. We are camped on Shenandoah Mountain . . . so steep you have to dig in your heels when sleeping to keep from sliding down. The sick are ordered to Buffalo Gap, so I think another move is in the making. Our destination is kept very secret by General Johnson. Who knows what will happen next?

DIARY—4/8/62

Camping at Valley Mills. Going is terrible. Rain and mud—very hard on men and animals. Marched all afternoon and into the night. Never so tired in all my life, just stumbling along, half-asleep. No mood for speech, no breath to spare. Only the continual slosh of marching feet, mud sucking on wagon wheels, creak and rattle of harness, blowing of horses, weary to the core. Always from out of the darkness comes the order, "Close up, men!"

I pulled a board off the side of an old shed and laid it in the mud to sleep on. Never found out a thing till dawn.

The Federal forces continued chasing the Confederate armies up the Valley. Ten to twelve thousand Confederate soldiers were flocking into town. Cannon and wagons plugged the streets.

It was barely light one morning as I stepped through the barn door directly into James' path. The bucket was knocked out of my grasp, and milk splattered everywhere.

"Sorry, Sis!" He sagged against the barn wall, gasping for breath.

"James! What is it?"

"Jackson . . . Jackson has ordered an evacuation. I just came from town. Everything is in an uproar. The hospital is filling railroad cars with patients, baggage cars are being stuffed with ammunition and army supplies!"[1]

I stared at him, petrified. "What should we do?"

"I don't know. I just had to tell you. I must go. Father and Mother need to know." He turned and fled.

In a daze I grabbed up the nearly empty milk pail. "John! Peter! Come running!"

We raced to the house. They needed no urging but quickly did what I told them to do. By the time I had the younger boys up and dressed, John and Peter were waiting by the back door, arms loaded with things for all of us to carry.

I ran my eyes over our assortment of bundles. "Are we ready? Oh! I must get the money pouch." I darted back up the stairway.

We were almost to the woods when Peter croaked, "What about the cow?"

"Oh, boys, I forgot! Is it too late to chase her down?" My heart sank in dismay. How could I have forgotten?

"I'll go." John dashed off before I could think to

stop him.

We were at the creek now. Andy's sobs brought me to my senses. I stopped to pick him up, and carried him, bundle and all, to the other side. There was splashing as the other boys carelessly followed in my wake.

"All of you . . . Quick. Run ahead to the cave. I'll wait here for John."

After long, anxious moments John appeared, Blossom in tow, and we hurried to join the others. We crouched without a word within the cave's entrance, straining to hear any hint of sound. All was quiet but for the distant ripple of running water and the steady drip of moisture onto the limestone floor. A thin tweet-a-tweet from high in a hemlock was answered in the mountain laurel thicket. From the grown-over hillside came the low cry of a mourning dove.

I spread out a blanket and motioned the boys to sit down.

"Mommy, what . . . what is after us?" Tears were streaming silently down Davie's face.

I forced myself to relax. "James stopped by to tell me that Staunton was to evacuate. That means fighting may be close by. In case there is, we'll just wait here till it's over. We'll be safe here."

Andy buried his head in my lap, and I stroked his rigid back until his body began to relax. Finally he fell asleep.

The minutes and hours dragged by. Several times I sent John to the creek's edge to check for any sign of activity, but each time he returned shaking his head.

It was late afternoon when he met James and

119

brought back word—everyone return home, false alarm.

I gathered my tired, hungry brood and started back toward the house.

Another week passed. The enemy now occupied the town of Harrisonburg, camping on the surrounding hills, helping themselves to anything they pleased.

The tension was making the boys jittery, and Davie began having nightmares. A letter from David was a bright spot in our time of uncertainty.

4/9

Dear family,

I'll take the rare privilege to send a letter your way. Mail is going out this afternoon. We have stopped at Valley Mills to recruit, and our ranks are swelling to full size once more.

My arms ache to hold you all. Things are happening fast. I don't know when I can get word to you again.

Ellen, several men were brought in last week—Mennonites from Rockbridge County.[2] I happened to be near Colonel Harman's tent when they arrived. It wasn't long before Harman stuck out his head and hollered, "Bezler! Peter Bezler! You still got one corner empty? Here's a fellow for you . . . and see if you can teach him a few good attitudes toward Yankees." He looked more than a little disgusted.

You can imagine how my heart leaped to hear of someone who refuses to take up arms. He is not allowed to communicate at any length with the enlisted men. What little I know is all gotten secondhand.

The men he was with just spent a month in jail in Richmond for their beliefs. It was finally decided the older church members could return home by paying a $500 fine for exemption privileges, but these young fellows were forced into service.

They insist they will not shoot no matter what happens. Our men scoff and cast sour looks their way, but they take it all in good grace and are friendly to all. They have something the rest of us do not.

Love,
David

P.S.: Have you heard any word from my folks? I keep wondering whether Thomas or Edward are among the Yankees headed our way. God help us!

"John . . ." I pulled him out onto the porch. The afternoon sun had warmed the worn boards at my feet. "John, something is astir. I can feel it. The pike has been jammed with soldiers and wagons heading into town all morning. I . . . I wish I knew what this means." I could not hide my worry.

"Let me slip over to Grandfather's and try to find James, Mother. He would know if anyone does."

I had not dared let the boys out of my sight all day.

The enemy had already been spotted ten miles west, and telegram messages the evening before had brought the terrifying news that Stonewall Jackson's armies were leaving in the opposite direction, heading east over the Blue Ridge mountains and leaving Staunton open for enemy attack.

With great misgiving I watched John slip out of sight across the field, then gathered the younger boys around. "In case of an emergency, we will head to the attic and hide behind the chimney. John should be back within an hour."

Their eyes reflected my fear. Too frightened to eat, they crouched silently by the window, watching . . . waiting. I paced back and forth behind them.

One hour went by, then two, then still another. Evening came, and still no sign of John.

At dusk I went out alone to do the chores. At the sound of horses coming up the lane, I left my milking and opened the barn door, my heart nearly leaping out of my chest.

Three men in gray were pulling their mounts to a stop by the watering trough. They saw me standing in the doorway.

"Howdy, ma'am. We need to water our horses. Hope you'll oblige us."

I nodded, swallowing hard. The slurping of the thirsty animals drowned out their brief conversation.

At last they pulled the horses back. "Ma'am, we're awful hungry. You wouldn't be so kind as to bring us out something, would you?"

The man's words were not rough, and I found myself handing them the milk pail and going to the house for several pieces of cornbread and a small piece of cold squirrel that was supposed to have been our evening meal.

The men ate rapidly and licked the bones clean, wiping their hands across the back of their pants. "Thank you, lady. We haven't had milk to drink since I don't know when."

Their courtesy gave rise to my courage. "Sir . . . Will there be a battle directly? Are the Federals upon us?"

The blond-haired man's eyes turned to steel. "We plan to keep those sneaking rascals away from you, ma'am. We're standing picket duty just up the pike from here. No one is allowed to leave or enter town."

I watched them ride away, then turned toward the house, my mind in a whirl. *Townsfolk not allowed to leave* . . . Had John been forced to stay? Had he been pressed into service as a baggage boy? I had heard of that happening. I moaned.

A gentle tapping at the door awoke me. Slipping off the chair, I walked to the door and called, "Who's there?"

"It's me, Mother!"

"John!"

I pulled him inside. My tears of relief dampened his shirt. At last I drew back and looked into his face. "I'm sorry, son. I was so worried. Are you all right?"

"Yes. I . . . I'm very sorry. Is there something I can eat? I'm almost starved."

In the morning when the boys got up, John repeated his story. He had met James heading to the telegraph office. The soldiers had poured in by railroad and on foot, sealing off the town.

"There were a lot of country folk who had fled into town for safety or food and were forced to stay. Some of them were frantic. They had children or family at home waiting for them. Some of them had also come in search of relatives in the army."

"Why were the soldiers so strict about it?" Peter scraped the last of the meager spoonfuls of mush from his plate and pushed back from the table.

John's eyes lit up. "Because Stonewall Jackson was in town, and they didn't want anyone passing the news through the lines to the Feds. I saw him myself."

I was confused. "But I thought his men had headed east out of the valley."

John nodded. "He's clever, Mother. All he did was march his men across the mountains to the railroad station and catch the train back to town. The Northern troops don't know where to find him. He left this morning before dawn, he and all his ten thousand men, gone without a trace."[3]

"Where is he headed now?"

"I don't know. West, someone thought. But whatever he does, he has some good purpose for it, you can be sure of that."

DIARY—5/7/62

Have joined up with Jackson's infantry, racing to catch up with Federal forces in the Alleghenies. Men all fired up for action. Impossible to decipher the General's long range plans. Running from one force to chase another.

Tortured mind, marching weary feet, tired to the bone. This can't be the way of righteousness—death and hell struggling fiercely up and down the slopes; billowing smoke; roaring cannon; yelling, screaming, cursing, dying men; gunpowder blackened faces; red, watering eyes; wild emotions; and parched mouths and noses.

Every body fiber is tensed to bursting, and a strange weakness sickens the stomach. Fierce surges of strength leave one wringing with sweat in minutes.

Many dead lie on the mountainside. What spared me? How could the ball that pierced the New Testament in my pocket, went halfway through my diary, and knocked me down, leave me with nothing worse than a throbbing shoulder?

I can find no sleep, even though exhausted. The pitiful moans of the wounded are enough to drive a man frantic. All the noise of battle reverberates through my mind.[4]

Camp Simmons

Dear Ellen,

Thank God I am well and can send this your way. We are in camp in the Alleghenies, eight miles back from where we caught up with the Union forces. It has been over a week since I took part in my first battle on Bull Pasture Mountain.

Now we are turned back again, and with Jackson as our leader, are to push the remaining enemy forces out of the valley.

I will spare you, dear wife, of all that has taken place, but O my God! The battle was a great horror of death! Although it lasted only four hours, it seemed we were at it a week.

I wonder if I will ever hold you again? After all I have seen, the possibilities look very slim, and yet perhaps my fortunate escape this time is a good omen.

Dear wife, if you've ever prayed for me before, pray now.

With all my love,
David

DIARY—5/17/62 Lebanon White Sulphur Springs

Camping here several days. Trying to get rested up for days ahead. Men washing out clothes and cooking extra food.

Rough marching to get here. Heavy rains. Wet as rats, and cold. No tents.

Feel sure we are heading into more bloodshed. Makes a sickening weakness in my gut. The men seem to brace up under this stuff and draw their courage from somewhere.

Is God watching now? To be on the path of destruction does something to a man.

DIARY—5/24/62

Life has become a maze of marching and weariness. The loveliness of the advancing season appears along the way as a dream from another world.

I have an irrepressible feeling that my time is fast approaching. Have found Jacob Wenger is from Dayton. Oh, God, my soul hungers for more in life than this—yet bodies get so tired, it becomes difficult to concentrate on matters of mind and conscience. Blind obedience, that's what the generals want. Talked with Chaplain Phillips.[5] His strong reasoning is convincing but brings no peace of mind.

Near the end of May, we received word Jackson's army had routed the opposing forces out of Winchester, pushing them thirty-five miles across the Potomac River.

Staunton was jubilant. The townsfolk came out into the streets, hugging each other with joy. Soldiers went from door to door ordering all wagons pressed into service to haul back captured goods. Ours was no exception.

I felt a strange mixture of relief and dread—relief for the greater distance between us and the Northern army, and dread that one of the hundreds of wounded being carried into Staunton by ambulance, wagon, or stretcher would be David. John made daily trips to the telegraph office to check the list of dead and wounded.

Then without warning, the tide turned. Peter came running up the front steps early one evening, a strange look on his face. "Mother, come here."

I wiped my hands on my apron and hurried after him onto the porch. The recent rains had made the fields dark mellow ribbons of plowed soil. The grass and new leaves hung limp and dripping. Mist rose from the hollows and the twisting course of Lewis Creek to the north.

On the muddy pike, a steady stream of wagons was sloshing its way toward town, the fatigued horses' heads bent low. No shouts or snapping of whips were heard.

"Weren't those the same wagons sent out to bring back things from the army last week? They're all empty!"

I rubbed my hand over my eyes. "I don't understand. Something must have happened."

As we watched, one wagon turned into our lane. Mud was caked between the wheel spokes, splattered over the sides, and smeared thick on the wagon bed.

The driver lifted his hat wearily, driving the horse around the house toward the barn. He was unhitching as Peter and I came up beside him.

He lifted his grime-covered face. He was just a young fellow, hardly older than Peter himself. And there was something familiar about his features. My mouth dropped open in surprise.

"James?" Peter stepped forward.

The weary lines broke into a brief grin. "I wondered whether you would finally figure it out."

I gasped, catching hold of the wagon's edge to steady myself. "James! How can this be?"

"Able men are awful scarce, Sis. I . . ."

"Why are all the wagons coming home empty?" Peter cut him short.

"Yanks following too close."

"Following? I thought Jackson just chased them across the Potomac."

"He did, but they have gotten reinforcements and are now closing in on both sides of him. They're out to trap him for sure this time."[6]

Fear leaped into Peter's eyes. "But they can't. Papa is with Jackson now!"

"That may be. But there's nothing we can do about it. I need some sleep before they get here. I'm dead tired. We've been driving straight for two days and nights."

James crawled up onto the broad back of the mud-splattered mare, lifted his hand, and was gone.

DIARY—6/3/62

Marching for our lives. Vicious storm drenched us all. Mud, shoe deep, smeared across man and beast. Yanks only couple miles behind. Only a fraction of time allowed for rest. We march more asleep than awake. When the call comes to halt, we drop where we are, asleep almost before we hit the ground.

Two armies are trying to converge forty-five miles ahead of us, to trap us between them. We owe our lives to our cavalry.

Jacob Wenger was captured in Winchester. What will happen to all those men who risked their lives for what they believed? What will happen to me—who no longer know what I believe?

DIARY—6/7/62
Passed Harrisonburg on the double. Feds close behind. Word of Turner Ashby's death just brought into camp. Men sobbing, unashamed, hats off.

My dear wife, if I could just hold you close and see your clear eyes and the innocence of little Andy and the other boys, maybe my mind could start to untangle all of this.

A low rumble broke the morning silence. I stopped short. Surely not thunder—not with such a clear sky.

I glanced at John just coming out of the blacksmith shop. He had heard it too.

"Do you think it's another battle?"

"I don't know." He stood rigidly, staring unseeingly toward the north.

I fought back the tight feeling rising inside me. It had been a while since we had heard from David. The words of his last letter came back, burning with their plea, "If you ever prayed for me before, pray now." I swallowed hard, tracing the horizon with my eyes.

The rumbling continued, increasing in intensity, until evening.[7] It was midmorning of the next day when a knock sounded on the door. Peter leaped to open it, then stepped back in confusion. Father stood in the doorway, twisting his hat awkwardly in his hands. I was at the door in an instant.

"Father! What a surprise to see you here. Won't you come in?"

He cleared his throat, running his hand over his gray hair. "No, I . . . Well, ah . . . yes, I guess I can." He came right to the point. "Ellen, you are aware that a battle was fought close by yesterday?" His face contorted, and he shielded his face with his palm. His voice was thick. "William was . . . was killed."

"Oh, Father!" My own brother, dead. I caught hold of the door frame. A horrible dread rose up inside. I forced the words out between clenched teeth. "And David?"

"Wounded in action. He is on the list of those brought into town last night."

The room swayed. Father's voice continued, but seemed to be coming through a thick haze. Dimly I could see the boys' white faces staring at me, then everything went black.

"Ellen. Ellen, can you hear me? You've got to be strong, my girl."

Cold water splashed across my face and dampened my collar. A heavy feeling lay on my chest. Something terrible must have happened. I groped to remember. My ·eyes blinked open, and the room swam into focus. Andy was leaning over me, chin quivering and eyes full of tears.

Father dabbed at my face again, but I pushed his hand aside. "No . . . no, Father." I wet my lips. "I'll be all right."

I sat up gingerly. My brother William killed. David wounded. I stifled a moan.

I let Father help me up. The roughness of his coat was against my cheek. The smell of leather and horses brought back memories. His touch held the tenderness of a parent for a little child. I could not hold back the tears, leaning hard against his arm.

"Now, now . . ." he looked embarrassed. He patted my shoulder awkwardly. "We can't give up now."

"I . . . forgive me, Father." I pulled the boys close. "We must be strong for Papa's sake."

I gulped for air. "How—how badly is he hurt?"

Father blew his nose. "I don't know."

"I . . . I must go to David. I must see him. But the hospital is on the other edge of town." My hands felt clammy cold.

"Mother and I are going to pick up the body. You could ride along."

"But the boys . . ."

"I'm going home to pick up Mother. I'll bring Tansy along when I come back."

I nodded, biting my lip till I tasted blood. He glanced distractedly at each of us, then stepped out the door.

Huddled together, the boys clung to me, sobbing.

We rode in silence. Mother sat stiffly in the middle, not looking to either side as the wagon rattled into town, passing men lying along the road's edge. Crowds of townsfolk spilled over into the street jammed with wagons and buggies.

David . . . David! Are you lying here? Are you one of these men? I shuddered, my eyes sweeping constantly over the scene before me: dirty bandages, seeped with blood; staring, powder-caked faces; lifted hands with moans of, "Water . . . water . . . !"

❧ Chapter VII ❧

"**E**xcuse me, please." I plucked timidly at
the sleeve of a passing orderly. He
turned impatiently, then seeing my
distress, the creases in his forehead
relaxed.

"Yes . . . ?"

"I . . . I am looking for my husband, David Shull.
I heard he was brought in last night from the battle
of Port Republic. He was part of the Fifty-second
Infantry."

"Lady, with the hundreds of men being brought
in here, how can I . . ." He sighed and pointed a tired
finger down the dim hall. "All newcomers are put in
the front room until placed elsewhere. Check there."

He was gone before I was certain which room he meant. I stood there stupidly, a statue in the stream of activity around me. Moans, sometimes a scream, came from doorways down the corridor. I shrank against the wall as a stretcher bearing a sheet-covered body jostled past. Smells of ether, blood, sweat, and death mingled in the stale air.

Oh, David! Must I find you in a place like this? I trembled, and my hands felt cold. I hurried along the painted tile walls and paused in the farthest doorway, steadying myself against the doorjamb.

The place was crammed with cots. Men were on the floor and in the aisles. Some were groaning and tossing; others were cursing. Others were lying still, not moving a muscle.

I instinctively shrank from walking among strange men, yet I had to find David. I forced myself to take one step, then another, heading toward a black-dressed lady with a large white apron, bending over a cot with a basin and bandages.

"Excuse me, ma'am . . ."

The lady straightened and turned. "Ellen!"

"Agnes!"

We clutched each other, the rolls of bandages falling onto the bed.

"You . . . ?"

I struggled to find my voice. "I'm here to . . . David's been wounded. Your husband?"

"Wounded in the battle of Kernstown. He had just escaped from the enemy before the fight. He lost his leg. I nursed him along for five weeks but . . ." She turned her head aside. "I've been working here ever since. Come."

I followed her up and down the aisles, forcing

136

myself to look at each face. Would I even know him? The feeling of dread grew into a tightness that squeezed my chest. I found it hard to breathe. Then I saw the chart with his name.

"David!" My scream was no louder than a whisper.

Blood was seeping from strips of sheeting wound around his neck and head. His eyes were closed, and his parched lips were drawn back, jaws held stiffly in place by a wire brace. Swathed in bandages, one leg was pulled straight, strapped to a board. He lay still, so dreadfully still.

Agnes squeezed my hand and turned respectfully aside.

David! My heart beat wildly. I leaned over the bed, shutting my eyes as I felt the room begin to whirl. I must be strong, strong for David's sake.

"David . . ."

He turned restlessly toward my voice. When his eyes opened, they were bright with fever.

My voice shook. "It's Ellen, David. I've come. I love you, David! I love you." My eyes burned with tears. I knelt on the rough wooden floor, reaching for his restless hands, clasping them tight.

He frowned, trying to concentrate, then a light sprang up in his gray eyes. The grip on my hand tightened.

I buried my face on his chest.

I felt torn in two when Father found me. He stood silently at the foot of the bed, the nervous twitching of his cheek the only sign of emotion.

I laid my cheek against David's hot one. "I'll be back in the morning, dearest. You must make it through. You must make it."

137

Then, tears streaming down my face, I blindly let Father lead me to the wagon. Mother sat woodenly on the wagon seat. In the back, a faded canvas covered a coffin. William, my own brother, dead. His wife and half-grown family back in Bridgewater, without a husband and father. How could this be real? I muffled my sobs in my handkerchief.

"Deah chile! You's all done in. Yer face is white as de inside ob a ches-se-nut." Tansy led me to a chair. "Dat man ob yours still liven'?"

I nodded numbly. Suddenly I felt drained. I untied my sunbonnet just as the boys appeared at the top of the stairway. They were beside me even before I sank into a chair. Not a word was said, though their eyes were asking a hundred things.

"He's alive, boys. Papa is badly hurt, but he's still alive."

"Where he hurt-en, Mommy?" Andy's little body pressed against me, shivering.

"His head and his right leg. They've wrapped his head, and his leg is strapped fast to a board."

"Is he hurt turrible bad?"

"Pretty bad, Andy. A doctor came and gave him some morphine for pain just before I left. They will do all they can for him."

I didn't tell them of the hundreds of others just as bad or worse off, or of the lack of supplies, or scarcity of attendants. I dared not even allow myself to dwell on those things.

138

The days passed in a haze—visits to the hospital, changing dressings, forcing thin gruel between swollen lips, sponging fevered face and hands. I was torn between the two desperate needs of my family.

A week went by, then two. Word came that Jackson had marched his men over the Blue Ridge through Jarmen's Gap to catch railroad cars east. Robert E. Lee needed their help near Richmond.

"Mother." John stopped on his way to the barn, took the hoe from my hands and led me to the shade. "You are wearing yourself out. Must the garden get finished tonight?"

I wiped my sweaty hands on my skirts. "We need every plant, John. I thought I'd work just a few minutes while the rest of you do chores."

"I know every plant is precious, but we can help you after supper. Go in and rest a while. You hardly take time to catch your breath these days. You can't go on much longer like this."

He picked up the milk bucket again. "Isn't Papa getting better? Is there no improvement at all?"

I sat down beside the well, leaning against its smooth sides. The cool stone felt good through my thin calico. I closed my eyes to hide the pain his words brought me. "I don't know, son. He is so miserable most of the time it's hard to hold a conversation with him. The doctor feels he should be showing signs of improvement but . . ."

"But what?"

I folded and refolded my hands in my lap. "I think he has an anguish more dreadful than the wounds he suffered."

"How bad are those wounds, Mother? You've never answered clearly when we ask you. I'm fifteen now. I ought to be able to know the truth."

My eyes grew misty. "You are becoming a man, John. This shirt is too small for you." I reached up, fingering the frayed ends of the too-short sleeves. "His leg has a big, ugly wound where a piece of shell went through and broke the bone." My mouth twisted painfully. "But the worst . . . John, he doesn't look the same. The doctor is letting me dress it now." I took a deep breath. "His face is swollen and discolored, and several teeth were knocked out on one side. They had to wire his jaw partially shut."

John winced. "Does he ever talk about . . . how it happened?"

I shook my head.

He waited for me to say more, but when I kept my eyes on the ground, he squeezed my shoulder and turned toward the barn.

I laid my head against the well's rim, letting the breeze blow cool against my closed eyes. No one else knew how hard it was to hear David's groans and watch his efforts to speak.

Every day another white sheet would be draped over another bed. The vacancy was filled as quickly as the orderlies took the body away. Just the day before, a work-worn woman across the aisle from me, with blond disheveled hair and dark circles under

140

her eyes, straightened up and cried out like an injured animal. She had thrown herself sobbing onto her husband's body. "Tom, answer me, Tom! We need you—the children and I. Oh, Tom, you can't leave us, you can't!"

She had rocked back and forth, her cries rising to a shrill pitch as tears streamed down her face. They continued until an orderly led her outside.

And Jonas Fisher. How could I forget him? I felt a dull ache even now to think of him.[1] He was just a young fellow from Georgia, hurt so badly, and yet so brave. He had been three beds down from David. Never complaining, he always had a cheerful word of greeting to all who came by.

I had written a letter for him one day while waiting for David to wake up.

"You must have it pretty rough, seeing your man suffering like he is. You have a family?"

"Four boys. The oldest is almost sixteen."

His eyes had lit up. "I have four brothers back home. Ain't heard from them for awhile though. Tell them to write me. I miss them like everything."

When I held the writing paper toward him, he shook his head laughing. "I never learned no schooling much. Ain't got no hand for letters. You write it all please, and I'll be much obliged."

There was quiet for the next few minutes while he dictated, and I wrote. At the close of the letter he said, "Tell 'em I'm getting along fine, and mebbe I can come home soon." His face lit up. "I'm getting a lot better, don't you think?"

I looked at his left leg, healing beautifully, but now inches shorter than the other. He had told me how the doctors had slipped the broken ends of bone together, lapping the ragged edges. An open cast made of layers of brown paper cemented together with stiff paste and baked around a stove pipe held it all in place.

When the cast was taken off, he discovered how crippled he would be the rest of his life. Although a bitter blow, there had been no hysteria.

"You have been a brave man, Jonas. Your father has every reason to be proud of you."

All the talking had tired him, and he lay back and closed his eyes. But the pleased smile on his face stayed there long after I resumed my other duties.

At my next trip to the hospital two days later, I was surprised to find his bed empty. Had he been sent home already?

I made my way toward Mrs. Mazzie Watkins, an elderly lady who came in regularly to help deal out tea and toast. Sometimes she managed to supplement the hospital's food with her own private concoctions of herbs, in an effort to speed healing and renew zest for living. The men amusedly tolerated her sincere efforts and never told doctors of the secret bottles she hid in the many folds of her brown skirts.

"Mrs. Watkins?"

"Um?" She turned from bending over a newcomer, her eyes squinting as she tried to see me.

"Mrs. Watkins, this was Jonas Fisher's bed. Was he discharged yesterday? I'm so glad if..." I stopped short at the puckered frown that came over her face.

"He's gone. And 'twas an awful way ter go. I tried to make him take my arrow root and calamus, but he would have none of it. Said his mammie didn't use sech stuff 'cept'en on stomachache and the grip."

I pulled her closer. "What do you mean?"

"I mean he up and died last night."

"Died!" I gave her arm a shake. "What happened? He was almost well. He was hoping to be sent home any day."

"I don't know nothin' 'cept what they told me. Bled to death last night, and the doctors nor the rest of 'em couldn't help him."

My mind was still in a daze when Agnes came in soon after the two o'clock meal. Her eyes were bloodshot and as soon as she saw me, tears brimmed close to the surface.

"I helped him walk last evening for the first time," she choked out when we had a minute to talk. "Everyone was so pleased. They were all cheering, and he was beaming like a young boy. But during my night rounds, I heard him cry out. There was a small jet of blood spurting up from his injured leg."

Her face was stricken. "I jabbed my fingers into the hole and called for the surgeon on duty. His examination showed that an artery must have been cut by a piece of splintered bone. 'No earthly power can save him.' That's what he said."

"Oh, Agnes! How awful! What did you do?"

"What *could* I do? He took the message so calmly, gave me some last words to his family, and then he took a long breath, looked at me bravely and said, 'You can let go.' But, Ellen, I *couldn't*. I felt I could stay there all night, or forever, even if my own life was in danger. But I fainted."

I grabbed her close, and we cried on each other's shoulders. Finally she pulled back and blew her nose. "I cried myself to pieces. It's hard to see them go, but when you think they've finally pulled through, it's worse than when they give up from the start. It seems there are so few that walk out these doors to live normal again."

So few that live normally . . . Panic rose within me. I fought it back and forced myself back to the present. Opening my eyes, I could see the cow being led out to pasture again. The chores were finished. The boys would be anxious for the evening meal.

It was late when I followed the boys up the stairs to bed. After closing the door, I sank into a chair without undressing. My whole body throbbed with weariness, and the knot in the pit of my stomach refused to relax.

The conversation with John this afternoon had made me face up to what I was unwilling to admit before. David was not making progress, in fact, he seemed to be getting worse. The tossing and turning, even while doped with morphine, never seemed to stop.

His eyes would light up to see me come, and his hands would clasp mine with an intensity that never failed to bring tears to my eyes. And yet there was something, something between us; something he could not bring himself to talk about.

What hell had he endured out there on that bloody field? I paced back and forth wretchedly in the darkness. Whatever it was, it would kill him unless something changed.

How long I walked the floor, I do not know, but when I finally crawled into bed, I was resolute. I would talk to a doctor tomorrow. I would plead for permission to bring David home.

"I'm here, honey." I took off my sunbonnet, and turning my back to the rest of the room, bent closer over David's still form. I reached out a finger to touch his cheek.

The eyes that fluttered open gleamed for a moment, then turned dull again. Wincing, he lifted an unsteady hand to grasp my fingers, lifting them to his lips.

"You . . . you shouldn't have come." He spoke with great effort.

"Why, David!"

"This . . . no place . . . for a . . . woman." He ran the tip of his tongue over dry lips. "Remember . . . how I said . . . I caused you enough . . . enough suffering already? It hurts too much to keep . . ." The last words faded into a whisper. A coughing spell overcame him, and he groaned as the effort made fresh blood ooze through his neck bandages.

I turned aside to hide my agony. *Oh, David . . . David, you've come too far to give up now. We love you; we need you . . . the boys and I!*

The man in the next cot caught my eye and beckoned with a gnarled finger. His gray, stringy hair straggled out over the pillow. His raspy voice sounded uncomfortably loud against the hum of activity in the large room. "He ain't got much chance anymore. I've seen it plenty of times . . . they give up; they're soon gone." He snapped his fingers.

145

I drew back sharply. How could he blurt that so callously within David's hearing? My answer was coldly quiet. "Sir, we don't plan to let that happen."

I turned back to David in the middle of the man's muttering, sponging David's face and lips until my angry indignation subsided.

"David . . ." I waited till his tired eyes opened again. "David, I am going to take you home. *Home*, David."

A trace of yearning passed over his face.

"I'm going to find a doctor."

He struggled weakly to say something, but I shook my head. "Lie still. I'll be right back."

The mid-afternoon meal was making its rounds. A large kettle of thin soup and a mound of cut slices of hard, dark bread was being pushed on a cart from one room to the next.

"Please, sir. I must talk to you." I felt my face flush under the doctor's irritation. His shaggy eyebrows scowled at me. His gray hair, though fluffy around his ears, was nearly bald on top.

His voice was clipped. "What is it? I've been called for emergency surgery in ten minutes."

I plunged on. "It's my husband, sir. He's not getting better, and I fear he's lost his will to live. I would like to take him home. Perhaps there . . ."

He pulled his watch out of his pocket, flipping open the case to check the time. "I'm sorry, lady. It's against hospital policy."

"They need never know!"

He rolled his eyes helplessly. "How bad are your husband's injuries?"

"A broken jaw and shattered upper leg."

"Mouth wired shut?"

146

I nodded. "Until recently."

"Leg beginning to knit?"

"I . . . I'm not sure."

His face softened as he saw my misery. "It happens all the time." He sighed. "I wish we could give out potions of 'determination,' but we can't."

"But, sir, perhaps in familiar surroundings. We have four sons at home. Maybe away from all this suffering, with their help . . ."

His eyes flashed. "Lady, you are asking the impossible! You think you could handle it. Well, let me tell you . . . you couldn't! Would you know what to do if he began to hemorrhage? And what would you give him for pain when the dressings need changing? He won't be able to eat solid food for months yet. You'll be at his bedside from dawn to dusk and all through the night. You have no experience or training to fall back on in case of emergency!"

I felt tears of frustration fill my eyes. "But I have love, sir." Without thinking I reached for his arm. "Don't you have a wife?"

"Yes, but . . ."

"Wouldn't you try the same for her if it were your last hope?"

His shoulders sagged, and he turned abruptly. "Come with me."

I followed him around the corner to a storage closet lined from floor to ceiling with shelves filled with supplies.

"Now we can talk without being heard." He wiped his brow wearily. "You think we don't care. Look at our supplies. It's hard to do with far less than we need. It makes a man tense and ready to snap at everyone. I've been working twenty-four hour days for longer than I can remember."

He straightened his sagging shoulders. "How far away is 'home'?"

"About five miles."

He stroked his mustache thoughtfully. "The trip is going to be rough. What's your husband's name?"

"David Shull, sir. He's in Room 102, Bed 36."

"This is against hospital policy, but I'll check him, and if I think there's the slightest chance he'll stand the trip, I'll let you take him home."

My eyes widened. "I don't want to get you into trouble."

"It's not the first time I've done things on my own." He gathered up a load of bandages and stepped to the door. "Be here promptly at six tomorrow evening. We'll see what we can do."

James was the kind one who carefully guided the horses through the streets, picking out the gentlest route home. Twilight coolness floated up from the lowlands by the creek as we passed, and I pulled the cover closer around David's shoulders.

He seemed to be in a stupor, and had made no comment as he was transferred from stretcher to hay-lined wagon bed. The light from the kerosene lamp cast a shadow across his profile—such a white face, and so still.

I felt my throat constrict and checked again the cardboard cone soaked with ether lying covered beside me. "Use only in case the pain gets too severe." The doctor had looked at me sharply as he placed it in my hand. "If he can make out otherwise, it will be the better for him."

"Making out okay?" James was peering back over his shoulder. "The section ahead has quite a few ruts. I'll try to take it slow."

I nodded, daring not to lift my eyes from David's face.

The shrill of crickets rose steadily from both sides of the road. Some jarring was unavoidable. David moaned, and I held a wet sponge to his cracked lips.

We were a mile out of town when a dark figure emerged from the dimness, giving me a jolt.

"Father!"

He looked sheepish. "I was just out for a stroll. Thought you might need help . . ."

By the time James brought the horses to a stop, David had lapsed into merciful unconsciousness. The men carried the stretcher into the living room, placing him carefully onto the waiting cot. With eager, yet frightened anticipation, the boys gathered to await his return to consciousness.

I followed the men to the door. "Thank you, Father, James. You have been a great help."

James' face was sober. "Shall I send Tansy down for the night?"

I shook my head. "This is something I must do alone. Maybe later . . ." I hoped desperately they could understand.

Father coughed dryly and cleared his throat. He said nothing, but gave a slight nod as he climbed into the wagon. James hung behind. "If anything happens, just send John to bounce a few stones off my window, and I'll be right over."

As the crunching of the horses' hooves faded into

the darkness, I could hear soft sobbing behind me. Suddenly waves of terror washed over me. What had I done? Did I bring their father home to die before their eyes? I bit my lips. I must be strong! I had to be strong! David hung on through that first night, and one day gradually crawled into another. I prayed desperately, not with confidence God would hear, but because I knew nothing else to do.

The telegraph office in town steadily clicked out news of the awful fighting going on near Richmond. Day after day, in rough wilderness country, the armies clashed, the list of dead and wounded growing to frightening lengths.

Grateful that David wasn't among them, I spooned broth through cracked and swollen lips, rubbed sore limbs, gently changed oozing dressings, and felt rewarded by any grudging bit of healing that showed itself.

But his spirit—even though his wounds showed signs of healing—remained crushed and broken, barely a hint of a smile, very few words, and most often his face toward the wall. The boys felt hurt by his lack of interest.

His moans and mumbling often woke me up at night. I would lie in the darkness, heart pounding, unable to sleep again.

"Mother, what's happened to Papa? Will he always be this way?"

"I don't know, son." The sun was already hot, even though the morning was still young. I stopped in the shade of the barn, setting down my end of the makeshift carryall, and straightened up sadly. It had been Peter's turn to help clean and dress David's wounds. He had worked carefully and without a word through the whole grim procedure. "I think Papa knows something we don't; something that has just about destroyed him."

"Why can't he tell us?"

I gingerly separated the rags that could be scalded and reused from those that must be burned. "He's trying to shield us, to carry some horror alone. We can only wait until he is strong enough to share it."

"Well, I hope he lives long enough to get it done!"

I was too stunned to reply. I fingered the hair so desperately in need of trimming on the back of his neck. "I'm beginning to think God is the only One who can help Papa now, Peter, the only One."

He didn't answer, but the hunger and confusion in his eyes haunted me. I couldn't tell him of my own struggle with the same aching questions. I must always be strong, going ahead with whatever needed doing with a cheerful outlook no matter how dark the moment.

The younger boys, too little to help with David's routine care, had come and tried to share bits of news they thought would interest him, but they had soon given up. They would again appear silently in the doorway, their eyes big with unshed tears, and then slip out of sight again. It cut like a knife.

The heat intensified all day. By evening, I was

151

exhausted, but it was too hot to sleep. I lay on my mat in the corner of the floor, careful not to move but unable to relax. Sullen night air ruffled the cotton curtains at the window, and I could hear the growl of distant thunder.

How could I go on like this? Helplessness overwhelmed me, and I thrust my face deep into the pillow, glad for the dark.

Thunder rumbled again, and there was a brief moment of brightness as streaks of lightning swept the sky. Then silence.

The breeze picked up, bringing a smell of rain. I thrust back the covers, huddling, arms around bent knees. David stirred restlessly in his sleep. The next flash of light illuminated his face, drawn and tight.

Tears slipped unchecked down my cheeks. If only I could do something to help. This loneliness was crushing me, carving caverns inside that frightened me with their immensity.

There was a splatter of rain on the roof, a pause, then it picked up in earnest, driving the spray in the window and wetting the fluttering curtains. I scrambled up, tugging at the shutters. The old hinges screeched. Had he heard?

I paused and glanced in his direction. All was dark and still. Then a crash of thunder shook the house, and the rain poured. Before the heavy shutters swung shut, the room glowed bright as day.

"No! Don't shoot! I didn't know it was you, Edward. I didn't mean to kill you!"

My heart pounded wildly. David was sitting up in bed, his eyes wide and staring.

"David, it's me, Ellen. You're safe, David. You're

here at home. Remember? There is no battle." I knelt beside him, reaching out with trembling hands.

He sank back weakly with a moan. "I didn't mean to, Edward! Oh my God! My own brother . . . !"

"David! What is this that is terrifying you? Tell me, David!"

Suddenly he went limp. In the darkness I could feel him pulling back. There was a deep shuddering sigh, then he spoke strangely, "I . . . I guess I was dreaming."

I reached for his hands, my breath coming in gasps. "David, please let me share in this thing that is killing you—yes, killing you, David. I'm . . . I'm your wife!"

There was a frightening silence.

I continued brokenly. "We can't even talk anymore, David. We're in two different worlds. Seeing you waste away and not being able to help is a lot harder than knowing. Please, David—for my sake, for your sake, for the sake of the boys . . . !"

The rolls of thunder were nearly continuous. I almost didn't catch his reply.

"You care that much?"

"Yes! A thousand times yes! We've never kept anything from each other before, have we? This is eating away at you till . . ." I caught the sob in my throat, "it can only end in death."

A trembling hand reached out in the darkness and drew me close. Our tears mingled together. "I . . . I don't deserve a wife like you. You'll hate me when I tell you what I've done. You'll be through with me, Ellen."

"No . . . no, David!"

"I killed my brother, Ellen!" His voice cracked.

153

"My own brother! I didn't know it was him. God knows I didn't know!²

"We were in a field. They were firing down on us from ridges on both sides. Men were falling all around me. It was confusion, noise, and death. I . . . I hardly knew if I was living or dead."

He stopped to regain control of himself. "A group of us were sent through the underbrush to capture a cannon. He was behind a rock, Ellen. All I saw through the smoke was a rifle aiming at us. We all shot." His voice broke. "He fell back and . . . and then I saw who it was! I couldn't go on. The others pushed on without me. I knelt down and cradled his head in my arms, begging him not to die, begging him to forgive me . . ." David sank back, overcome with emotion.

I was weeping too hard to speak. *Oh, God in heaven! Has it come to this?*

"His . . . his blood was running down over me, and his eyes were glazing over. But he smiled at me, Ellen. He smiled at me, and with his last breath he said my name.

"I was beside myself! War is hell, Ellen! It was then a ball knocked me flat, and I felt blood on my neck. I could hardly breathe and everything started to swim."

"Oh, David!"

His voice was getting weaker. "When I came to, they had carried me down into the field and laid me under a tree. I begged them to find Edward . . . to bury us side by side.

"The next thing I remember was waking up in the hospital and wishing to die. I can't forgive myself, Ellen. It torments me day and night. I think I am los-

154

ing my mind!" He groaned and his head fell back.

I was trembling. Crying. Praying. I kept patting his hand, grateful at the moment for the darkness that filled the room.

❧ Chapter VIII ❧

The stifling heat of summer settled over the valley. All through the tall grasses bending in the scorching wind, the shrill sounds of insects rose and fell. Puffs of dust rose from every traveler on the pike. The air shimmered across the pasture and hung heavily inside the house.

It gave me the same smothered feeling I had had as a child when I pulled the covers over my head in the face of an approaching storm, feeling the sweat trickle down my neck in the darkness, yet afraid to poke out my head for a breath of air.

Mercifully, the war had moved elsewhere, leaving the land to restore its mangled acres. Mutilated trees made half-hearted attempts to cover their splintered

157

and bullet-pocked limbs with a sprinkle of fresh leaves. Torn and burned grasses struggled to sprout timid green tips to hide the many bare graves, some with markers, many with no identification. Their occupant's families would never know their ending agony.

Word was slow to reach us of the fighting near Richmond.[1] Occasional distant rumbling of cannon, and the mournful whistle of eastbound trains loaded with supplies for those at the front were grim reminders of what was happening on the other side of the mountain.

Nature would heal itself as certainly as there was life. With people it would take longer. But it would come; it must come. One must keep on living, trying to find courage and hope for something beyond the awful past.

One hot afternoon I gathered up my mending and stepped barefooted onto the porch where John and I had settled David an hour before.

"Come join me, dear." David propped himself up on one elbow, patting the edge of the cot. "Where are the children?"

"I let them go to the creek. It's so hot!" I fanned myself with my apron.

"Do you think it is safe?"

I felt startled. "Do you think there's danger? Things have seemed so quiet the last while. I guess I . . ." I lifted the wisps of hair off my neck. "I was going to ask you first, but you had dozed off."

"They're probably okay. It's just that . . ."

I stroked his arm. "I'm sorry, David."

He looked away. "If I could just find peace! I've relived it all a thousand times. I've told God I'm

158

sorry. I've wept, I've prayed, I've . . ." He took a deep breath. "There's no need to say all of this. You know every bit of it already. I need help—*help*, Ellen!"

He picked up the Bible from where it had slid down onto the porch floor. "I've been looking. God knows I've been looking. Maybe one of these days He will help me forgive myself."

I jabbed my needle fiercely into the shirt in my lap, not able to look at him through my blurring vision. But his eyes were on the Book before him. "I found the verse the chaplain loved to quote to us before a battle, 'I came not to send peace, but a sword.'

"But look at these, Ellen. Why didn't he ever read us these, 'Love your enemies, bless them that curse you, do good to them that hate you and pray for them which despitefully use you and persecute you.' "

I shook my head helplessly. "The women in town say those verses are outdated, that no one really lives by that today, not during wartime."

He didn't answer right away. Leaning back on his pillow, he closed his eyes with a sigh. I traced the ugly scar along his neck with my fingertips. "We've read over so many verses, David. In one sense it seems so plain to understand, but on the other . . ."

He rubbed his eyes. "A few months ago I would have thrown it aside as ridiculous, fulfilled my duty to the state, and felt justified in doing so. But now I'm not so sure."

He opened his eyes to stare at me. "If the Bible works, it should be true for all times—or it's not true at all!"

I picked up my mending once more. "But who would be so radical, David? There isn't anyone, is there?"

"Perhaps."

"Perhaps?"

"Perhaps there are. Remember? That Mennonite fellow. He said they still hold to this teaching." He gripped my hand. "Ellen, you said we were in this together. Would you be willing to make a commitment to truth—pure, unadulterated truth?"

My eyes widened. "You know I'll stand beside you always, David."

"Ponder it, Ellen. It may cost more than you'll care to pay." The intensity of his eyes made his face more gaunt than ever.

A puff of air stirred the leaves beside the porch, and I drew my breath. *Willing to pay? What would I be willing to give for David to find peace—to find peace in my own soul?*

I wet my lips. "It frightens me, David. It frightens me almost to pieces. But there is something inside that hungers for more than what we've known and been taught. I am willing—if you are."

"We don't know where this may lead us, Ellen. Or how it will affect the family."

I felt tears coming. "But what will we have without it, David?"

His face suddenly relaxed, and he gripped my hand. "Then let us pray."

His prayer was very brief and fervent. "O God of heaven, here we are. Show Yourself to us, and we commit ourselves to follow."

A few garden things managed to survive the dry heat of the summer, and we put all our efforts into harvesting them for the winter months ahead. Carrots, carefully dug and placed in a bucket of dirt were buried in the crawl space under the house. The half a dozen heads of cabbage and bags of potatoes were set alongside them.

Beans and corn, laid out on screens in the hot afternoon sun to dry, filled jars and crocks on the kitchen shelf. Strung-up onions and apple slices hung from the attic rafters.

One evening Andy and Davie pulled me away from where I was sitting on the steps, stringing up bunches of tea Peter had harvested along the creek banks. Except for an excited giggle, no word of explanation would they give.

In the tall weeds behind the barn, long curving briars tore at my skirts and scratched my bare legs. "Whatever could you want to show me out here? Aren't you getting scratched up?"

They were too excited to notice. "Over here, Mommy!" Davie was panting. "Look what we found!" He almost dragged me through the worst of the thicket to a pile of old manure David had cleaned out of the barn a year or two before.

There on the back side, almost overgrown with towering ragweed and jimson, trailed a healthy looking vine with large green leaves.

"Not . . . not a pumpkin vine?" I could hardly believe my eyes.

"Yes, see here!" Andy pulled back the tough weed stalks and pointed eagerly. The pumpkin lying there, orange and fat in the twilight, was a bit lopsided, but beautiful nonetheless.

"Why, I was just wishing for pumpkin! However did a seed fall here? We didn't have any seed to plant this year at all."

There were two of them, and together they filled the washtub. All four boys were needed to carry the rich booty to the house.

Along with the cooler days of September, I watched David struggle to regain his strength. There was purpose behind his shaky efforts to sit up, and every night I rubbed the shrunken, stiff leg muscles, wincing along with him as he sweated out the pain.

John brought him a smooth piece of hickory, and he spent hours carving out an oblong picture frame. He shaped ivy leaves along its fluted edges and rubbed it with a broken piece of glass until it felt as smooth as silk to my fingertips. He would not tell me what it was for.

Last of all he had Davie bring him a dab of axle grease, working it into the grain until its darkened wood gleamed in the lamplight. It was lovely. It would always be treasured.

One day I stepped inside the front room with a stack of freshly-folded clothes and caught him standing beside the cot, his face white with effort.

"David!"

Guilt clouded his face. "You weren't supposed to

162

see."

"You're going to hurt yourself. Here . . ." I flung down my load and caught him before he fell, lowering him gently onto the cot once more.

"You're too weak to try that yet!"

"You don't understand, Ellen. I've got to push myself."

"But . . ."

He caught my hand. "You've done so much, Ellen. There are some things I must do alone. You must let me try. Now, see what I was doing . . ." He pointed to the finished frame laying on the pillow. "It's our marriage certificate, finally trimmed out properly. There's even room to press some of those posies you like so well and place them around the sides."

I felt color creep into my cheeks. I bent over, cupping his face in my hands. "I can hardly find a place not covered with whiskers." I brushed his face with a kiss, laughing shakily. "I'm just happy to have you here and know you still have the spunk to try things on your own. Persistence is becoming to you, you know."

"Is it?" For a moment his old grin brightened his face.

"That's what made me love you in the first place. You know *that*, don't you?"

"I couldn't help it. I was smitten by your lovely green eyes."

"Not green!"

"Hazel, then. You were too shy to say a word. Too refined. Remember?"

"Perhaps." I stroked his hair. "David." I bit my lip. "Will you . . . are you still wishing to go?"

"Go where?"

"You know."

He stared out the window. "Who knows, Ellen. It would have to be secret. And it can't be for a while. I must get my strength back, get strong enough to go before the recruiters come checking on me again."

"It would be so dangerous!"

"I know. But we've committed ourselves." He turned to face me. "Or, do you wish to turn back?"

I took a long deep breath. "No, of course not, David."

Forward was the only way to peace. But the cost—could I bear the cost?

The rain showers of the day before had stopped during the night, and the morning fire felt good as I knelt to scoop up the ashes along the front of the hearth.

I frowned. The fireplace needed scrubbing. The whole room did. Even as the flames leaped higher, I was embarrassed to see cobwebs trailing several places from the beams overhead. I hadn't had time all summer to concentrate on extra cleaning. With David's improvement, I no longer had any excuse.

I thought back to my girlhood. Housecleaning was always hired out. My stepmother always scrutinized the results, making sure her standards of cleanliness were met. I hadn't thought about it being otherwise until one morning I had found Silas, with rag and pail in hand, limping toward his cabin.

"What are you going to do, Silas? I slipped out to

bring you some fresh tarts from the kitchen. Tansy's in a baking mood today." I handed him the folded paper, steam still drifting from the corners.

"I guess I's in de scrubb'en mood, Miss Ellen." He took the paper, grinning a toothy thank-you.

"House cleaning? Why, Silas, that's women's work. You're the farm overseer."

He chuckled at my wrinkled nose. "Wuhk nebber hurt 'eny one."

"But why don't you wait till Tansy is free to help you—or little Willie?"

The old man hooked his cane over the pail's rim and reached for his door. "I jus' hiahs mysef. I figures dat's de cheapes' way. I's been do'en it mysef for nigh twenty yeahs now. If'en it be jus' me an' mysef, we don' hab no squabbles. If I hab any question, I jus' ax mysef and we come to quick agreement."

"But, women's work?"

He tapped one gnarled finger on his chest. "De real Silas is not made liddle by any kind of honest wuhk. De real Silas only made liddle if he act in a se'fish way."

I smiled, remembering his choice of words. He had never found a job that needed doing that was below his dignity. And no one could fault him for not doing it well.

Even when he became bedfast the summer before I left home, he had often asked for help to get into the lone chair by the window, his trembling hands tenderly dusting the sill and the geranium sitting there.

After three days of thorough cleaning, the boys and I were glad to leave scrub rags and buckets behind and head for an outing in the woods. As much as they begged, I would not tell them the reason for our expedition.

"You've all worked hard helping with Daddy, as well as cleaning. You deserve a break." I swung my pail back and forth on my fingers.

"Even Daddy is entitled to some peace and quiet. I think he was beginning to be afraid we would attack him next with all our cleaning paraphernalia."

"Pair of *what*?" Davie reached for my hand, skipping along beside me.

Peter threw back his head and laughed. "She means all our scrubbing tools. Well, I am glad enough to leave that behind. I never did care for women's work, and I don't 'spose I ever shall. Will you, Andy?"

Andy panted to keep up. "But . . . but she's still got a bucket."

I chuckled. "Over there in the bend of the creek is what we are going to use our bucket for today."

Andy followed my extended finger. There at the far edge of the pastures grew three large persimmon trees. A hard frost two days before had changed the tartness of the dull orange fruit to a wrinkled sweetness. I planned to experiment with the pulp, mixing it with cornmeal to make a type of bread Indians used to make. If I hurried, we could have it for supper along with the regular boiled potatoes, stewed carrots, and cabbage.

As I was placing the finished dish on the table that evening, James' familiar figure came around the back of the house. Andy and Davie were skipping along beside him, talking simultaneously. James was smiling down at them both, but when he looked up, I could see a soberness in his eyes.

I wiped my hands on my apron, conscious of the rust-brown stain on my fingers. "Good evening, James."

"Hi, Sis."

"It's been a long time since we've had this privilege. Where have you been keeping yourself?"

"Helping with the fall work. Hiram and Tobias ran off, you knew that, didn't you?"

"Ran off! No."

He nodded. "Followed a group of bluecoats north. It leaves all the farm work for the two of us. Keeps us hopping till sundown and then some."

"You should have told us."

"What could you have done? David isn't . . . By the way, how is he doing?"

I brightened. "Better. Step in and say hello. He'll be glad to see you."

He followed me into the house. "Dad and Mother been down since all of this?"

"Father stopped in Tuesday on his way home from Harrisonburg. He brought me half a pound of salt he managed to get in some sort of trade. I was so grateful."

"Yes, some salt was being distributed in town a week ago,[2] but each person was only allowed to buy one pound." James grinned wryly. "Tansy was having a fit trying to cook without it. Said the food tasted like it had been washed through dishwater before setting it on the table! Father brought about ten pounds from Harrisonburg. Some friends of his went to Kanawha County for salt. It cost an arm and a leg."

"Kanawha County? That's in . . . !"

"West Virginia. But salt isn't the only thing that's out of sight. I priced a barrel of flour at fourteen dollars the other day, and butter is seventy-five cents a pound."

I led the way to David's cot. "Yes, we aren't the only ones 'scraping the barrel' as they say. And I'm sure those in town have less laid by for the winter than those of us fortunate enough to have a garden, however skimpy they may have been."

"Well, look who's here. Glad to see you, James." David thrust forth a thin hand. "Sit down. A man gets mighty lonely without other menfolks to talk things over with. What's the news?"

I slipped outside to get another head of cabbage and two potatoes. Surely James would eat with us if he were invited.

When I returned, James' back was toward the door and his voice was raised in emphasis, "That's what I heard. Lee has taken his men into Maryland. Things never looked better for us than now. The Confederates are taking the offensive. All we need is more men. I . . ."

"Is it true we won another fight at Bull Run?" It was Peter's eager voice.

"Yes, and then captured Harpers Ferry again. We have two good leaders. Our gray coats would follow them anywhere. I'm going to go too. I'm almost eighteen now."

I almost dropped the knife in my hands.

David's reply was grave. "Your father can make it without you?"

"The fall work is just about finished. I've worked hard. I want to get in on the action before it's all over."

168

"You realize what you're getting into? War is not a glamorous game."

"I know that," he answered impatiently. "But you're still laid up; you can't go. You've given your time. Any able-bodied man is duty bound to help now while the stakes are so high. This just may be the beginning of victory!"

There was silence. Finding my voice, I stepped to the doorway and spoke, "Supper is ready. James, you'll stay and eat with us?"

He started to refuse, then hesitated. "I'll sit down a little." He jumped up, and in one swift movement was at David's cot. "You're going out too?"

"I've been trying to the last while."

"Great! Here, let me help you." With John on the other side, they slowly maneuvered David around the corner to the table.

Davie danced around them. "This is mag-nis-i-cant! . . . fairly mag-nis-i-cant!"

I smiled at his joy, yet couldn't keep back a twinge of fear. No one else knew why David pushed himself till he was weak with exhaustion.

"You're looking a lot better than you did three months ago." James helped push David's chair up to the table, then stood leaning against the wall grinning. "A wedge nailed onto your right boot would help that limp."

David grimaced, rubbing his twitching muscles. "That leg must have shrunk a good inch or more. I was hoping it would stretch with time."

He looked fondly around the table. "But what is that when we have everyone here together. Have a seat, James, and let's bow our heads."

A full moon had just cleared the mountain tops,

and the night air was growing chilly when James finally headed for the door. I followed him out and stood leaning against a post, shivering. The whole valley lay quiet except for a pack of dogs baying in the hills.

"James . . ."

He stopped as though he had expected me.

"Are you . . . are you in a hurry to get back?"

He turned, his face outlined by the lamplight shining faintly through the window. "No rush. I told Father I was coming down to say good-bye. He won't expect me back till late."

Tears sprang up in my eyes. "Oh, James!" My feet stumbled on the porch steps and he stepped up to catch me before I fell, pulling me against him in a boyish hug.

"Now, Sis, don't make it hard for a fellow. We boys have to grow up sometime."

I fought to control myself. "But . . . but you're so young. Must you go?"

"I feel duty bound, Ellen." He patted my back clumsily. "Father says he can't stand in the way if I'm determined to go."

"And Mother . . . ?" I pulled back and looked into his face.

He laughed ruefully. "She's all tore up over it. One minute she's proud as she can be. The next minute she's all sharp-tongued and snapping at me. I guess it's the only way she has of showing her fear. I reckon she'll make it."

"Where will you go?"

"There are fellows passing through town regularly heading up the pike. I want to join up with Jackson's army near Harpers Ferry."

170

"That's a ninety-mile walk!"

"I'm young and strong. And I might as well get used to walking. A soldier's got to be able to endure a lot of marching."

I sank to the step, wrapping my skirts about my bare feet. Surely he had mixed feelings about whether war was right. Kill his fellowman? James had found it hard to even kill an animal!

Memories rushed through my mind: the newborn pup, left by a stray in the barn; James squatting beside it, willing it to live; then one day finding its back broken by a wagon wheel, taking it behind the woodpile to finish it off mercifully, and his tear-streaked face when at last he returned. The bloated calf, lying on its side, bawling and fighting for breath, its legs thrashing the air, and James suddenly finding work that needed doing elsewhere until it was all over. I shuddered.

He coughed awkwardly, rubbing his boot in the dust. "Don't worry. I'll watch out for myself."

"Perhaps."

"Ellen, I've got to get away. Mother is getting harder and harder to live with. Father and I can't keep the farm in tiptop shape by ourselves. It's impossible. Seeing the farm deteriorate from lack of help is awfully frustrating to her. She's trying to keep control of the farm, plus all her meetings in town. Before, she could. Now things are driving her crazy.

"You know she had big plans for me—go some-where, continue my schooling—but the war has changed all that. I never wanted that. Don't you see? Don't you remember how you felt?"

I hugged my arms tighter about my knees. I tried to laugh but couldn't. I wet my lips. "Well, James. I

171

think I understand more than what you would believe. It's just that . . ."

"That what?"

"It's that David and I have some real doubts about whether war is right. There may be a lot of people guilty before God of murder."

"Ellen! You could be arrested for that."

I pressed my hands against my forehead. "Oh, James. I'm confused sometimes, but how can loving all men fit with this kind of destruction?"

"You're just beside yourself, Ellen. This ordeal with David has left you worn out and unable to think clearly. Why, we can't just let the Yankees run all over us without resisting at all. What would happen to us . . . to our families?"

I rocked back and forth. "You haven't answered my question."

"Well," he cleared his throat awkwardly. "Going out to support your country is different than going out on your own and killing someone for personal reasons. I don't *hate* the enemy."

"You kill those you *love*? I don't relish being loved like that."

He thrust his hands angrily into his pockets. "You just can't tie the two together, Ellen. Everyone knows that. Those Bible teachings are good in peace time, but not in a time of war.

"Our state needs me, and I'm going. You have to figure out your own conclusions." As he turned on his heels, I reached out quickly in the darkness.

"Don't be angry with me, James. We wish the best for you."

His voice softened. "I know."

"It will be hard to see you leave. I've depended

on you a lot."

"You've got David now and growing boys. I'll try to write now and then. Watch for me on the pike tomorrow morning, or some morning soon after that. Take care . . ."

He patted my shoulder, then turned and walked away. I stood, head bowed, listening to his footsteps fading into silence. After a few moments, I stepped back inside.

"He's gone?"

I sank onto the bed with a sob. "Oh, David! What will happen to him? He's merely a boy!"

He shook his head.

"And our John, David. Next month he will be sixteen. If the war continues . . ."

"We've got to get this thing settled for John's sake. I must make that trip. Jacob said there are Mennonites at Spring Hill. That's only a couple miles from Uncle Fred's. If these people don't live the way Jacob said, then we have no other option, but if they do . . ."

"Then . . . ?"

"Then we have a choice, Ellen, a pretty serious choice. A choice to join them, and suffer the consequences, or not. Either the Bible is worth staking our whole life on, or the Mennonites are a farce."

I trembled. "What will my folks think? What will they *do* to us?"

"The most they can do is turn us out, nothing worse than what we've experienced before. But perhaps I will get back before they find out."

"But surely sooner or later they will know. I don't know if I can face that again." Tears slipped down my face.

His reply was gentle. "We have to make our decisions and live one day at a time."

"I know, David. It's just that, after all these years of leaning over backwards to build a relationship of sorts with them . . . to throw that all away, I just can't . . . can't . . ."

"Why, Ellen!"

"What if they turn me out before you get back, David. What if something happens, and you never return!" I couldn't control my rush of emotions.

"Ellen, Ellen. We're in this together, aren't we?"

I hid my face in my hands, keeping my voice under control only with great effort. "We vowed if you came home alive, we'd never separate again. Can't we all go, David?"

The question was ridiculously impossible, and I knew it.

His shoulders sagged, and he opened his mouth to speak, then closed it again. I felt guilt, even greater than my panic, rising within me. I hated myself for asking.

"Now, Ellen," he said. It wasn't an answer at all, and yet to me it was a very definite one.

He pulled me close. "I know it's hard. I hate to leave, but I feel this is what I must do. You won't stand in the way, will you, dear? Not my brave wife."

I smiled, though I felt dead inside. "I'm sorry. Of course not, dear." A frozen calm settled over me, squeezing my emotions into nothing.

I couldn't respond to his tenderness. I fled to the bedroom and threw myself on my knees. I pressed my face into the sheets, fearful that if I started weeping, I wouldn't be able to stop. Must the stakes be drawn so high? Was there no easier way to peace?

❧ Chapter IX ❧

Lee's advance into Maryland ended in disaster. The battle of Antietam Creek resulted in more killed and wounded than any single-day engagement the country had ever seen, twenty-three thousand men sacrificed to the goddess of patriotism!

While the Confederate army was retreating southeast toward Richmond and Fredericksburg, we watched the road to town become filled once more with conveyances crowded with wounded. Many more were walking or hobbling with crutches. They were dirty and barefooted, wearing bandages and slings, each needing a place to recover or a means to get home.

At any hour of the day I could expect a knock at the door and see one, two, or a group of them, leaning wearily against the porch railing, asking for a drink or any food we could spare. I almost dreaded to see another day, knowing our carefully stockpiled supply of food was dwindling dangerously fast.

And still David pushed himself, walking to the far corner of the pasture and back after everyone else had gone to bed and getting up early to do it again. He didn't tell me until the morning he planned to leave, about his startling conversation with the red-haired man with whom we had shared supper a week before.

Jesse Treisen had been alone, which was unusual, and he had the table manners and courteous ways of a gentleman. He told us he was from Lexington and had been given four weeks leave of absence after being shot in the foot during the last battle. The most unusual thing about him was his left ear, which was split halfway up the outside edge and healed in a jagged scar, making a drooping flap which he fingered repeatedly during the meal.

Much to my embarrassment, Jesse noticed Andy staring at his head. Grabbing Andy up on his knee, he explained what had happened. As a cavalryman, a branch had sliced into his ear the summer before while he was being chased through a dense oak woods.

"I thought it would be a shame to bleed to death from an ear, so I just daubed some clay on it and kept going. Never gave me no trouble except the way it healed. Do you suppose my boys will be bug-eyed too?"

Andy was too bashful to answer, and Jesse didn't

insist. He just laughed and pulled a homemade flute out of his jacket pocket. The rest of the evening was spent in light conversation instead of war news.

When Jesse got up to leave, David followed him to the door. "You can sleep in our barn tonight," he said, lifting down the lantern to show him the way.

My husband stood now, his free arm around my shoulder, the other hanging onto a small bundle of extra clothes folded up in a blanket, along with food for a meal or two. It was still dark, though a faint glow over the mountains in the east promised to bring light within the hour.

"I must be going, Ellen. With God's help, I will return. Jesse Treisen told me the armies have pulled into quarters to rest and reinforce their ranks. Any day now they'll be stopping here to check on me. Thank God you will be able to tell them I'm not here. Jesse said two men from Rockingham County were shot."

He saw my alarm and cleared his throat. "They were shot for desertion a week ago.[1] But Jesse also said there's word the Mennonites and Dunkards have been granted an exemption, providing they pay a fine. Understandably, the soldiers don't like it much, but that's good news, Ellen. That's what we were wishing to hear, weren't we?"

I steeled my emotions, lifting my eyes to his. "Yes, David. May God be with you . . . and have mercy on us all."

"You're a brave woman, Ellen."

"Not brave, David. I'm terribly afraid. I lost you once, and God brought you back."

He kissed me good-bye. "I hope to be back within a week. And if these people are anything like we hear, we'll make the move together. We'll find somewhere among them to settle." He squeezed my hand. "Think of it, Ellen. To be rid of this maddening guilt, to no longer be alone in our search for truth."

"Mother . . ." John paused, embarrassed, in the doorway.

I turned over and sat up, hastily smoothing the wrinkles out of my dress.

"Mother, are you all right? It's after sunrise."

I scrambled to my feet. "Yes, John. I don't know how I went back to sleep."

He stood there watching me hurriedly brushing out my hair with long strokes.

"Where's Papa? Out on his early morning walk?"

I bit my lip. "He's gone, John."

"Gone!" His face whitened. "Did someone . . ."

"No, son. We had to keep his plans a secret. But now that he's gone, you are old enough to be trusted. We've had a lot to think about since Papa came home. You know that already. We've cried and prayed and talked for weeks—for months."

"But he was better, better than at first . . . remember?"

"I know. In many ways he has recovered, but there is still a terrible weight he needs help with, John." I pressed his arm to steady myself. "John,

178

Papa met his brother Edward on the battlefield, saw him shot and killed."

"Mother!"

I formed my words with difficulty. "Papa feels responsible. He held Edward in his arms as he died. "Edward was his youngest brother. Growing up, Edward always tagged along after Papa and was very special to him. It has nearly killed Papa, John."

The fresh horror of it all washed over me, and I couldn't hold back the tears.

"How horrible!" John was shaken.

"Papa knew he would be required to go back into the army as soon as he was physically able. After all he's gone through, he's completely convinced war is wrong."

John blinked, unashamed of the tears glistening on his cheeks.

"I know all we've heard is the right of our state to protect itself from invasion, and the blessing of God rests upon our cause, but somehow that no longer satisfies us. I don't know how to explain, but it doesn't ring true—opposite sides, both praying to one God for victory in battle.

"Papa met a young fellow in camp who belonged to a group called the Mennonites. They don't believe in fighting and killing. Ever since his mind has cleared, he has been pushing himself, working toward getting his strength back so he can try to make contact with these people. We've heard of a special law being made that would exempt these people from fighting."

I did not mention the indignation of southern loyalists.

"What will Grandfathers say when they find out

where Papa's gone?"

"He's going to stay at Uncle Fred's. We can just tell them that. But if they aren't satisfied with that explanation . . ." I stood and reached for my shoes, "We will deal with that when it happens."

"Mommy! Come and see!" Davie tugged at my skirt impatiently, fairly dancing with excitement. "There's horses, lots of horses!"

I wiped my hands and pushed myself up from the tub of steaming, sudsy water. My knees felt stiff from kneeling so long. "Horses, Davie?"

"Yes, out on the pike."

I grabbed my shawl and followed him out the door. The air was cold and a stiff wind was blowing. Each night dipped below freezing now, bringing leaves to the ground and nipping colors from field and meadow.

John and Peter were already at the end of the lane watching the slow-moving mass shuffle past. There were over fifty, dirty, limping, skin-and-bone horses being herded toward town.

"What is it, Mommy? Where are they going?" Andy reached out a hand to grip mine, huddling close for protection from the wind.

"You boys need your coats." I knelt down, pulling my shawl around them both. "I think they must be returning worn-out horses. They'll be replaced with fresh ones. We've seen them do this before. Remember?"

Andy shook his head uncertainly. "I don't."

180

"I do!" Davie's eyes lit up. "And they took the rest of Grandfather's horses, didn't they?"

I nodded. "They left him with two worn-out ones that looked half dead already."

"But he fixed them up, didn't he?"

"Yes, he kept working with them till he built them back up. And they make good carriage horses, even though they don't match in color. There's nothing your grandfather likes more than the challenge of nursing back a run-down horse to top condition."

"Hey, hey! Get up!" There was angry shouting interspersed with the cracking of a whip. Horses milled in confusion, bringing the whole procession to a halt.

"What are they doing?"

I stood up to see better, but my view was blocked by all those who had gathered around. "I'm not sure. Slip up to the house and get your coat, then you can sit closer and find out. Get coats for both of you."

By the time Davie returned, the caravan was moving again, and Peter and John were kneeling beside a mule sprawled at the edge of the road.

Peter looked up at our approach. "They left this mule behind." He frowned. "Looks like it's going to die."

The brown mud-caked legs jerked convulsively, and the angular head was drawn tautly back. Ribs showed prominently beneath shabby skin, and even above the shouts of the departing men, the raspy breathing sounded uneven and desperate.

John lifted the sagging head and nodded toward the vacant eyes, the fluttering nostrils, and the saliva-smeared mouth. "He's about had it. Davie, could you bring some water? No, Peter, you hold his head, I'll go."

Somehow we managed to get some of the water to trickle down his throat, then waited tensely. As the moments dragged by, there was little sign of returning strength. I gave up and went back to my washing. The boys insisted on continuing their efforts. To my surprise and their great delight, by nightfall they managed to rouse the animal enough to prod it to the shelter of the barn.

We had a late supper of potatoes and stewed pumpkin. As excited as they were over their good fortune, the boys couldn't help comparing the mule with Ginger.

"I wish we still had Ginger. Whatever do you think happened to her, Mother?"

"I don't know, son. But as well trained as she was, I'm sure she gave someone good service as long as she was able."

"What shall we call him?" Davie scraped out his plate carefully and checked the pans for any trace remaining.

"He looks the color of that muddy clay along the creek bank below the persimmon grove. Claybones would be a good name for him." Peter grinned, pushing his chair away from the table.

There was a knock, and Peter jumped to open the door. A young man in uniform stood on the front porch, holding his cap in his hand.

"Is this the Shull's?"

My heart leaped in my throat. "Yes."

"I have a letter a fellow gave me up the pike a ways . . ."

"Oh! Thank you!" I reached an eager hand, almost snatching it from him. Then catching myself, I continued, "Won't you come in? We just finished supper, but I'll be glad to fix you something to eat."

"No, thanks. I must get into town before dark."

He was gone before I could say more.

The note was scribbled on the inside of a piece of wrapping paper.

Dear family,

I arrived at my destination last night, but I don't know when there will be a chance to send this your way. Hopefully Uncle Fred can find someone heading south.

Freds were glad to see me. Their son Andrew was killed three months ago in the battle of Gaines Mills. They feel very much alone. They have really aged.

I will stay here till my strength builds up again.

Miss all of you so much! Thanks for your love. Pray for your papa tonight.

> Love,
> David

The next word was four days in coming. It was a letter from Aunt Malinda. I held the wavy writing up to the light to see better.

My dear Ellen,

We are doing as well as possible, though we miss you. Three years seems like a long time. We are not able to do much around the place but are making out the best we can.

Maybe you've heard that our Andrew was killed back in the summer. It seems we've lost all reason for living, yet we must somehow keep on. David said to send you word that he is continuing his business trip today. Hopefully a return to you within a week will be possible.

Take care, and please write sometime.

Your Aunt Malinda

I read the letter once again, slowly. Andrew, poor young Andrew, only eighteen years old. He was Fred and Malinda's only child, born in their old age, now cruelly snatched away!

And David . . . if only I could be there with him! It had been two long weeks since he had stepped into the night.

"You're a brave woman, Ellen," he had said. But I wasn't. I turned to the window, watching the shine of icy rain coursing down the darkened pane. I hadn't told him what I suspected to be true. He didn't know. My fingertips briefly touched the growing form within me, and I buried my face in my hands. I had never felt more alone.

Time moved slowly by. The boys again took the crosscut saw and scoured the edges of the field, picking out dead or fallen trees for firewood. Claybones limped along after them, cropping grass close by and slowly adding flesh to his thin frame.

I found it hard to drag myself around. Weariness

and fear knotted in my stomach. It was harder still to pray. Was no news an assurance all was well? Or . . . my mind darted away from other possibilities like a frightened rabbit.

One early morning, a sharp knock sent me scrambling off my knees before the hearth. When I opened the door, a sudden shock went through me. It was my stepmother with a heavy cloak thrown around her rigid form.

"Why! Good morning, Mother!"

"Aren't you going to invite me in? It's cold out here."

"Yes, surely." Flustered and nervous, I pressed my hands together to hide their trembling.

Mother stepped inside and walked briskly to the fireplace, holding her hands out to the feeble blaze. "Is this all the better you can do for a fire?"

My face flushed crimson. "I was just getting it started, Mother. It needs a little time." I reached for another piece of wood.

"Where are the boys? Aren't they up yet?"

"I was just going to wake them."

"No, no. Don't bother. I want to talk undisturbed. I . . . I need John's help this morning."

"John?" I couldn't hide my surprise. John had offered his help after James had gone but had been turned down.

"Yes." The older woman's face twitched nervously. "Bernard had a . . . a heart attack yesterday and . . ."

I reached for a chair. "A heart attack?"

"The doctor was out last night. He's very weak and can hardly talk. There's only Tansy and me to keep up with things." Her eyes glistened, and she dabbed at them with a handkerchief.

My heart went out to her, and I reached out a hand. I was seeing a rare glimpse behind the carefully polished armor. "Of course, we'll help any way we can. I'll call John right away."

Mother fumbled with her handkerchief, then pulled at the strings of her bonnet. "Well, er . . ." She cleared her throat. "How is David getting along? Would there be any chance . . ." She coughed uneasily and fanned herself with her hand.

So that's what it was. Mother needed help, a man's help. Out of desperation she had come looking for it where she most despised admitting a need. It was nearly killing her.

I felt a trace of pity with the dread that had begun to form in my stomach.

"Well, Mother . . ."

"Is he still in bed?"

"No . . . no."

"Well, where then? Out taking one of his walks?"

My voice was feeble. "No, Mother." My mind clutched for a suitable answer. "He . . . he's not here right now."

Mother looked up sharply. "Gone back to his regiment? No?" An angry gleam came to her eyes. "He's not hiding, is he?"

I shook my head, clearing my throat. "Have a seat, Mother."

Mother stood as though she had not heard. "Explain to me."

"Well, Mother, it's . . . he has gone on business up the Valley."

"Business?"

My shoulders slumped. "I'll not try to deceive

you, Mother. He's looking for peace among those who live up to what we feel is truth, the Mennonites." My gaze didn't waver, although my heart shrank back at the anger that flashed in Mother's eyes.

"Peace! Peace?" Her face was growing red. "Peace indeed! Deserter!" The ugly word spat out.

"Please be calm, Mother. I don't want the boys to hear all this." I fumbled with the buttons on my dress. "David has suffered tremendously. Physically, yes, but also mentally and spiritually. We have gone through a lot while he was recovering. We need help in our determination to seek after God, and he's gone to the most godly people we knew to find it."

Mother's face turned crimson with rage. "Help? He wants help! He'll wish he had help till this is over!" her voice rose shrilly.

"We've all suffered through this worthy fight for liberty. Who hasn't given up members of their family for the cause? But do we give up? No! You think you've suffered more than the rest of us?"

She snorted. "The idea! Leaving his responsibilities and running off to find 'help.' A deserter; that's what he is! I should get rid of all of you but . . ." She was breathing hard. "But I need you right now. I'll make you an offer. You are about out of money, and this winter is going to be tough without it. I'll help you out with money and food. There's only one condition—you will *disown* him!"

She looked triumphantly at me, confident there was no other way but to accept.

I dropped my head, feeling strangely dizzy. Had it come to this?

The silence drew out for several moments. There

was no turning back now. I found my voice. "No, Mother, I am with him in this. I too must have peace."

"Peace!" She laughed harshly. "You'll know nothing of peace after this! You have twenty-four hours to get out. I'll find someone to live here who knows a good offer when he sees one."

I fought for breath and pressed back the sob rising in my throat. "Very well. And, Mother, please remember this. We don't hate you. We are only doing what we have to do."

But Mother was too angry to listen. "Leave me," she shouted. "Leave me and join that deserter husband of yours. We helped you out once. This time you won't get any help." She marched toward the door.

Weeping, I watched her go.

The full moon was temporarily blotted out by fast moving clouds, and the bare tree branches swayed. I pressed the package tighter to my breast, almost stumbling through the thick matted grasses of the field, their color long faded. My last errand; then we must leave. A moan rose within, and I bit my lips.

Oh David, David. How can I find you? Why did we part with one another even for a day?

After Mother had left, I had gathered the boys around, carefully explaining our options. Although they didn't understand it all, they immediately wanted to go to David.

Then I had pushed myself, working all that day as

in a feverish trance, forcing my hands to hurry, packing a few essential things to take along: food, a change of clothing for each one, my most prized possession—the roses clock, and a few baby things hidden away in the bottom of my own bundle.

For once, I could be glad the soldiers had picked up and taken so much in their forays over the farm. David's blacksmith tools, the wagon he had labored to make, even the pitiful mound of remaining hay, all were gone. There was little to leave behind.

John was sure poor, bony Claybones could make the trip. His gait was a slow hobble to be sure, but we could pack a few things on his back. Otherwise we would have left almost penniless.

I had worked long after the boys had finally settled, then gathered pen and paper and wrote swiftly. I couldn't leave without leaving some letter, some word for James, if he returned—and for Father. Father, what would become of him? Must I leave without seeing him one last time? I folded the letters carefully, then grabbed some wraps before slipping out the back door.

As I approached, the large house was dark except for the dim glow of a candle in a second story window. I hurried around the back, muffling my heavy breathing in the shawl wrapped around my head. I pulled my coat closer, leaning against the carriage house wall to catch my breath.

There. A flicker of light passed through toward the back of the house into the kitchen. *Oh, let it be Tansy!* I thought as I crept closer. Peering between the curtains, I saw her. I tiptoed up the steps and tapped softly on the door.

"Oh, my chile, do you hab to?" Tansy wiped her almond face with the apron clutched in her large hands. "You's such a wee lady, and now wid a lambie on de way . . ."

She shook her head, pulling me once more against her plump softness, stroking my back, crooning sadly. "You need a good mammy to watch ober you jus' now. I's haf a notion to go wid you."

I kissed the wrinkled cheek, tears in my eyes. "No, Tansy, your place is here. Father and Mother will need you now more than ever. We will make out. John is sixteen now. We'll go to Uncle Fred's. I must go back now before Mother finds out I came. You will make sure Father gets the letter when he recovers?"

"Oh, yes, chile." She patted the folds of her calico dress. "Dis paper will stay right heah till it go right into Massah Bernard's hand. Don' you worry none 'bout it. De doc-tah say Massah Bernard need plenty ob res,' and I aim to see he gits it. I be keepin' Missis Bernice so busy, she not hab no time to be a'steppin' 'round in his room—wid her frizzled ways—so help me.

"An' de viney frame," she fingered its smooth edge admiringly, "id goes straight to my own room, an' der it stay till dis heah war be ober, and you kin come home. Ain't nobody's hands gonna touch dis 'cepin Tansy's hands."

I hung on to her steadying arm. "I know I can depend on you, Tansy. I just couldn't leave without assuring Father we still love him. He will feel responsible when he finds out." I turned toward the door. "I *must* go. We will leave early in the morning. If James comes home . . ." I stopped, catching a sob in my throat, "tell him . . . tell him how much I love him. He will always be my baby brother."

"I do dat sho. Now, don' fo-git dat basket." She picked up the parcel on the floor filled with fresh biscuits and food she had grabbed together.

"You shouldn't have, Tansy."

"You's gonna need dem. I's be prayin' all de days dat de good Lord watch ober you and yer lambs. He won' let you down."

When I returned home, I looked again over the bundles lying on the floor, then stumbled upstairs. Sleep would not come, and I lay there, dozing fitfully till dawn.

❧ Chapter X ❧

All morning we pushed ahead, a curious spectacle of overstuffed figures decked out with several layers of clothing, shouldering odd-shaped bundles, with a gaunt mule bobbing along behind, coaxed by the rope tied to John's wrist.

The long shadows cast by the bare mountain ridges retreated slowly. The forested sides were now stripped of leaves. A bluish haze at their peaks faded into the clear, chilly sky. The road before and behind curved and dipped out of sight. It was becoming difficult for the younger boys to keep up.

"Easy, boy, easy . . ." John patted the mule's homemade halter and rubbed his hands briskly together to increase the circulation. He shaded his eyes to follow the curved row of trees snaking across the pike below the next hill. "I believe there's a creek up ahead. We can stop, eat our lunch, and take a well deserved rest. Claybones is starting to limp again."

He ran his hand along the mule's withers, feeling for the swelling that had bothered the animal ever since his second chance at life.

Claybones snorted and laid back his lips, showing yellow worn teeth. His bones still protruded awkwardly under his shaggy winter coat.

Andy giggled. "I'm glad we didn't have to carry all the blankets he has piled on him. He looks like a skinny camel with a hump on his back."

"No, he doesn't. I wish we had Ginger instead of him."

I caught the quiver in Davie's voice and smiled brightly to cover my own weariness. "We don't have Ginger, but we have each other. That's worth more than a horse to me." I pulled his coat collar higher and patted his arm. "That reminds me of what some boys about your age said years ago when I was still at home."

Davie's eyes flickered with interest and he lengthened his stride to keep in step with me. "What did they say?"

I rubbed his cold hands between mine. The scene came easily to my mind. At the time it had seemed funny, but now, I felt only a sense of pity.

My fingers tightened over his as I told the story. Mother, James and I had taken the carriage to Bull's Tavern to meet the afternoon stagecoach. A slave trader who did business in the deep South was scheduled to arrive, and Mother hoped to pick up another farmhand for us.

The coach was late as usual. While we waited, I took James to Hill's pump at the corner to get a drink. Several young Negro boys were messing around the pump, buckets in hand, presumably there to get water for their mistresses. James was fascinated by their talk and an on-going spitting contest. He would have followed them without a thought, his own thirst forgotten.

When the rumble of the stagecoach was heard, all the boys went running toward the tavern. By the time we got our drinks and returned to the front of the tavern, there was a crowd of people around the coach. The young Negro boys pointed at a stately looking man stepping down, with a clear-featured young mulatto in tow. The tall youth's eyes swept contemptuously over the crowd.

"He paid a pile ob money fo dat man."

"Aw, don' you be talk-in 'bout what you don' know. I bet he jus' a poht'ah fo de house. He don' hab to wuhk so hahd."

"Yeah, but dem muscles, he know how to use dem things. He be wuth a heap." The dark-skinned boy rolled his eyes and raised his bucket of water high above his head. " 'Cause, I's wuth perdy much mysef."

His taller companion swatted at the bucket with his hat, making the water slosh over them both. "You ain't wuth ah hundud dollah."

The bucket was set down in a hurry. "Now, jus' look what you did. How much you think *you* wuth?"

"Me? I's wuth *five hundud* dollah."

James had been all ears. He stepped closer. "What am *I* worth?"

The bucket swinging stopped, and the boys circled to look at him. "Aw, massah suh—you white; you ain't wuth nuthin'."[1]

Davie's mouth fell open. "What did James say then?"

"He was too surprised to say anything. Of course, it wasn't true. In God's sight we don't measure people by skin color or muscles. But that's all those boys had ever known."

Peter waited till we caught up with him. "Did Grandma buy that fellow?"

"Yes, we took him home with us, but I was always a little afraid of him. And he was there less than four months before he ran away. Father never could trace him down."

As we walked along in silence, I kept puzzling over the incident. Father made sure the young man was treated fairly. We never had more than half a dozen slaves at one time, and I never knew Father to mistreat any of them. Indeed, most of them had been with us so long I thought of them as family.

But nothing could gloss over the ugly stain of slavery, not kindness or care or even Christian teaching. There is something within every soul that cries out to be free, to stand before God and man on his own merit.

When we came to the creek, John turned Claybones through an opening in the brush. The rest of us followed and came out in a large clearing. A dead willow skeleton stood to one side, its brittle branches hanging into tall briars edging the path. From the charred wood scattered about, it looked as if the place was used often. A forgotten canteen and a discarded pair of worn-out boots stuck up through the weeds.

"Looks like a camping place." Peter walked around the clearing. "Probably soldiers. I was surprised we met only three this morning. The one with the sorrel mare sure asked a lot of questions. Were you worried?"

My reply was deliberately casual. "We've met a number of families on the move so far. It must be quite common. He was just curious, I guess." I grabbed a corner of the old blanket I had pulled out and flipped it onto the hard-packed ground.

When the biscuits and cold side-pork from Tansy's basket had been shared around, I pulled my legs up under my skirts for warmth and leaned wearily back against the willow. Every part of me ached.

"Can we look around, Mother? We won't go far."

I roused myself. "Yes. Just stay close. We must leave before long."

The slight breeze carrying the murmur of the boys' voices and the creek's constant gurgling were a soothing lullaby. My shoulders slumped. I fought to keep my eyes open. Then unable to resist, I dozed.

❧❧

"Mother!"

I jerked awake. John was standing over me. "Mother, men are coming!"

Feeling foolish, I scrambled to my feet, brushing sand from my dress. They were upon us before I could even glance around and locate the boys.

"Looks as though we aren't the first ones here."

The full-bearded man in a gray overcoat nodded curtly, prodding his horse past me to an opening in the mulberry bushes along the creek's edge.

The heavy rider with a sagging stomach, held back. His pudgy face was accented by high cheekbones and deep-set wrinkles. The pale blue eyes swept over us, remaining longest on John's growing frame. "Where you from?"

"The edge of Staunton, sir."

"Heading where?" The eyes narrowed.

"To visit relatives near Spring Hill village."

"Where's your husband?"

My voice faltered. "I . . . I'm not sure."

"Not sure? He's not a deserter, is he? That's our business, rounding up those slippery creatures. This part of the country seems full of them."

My heart thumped wildly. I forced my gaze to steady on his face. "My husband joined the Fifty-second Infantry, sir. I'm not sure where they're at right now . . ."

He nodded, satisfied. "Fine group. Near Bunker Hill I understand. Hope you receive word from him soon."

As his mount cantered past toward the creek, I began to tremble. There was a queer look on John's face. "I . . . forgive me, John. I didn't mean to lie. He didn't give me time to explain . . . it happened so suddenly. I . . ."

"Let's get out of here." John hustled the younger boys into motion, leading Claybones ahead at a brisk pace. His sense of urgency did not diminish until we had put a good distance between us and our stopping place.

The afternoon sun arched toward the edge of the

198

winter sky and hung shimmering for a time on the mountain tops. Weary as we were, we pressed on, mingling with others traveling north and south.

Now the air was turning colder, and Andy was crying from weariness and cold. Davie's face was puckered up in an honest attempt to hide his growing desperation. My heart went out to him.

"Davie, do you see that house back in the trees ahead? Let's see if those people have a place to put us up for the night."

An ancient barn crowded the side of the rutted lane. I stopped in the open doorway. Stained by sun and rain to a mellow gray, the sagging building stood empty. Only a small mound of hay was left in one corner.

"Why don't all of you wait here while I go and talk to the people." I gathered my frayed courage. "John, pull out a few dried apples to suck on till I return."

Several children darted away at my approach, their bare feet exposed to the cold. I smoothed the loose strands of hair back inside my bonnet, placed a smile on my face, and straightened my coat.

"Is your father or mother at home?"

There was no reply. The children gawked silently from their places on the porch.

"Is your mother at home?"

Finally the oldest stirred. "Yeah."

"May I speak to her?"

"I reckon might as well." The sandy-haired lad led the way to a run-down lean-to tacked onto the back and jerked on the door. "Ma! There's a lady here to see you."

I moved cautiously forward. The children did not move until I reached the steps. Then, in an instant, they all slipped out of sight behind the half-closed door.

The spare, slovenly figure of a blond-haired woman appeared at the threshold and looked warily down at me. From the drooping hair and loosely pinned bun to the hem of her faded dress, she looked suspicious and unfriendly. Scotch, I was sure of it. There were a lot of them in the Valley.

"Hello," I began more heartily than I felt. "I'm a mother with four children, Ellen Shull by name, moving up the pike a ways. We've come this far today and are looking for a place to stay the night."

She took a step toward the porch edge, and I saw she had on men's boots. Her voice was brusque. "Don't know as we have any extra room. We're right cramped for space as it is."

By now I was standing on the bottom step. "Oh, all we need is a corner on the floor to lie down on, just to get inside for the night. I left the boys out in that building by the road. They are miserable with cold . . ."

She crossed her arms and turned as if to go back inside. "Never had much to do with strangers. Don't know who to trust these days."

Oh, God, she is going to turn us away! I thought. How could I go back to the boys with no for an answer? In desperation I climbed the steps, dodging holes left by broken or missing boards, and put a hand on her shoulder. I felt her flinch in surprise.

"Please, ma'am. We were turned out of our home next to Staunton and are going to relatives in hopes of finding shelter. I . . . I . . . you're a mother." I placed a hand on my stomach. "And I'm in the 'mothering way' and feeling mighty anxious for a good

200

resting place."

Her eyes swept over me as if doubting my words. She said nothing, but stepped out of reach.

"We won't be a burden to you. We have a little food along, and we'll share what we have."

Her shoulders relaxed and a hint of a smile touched her lips, then was gone. "Wa'll now, it may be we could push some things aside and make a bit of room for the night. Bring them on."

"Thank you, ma'am! You don't know how much we appreciate this!"

But she had already gone inside and pushed the door shut behind her.

As I retraced my way down the steps, I could hear her sharp voice giving orders to the children. A baby's whimper rose and was quickly shushed.

I hurried back to the barn, shivering from the cold. The moon had come out early tonight, turning the twilight all silver and blue. Silent and unmoving, the shadows of giant poplar lay in long black columns across the roadway.

I stopped in the entrance. The boys were all crowded together on the straw. "Boys, we can stay the night. Think of getting warm all the way through! Is Claybones tied well enough to hold him till morning?"

John gave a tug on the halter rope. "I think so. We'll take out covers?"

"Yes, and I said we would bring some food to share with them." I hurried on at Peter's look of disapproval. "We wouldn't have been welcome otherwise. Pick out a dozen potatoes and the last of the dried cabbage. It's the best we can do."

The inside of the cabin consisted of only one tiny

room. It was crowded with an assortment of ancient handmade furniture, dirty clothes, and a broken spinning wheel. A large, smoke-blackened fireplace filled one end and a carelessly nailed together ladder climbed the wall at the other, leading to a small opening in the ceiling. Dark rafters stretching overhead hung with anything from buckets and dippers, to clothes, dried herbs and kettles.

I counted eight children's heads poking up from the one bed in the corner, and though their eyes followed our every action, they didn't move as much as a finger.

After introducing ourselves, I held out the bag of food. "It isn't much, but perhaps it will help."

I thought she had to restrain herself to keep from snatching it out of my hands. "They call me Widow Downey. I be obliged for the vittles."

She dumped them into the large iron pot over the fire and motioned to the child nearest the back door. "Fergus! Get a pail of water for the kettle. Can't you see we be nearly to eat?"

The stew she ladled out was hot and filling. Mixed among the cabbage and potatoes were small chunks of meat I didn't recognize.

"Your food, it's very good. But the meat, I never tasted any like it before. What is it?"

She shot a sidelong glance at me, and her lips parted in a rare smile. "My Vancey caught 'em in the barn, he did. They was after the corn my man had stored there. Three of 'em, fattest rats I seen in a year."

My stomach suddenly knotted up. I pushed my empty plate back on the warped table and sat down again on my blanket in the corner.

The boys joined me, and we watched the children fighting over the scrapings in the bottom of the pot. For the moment, they seemed to have forgotten we were there.

John leaned over, his lips brushing my ear. "I think I should sleep in the barn with the mule. As hungry as those children are . . ." There was a flicker of amusement on his face, but his intention was serious. Though it worried me, I knew keeping the mule and our belongings safe was important.

I gave John as many covers as we could spare, and he slipped out the door. Then I helped the others wrap up close to the fireplace. My offer to help with the dishes was refused. "Hit's dark, an' I ain't got no more water drawed up anyways."

The Downey children gradually straggled up the ladder to bed, and the widow woman sat, pushing herself back and forth in a cane-back rocker, staring wordlessly at the fire. I pulled my coat around me as a cover and lay down. The fire died to coals and cast flickering shadows across the stacks of dirty pots and pans by the hearth. There was no sound except the faint sigh of a cold draft through a crack near me and the occasional pop of tobacco juice hitting the hot coals.

What was this woman living on? There was no garden, only a weed patch on one side of the house. I had seen no farm animals. How was I to know whether the little she had said about herself was true?

I closed my eyes, then opened them a slit. Her gaze had shifted to my face. Suddenly I was afraid— afraid for us. Afraid for John alone with the rest of the food and baggage.

*Dear Lord, if you can see us, please watch over us
... and David!* I was hardly aware I was praying, and
yet I desperately reached for help beyond myself.
Surely by the next evening we would be reunited,
and everything would be all right.

I lay tensely, knowing I could never go to sleep.
Yet later I awoke, and rays of moonlight were filtering through the oilcloth window. Something had
awakened me, but what?

It came again; furtive footsteps on the porch; muffled, angry voices; and a woman's whispering.

"Why'd you . . ."

"I ain't had no reason to know ye was coming. Ye
been gone two weeks and the young'uns was
hangry."

"Confound it, woman! We've been riden' all night;
we aimed to come in an' warm a bit."

"Ye should have come days ago. What'd ye bring
this time?"

There was a scuffle of footsteps and someone
moved off the porch.

The widow's voice came again, this time in a hiss.
"Ye can't let me sit jest 'cause one time went bad. She
had food with her, and we had to eat."

There was a lull, then a thump as something
heavy hit the ground. Then a rapid clatter of hooves
faded into silence.

I squeezed my eyes shut as the door opened. The
bed creaked as weight settled onto it—then silence.
For a long time I lay, heart pounding, not daring to
move. Finally I opened my eyes. I could just make
out a mound under the bedclothes in the corner.

Sleep did not return. My mind raced. This must
be a stopping place for nightriders, groups of men

who roamed the land, living off the spoils of others, and hiding in the hills when threatened with discovery. If they found John . . . !

Could one of them actually be her husband? What kind of woman would shelter so many strange men at night? I swallowed at the revulsion thick in my throat, and held myself still until the shadows of the room began to pale, and the occupants beside me and in the loft began to stir.

"Here, Andy, your shoes. Peter, your coat is underneath your cover." I was folding up bedding as fast as I dared without appearing frantic. I felt a desperate urge to check on John, to get away from this eerie place.

Overhead there was scuffling and giggling mixed with thumps and an occasional grunt. All the while, those cool blue eyes gazed at us unflinching from the moving rocker. She made no sound or offer to help.

Lining the boys up at the door, I turned back to see whether anything had been forgotten. My coat! I took a step toward the corner where I had slept. It was empty. Confused, I looked back at the boys, wondering if we had somehow wrapped it up by mistake in the blankets.

Then I caught sight of it—draped securely around the Scotch lady's lap! When my surprised look stopped at her face, her baleful stare showed no guilt and challenged me to mention it. The rocking continued as I gaped at her. Turning around, I took the warmest cover and threw it over my shoulders.

"Thank you very much," I said. "And good-bye."
She nodded coolly, making no reply.

I pulled open the door, and we almost ran as we made our way down the frosty steps and across the yard to the barn.

John was waiting for us a short way up the pike. His face showed great relief at the sight of us. "Are all of you all right?"

"Yes, John! And you?"

He nodded, starting off at a rapid pace. "Here's the last of the bread for breakfast. I'd feel better if we'd eat on the way." He divided it out carefully. "Here, Claybones, keep a move on. We have a good ways to go today."

I matched my steps with his. "You didn't have visitors last night? No one harmed you?"

He threw me a sober look. "I had visitors, but I wasn't at home."

"John! What happened?"

"What happened to your coat?"

"She . . . took it as payment, I guess. I was afraid to ask for it back. I'll make out."

He shook his head. "Scandalous! But we can be thankful we didn't lose everything.

"After I left the house, I made myself a nest among the bundles, with Claybones as a backrest on one side. I was actually right comfortable, but couldn't go to sleep thinking the woman might come. Finally I got Claybones up, loaded everything, and led him across the road where I remembered seeing a fallen tree lying across a large boulder about 100 yards back. I stuffed everything underneath, tied the mule to a tree, and was nearly back at the road again when I heard horses. They weren't in a hurry, just trotting along slow, then stopped right on the other side of the tree where I was hiding. Talk about scared!"

Peter shifted his bundle higher up on his shoulders. "What did they do?" he asked wide-eyed.

"They talked, and I could hear every word they said. They were arguing whether to stop at the house or not. A couple of them went to see if all was clear while the rest of them stayed in the barn. I tell you I was worried."

I wiped my forehead with an unsteady hand. We escaped with only the loss of a coat! "We were not alone last night, boys. Always remember that." God did hear prayer. Despite my clumsy petitions heavenward, I was becoming convinced of it.

It was late that evening when Uncle Fred's farm came into view. It was all I could do to keep pushing one step in front of another. When the front door opened, I was glad to let the wrinkled old hands half guide, half carry me into the delicious warmth of the kitchen.

I lay back against the pillows, too exhausted to notice the shocked looks on their anxious faces. "It's . . . it's so good . . . so . . . good . . ." My eyelids strained to stay open, but it was a losing battle. Two nights with very little sleep could not be held at bay any longer. The room was hazy around me and my mind numb beyond feeling. We were safe. We had made it to safety, and David would be here soon. I drifted into oblivion.

"But, Fred . . ." The frightened, wavering voice was cut off by a gruff whisper.

"Hush, Lindy!"

There was a muffled sound of tiptoeing past the door, and my eyes fluttered open. Morning sun was streaming through the window, lighting up the tiny dormer bedroom where I lay. I turned toward the sound.

"Fred, Malinda! Please come in."

The thin, stoop-shouldered woman entered, followed by Uncle Fred's bent figure.

"Now we done woke you up with our noise. How are you feeling?" Malinda stepped closer to the bed. Her gray hair was wrapped in two thin braids around the back of her head. In his loose-fitting clothes, Fred seemed shorter and more drawn than I remembered. His straggly mustache twitched with emotion as he laid a gnarled hand on his wife's shoulder.

I reached out to warmly encircle the bony hands nervously twisting the apron. "I feel better, much better. Last night is kind of hazy to me."

Fred cleared his throat. "I thought so." He hooked his thumbs into his suspenders, his eyes not meeting mine. "Don't know how you made it this far."

They were distressed about something. A sudden fear clutched my heart. I propped myself up on one elbow. "What is it?"

He pulled out a tattered handkerchief and blew his nose noisily. "You came after David?"

I leaned forward. "Yes. He said he'd stop back by your place on his way home."

The look on their faces startled me. "Hasn't he been here yet?"

Uncle Fred's mouth contorted. A coughing spell

shook his slight frame, and he motioned helplessly to his wife.

Malinda wrung her bony hands in distress. "I don't understand. He just left, Ellen. He just left yesterday morning, heading for home. You didn't see him?"

"No, no! Heading for home, you say? But it can't be!"

I fell back onto the pillow, tears stinging my eyelids. Oh, how could this have happened to us?

I must not panic. Fred and Malinda were almost beside themselves. Fred paced back and forth in agitation.

"We wanted him to stay a day to rest. He had just gotten back late the night before. He didn't even tell us where he'd gone, except on business, and to visit friends."

"He was worn out, poor boy." Malinda's eyes were red from weeping. "He said he had to start back. You would be worried about him."

The walls seemed to be crushing in on me, and the faces bent over the bed seemed to recede and waver in the slanting light.

Aunt Malinda began fanning me with her apron. "Fred, get her a drink. The poor girl."

I struggled to sit up. "I . . . I'll be all right. No . . ." I motioned away the cup Fred offered. "Tell me more. How did David seem? Tense? Worried?"

Malinda stopped her fanning for a moment and dabbed her eyes. "No . . . no, rather calm, wouldn't you say, Fred?" She looked at her husband. "We talked about it after he left."

"Peaceful, real peaceful."

I took a deep breath. Some of the tension went

out of my body. "Tell me everything you can remember."

Fred lowered himself heavily into a cane-back chair in the corner. "We had already gone to bed, Lindy and I. He knocked on our window to tell us he was here. I reckon we stayed up an hour talking." He glanced at his wife, who nodded.

"He said his business quest was a success, and someday he'll tell us all about it.

"The people he went to see took him in and were real good to him, doctored him up. Guess he was pretty petered out till he got there."

I nodded eagerly. "And then . . . ?"

"He didn't tell us more, only that he was going back to . . . you and the boys." Malinda smoothed down the covers wretchedly. "If only we would have made him stay."

I tried not to think of what might have happened. "Maybe he stopped somewhere to rest, and we just happened to miss him. Please don't blame yourselves." I tried to focus my whirling thoughts. "We should try to catch up with him. Maybe if we leave right away . . ."

"No." Uncle Fred shook his head. "You're in no shape to start anywhere anytime soon. I'll go out and see if I can find him."

I dropped my eyes. I would have to tell them the real reason for David's trip. "I . . . I guess I must tell you. We didn't have much choice. Mother was furious when she found out David was gone. She turned us out. I . . ."

Malinda cut me short. "Turned you out? In your condition?"

"She didn't know. She gave me the option to

disown David or get out."

"After all you've done for them?" Malinda sniffed. "Whoever thought a body could be that thoughtless, and just for a business trip! Well, don't you worry none. We'll take care of you. Fred, I'm going to get these people something to eat. I hear the boys rousing."

She rose, clearly finished discussing it for the present. I closed my eyes. I felt too weak, too shocked to explain everything to them. There would be time later.

Fred saddled up his old mare and went out, but found no trace of David that day nor the next. The first winter storm came whirling over the mountains. Freezing rain changed into mingled sleet and snow. For now, further searching was impractical.

And so we waited, day after creeping day, hoping against hope to see his limping figure trudging in the lane or to hear a knock announcing his arrival.

A week later Peter came charging into the house, hardly stopping to knock the snow from his cracked shoes. I looked up from where I was mending socks in the corner. "Peter, do watch yourself. Now you've tracked in snow, and Malinda was just finished mopping."

"But, Mother, look here!" Peter waved a white envelope triumphantly. "A letter for them. It's from Daddy. I know it is!"

My heart gave a leap. My sewing dropped forgotten onto the floor. "Are you sure, Peter?" I almost grabbed the creased and dirty piece of paper from his hands. I could hardly hold my hands steady enough to read the address written on the side.

"Yes, yes, son! I think you're right. Oh, go get

211

Malinda quick. But however did you get it?"

"A man dropped it off, a man on horseback." He flung the words over his shoulder as he sped up the stairs.

> Dear Fred and Malinda,
> May God protect this letter until it reaches your hands! I am sick with worry for my dear family. I was captured . . .

Fred's quavering voice broke.

> . . . captured the first evening on my way home, and escorted back to my regiment. A thousand agonies I have suffered since, thinking of Ellen's desperate situation. Neither letter I was allowed to send her has been answered, and I can hardly think of anything else for worry.
> Can you please help me get word to her? We are in winter camp at Bunker Hill (Port Royal) near Fredericksburg. I am constantly under guard and looked upon with scorn, but am standing firm on my conviction that I cannot fight.
> I cannot share more at this time. Please let me know as soon as you learn anything about my family. I pray for them night and day.
>
> David

"Mommy!" Davie flung himself onto my lap in a torrent of tears. "They got my Papa! They got my Papa!"

I pulled him close, hardly able to see through the blur in my own eyes. I stroked his back helplessly, the other boys looking on with white faces.

Uncle Fred was quiet as he folded the faded piece of paper. "It's . . ." he coughed awkwardly. "It's too bad he got taken now, 'fore he knew 'bout you leaving home. But you can stay here . . ." He glanced toward his wife.

"Why, sure."

"You'uns stay here as long as you need to. He's where it is his duty to be. We can just be glad they ain't shot . . ." He caught himself then went on, "Ain't been too mean to him. But what's he mean . . . can't fight? Won't fight 'gainst them keeping him under guard?"

My mouth opened but no sound came out. I swallowed hard. How could I tell them David could no longer fight after they lost their own son? And yet I must, and if they turned us out . . .

They were looking at me strangely. I cleared my throat. "Well, Fred, Malinda, I know David didn't tell you all he suffered during his time in the army. He didn't feel free to tell people." I hurried on. "But you have a right to know.

"Last summer David was in the battle of Port Republic." I could feel my eyes getting misty. "His group of men were trying to take a Union cannon when they were fired on from behind some rocks. They shot back, and when David stumbled over one of the Yankee sharpshooters, he was horrified to find it was . . . it was his own . . . brother!"

Malinda clutched at her throat as if frozen. Uncle Fred swore softly under his breath. "Killed him? Which one?"

"Edward." I huddled over Andy's body pressed tight against mine.

"The youngest!" He slammed his hand on the table, eyes flashing. "War is awfully unjust. Our Andy taken, and the Uberwassers up the road with five sons haven't lost a one. They're all alive." He shook his fist in the air. "Who'd a thought it. David meeting his own flesh and blood. He never . . ."

"Hush, Fred." His wife shook his arm. Her mouth trembled. "Tell us, Ellen."

"David held him as he died. That's . . . that's when he was wounded himself, almost killed. And when we brought him home, it was always on his mind. It nearly drove him crazy."

I took a deep breath. Fred had his head down between his hands, and the tears were rolling unchecked down Malinda's faded cheeks.

"It was quite a while before he shared it with me. Together we committed ourselves to finding a different way. Guilt had just about killed him. Don't you see? It was either find help, or . . ." I stopped suddenly.

Fred and Malinda sat silently. Finally I continued. "This business he was taking care of, these people he wanted to visit . . . it was the Mennonite people. He had contact with one for a couple months last spring, and he felt he had to learn more about their beliefs. We were thinking of joining them."

I sat with head bowed. The room was still. Then Fred's chair scraped hard on the floor, and he got up, shoulders sagging. Without a word he walked out of the room. In a moment I heard the outside door close behind him.

Frightened, I glanced at Malinda. "I'm sorry, I've

214

upset him."

She was working her knuckles nervously. "Maybe not." She wiped her eyes with the back of a hand. "Likely it's too much for him to bear right now. He ain't one to storm into somebody, does he disagree with them."

I turned away. "You are kind, Malinda. Very kind. You have already suffered terribly losing Andrew. I'll understand if you want us to leave."

I took a deep breath, praying for help for the questions I guessed would come when David's uncle came back inside.

"May I come in?" Candle in hand, I knocked softly on the door opposite my own. Crowded under the eaves, this room was hardly larger than the one I slept in. In all the years Freds had lived here, it had been used as a storage room. There was just enough room for each boy to roll out his blankets without his feet sticking into another's face.

Taking the muffled reply as a welcome, I shoved on the rough boards, careful to lift as I pushed to keep the sagging door from scraping and waking the elderly couple below.

All afternoon Fred had stayed out in the barn. When he came in for the evening meal, his face was set and blank, and I could not tell what he was thinking. Only once had he made a comment, and that was because of his wife's nervous movements during supper. "Fer lands' sakes, Lindy, you'd think the bandits were after ye, the way yer jumping up and down and can't keep still!"

After we made our way up the narrow stairs to bed, I had heard the murmur of voices below me. Even out of Fred's presence, I felt as nervous as Malinda. How could we stay and cause pain to those sacrificing for us? Was this to be a repeat of two weeks ago? No, it would not be the same. As much as they disagreed or felt cut by our differences, they were not the kind to force us out or give us reason to feel mistreated. No, they were too loyal to David to do that.

After the voices below had at last grown silent, I lit the candle and stepped across the hall. The boys' eyes showed relief, and I knew all of them had been unable to sleep. I sat on an ancient black chest with brass clasps.

"Boys, we need to talk some things over tonight. This is not an easy time for us." I cleared my voice to steady it. "But at least we know where Papa is."

"Will they kill him, Mommy?" Andy's small hand tightened on my knee.

"We . . . we hope not, Andy. There won't be a lot going on during the winter, because the roads are too bad. That's to his advantage. I will write Papa tonight. Think how much better he'll feel when he hears we're okay."

I sagged back against the wall. "There is something we need to realize though." My eyes lingered on each face. If only I could shield them from the trauma of these months. War! It made old men of little boys and wrecked or hardened everyone who took part in it.

I turned toward the dark window crowded under the rafters. It had started snowing an hour before. In the candle light, the flakes swirled strangely against the rippled glass as though mocking what I was about to say.

"You know Papa no longer believes it's right to fight. Uncle Freds can't understand this. Although they don't like war, they feel everyone is duty bound by God to obey the call to arms. I'm not sure I can explain it, but I do know we want to do what we believe is right, even though people around may not agree.

"Uncle Freds have been good to us, very good. If need be, they would share their last piece of bread with us. But I cannot feel right staying when our being here brings back all the hurt of losing their own son. Not only that, we are running them low in food, and it's a long time yet till spring."

No one spoke for some time, and I hid my cold hands under my skirts, gripping my fists until they felt numb.

"What about the food we brought along? The dried apples and that bag of flour? The turnips?" Peter asked in desperation.

"We've used quite a bit of that already, Peter. With skimping it should last a little while yet, but . . ."

"Will we starve?" Davie's chin was quivering.

"No. No, son!" I pulled him against me. "Remember how God protected us on the way here? As much as I love you and want to provide for you, so much more does God."

John pulled himself to a sitting position. "What choices do we have, Mother?"

I felt encouraged with the quiet way John dealt with the facts. That would be David's way, not panic or hysteria, but an objective look at possible options, laying them out one by one until the answer became clear. I smiled at him.

"Thank you, John. That's how we must do, look at things without getting upset. What would you say?"

He ran a hand through his rumpled hair. "Well, we can't go back to Grandfathers. Grandmother made that impossible."

I nodded.

"And if we can't stay here, then there are only two ways to go: north to try to find the same people Daddy made friends with, or back south to Staunton and try to find a place to stay and work to pay our rent and food. We boys could try to find work in town."

"Maybe there'd be a farmer along the way who needs help that would let us stay for awhile." Peter frowned, drumming his fingers on the floor.

John shook his head. "Not too much chance in the winter. Now if it were summer . . . No, I think town would give us a better chance."

"One thing we mustn't forget, John," I sighed. "You're old enough it's not safe for you to be seen in public. If we believe it's wrong to fight, come springtime, you could be grabbed as a fresh recruit for the army. We've seen how desperate they are."

"Then that doesn't leave much choice." Peter's reply was quiet.

"It seems that way. But we don't have to decide tonight. Let's think about it, pray about it, and try to make a decision very soon." I stood up. "Good night, boys. Get some sleep, and snuggle under the covers to keep from getting too cold. I know the way will be clear for us at the right time."

With a light squeeze on Davie and Andy's shoulders, I left the room, pulling the door shut behind me. Tiptoeing into my room, I set the candle on the crate serving as a stand beside my bed.

This room had belonged to Andrew, Fred and Malinda's beloved son. There were still evidences of a boy's presence: a squirrel's tail tacked to the window frame, a single deer antler with a broken tip protruding from a small corner shelf with candle drippings, and pegs for a gun. A half-plaited horse bridle hung next to a small picture of Andrew himself, his serious eyes looking out at the world.

Where was Andrew now? What happened to these young men, seriously committed, feeling they were serving God? Did God approve of their sincerity and overlook the teachings of Jesus? Was it really outdated to avoid all participation in war? If a person didn't accept the Scriptures as given, how could you know what to believe? I shuddered.

❧ Chapter XI ❧

DIARY—2/3/63, Bunker Hill.
Oh God, help me stay true to You. The guardhouse is filling up. How can one feel so alone surrounded by so many men? They sit around and tell of their families' desperate needs. Many of them had slipped home for their children's sake, but tightening "man searches" hunted them down and brought them back.

Others are here because of drunkenness or carelessness on guard duty. At least they know where their loved ones are. God have mercy on Ellen and the boys!

The snows began in earnest. John and Peter threw themselves fiercely into every job that needed doing, trying to bridge the gulf between us and the ones who had taken us in.

I ached as I looked on. Again, the children suffered because of their parents. Had we made the right choice? Thus far it had brought only pain to the family. And yet, something inside me yearned for more of this new awakening, this inner awareness that spoke so clearly to truth. After a taste of this, how could I go back to the shallow piety I had known before?

In spite of all we did, the atmosphere remained stiff and cool. Often after going upstairs, I wept my tension into the pillow. Yet I knew I should not take it personally.

The old couple *was* softening. In spite of their resistance, I could sense the boys' efforts were not in vain. But then, love is never in vain; surely it wasn't. Even if Fred and Malinda remained aloof for the length of our stay, it would be better to love than to nurse hurts and harbor bitterness. Hadn't I read a verse a few days before promising that even a cup of cold water given out of love was remembered and rewarded by God? I must find that verse again.

There was one bright spot for our family. After all these weeks, we received a letter from David. He rejoiced to hear of our safety and pleaded with us to stay where we were. And then he said:

Maybe the war will soon be over. That is the feeling in the camp. Soon after I was brought here, the Northern forces were repelled from Fredericksburg under heavy fighting. Southerners think they smell victory!

I long to sit down and share with you all my heart, but the letters are censored before they're mailed. I find solace in reading my New Testament. Am hoping you are doing the same.

All my love,
David

DIARY—2/5/63

Time hangs heavy here. Four walls, the cold, and a minimum of food are hard on a man. No place to be alone. My only comfort is my Bible. It is becoming quite frayed.

They are gradually allowing the others to return to active duty, but tell me I have not shown the proper remorse for the stand I have taken. I am accused of being worse than James White, the lieutenant who deserted on the tramp from Shepherdtown to here.[1]

DIARY—2/10/63

My hip is bothering me so I can hardly walk. Was checked out yesterday by the camp surgeon. Just a young fellow, scarcely over twenty. He says it's rheumatism setting in because of inactivity and cold quarters.

Found out his dad used to bring horses to the shop for me to shoe. Seemed pleased to make that connection. Promised to see if he could make it easier for me.

The food situation remained desperate, but there was no way we could leave now, even if we knew where to go. We could never tell when another storm would come sweeping over the mountains, covering us with more powdery whiteness.

We dropped back to two meals a day, going to bed earlier and waiting to get up till the sun had risen. I knew I was too thin for a woman in my condition, but food was limited, and my appetite was poor.

"It isn't right that we are running you so short, Malinda." I pulled her aside one evening toward the end of February.

She shook her head shortly. "We all need vittles, and we'll do what needs doing and spend no time moan'en about it. You added what you had to the meals too, ye know."

I knew what she said was true, but the guilt I felt still haunted my waking moments, even following me into my dreams.

And then we heard of Mr. Cochran. Uncle Fred met him on the pike one Monday evening, and learned through a slip of his tongue, that he had some surplus food hidden in his icehouse. Fred offered him a load of hay, enlarging the amount until the old man promised to make some kind of deal, were the hay in good condition and delivered to his barn.

I stood by as John slipped on his coat and thrust his hands deeper into the homemade rabbit-lined gloves I had given him. I felt my lips tremble. "You'll be careful, son?"

"Yes, Mother." He reached out an awkward hand. "I'll keep Malinda's shawl wrapped around my face and remember to sit low when we meet anyone."

I pulled him close. "Don't take any chances."

Fred shuffled into the room, rubbing his stiff muscles. "I reckon we better leave 'fore it gets much later. We'll try to get our tradin' done so we can get back a'fore nightfall. We're lucky it ain't snowing today. Stars were out clear when we came in from milk'en a bit ago. Lindy, you got the bricks hot?"

The firelight flickered on his wife's face as she bent to wrap the row of worn bricks lined up along the hearth. "I hope you stay warm enough, Pop. It's eight long miles to Henry Cochrans. Wonder if his wife still has that recipe for potato pie.[2] You might ask him, if you think of it. I mislaid mine some years back."

His thick eyebrows knitted. "It ain't the miles I'm afeared of. It's . . ." He coughed and hitched his overalls a mite higher. "It's them stragglers who hang around in these mountains and make life rough for friend or foe. A fellow down the road—Jack Peters— had them swarm over his farm, Henry told me, and . . ." He hesitated as he caught Malinda slightly shaking her head.

He rubbed his ear gingerly. "Anyways, he told me Jack said he had half a notion to do like his grandma used to do when the Indians was maken' so much trouble in these parts. You recollect that story, Lindy?"

"Jack Peters' grandma? Never heard of her."

"Well, his grandma had a little cabin all by herself back up on Jennings Gap. There come a time when the Indian raids got so bad, Jack's folks begged her to come on down and live with them, but she wouldn't. She had a little corn patch, an old cow, a couple chickens, and some bees.

"Said she'd been there going on twenty years and ain't no redskins gonna get her to leave now."

He pulled his boots over his stocking feet and reached for the muffler his wife held ready. "Yep, she just had one door, the front. She set her beehives smack in the front yard, and fastened herself a long cord from the hives to the kitchen window. Whenever she'd hear the first hint of trouble, she'd jest jerk that rope and the bees would come out fighten mad."[3]

He chuckled and reached for the doorknob. "I reckon the sky is nigh light enough. You ready, John?"

The day was spent making candles. Carefully hoarded wax and resin had been melted together. Each candle was allowed only several dips before being hung aside to dry.[4]

"We'll do like my mom used to when I was a child. Pop and you boys can fashion wire holders to keep them stand'en in place while they burn." Malinda handed the last row of dripping tapers to Davie to hang. "We won't need many anyways. A body that goes to bed at the right time doesn't need much more than sunlight."

Andy came away from the window where he had been keeping an eye on the road. "It's starting to snow, Aunt Malinda."

I groaned. "Snow? It can't be. The sky was clear an hour ago." I hurried to the window.

David's aunt shook her head. "You never can tell what the weather will do here." She hobbled over to stand beside me. "It's not snowing hard yet. Mebbe it will hold back till they get here." She clasped her hands together, her faded blue eyes betraying apprehension.

"Shall Davie and I go ahead with chores?" Peter was already reaching for his coat.

She gave a startled glance at the clock. "It's a mite early, but I suppose that would be best. My, I don't know where the day all went to!"

"Let me go along out, Malinda. No, it won't hurt me. It will do me good to get some fresh air. And we'll get done quicker." I gathered up the drying racks to put away.

Doubt clouded the wrinkled face, but at last she turned back to the kitchen. "Well . . ."

"If we get a pint of milk, we can add a bit to potato soup for flavoring. We do have a few potatoes left, don't we?"

"A few, I think. I'll go down to the cellar and see. Andy, you can carry the light. Careful now."

We did the chores hurriedly, taking no time for words. There wasn't much to do. The milk Peter got covered little more than the bottom of the pail.

I stopped in the barn doorway, watching the snow spiraling down out of the darkening sky. There was still no rattle of wagon wheels, no sound of horses' hooves coming up the dirt lane. I pulled my coat around my growing figure and felt a stab of fear inside. Where were Uncle Fred and John? As much as David's uncle liked to visit, he would know better than to take any longer than necessary today. I turned quickly toward the house. It would do no good to fret.

There was Peter carrying the milk pail just ahead. He stopped so suddenly, I almost ran into him.

"Did you hear that?"

"Hear what?" I stopped and listened too. The white flakes burned cold on my cheeks, melting to a black wetness against my sleeves.

"There, I heard it again, out that way." He pointed down the hollow where the road wound along the creek bottom.

Then I heard it too, horses' hooves coming at a gallop, wagon wheels clattering crazily. I clutched his arm. "Peter, take the milk into the house."

"But, Mother . . ."

The dog started barking, and I gave him a frantic shove. "Please, right now!"

When the door closed behind him, I crowded against the corner of the house, hugging the shadows. Whatever it was, was coming up the lane now. I could hear a horse blowing. Then Fred's voice called out, hoarse and panting, "Whoa! Whoa there. Easy now. That a girl . . ."

Suddenly I was running through the blinding flakes toward the dark shape of the wagon pulling to a stop beside the barn.

"John! Are you there? Fred! Are you all right?"

The back door jerked open, and four shivering figures stood in the shaft of dim light stretching across the lane.

"Whoa, girl." Fred was beside the horses, rubbing their necks, calming their pitching heads. "Yep, Ellen. We're okay. The horses jest had a scare down the road aways."

Avoiding my eyes, he turned back toward the panting animals. "Tell Lindy to have something hot ready for us. We're a mite hungry, ain't we, John?"

Even in the half-light of evening I could see fear and exhaustion in both of them, but when they entered the house ten minutes later, they were carefully relaxed. Supper was eaten in silence. My frowns kept the boys from asking any questions, but as soon as Fred had moved to his armchair by the fireplace, Andy crowded up to him. "Uncle Fred, why were you going so fast?"

Fred grunted without replying. Andy insisted, "Uncle Fred, why . . ."

"Ole Claybones and Patsy . . . ," Fred interrupted, "spooked, I guess." He finished whittling out a toothpick and poked it absentmindedly among his few remaining teeth. "An' since we was getting right chilly, I figured we might as well jest ride along."

His eyebrows raised. His usually sober eyes were almost twinkling. He stuck his feet out in front of him. "I see Lindy has my slippers warming on the hearth. Wonder if you could bring them fer me?"

Davie scrambled to help with the putting-on

229

ceremony. "Did you unload the food already, Uncle Fred?"

David's uncle looked nervously up at his wife. "We won't worry about that right now. I'm jest getting comfortable, an' I don't feel too tolerable toward going out in the cold again. We traded fer meal an' 'taters. And I feel it's quite promis'en we can get more later. He seemed pleased, the miser." The old man cleared his throat loudly. "He ought to be. He drove a hard bargain."

Malinda came to stand beside him. "Did you 'member my recipe?"

"Recipe?"

"Recipe! For Sadie's potato pie. Did you go and fergit it?"

"Well, if that ain't the limit." He slapped his leg in disgust. "That woman didn't give it to me, now did she, John? I asked her 'bout it. John is the one that reminded me of it. What did she say?" He frowned, twisting his mustache with a wrinkled hand.

"It had a lemon in it. I remember that because it seemed so strange." John shook his head. "She was going into the house to look it up for sure, but she never came back."

"Yep, that's what 'twas. We got to looking at the sky, and I knew we best be heading back. Tell you the truth, I plumb forgot 'bout it. Sorry, Lindy, but that's a fact. An' they say, the truth 'bout the facts is, that the facts is the truth."

His wife opened her mouth to say more, but Fred had already begun telling stories of hard winters when he was a boy.

When Fred was six years old, he was sent to the mill on horseback with corn to be ground. The miller

230

loaded the horse carelessly, and the bags of meal fell off halfway home. Not being strong enough to reload it, Fred had to wait till someone came to help him.

"That was the first part of April," Fred said, "and no one expected to see a snow come anymore that year. I tied that ole mare to a tree and nigh crawled under her belly, try'en to get warm. I tell ye, I thought the snow would kever me and the horse up too a'fore my older brother came along looking fer me."

With everyone's attention, Fred began telling how during his teens he made snowshoes out of four-inch maple saplings and strips of cowhide, and ran a trapline for several miles every winter. Encounters with bobcats and wolves kept the boys clustered around his chair for more than an hour. I had never known him to be so talkative.

By the time he was through, I could tell the youngest boys had totally forgotten about the runaway horses. It wasn't until everyone was settled for the night that I learned more. There came a hesitant knock on my bedroom door.

"I was expecting you, son." I could just make out John's face in the darkness. "Tell me everything."

He swallowed hard. "We were robbed."

"Robbed! Where?"

"About four miles from home. Six men coming from Burke's Mill way. They swung in after us when we turned off the pike."

I sank back, trembling. "So that's why the wagon was empty."

He nodded. "Uncle Fred figured they were up to no good, but there was nothing we could do but keep going. They caught up with us next to the river."

I grabbed his arm in the darkness. "Did they try to hurt you, John?"

"No . . . no. They had guns, but weren't mean. They wanted any food we had. We had to give it to them, Mother. That bag of cornmeal and some salt and potatoes. All of it gone . . . all those miles for nothing!" His voice cracked and he hung his head, shoulders slumped.

I squeezed his arm tighter. "Well, son, we'll make it somehow. Do you think that was the same group of men you saw before?"

He did not speak for a while. Finally he cleared his throat and continued huskily, "They looked more like army men. But that's not the worst. One of them kept looking at me, and finally asked how old I was. I had to tell him. And then he wondered where I lived."

"Oh, John!"

"We're not safe here anymore," he rasped. "That is, I'm not."

After comforting John as best I could, I sent him back to bed, feeling fresh terror within me. It seemed fate was against us.

We must leave. But to go where? And how, at this time of year? I tossed and turned. I prayed desperately. If only David were here to tell me what to do!

Finally, the tension was more than I could bear. I pulled myself out of bed, and fumbling in the darkness, lit the candle on the shelf and reached for David's Bible. I could feel the cold seeping through the cracks in the wall, and my fingers grew numb as I flipped from page to page, wishing, hoping for some word to jump out at me. Nothing came.

At last I bowed my head. "Oh God, please heed a

poor woman's prayer. There are a lot of things I don't understand, but this I know, I need You. And I want to be Yours, whatever that includes.

"I know I don't deserve anything, but unless You give clear direction, I cannot go through another day. Have mercy on me, O Lord; on me and my four sons, and on David . . . dear David . . ."

I don't know how long I sat there, eyes closed, with the Bible open in front of me. Gradually my frantic thoughts quieted, and from somewhere a sense of calm took over. Part of a verse I had read several days before came to me. "Behold, he goeth before into Galilee . . ." *Galilee,* for Christ it had been a place further from the public eye, a place safer from the enemy.

Impulsively I rose, and crouching under the slanting roof, peered through the small window. The snow had stopped, and dark clouds were scudding across the moon, casting murky shadows on the snowcovered ground. With my eyes I followed the lane between craggy black oaks standing stiff and tall down the hill to where it twisted onto the dirt road.

The road stretched both ways out of sight. There was no way to know what lay beyond the bend, but it no longer mattered. *He* knew . . . We would go. He would show the way.

The parting was hard. The boys stood beside me with their bundles strapped onto their backs. Claybones wrinkled up his nose, showing yellow teeth. I hugged Aunt Malinda tightly, feeling her tears against my cheek. "We can never repay all you have done for us." I could hardly speak.

Uncle Fred wiped his eyes with a wrinkled handkerchief. He busied himself checking the cinch straps. "Wish you wouldn't be so all fired ready to leave. I can hardly stand to think of you walking this a'way. If you could jest wait another day or so, I'd have that torn harness fixed, and I'd take you in the farm wagon."

I smiled at him. He had already offered this half a dozen times since we got up this morning. "Thank you, Uncle Fred. I know you would. It's not your fault the harness tore coming in the other night. But I'd rather go ahead. We'll take it slow, and with your directions, I don't think we'll have any trouble."

I mentally went over them again. *When you get to the pike, jest head north about five miles until you get to Burkes Mill, then take a left toward Weyers Cave. I've heard say there's a preacher lives about a mile the other side of the Valley Railroad. He could probably help you.*

We had lingered as long as we dared. We must get past the pike before traffic picked up.

"Come back anytime . . . !" It was Malinda calling after us. I held onto my smile until we waved the last time and were around the bend out of sight.

The day became surprisingly warm for February. The sky was fast taking on a brilliant blue. Wispy clouds stretched high overhead, still bright with the pink of dawn. For a long time there was no sound other than the tramp of our feet and Claybones' wheezing.

The fresh snowfall which had covered up the dirty ruts and mud holes was already mutilated by yesterday's traffic. John went ahead to pick out the easiest footing. I was deeply grateful for the cloth-covered package under my arm. Malinda had insisted we take along the last baking of bread and six eggs she had saved from a week's gathering. I had protested vigorously, but to my amazement, Fred backed up his wife's offer.

"Don't be foolish. You have more mouths to feed than we do. I'll take another heap of hay soon, and we'll make out fine. Don't you worry 'bout us."

I marveled at their kindness. It was a reassurance that God would indeed provide for us. Whatever happened, He would provide.

Twice during the next hour, Peter shinnied up a tree to survey the road ahead. The first time he saw nothing, the next, he motioned us frantically into the underbrush where we crouched, breathless, while a small group of cavalry rode briskly by. At the bottom of the hill we watched them overtake a horse and wagon stopped by the road, split to ride around it, and continue out of sight.

As we came closer, the boys eyed the vehicle with interest. The back was empty but for a long blanket-covered form and a wooden trunk crowded into one corner. An elderly couple sat on the wagon seat, the old man trying to hold a steaming cup to his wife's lips. The remains of a meager fire smoldered in the snow beside the wagon wheel.

"Good morning." In spite of the urgency to hurry, I could not pass them without offering assistance. The man was having trouble getting his wife to respond.

He looked up startled, almost spilling the tea.

I stepped to the wagon's edge, "We are friends.

Are you in need of help?"

He started to speak but couldn't. He grabbed for his wife as she began sinking to the floor.

"Davie, Peter . . . !"

But they were already scrambling up and bracing the woman from behind. I took the cup from the man's hand.

"I'm Ellen Shull from Staunton. We are moving north of here. May we help you for a ways?"

His watery eyes blinked. "She . . . she can't make it much longer, all this snow and cold. I'd be much obliged to you. We're hoping to make it to my nephew's place near Scotts Ford."

Then he caught himself. "Pardon me. Name is Tom Newby, and Mommy here, Myra. She's had such a shock, she's not herself. If you could, I'd be a-pleasured to you."

John tied Claybones to the back of the wagon and took the driver's seat. Tom's story came out in bits and pieces over the next four miles. They lived west of Staunton on a small farm with two sons; one at home on leave, and the other just recently left to join Imboden's Artillery.

"Two days ago, they come. The terrible creatures ransacked the house and shot my Demsey in cold blood on the hearth!"

He choked up, motioning to the blanketed body on the wagon bed. "They took whate'er they pleased, and stood in the doorway mocking Mommy in her bed. Held me back from going to either one till they had taken all they wanted."

He clawed at his throat. "I aim to shoot everyone I get close enough to. Shoot till they finish me off." He shook his fist. "There is nice soldiers and respectable ones, but Yankees are no better than animals."

All the while his wife sat hunched over, held on both sides by the boys, never saying a word.

I felt sick. What degradation man could sink to. And yet hate, how could that better the situation? That was what caused men to act in such despicable ways in the first place.

I opened my mouth to speak, grasping for something to say. And then it came to me—that's all he has left. Hate is the only weapon this old man has left.

As we neared the crossroads, I interrupted his muttering to lay my hand on his arm. "Sir, I cannot imagine what you are going through. But isn't it better to suffer injustice than to administer it?"

He looked blankly at me. I knew he didn't understand what I was trying to say. We pulled up beside the mill. With the boys' help, Mr. Newby settled his wife into a corner on the wagon bed. I wrapped one of our blankets around her body.

"May God help you," I said sincerely, smiling into her vacant eyes. Her staring eyes latched pathetically onto me. Her sagging lips parted, and she clutched at my arm. I hesitated, then feeling like a traitor, carefully peeled her fingers loose and stepped down beside the boys.

The old man was coming out of the front entrance with several Negroes and a young boy about Davie's age. At least one of them would accompany the wagon to its destination.

Seeing he had all the help he needed, I extended my hand in parting. "May God somehow grant you peace, sir."

He turned his eyes away from me and stared

straight ahead. "No peace while Yankees run loose. I'll kill . . ." He struggled up on the wagon seat and clucked to the horse. "I'll kill everyone of them I can get hold of."

They headed north up the pike. I watched until the wagon wheels drowned out his muttering.

❦ Chapter XII ❦

Dear David,
How I long to have you here and look into your eyes again. Can they still twinkle? I miss you.

I must tell you, oh David! My prayers have been answered! God has smiled upon us and given tender mercy in time of need.

We left Uncle Fred's a week ago yesterday. Some men had looked at John suspiciously, and we felt it best to move on.

God led us to a small, white house two miles off the pike just north of Mt. Sidney, where a Mennonite minister, Mr. Isaac

Grove, and his family live.[1]

They graciously fed us and let us sleep there overnight. When I shared our story, they insisted we stay until someone could be found with more room.

We had long discussions by the fireside. David, these people stand for all my soul has been longing for.

Two days ago, with John underneath the baggage, they took us further east by wagon to where an old man and his wife live— Wilhelm and Rebecca Gochenour— German people.

Just walking in their door, I felt wrapped with a beautiful peace. They have taken us in as if we were family members. Between our efforts and what they were able to store up for the winter, I think we will be able to make it through the remaining weeks until spring.

I stopped, pen poised in midair. Were we crazy to impose on this Mennonite couple this way? My emotions fluctuated between embarrassment and resignation to the kindness of others.

Finally I lay the pen down and snuffed out the candle. I would finish the letter in the morning. I lay back in the darkness, listening to the murmur of voices in the next room.

My mind immediately jumped back to our meeting several mornings before. I had been very nervous. Who would be willing to take us in—especially a woman in my condition?

When the wagon came to a stop, Mr. Grove knocked on the door of the rough-hewn cabin set against the wooded edge of a hillside. Smoke rose steadily from a chimney at the far end. The snow was neatly scraped from the porch and a narrow walkway running to the yard's edge.

On the left side of the path, the remaining stalks of an ample herb garden stood stiffly upright inside a low picket fence. A gnarled grapevine was trained up over the porch railing.

The white-haired, full-bearded man who came to the door extended a ready hand. "Guten tag! Bringen sie freunde zu uns?"*

I couldn't understand their conversation, but as the older man disappeared inside, Isaac smiled down at us from the porch. "You be welcome here, as I knew you would. Come."

John sat up quickly, pushing the bundles aside. "Here, Mother." He reached for my elbow.

I found myself being ushered up the steps and my hands enclosed in the warm grasp of a gray-haired woman slightly shorter than I.

My first thought was of the softness of a summer dawn. Her eyes were the clearest blue I ever remembered seeing. Her dove-colored dress reached nearly to the floor; only the tips of her black shoes could be seen. A white muslin cap covered most of her still thick hair.

She started to say something, caught her breath, and an odd look flashed over her face. For an instant

*Good day! Do you bring us friends?

241

she stood there, still holding my hands, then caught herself. "Oh, forgive me . . ." She glanced at her husband. "Do come in. I know you are weary."

She led the way to a chair by the fireplace. I looked around in disbelief. The room was small, but in the firelight, warmth and color gleamed from every corner. The floor held a butternut-brown oval rug, braided, I learned later, by Rebecca herself. Through an open door, I could see a post and spindle bed with plumped up pillows covered by a quilt with a patchwork of blues and grays.

Savory smells issued from a large iron pot thrust to one side of the hearth. Copper fire tongs and a shovel stood sturdily in their holder along the other side. A bucket of pink geraniums sat on a wooden stand by the window. A dried bouquet of pussy willows decorated the kitchen table.

I sank into the cushioned rocker held out to me. "It . . . it's lovely."

Rebecca was hurriedly adding more water to the kettle. She knelt and began shaping cornpones on the iron griddle already waiting hot by the fire. "Wilhelm, we shall add some herbs and broth to that pot of cabbage. That will make soup for our noon meal. You are staying for dinner, I hope?" She turned to the minister standing, hat in hand, on the doorsill.

We felt acceptance from the first—acceptance, and a mutual feeling that the strife bringing so much destruction was wrong.

"But how can you do this, take in strangers whom you have never seen before? You don't have an abundance of provisions. You already admitted that." I spread my fingers wide on the table top that evening after the boys had been shown to the lean-to at the back side of the cabin.

Laugh lines creased around Wilhelm's eyes, and he stroked his beard with a work-worn hand. "You haf forgotten you said you luf the same Father? Then we be uf the same family."

His wife hesitated, then spoke. "We . . . we had a daughter, our youngest . . . When I saw you first, it gave me a start. You looked so much like our Susan." A smile lighted her face in spite of tears glistening on her cheeks. She reached across the table, touching my hand. "You were sent here, Ellen. You will be like a daughter to us."

It was still dark the next morning when I awoke. I pulled the covers closer about my shoulders, listening to the sounds through the closed door: someone stoking the fire, whispering voices, then the door opening and closing.

I could smell the drying onions and peppers hanging from nails along the slanting rafters. There was the dusty fragrance of herbs, the tang of tea leaves, pennyroyal perhaps, and the faint mingling of other odors I couldn't quite place.

I lay there awhile, then climbed shivering out of bed and reached for my clothes. I dressed slowly. Pulling my shawl around my neck, I opened the door and stepped out into the front room.

A single candle burned on the mantel, casting bobbing shadows over the face of the clock I had unpacked and set in place the evening before. Already it seemed at home, softly, cheerfully ticking on, none the worse for all its travels.

Rebecca sat in the rocker, eyes closed, with a blanket draped over her shoulders and her Bible open in her lap. She looked up at my entrance. "Good morning, Ellen. Come." She patted the stool beside her.

"I'm afraid you were resting."

"No. No, child. I was just listening. I have already spoken to Him, and now He speaks to me." She smiled. "Here's what He was showing me this morning." She lifted the Bible close. " 'If I take the wings of the morning and dwell in the uttermost parts of the sea, even there shall thy hand lead me and thy right hand shall guide me.' "

The words were beautiful. Yes, wasn't I beginning to realize this? All along, His hand had led us; His kindness had blessed us. I leaned back against the wall thinking. The silence that followed did not seem out of place.

"Rebecca . . ."

The older woman stopped her gentle rocking. "Yes?"

"I have been wondering about some things." I leaned forward.

If she was surprised, she didn't show it, but merely smiled. "What are your questions?"

"I thought you people would be . . ." I stopped, confused. " . . . uncordial toward those different than yourself. Surely you've felt animosity the last two years."

"Yes. Yes, we have. But the Lord was gentle toward seeking ones. We could not do otherwise." She rocked back and forth slightly. "We are not perfect, Ellen. Do not think that for a moment. Within

244

our people you will also find struggles with selfishness and pride.

"But our goal is to love all men and to live out the
Word, just as it is given. This war is testing us to the
limit. Some are finding they are not ready to live out
what they said they held dear."

I tried to read her face. "You mean, some have
gone to war?"

Her head dropped. "It pains me to admit it is
true. But you must understand there has been much
ridicule and pressure, even physical abuse for some.
For the most part, our men have remained true." She
stopped short. "A purifying fire cannot bring out
what was not there to start with."

"You mean . . ."

"Heat reveals the dross, but it will not produce
gold of stubble."

My eyes followed the flicker of flame across the
room, pondering what she had said. "Have *you* faced
physical mistreatment?"

"Not yet. The Lord has been merciful. But we
must always be prepared for it." She smiled at me,
though her eyes remained sober. "But what other
question do you have?"

My face flushed. "I . . . I guess I was surprised at
the beauty you have created here. I . . ."

She gave a low chuckle. "You thought we would
be drab and colorless? I think no, though we enjoy
the simple beauty instead of finery and jewels.

"I was not raised a Mennonite. And at times
Wilhelm must curb my impulsiveness for beauty.
'We do not display God's handiwork in a way that
offends others,' he will say." She smiled. "And I
agree. But it cannot be wrong to bring a bit of His

wonder inside for us to enjoy."

"Oh, I love it!"

I saw amusement in her eyes. "But you are still not finished."

I bit my lip, then plunged in. "Your daughter. Tell me about her."

She smiled in reply. "You have been aching to ask. I could see it." She waved aside my protest. "No, don't feel embarrassed. I want to tell you."

She picked up her Bible once more and stroked it thoughtfully. "To give meaning to what I tell you, we must go back a number of years. Wilhelm's parents moved over from western Germany, the Palatinate, when he was nine years old. They settled in the fertile lowlands of Pennsylvania and started farming. In time they grew quite prosperous.

"We met there, Wilhelm and I. We were married, and over the years, had seven children. Two died at birth, five of them—three boys and two girls—grew up, married and settled around us." Her words were calm, carrying no trace of bitterness.

"We were happy there, very happy. But my Wilhelm has always dreamed of the snow-capped mountains, the rich valleys, the mountain streams of his childhood. When Susan married, and her husband became interested in moving here to the Valley, we said we'd come too."

"You sold your farm?"

"Yes, the remaining children bought it, and we gathered the belongings we could handle into wagons. It was in the spring when we moved; the mountains were bright green with new leaves, the streams were full and laughing, wild flowers and azaleas were in full bloom . . ." She smiled. "It was love at first

246

sight. We bought land together and lived out of our wagons for a while so that we could plow and put out spring crops. This was virgin land, rich and dark, never having felt the cut of a plow.

"Susan's Edward was a tall man, wide-shouldered, with a rolling laugh. He labored long and hard, and you could often hear him break into singing as he worked.

"That first summer was full, very full: field work, garden work, and building houses for us both . . ." She paused, rocking silently for a moment. "There was a little one on the way, and we would often sit together in the evenings, Susan and I, knitting and sewing in the twilight. Edward would rejoice that his son would have a place such as this to grow into manhood."

"A son? How could he know?"

Her eyes took on a soft, distant look. "He couldn't, of course. But he loved that baby, we all did, even though we had never seen it.

"The men were out in the fields pulling corn the day late in October when the pains began. Susan was in that very room." She gestured to my bedroom. Her eyes were wet. "The hours went by, and she needed help. Edward was off in a frenzy to find it, but it was not to be. She . . . she drew her last breath before he returned."

There was no hysterical weeping, only a bowed head and a rapid rising and falling of her chest. I felt the tears sting my eyelids and trickle down my cheeks.

"And the baby?"

"It was born dead." She nodded at the question on my lips. "A son. It was the hardest thing I've ever done to open the door for Edward when he returned.

He was beside himself with grief. We worried for his sanity. He put himself into the work so hard, I was afraid he would collapse.

"One evening after the fall work was over, he sat at the table with head in his hands, completely discouraged. We let him talk it out, and were not surprised when he said he thought he should move back. This place was too painful; the wounds were too fresh.

"And yet we wanted to stay. We had made friends. The small church was beginning to grow. The land was good. And Wilhelm could not bring himself to leave the wild beauty of the Valley. The Indians call it 'Daughter of the Stars.' It reminded him of his boyhood days. Pennsylvania was becoming too grown up for him. We would not return.

"And so Edward sold his quarter of land and left. We loved him like a son. It was hard. But the years have gone quickly. The children have visited, and we would not have it any other way."

"You are a brave woman, Rebecca."

"Not brave, Ellen. Do not shower me with words I do not measure up to." She shook her head. "Not brave . . . just resting on the wings I read about."

She leaned back and looked me full in the face. "Now tell me, daughter. Do you know Him?"

My gaze faltered. "I . . . I feel He has led us here. And I know He was there when I had no one else."

She smiled. "He is, as always, the faithful One. But He wants to be more to you than a helper; He wants your whole life, to cleanse and direct all your paths. Our way of entering into this relationship is through His Son of Light, the Lord Jesus Christ. This kingdom of light, of forgiveness, and joy, is *His* kingdom; the love we share with others is *His* love."

There was warmth in her voice. "The God-man, Christ Jesus, was given so that we weak mortals could see the Divine thought and purpose lived out in a human form. And His death . . ." her face turned grave, "His death was to span the breach of sin you and I had no way of closing.

"The failure to live above hate, selfishness, and evil includes us all. You have wrestled with it also, Ellen. I feel sure you have. The struggle has left our spirit utterly destitute—held fast in the talons of a force that cannot but destroy us.

"But . . ." her face lit up, "at our invitation the Lord, who is all powerful, steps in, washes away the evil of our past, and begins to take control. Our part is to daily choose to allow Him to do this. We no longer live for our own desires, but for His.

"Is it a confinement?" her hands spread wide. "No, never! If ever we find it so, it is because we do not listen closely enough. He always gives that which brings the deepest peace, the highest joy, the most lasting satisfaction."

I started to open my mouth, but she continued. "You shared about your husband's search for forgiveness. It is all for naught unless we come to God. The greatest crime, Ellen, is not the fighting of a war; the greatest crime is not accepting this offer of peace."

She paused. "Do you understand, my daughter?"

I bowed my head. "My sins are many. I admit it." My eyes filled with tears. "I want to invite Him in, not just as a friend—but as my Lord."

Dear Ellen,
   I received your letter at long last and have read it over many times. To know we

249

stand together shrinks the miles separating us into something I can more easily bear.

I am happy to say I am no longer alone in my stand. A Manassas Heatwole is now here, and we have talked a lot together. He had been forced into the army last spring but escaped after only two weeks. Somehow he managed to keep from being caught until this year.

I am treated with more respect and have been taken out a number of times to help with horses. Things are in a turmoil about the opening movements of spring. Feelings generally run high, with expectations being that we have a good chance of bringing the war to a quick end.

With warmer days and more exercise, my leg is slowly improving.

Two days later, just now got back to write again. I was called out to help a mare with a broken leg, and was kept busy ever since. It's a hive of activity around here.

Yesterday as I was being escorted back to the guardhouse, the officer of our regiment, Michael Harman, rode past. He called me into his cabin for a talk. Ellen, I was able, for the first time, to share with him my heart's convictions without feeling he was antagonistic.

When I was finished, he pushed back his chair and stood up. "Well, Shull," he said, "if all men felt as you do, there wouldn't be any need for war. But as it is, we'll have to fight this out to the bitter end. You seem to really believe what you are saying."

"Yes, sir, I base my life on it," I told him. He looked at me for quite awhile.

Finally he said, "We need a man like you to be in charge of the horses, getting them shod and ready for the opening campaign. If you give me your word of honor you will not try to run off, I'll get you out of the guardhouse."

I'm excited. To be out of the dark and smell of that room where sickness and dirt mingle so freely seems too good to be true. I accepted his offer,[2] but assured him no matter what, I will not take any part in fighting.

I hope I did the right thing. I do not know what they will do to me when we break camp. May God give me strength to hold fast.

I thank God for your safekeeping. May He keep you and protect you all!

Love,
David

Even though temperatures fell below freezing at night, by midday the sharp chill gave way to balmy air, bringing a softness to the land that touched every tree, every open field, and every stream and meadow. I could tell it in the warmth of the sun upon my face, the hint of green displacing yellow in the long fronds of distant willows, and in the flock of robins that arrived one morning and spread across the pasture land. Winter's icy grip was broken.

For Rebecca, it meant spring tonic time. She spent a day gathering plants she knew were good for colds and winter peakedness.

"When a boy's face looks the color of a toad's underbelly, then you know he needs a good dose of sassafras or spicebush tea." She unloaded her basket onto the kitchen table and carefully separated the twigs and roots she had found.

I came to stand beside her. "I've used these before." I reached for the red-orange roots of sassafras, holding them up to sniff at the familiar sharp aroma. "But I don't recognize the others."

Rebecca picked out a smooth green stem from the pile closest to her. "You can't forget this fragrance once you become acquainted with it. I call it Benjamin Bush. Most would call it fever bush or spicebush. It has honey-yellow flowers in the spring before the leaves come out and bright red berries in the fall of the year. But it's the twigs and bark that you want to use."

I got a whiff of the strong camphor-like scent. "Yes, I see. But what do you use it for?"

"It's good for tea. I sweeten it with honey. And then, of course, the greens." Her fingers flew, cleaning and trimming the different specimens and cutting them into a large pewter bowl. "Dandelion, sheep sorrel, and garlic, wild strawberry leaves . . ." She put these into a separate container. "I've heard they make a delicate tea good for infection. I want to try it."

I thought of Andy. "Andy's cough is getting worse. Do you . . ."

The older woman nodded quickly. "I heard you up with him last night. Where is he now?"

"He spent a good part of the afternoon lying down, but right now he's out with the others watching Wilhelm boil down the last of the maple syrup."

Rebecca stepped into the side room and returned with a covered bowl. "I hope he's wrapped up well." She held up the container. "When he comes in, we'll doctor him."

As the snow had melted, the big boys worked from dawn till late in the day helping collect the year's supply of maple sap. The trees were few and far apart. After the first day, Wilhelm had sat down and fashioned a map to mark the scattered locations. Meager as it was, he had done this every year since they lived in the Valley.

"*Alla bis'l helft, hot di alt frâ gsât.* 'Every little bit helps, said the old woman.' That is vhat my mother would say." Wilhelm pulled Andy onto his lap as we gathered around the fireplace that evening for a time of reading and prayer. "I think we haf fifteen crocks full uf the syrup. That makes five more than I get by myself. *Viele händ machen schnell ein ende.* 'Many hands make the end come quickly.' "

He smiled around the circle. My mind went to the value of those containers of sweetness. I knew a crock was slightly less than a quart. So it would have taken over ninety gallons of sap to produce that much. I could see why people called syrup-making brewing liquid gold.

Wilhelm had opened his Bible and was leafing through the pages. "But we haf something uf far more value than syrup, or money, or anything we can see. I am thinking uf the verses that talk uf the Kingdom as our most precious possession."

I let the words soak in. "Again, the kingdom of heafen iss like unto treasure hid in a field; the which when a man hath found, he hideth, and for joy thereof goeth and selleth all that he hath, and buyeth that field. Again, the kingdom of heafen iss like unto a merchant man, seeking gootly pearls: who, when he had found one pearl of great price, went and sold all that he had, and bought it."

The white-haired man stroked his beard and his voice softened. "Only those who sell all—find all. If the price iss too much to pay, we haf the Kingdom in name perhaps, but not in joy."

I closed my eyes for a moment. The phrases were beautiful. David had done that; we had done that. And in spite of the ever-present ache I felt in missing David, I was beginning to learn of the joy. I did not have what this old couple was experiencing, but I knew it was there.

❧

I stood in the doorway, dishtowel in hand, facing the sun's glow. Along the sloping hillside next to the barn, I could see the older boys and Grandpa and Grandma, as we called them now, carefully planting precious seed Rebecca had hoarded on a shelf in the corner cupboard.

There was a soft padding of feet, then Andy put

254

his arms around my growing waist. He laid his head against me and sighed contentedly.

"Like the sunshine?" I smiled, rumpling his hair.

He nodded, grinning.

"You're looking better. I didn't hear you cough last night at all."

"I feel better. And I'm hungry. Where's the boys?"

His eyes followed my finger to the plowed strip of land. He blinked. "They's planting garden?"

"Yes. What little Grandpa Gochenours have to plant."

"Spring is here?" There was fear in his voice.

"Yes, son. Isn't it lovely? Look at the tint of green sprouting up from the dead grasses and the violets! Do you see the violets under the trees? There are spring beauties too, up on the hill."

"But, Mommy." His lips quivered. "You said Papa would be safe until spring. What will happen when the armies start fighting again? Will . . . will he be killed?" He hid his face in my skirts.

I swallowed twice. Hard. "Son, look at me." I waited until his eyes, large and wet, turned upward. "Don't you remember all the people God has given to care for us? Uncle Freds, the dear minister and his family that took us in even though he had never seen us before, and now Grandpa Gochenours. God won't let us down now. Come, let's go and join the others."

DIARY—4/6/63

How unusual. Snow all Saturday night and Sunday till noon. Six inches on the ground. Very cold and windy. Men grumbling. I, for one, glad to postpone spring action.

Have moved closer to Fredericksburg. News has come through that the Yankee leader, General Burnsides, who was overwhelmingly defeated in December, has been replaced by a "Joseph Hooker." He is the fifth commander of the Army of the Potomac since the war began two years ago.

The men greatly enjoy tearing this man down, saying he is a coward as all the preceding ones have been. I dare not say anything, for or against, which they find strange.

With all due respect, I believe our commander, General Lee, is a true gentleman, an intelligent planner, and skilled for his job. The men almost worship the ground he walks on.

How can I then, stand against their patriotism? Our chaplain can very convincingly argue his side for hours. I have no witty words or well-phrased statements. All I can tell him is that I have a higher ranking Commander than army officers, and it is to Him that I must answer. I must answer in the way I feel is best.

They say they are not responsible for

the awful slaughter; they are merely obey-
ing orders. But who will reap? I fear we all
are in for a bitter harvest—reaping for
years after the last shot has been fired, the
last casualty has fallen, and the last grave
has been dug.

❧ Chapter XIII ❧

I leaned back and closed my eyes, warm sunshine spilling over my face. I could smell the mellow dankness of wood dirt and decaying leaves. From somewhere came the gurgling of a creek, waters full of juices from last year's grasses and flower stalks.

Rebecca had been right when she suggested this outing. "You need to soak in a bit of His tranquility, my child."

A cold soaking rain had kept us inside for close to a week. On the next sunny day, Wilhelm had pushed back from the table and reached for his hat. "Maple buds haf opened. The warmth will bring out the bees in a hurry. I must clean out the hifes for the new supply uf honey. You wish to come along?"

There was no need for a second invitation. Carrying a couple wooden buckets for any unused honey, the boys were soon following Wilhelm to the far side of the meadow.

I couldn't have asked for a more pleasant day. If only I could wipe out what I had heard the evening before. William Coffman, a young man from Rockingham County had been tried for desertion and sentenced to death by hanging. Two others were caught after hiding out all winter and shot to death.[1]

With a growing shortage of men, was the government ignoring the exemption status law passed last fall? Was this a scare tactic to pressure the Mennonite men to give up this "cat and mouse" game as some called it and join the army? I shuddered. Even an exemption law would not help David. He was not a church member.

Sometimes my new joy seemed elusive; today, I was ashamed to admit, my joy was almost nonexistent. The short cry of a bird high above made me open my eyes. Without thinking I whistled a reply.

Rebecca smiled, pointing to the tiny, olive-gray body flitting from one twig to another. Then a cluster of twittering birds joined the first, mingling excitedly among the branches.

"Yellow warbler." She reached out a hand as a tiny feather floated down. It clung to her palm lightly until a breath of air caught and carried it away. Rebecca picked up her darning needle again. "They are returning north. Every year I look for them. They've traveled a long way already. And to think that 'not one of them shall fall to the ground without your Father.' "

I looked up from my hands twisting in my lap. She was sewing so peacefully.

"How can you say that?" I pressed my lips together. Did this woman know at times I could hardly keep from crying? How could she sit there so calmly?

" 'Tis the news of last night?"

I nodded, not trusting my voice.

The older lady was silent for a moment. Then she said, "Did you ever see a cow bunting's nest?"

I looked up sharply. "No. I used to watch birds on Father's farm, and there were many buntings, but I never saw one's nest."

Rebecca nodded knowingly. "And there is a reason why. For some reason, this bird does not care to rear its young. It lays its eggs in another bird's nest, the nest of a bird smaller than itself."

Her mouth twisted in a bit of a smile. "Not knowing the difference, the parents feed the one who lifts his head the highest, and the rightful nestlings are pushed aside, crowded out, or starved to death. The parents will push out the dead bodies and give all their energy to feeding the intruder."

"How cruel!"

"So it seems. And you don't like cruelty. But something is happening within you that is even more heartless."

"To me?"

"There is something wishing to crowd out of your heart that secret chamber where faith would want to grow. And you are allowing it to take place."

My face flushed. "I'm not sure I understand."

Her hand touched my shoulder gently. "There is no way to avoid the turmoil and fear that comes from not knowing. But for faith to grow, it must be fed. Take care not to feed it harmful thoughts."

I sat, letting the words soak in.

"If a bird recognizes the bunting's egg, it will build another nest over the first and leave the bunting egg undeveloped underneath. It sits there, so close, but never has a chance. The whole while, the true eggs develop and hatch."

I wrinkled my forehead. "You speak of faith, of feeding faith, as something as effortless as . . . as feeding a child."

"It is not that simple, I know it, daughter. And yet, in a sense, it is. To not know the future, or to fear things beyond our control, demands that we rest it all on God. Our focus must be on Him. He must be more real to us than all the darkness around us."

The sound of footsteps and voices came faintly from around the ridge. Rebecca stuffed her sewing into her basket and got up, bending over to give me a helping hand. She took my face in both her hands. "Do you know He is near, Ellen?"

I nodded hesitantly, touched by her tears. "I know He is, though the feeling is not always there."

She smiled. "Ah, that is faith. And it is my duty to make sure you nurture it well."

Between them, the boys had gathered one bucket three-fourths full of the dark, unused honeycomb, dripping with sweetness. Davie's eyes were bright as we carefully picked out bits of trash and ashes sprinkled throughout and dipped the clean honey into crocks to store.

"I wish . . . I wish I could eat a whole big handful right now!" Davie sighed wistfully.

"And I wish I dared give you exactly that much," Rebecca's mouth twitched in amusement. She set the last container onto the shelf, then scraped out enough from the bottom of the bucket to generously spread onto the cornbread left over from dinner. "Here, this will give you a taste. Did Wilhelm tell you how he first got started with bees? No? Well, go ask him."

I carried a chair to the far side of the room to listen.

Wilhelm chuckled. "So, you want to hear the bee story." He bent down to unlace his shoes, and Andy reached eagerly with still sticky fingers to help. "Ah, thank you, son! Age makes for rust in the choints."

He moved his stockinged feet back and forth appreciatively. "Well, it's been, maybe eight years ago. It was spring, chust as now. I left for a neighbor's one morning, who lived ofer the next ridge. His name was Fredrick. I wanted to trade some meat for a piece of cowhide for making shoes.

"When I got there, I saw him out in his orchard cleaning out his hifes chust as we did today." He rubbed his hand absentmindedly across Davie's arm. "Did you tell your mama how we went about getting that honey?"

Davie shook his head eagerly. "He lifted the lid off and took his saw and just cut it out! An' the bees were swarming all around . . . even crawling on him."

"No one got stung?" I asked in disbelief. My experiences with bees were not pleasant memories.

"No." Then he giggled, "But I hid 'hind a big tree."

I couldn't help smiling. "Wilhelm, can you explain this?"

His eyes were twinkling. "One way to be safe iss to stay behind big trees. But if you want to haf the honey, you need to get *ein wenig näher,* 'a little closer.' The boys here, they helped." He waved his arm at John and Peter. "A lot easier it iss than doing it yourself."

Peter held up the ladle he was carrying, squinting along its length. "We used smoke, Mother. We wrapped old rags around a stick, started them on fire, and wedged it in their doorway."

The old man nodded, stroking his beard. "Some folks use pine needles or locust bark. The bees inside are goot and sleepy. No worry for them. It iss the bees coming back who don't forgif you. I like to work fast."

"You didn't act scared." Davie's eyes still held admiration for what he had seen. Then for my benefit, he added, "Grandpa said the bees can tell when you are afraid of them. John held the bucket, and Grandpa just lifted out the honey in one chunk and dropped it in."

"Then you shake off the bees," Wilhelm explained, "put the lid back on, and there you are. Ready for another year of honey making. But what was I talking about? Oh yes, my old neighbor, Fredrick.

"Fredrick looked rather snappish, and I said to him, 'Fredrick, what's wrong? It looks like some bees crawled under your collar.'

"He was chust a little Scotsman with a swipe of sandy hair left on top, and he flared up like a mad rooster. 'I'll have you know, Mr. Goch-e-ner, that it's

my most prized queen done left and swarmed somewheres, and I've been looking all day and not found
a trace of 'er. An' she a de-sen-dent of the one my
grandpappy brought cross the water.' "

"What does 'swarmed' mean?" Andy interrupted.
Peter spoke up matter-of-factly. "When the bees
leave the hive. Now let Grandpa finish his story."

The old man cleared his throat. "A queen leefs
looking for a new home and takes her whole family
right along with her.

" 'Well,' I said, 'I'll help you look.' So we did. We
looked all over the hayfield and the edge of the
woods, the barnyard and behind the house. When I
lef' we still hafen't found the bees.

"Very soon after, I was cutting firewood on the hill
and sat down against a big black oak to eat my lunch.
All of a sudden, the wind died down and I heard like
an engine letting off steam right abuf my head."

"The bees!"

He chuckled. "I was chust about blocking their
front door. I chumped up; the bees were swarming
all around, stinging and buzzing through my hair. I
headed for the creek faster than I run for a goot
while. Didn't stop to see if they were following. I
chust chumped in and plastered mud on my neck
and ears—everywhere they had gotten me, then
waited till they had time to calm down.

"I went back and found the hole, and by the ef'n-
ing sun, I could see the mass of bees squirming
inside. I stuffed my wet socks into the crack and
headed straight to Fredrick's. He was so excited. He
threw an arm 'round me, and I had to trot to keep up
with him. We smoked them up goot.

"By then it was dark. We built up the fire for light,

and we sawed that tree right off and took it home. Fredrick was so glad, he gif me enough bees to start four hifes. And we haf honey efer since." He chuckled.

"Didn't the stings hurt?" I asked.

"Yes, they hurt." Rebecca came to stand behind him, wiping her hands on her apron. "I had gotten so worried, I started out with a lantern to look for him. By the time he got home, his neck and ears were so swollen I hardly recognized him. The fingers on his right hand were stuck out like red peppers on a stalk, and one eye was completely swollen shut. It was several days before he was able to do much of anything."

Wilhelm passed it off with a laugh. "I've been glat efer since for our bees. What would we haf done in this war if we couldn't haf had honey. And Grandma can make the tastiest cakes and bread on this side of the mountains." He winked at Andy.

"Now, Wilhelm!" His wife's eyes were bright. "It's just in being thankful with what one has. Soldiers got our cows and most of the sheep last year, but we had two ewes ready for birthing penned in an old shed in the back pasture. We were able to save them."

"And they each had twins." Peter grinned.

"Yes, and though the chickens were all taken, our little Banty hen sat hidden in a corner of the loft without batting an eye, and they never found her. Six of the eggs hatched to give a start with chickens again. So, with our goat and the garden, we have not suffered like you who lived closer to town. We're glad to share what little we have. The simpler our lives are, the more room we have to grow spiritually."

I mulled over her words. Although it seemed

266

backwards, it was true. "Isn't it strange. I grew up in prosperity, yet my family was poor in the simple things that make you rich . . . except for Silas!" I smiled faintly, remembering. "Let me tell you about old Silas."

I had a cough, not an ordinary cough, but a hacking cough from deep inside. It felt like hot coals being raked over my chest. When Wilhelm and the boys went out to finish shearing the sheep, Rebecca led me back to bed. "I don't like the sound of that cough. Lie down and soak up some rest."

"But I should help. You'll be extra busy with the wool to clean."

"There is no rush to get it done. The boys can help. They did excellent yesterday with the shearing. There are only the two young sheep left. You just lie down, and I'm going to fix you up with a hot poultice and my sage and vinegar tea with honey. I don't want you run down when the baby comes."

I lay back against the pillows, too grateful to protest. The last while my strength seemed to disappear before a day had scarcely begun. I had only seen the first sheep being sheared the day before, and I was ready to come back to the house.

I closed my eyes. *David . . . oh, David!* This was his child, and he couldn't even be here at its birth. Was he thinking of us these days? Was he still . . . I forced my thoughts elsewhere. Hadn't Rebecca said faith couldn't grow by feeding on doubt? Wasn't God still right beside him?

267

There had been no letter since the one written the night before his regiment pulled out. It had been very brief.

> We are pulling out in the morning to help back up General Early's army. I know not what lies before me except God's love and your prayers. May God keep you is my hourly prayer!

My thoughts were interrupted by Rebecca stepping into the room. Steam rose from the porcelain cup held in front of her. I drank the bitter brew obediently, grateful for the tender hands cool against my forehead.

"I'm going out to see how the men are getting along. Just rest now. I'll be back in just a mite." After smoothing down the sheets, she stepped softly to the door. She paused and looked back with smile lines around her eyes. "Know He is with you."

I smiled back, then shut my eyes once more, allowing my body to relax into the soft bed. What had I been thinking about? Ah yes, David's letter. *I know not what lies before me except God's love and your prayers.* My mind jumped from one thought to another, seeking assurance God would keep David safe. I also knew there was no promise I would see David again, or that he would ever know this child.

I had not told him. Somehow, I could never bring myself to add that weight of responsibility to the load he already carried. No, there would be time to tell him later . . . if there was a later.

Rebecca had said when we have nothing certain to hold fast to, we are forced to grow, to embrace the only unchanging security, God Himself.

"My mother used to say we are all born with a nature that resists all efforts to change it. We feel it safer to stay inside the secure walls of our hearts than to open them, and let God work in our lives.

"But when we do, God begins to work something of rare beauty." Her face had glowed. "You are standing on the threshold of something big and wonderful, Ellen, and all God asks of you is to take the first step."

These were not lofty, pious sounding words. These were words of experience, unfeigned and beautiful in their simplicity.

I bit my lip. "But what if I'm afraid?"

She had smiled. "We all are. It's a fearful thing to let go. It is not unlike pushing a boat out into a vast ocean, letting go of all your moorings.

"There is only one thing great enough to give us the courage to do so. Here . . ." and she had carefully torn off a corner of a newspaper Wilhelm brought home two days before. What she wrote took only a moment. "Read this sometime," she said as she had handed me the paper.

The paper had waited until I was alone. Now I pulled it out and smoothed down the crumpled edges. There in Rebecca's careful handwriting was a Bible reference, 1 John 4:18.

I reached to the nightstand for my Bible and eagerly turned the pages, running my fingers along the verses until I found it. I held the words closer. "There is no fear in love . . ."

Love—yes, of course. I dropped my Bible onto the bed and stared out the window. Love was the key to glad surrender, to giving God room to work, to bring about whatever He thought best. He warmed our spirits with His life, and helped us become soft and elastic, willing to become—to become what?

I glanced down again. "... for perfect love casteth out fear because fear hath torment. He that feareth is not made perfect in love."

If fear and love could not coexist, then how could a person have both within at the same time? I loved God. In my heart I knew I did. But then why this fear—fear for David, fear for the future? Because my love was not perfect? What is perfect love? How could imperfect people ever hope to obtain perfect love?

I closed the Bible with a sigh. I would have to wait for a chance to ask. It seemed too hard to understand.

Wilhelm and the boys came in for lunch sweaty and dirty. Their clothing smelled of lanolin from the wool. The May sunshine had already sunburned the boys' arms and necks.

"I need to build a fire to heat water to start washing wool this afternoon. Andy, would you like to come along?" Rebecca stood up and began gathering empty dishes from the table.

"Yes!" Andy shoved himself off the makeshift stool and rubbed his sleeve across his mouth.

"Just leave the dishes. I'll do them." I pulled

myself to my feet, waving aside Rebecca's protests. "You go ahead. My rest and your care this morning made me feel much better. It will be good for me to move around a bit."

The older lady stood undecided. "Only if you promise to lie down as soon as they are done. We can all help clear the table."

In a few minutes, the dishes were stacked and waiting, and the older boys were picking up the heavy, grimy bundles of wool and heading toward the barn. Wilhelm stood up, walking slowly after them. His wife pushed him gently back. "Rest a bit, Wilhelm. You are worn out, I can tell."

She led him to the rocker, and he sat down heavily. "I am a mite tired. I'll rest for chust a moment."

Rebecca passed a knowing smile my way and closed the door carefully behind her. As I reached for the teakettle of hot water, his head was already beginning to nod. I muffled my coughing in my sleeve.

"Daughter . . ."

I turned, startled. "I . . . I didn't hear you. I thought you were still dozing."

He chuckled, then sobered. "You are troubled."

I twisted the dishcloth into a tight knot. "Yes, I . . . I am. I have this fear inside—fear for us, fear for David."

I fought to control myself. "I am so confused. For a time I felt peace. Now I'm not sure I have what it

271

takes to hold fast. What if David doesn't have what it takes? I . . . I know I sound childish . . ." I was crying now. ". . . and silly, but . . ."

He let me talk, showing no surprise at my questions. This time I was telling everything.

Finally I wiped my eyes and looked at him standing there, bearded chin bowed against his chest, white hair beginning to curl where it met his ears. His silence had more meaning than any protests he could have made. A rush of affection came over me for this humble man. What was he thinking?

"I—I shouldn't have said all that. I'm sorry." I said hesitantly.

"Any normal person would feel the same. Life iss not easy. And one does not always haf the assurance that he has made the best choices." He rubbed the back of his neck slowly. "It iss goot to question them betimes."

My disbelief showed on my face. "But that—that shows a lack of faith; a need for, for . . ." I searched for words.

"Perhaps it iss more important to our Gott that we come to see our need than that we haf no qualms about the way we haf taken."

I was struggling to follow him. *More important to realize our need?* I unfolded the dishcloth, draping it over the basin's edge.

"You don't understand." He smiled. "Come sit down." He retraced his steps to his chair and picked up the piece of wood he had started working on the evening before. He worked slowly and carefully. The wooden screw which held the spindle on the spinning wheel needed replacing. Rebecca would be needing the wheel before long.

"These things haf bothered you since you came. It is goot to haf it out in the open."

"You don't have time to waste like this."

"I haf time for anything important, and this iss important. You are worrying whether you did the right thing to come here and impose upon us. And you are wondering if David made the right choice, and if so, why Gott didn't keep him from being caught."

He smiled at my look of surprise. "You are wondering how we can hold steadfastly to our peace stand when others around us seem blessed by Gott. Does Gott require such strict obedience as this? And, pardon for saying this, but sometimes deep in here," he tapped his chest, "you perhaps feel anger at Gott for not changing things, not?" He paused.

I glanced down at my hands, carefully folded in my lap. How could he have known?

"Ef'ry time we hear about army movements, you haf struggled with this again." His voice softened. "You cannot build faith on darkness, Ellen, or confusion."

He sat there motionless, gazing far away. He was not a stranger to suffering; I knew that. Yet he seemed so peaceful, so unscarred by past hardships. *How could he do it?*

As if he had heard my question, he cleared his throat and continued. "I was nine when my family started for America. It was a long hard voyage. I can still smell the salt spray, and hear the waves crashing onto the deck. Father was seasick much of the time, and my mother ran herself ragged trying to care for us all.

"About one week out, two uf my brothers came

down with a fever, and in no time," he snapped his fingers, "they passed away, my baby sister following them. All in one day."

His lips quivered. "I stood beside my mother on the swaying deck when the sailors threw the cloth-cofered bodies oferboard. As her little girl was carried to the edge, my mother was so broken of heart," his voice sank to a whisper, "she gave a lunge. I grabbed her, holding her back. She was sobbing, 'not my baby, not my baby.' "

He passed a hand over his face as though trying to erase the pain. "My mother turned very ill herself, but Gott was merciful and spared her life. The trip took most uf the summer.

"Three years later, my father was killed in a milling accident, and as the oldest son, I was placed out to work for a wealthy Lutheran neighbor. He was goot to me, and taught me the manhood skills uf making a living in a new country. I worked for him for five years, and in the end, married his daughter."

He smiled. "They didn't say much when Rebecca chose to choin with the Mennonite faith. No, they were too godly to do that, but it hurt them deeply. We did not feel welcome to visit them often after that."

"Then you know what it is like to feel rejected."

There was sadness in his smile. "Yes, my child. We haf not been foreigners to suffering. But neither was our Lord. We all haf sorrow and at times, choy. Life iss not fair, but the difference is, God's children are not alone."

He leaned forward. "You ask about not fighting, doing no violence. Many are the sincere people gifing their support, their money, their sons, their husbands for the cause, but we must not forget, we haf a greater cause, Ellen. A cause that iss far grander than one goot for only a few short years. And to this cause we haf given everything we haf—families, money, possessions, time, ourselves—not chust for a bit of time, but for *die Ewigkeit,* 'eternity.'

"This iss the cause of Jesus Christ. And it iss our humble duty to do chust as He did in all of life, in wartime or peace; it makes no difference. He does not teach a double set of rules to lif' by. His ways are gentle ones uf luf and light, uf helping, uf ofercoming evil with goot."

He settled back in his chair. "Let me ask you, Ellen, can a man pray for his enemy, and at the same time blow out his . . ." He gestured to his head. "Can you show luf by dealing out hate? Iss this what we learned of our Gott?[2] Can we ofercome evil with more uf the same?" He shook his head. "I think not."

I sat quietly, thinking over what he had said. It seemed so clear, the way he explained it.

"There are many, not taught as we, who feel duty-bound to go and say they can feel the touch of Gott on the field of battle. I haf talked to such. There are mothers who pray for their loved ones and beseech Gott's mercy upon them as they fight.[3]

"I am not here to dispute their claims, but I will say this, Gott iss not a respecter of persons. We each," he pointed to his heart, "are responsible to Him for all that we haf been taught and know, yes, and all that we haf an *opportunity* to know. Only a Gott who knows all these things can be a fair judge to all men.

"Many on the battlefield find fighting and hatred fit well with the condition of their souls.[4] But there

275

also are men, I am sure of it, who are living up to the highest truth they haf been taught.[5] They will be the ones most pained by the evil they partake in.

"I choose to live by the highest standard uf truth Gott gifs. The highest level calls for the greatest sacrifice." He lapsed into silence.

I had never heard it explained this way before. I tried to absorb it all. But there were a few things yet that troubled me. "God could have prevented the war, couldn't He? Why did He allow such a terrible thing?"

His answer did not come quickly. "We all be creatures of choice; you know that, Ellen."

"Yes, but . . ."

"If this be true, then He will not, He cannot, oferride man's decisions, even if it iss for his own goot.

"We all are to blame. The trouble has been building for years. And instead of choosing Gott's way, things were handled selfishly. Even we, as Mennonites, haf been too busy making life easy for ourselves instead of reaching out to others. One hundred years ago, we were struggling to get a start in this new land, and many were massacred by Indian attacks, but no longer.[6]

"Perhaps Gott wanted us all to feel the results of being left to our own devices. Gott did not say we are to adopt other's standards and adjust His Word to man's dogma. We haf to start from the Holy Writ. All uf life must be regulated to fit the *Word*. It iss the only way life makes any sense at all."

"Yes, but what about David? He made his choice for the highest level of truth. Why did God let him go?" I pressed my hand against my lips.

He rose to his feet, momentarily reaching to the

wall to steady himself. "I did not say life iss fair, daughter. Choosing Gott's way does not open the door to *die Ruhe*, to 'ease.' I haf not all the answers. Perhaps it iss to prove that he didn't choose this way just to escape hardship.

"Those men need to see Gott's truth also. What better way than to lif' it out among them. We must trust Gott's love for what we cannot understand."

In the night I called Rebecca into the little bedroom.

"Yes, Ellen?"

"Light the lamp. I . . . I need your help." I spoke through clenched teeth.

Her hand was cold on my forehead. "How long have you been awake?"

I stifled a groan. "I . . . I'm not sure."

"You should have called me sooner," she reproved me gently. "I have everything together. I'll bring it in."

The room darkened as she stepped quickly out. I felt another wave of pain.

I lay back on the pillows, exhausted. Rebecca was bending over me, her eyes shining.

"God has been good to you, Ellen." She held out a tiny bundle. "You have a daughter."

"A daughter?" I reached out hungry arms, not daring to believe it was so. With shaking fingers, I pulled the blanket aside. There I saw a head of dark hair, tiny features, closed eyes, and a mouth drawn up in a grimace. Her tiny cry was like music to my ears. I placed my cheek against her soft forehead. All my love enveloped this wee new bit of life. Overcome with emotion, I buried my face in the blanket.

Rebecca had tears in her own eyes. " 'My soul doth magnify the Lord, and my spirit hath rejoiced in God my Saviour. For he hath regarded the low estate of his handmaiden . . . .' "

The words were like a benediction.

She laid a gentle hand on the two of us. "I will leave you alone now, Ellen. It is time to wake the boys. They will be anxious to meet their new little sister."

As the door closed, I pulled back the blanket and caught one small hand in mine. "I . . . I can't believe this!" I ran my finger over the fuzzy head. "How I've longed for you, and wondered who you would be." My whisper turned into a shaky laugh. Who would have dreamed? Me with a daughter! All my life I had wished for a sister, a mother, a feminine "comrade-in-hearts." And now this! What incredible joy!

Soft laughter welled up inside me, shaking me till tears came to my eyes. And suddenly I was crying, hardly able to muffle the sobs. "Poor little thing, coming into the world without a piece of clothing to call your own. Your father doesn't even know you exist." I hugged the bundle closer. "No home, nothing fancy to wrap you in. But you'll have love . . . all the love my heart can pour out. You're a miracle—a bit of heaven itself!" I pressed my lips against the

278

swollen face.

There was a scuffling of feet, then the door jerked open, and two faces peered inside. Their eagerness turned to bashfulness as they tiptoed in and stood beside the bed.

Andy reached out a hesitant hand and touched the baby's head. "Are you glad?"

My eyes met John and Peter's grinning faces in the doorway. My answer was hushed. "Very, very glad, Andy. Are you?"

"Yes, I guess so. Even girls are good for some things."

"Are you all right, Mommy?" Davie stroked the folds of blanket.

"Yes, son. I'm very tired, but I am happier than I've been in a long time. Here . . ." I placed the tiny bundle into Davie's arms. "We will name her Susannah Faith. Susannah after Papa's mother, and Faith because of what Rebecca has taught me. But we shall call her Susan after . . . after . . ." Though I couldn't finish, I knew the older woman standing in the doorway understood.

That evening Rebecca came in with a cup of tea and a tray of chicken dumplings and gravy. "To build up your strength, Ellen. And I have something for you."

She pulled up the heavy lid of the trunk in the corner and lifted off the drying branches of cedar spread carefully over top. "I asked Wilhelm, and he said yes."

She drew out a blanket-covered parcel onto the bed. My eyes widened as I saw what was inside.

"Oh, you can't do that!"

"It was meant for you, Ellen, for little Susan."

I fingered the dainty dresses and soft baby things. The faint cedar smell still clung to their folds. "How can you bring yourself to do this? Your Susan put literally hours into these for your own grandchild. They're . . . they're lovely! But no, I can't accept them."

"And why not, child?"

"You've made us feel accepted, like one of the family. You've done everything for us, but this is too much. These little garments are a sacred memory you have stored in here. I . . . I can't."

"There will be no one else," she said simply. "God meant it for you."

DIARY—5/16/63

Have just been through what some of the fellows say has been the heaviest fighting yet. Must write to the family and say I am okay lest they worry.

My arm is in a sling. During the four days of fighting at Fredericksburg, I was detailed to ambulance service. To run in among the whining shells, neighing horses, and screaming men is something I do not care to relive in my mind. I doubted I'd be spared, but God is very merciful.

During the last day of battle, several of

us were sitting on a pile of rails eating our rations when we saw a cannon ball rolling our way. Figured it was a solid shot so paid no mind, and then it exploded. A fragment caught me in the shoulder. Did only surface damage. Should soon heal although it is very painful to move.

They say there are about nine thousand prisoners at Guinea Station taken in the fight.

There is great sorrow among the men because of Stonewall Jackson's death five days ago. He was a brilliant leader and very conscientious in his own way about religious things. He made a valiant Old Testament warrior, but what about a soldier of Christ's Kingdom? "If my kingdom were of this world, *then* would my servants fight . . ."

I respected him, and yet in God's sight isn't the death of any private just as important?

Washing out the wool in warm sudsy water, then in cold, was a job that spread out over a number of days. When the finished bundles lay white and fluffy-soft on a pile, Rebecca covered them carefully and placed them in the barn loft.

Two weeks later the tall spires of poplar were covered with the green of unfurling leaves. Along the river, the fuzzy yellow-gray of oak and birch con-

trasted sharply with the red seedpods of maple on
the surrounding hills. The whole world was growing
soft with the gauze of spring.

I loved this time of year, dawn with the twittering
of a hundred birds, pale shoots of growing things
thrusting up their heads in straight rows across the
garden, and dew turning the soil dark and rich with
moisture.

Faint masses of creamy pink and rose told of wild
azalea and mountain laurel blooming on the western
slopes of the distant mountains. Dark spruce mixed
with lighter pine climbed the higher slopes until
every color faded into a bluish haze along the peaks.
The beauty took my breath away.

My thoughts went to David. Was he able to enjoy
the beauty as I was? What would the advancing season hold for him?

Dear family,

I am writing this, leaning against a
wagon wheel in a large field filled with
men, horses, and tents. We've stopped for
the night near Culpeper. No one knows
our destination for sure, but I, for one, feel
Lee is on the offensive, and we will cross
into Union territory before long.

For one thing, we are running out of
provisions. The horses need fresh feeding
grounds, or they will be in no shape for
action.

A train pulled out heading south about

an hour ago. I think it was the loneliest sound I've ever heard. I longed to jump a ride and let it take me where I ache to go.

I have not heard from you for so long. Does that mean all is well? I pray to God it does. I do not know where to tell you to send any mail.

Although I am watched very closely, I still help care for the horses.

My limp makes it hard for me to keep up. Usually they give me permission to ride in a wagon hauling cooking supplies.

Tell the boys I love them all. May God bless the kind people who have taken you in.

Love,
David

✺ Chapter XIV ✺

The boys were growing out of their
clothes. I had patched and repatched till
I was embarrassed. I noticed their pitiful
condition again as I gathered the dirty
garments onto a pile to carry outside where Peter
and Davie were filling the iron washpot with water. I
must figure out a way to make them last longer.

I dumped them onto the ground, then straightened up to call across the yard where Rebecca had
disappeared, "Rebecca, do you have some things to
add to my collection?"

"Perhaps a few." Her voice came faintly from
within the springhouse where she had taken the
goat's milk to cool. She stepped into the sunshine

shading her eyes against the morning brightness and walked toward me. "Are you sure you're up to this?"

"Yes, I feel . . ." I took a deep breath, letting the clean fresh air fill my lungs. My eyes drank in the life and beauty around me. "I feel at peace again. And the warm weather and spring food have made us all feel like real people once more.

"War and bloodshed seem far away . . ." I stooped quickly to add more kindling to the fire under the wash kettle. "It is true that General Lee has crossed the Potomac into Maryland?"

The gray-haired woman nodded. "We have heard so. We pray night and day for David, my daughter. But God has been good to you. Little Susan is proof of that."

"Oh, yes." I managed a smile. "God has been merciful to us . . . merciful and so good. I'm not belittling His blessings. He has kept John safe, and we all love Susan. Sometimes it almost frightens me how much I love her.

"And this . . ." I touched the white cap Rebecca had made for me a week before. "My heart is at peace about the way we have chosen."

She nodded approvingly. "It is not easy to change, I realize that. It is becoming on you, daughter, but more than that, I see the beauty of a peaceful heart. 'Tis your outward sign of submission. God will bless it.

"And it helps to keep busy, does it not?" She lifted down the battling board from the springhouse wall. Made very simply, it consisted of a large oak log split in two and held up by three legs notched at the top and pegged fast. Its top was worn smooth from much use.

I looked at it with delight. "How ingenious! But why three legs instead of four?"

Rebecca set it closer to the fire. "Wilhelm made this for me when we couldn't buy another one. Three legs won't tip, even on this slope. We'll just set it here and . . ."

"Mother, Susan is crying." Peter came up behind me with a bucket of cold water for rinsing. "Where shall I put this?"

"Here," Rebecca pushed forward a wooden tub. "Ellen, you take care of the little one. I'll start washing. Peter, could you bring me the soap bucket from the cellar?"

By the time I got to the house, Andy and Davie had already reached the cradle and lifted baby Susan out.

"Mommy, I think she wanted me." Andy frowned as I reached out to Davie for her.

"Sit down, and you can hold her a bit." I placed the squirming bundle into his eager arms and smiled as the crying intensified. One little fist closed around his finger while the other waved wildly back and forth. Her face grew red with her screaming.

Andy looked distraught. "She doesn't like me."

"Of course she does. Here, let me change and feed her, then we'll fix a little nest for her outside where you can watch her. Can I trust you to not let anything happen to her?"

"Of course! I'm gonna tell Grandma." He skipped out the door, and Davie came closer, leaning over my neck.

"I wish Papa could love her too."

I swallowed the lump in my throat. "I know, dear. We'll just keep praying that someday he can hold and love her too. But until then, we'll love her, won't we?"

"Yes, lots!" He smiled and took a deep breath. "I guess I'll go help Grandpa."

"What is he doing this morning, son?"

He rubbed his bare toes along the crack in the wooden floor. "I think he is sharpening the scythe. He said it's time to cut the first hay in the meadow. Peter and John are going to help him rake it up."

"And I'm sure he'll be glad for your help too." I smiled, fingering his sleeve gently. "You are a big help to him, Davie. He has told me so."

Davie's eyes shone.

When I got back to the wash yard, Rebecca was already dipping the first batch of clothes up and down in the boiling water. Her sleeves were rolled up and clouds of steam rose around her head. She looked up in surprise. "Back so soon?"

"She just needed feeding. Andy is going to watch her. I fixed a nest in the shade of the apple tree." I reached for the long wooden paddle. "Here, let me do that."

We worked together in silence for awhile, then Rebecca stopped to wipe her face with her apron. "How would you like to attend church services with us?"

I paused as I lifted a steaming pair of trousers onto the battling board. "When?"

"This Sunday. Wilhelm met one of the brethren, Jacob Harshberger, going by yesterday. He was riding around giving out the message." Her face lit up. "Since the war began, church services have been few and far between. And over winter we often just met in homes. What do you say?"

I let the trousers drop and wiped back wisps of hair the steam had loosened. "I . . . I don't know. Would they welcome an outsider? Maybe it would make it harder for you."

The Mennonite woman put her hands on my shoulders. "Our people will love you, Ellen."

I dropped my eyes. This kind of acceptance was still foreign to me. "I . . . I think we would like to go."

The boys came in hot and dusty for dinner. Rebecca had carefully dug under the growing potato plants and fingered out enough new potatoes to mix with spring greens for the noon meal.

"There are not many, but enough to share around. And we have plenty of biscuits and gravy from the grouse you killed yesterday." Rebecca looked at John approvingly.

"Yes, we haf plenty of food, and plenty of helpers too. John and Peter, they learn well for boys their age." Wilhelm ran a wooden comb through his white hair and dabbed his beard dry before the small looking glass in the corner. "Soon we will haf the neck uf the meadow cut already."

"Maybe it was best that soldiers took our cows last fall. We had not enough hay for them anyway. And Wilhelm trying to do the haying by himself . . ." Rebecca shook her head. "I helped rake as I could, but it's too much for two old people to do by themselves."

"You forget our horses were taken too. Now we haf a mule to feed hay to. And we can use him to pull

289

plow and wagon." Wilhelm dipped out the spicy gravy from the pot in the middle of the table. "You haf asked Ellen about Sunday?"

"What about Sunday?" Davie sat up straighter and reached across Peter for the water jug.

"Say excuse me, Davie, and don't interrupt." Peter started to say more, then stopped as he saw my eyes on him.

"Grandpas have asked us to go along to church with them." I looked around at the boys.

"Is the mule and wagon a goot enough stage coach for you, Davie?" The old man rested a friendly hand on Davie's shoulder and chuckled.

"Why, sure. Papa took us lots of places in our . . . our wagon." He faltered and looked in my direction. "Would . . . would Papa want us to go?"

"Yes, Davie. I think he would be very pleased. But what about John?" I worried. "Would it be safe to have him exposed that much? Where is the church?"

"Only a few miles south. And things are quiet enough, I feel he will be safe. If someone comes, we hand him the baby and wrap a shawl around his head. He will be *kindermädchen*, 'a nursemaid,' no?"

Bright June sunshine through the trees formed splashes of sun and shade as the wagon bounced and jostled in and out of ruts. The flickering light and shadow made me blink.

In places, pine needles carpeted the road like a copper-colored mat, muting the sound of Claybones' hooves. The trees were massive—hickories, giant oaks, and spreading chestnut and pine. Wilhelm had said some of it was virgin timber. These stately sentinels had stood guard over Shawnee, Delaware, and Cherokee Indians who had loved and hunted this valley and crouched by flickering campfires weaving legends about its beauty.

One hundred and fifty years ago, these same trees had seen the first white men trailing down from the North, looking for places to settle, their families and earthly possessions squeezed into wagons, struggling along the Indian trails or following the winding river.

The woods gave way to rolling fields and meadows sloping to the east. Less than a mile away I could see the south branch of the Shenandoah River, a silver thread shimmering in the sunshine.

Each person sat lost in thought. I stole a look at the old couple beside me on the wagon seat. Wilhelm, with freshly brushed, broad black hat and complementing suit, was holding his worn Bible in one hand and the reins in the other.

A fringed shawl hung from Rebecca's shoulders and a stiff bonnet framed her tranquil face. Holding a white lace handkerchief lightly in her lap, she looked as peaceful and calm on the jostling wagon seat as she did in her rocking chair at home. She always seemed in touch with a source of peace beyond herself.

"When you are in the presence of peace, nothing need surprise you, Ellen," she had said once. "Everything is merely unfolding as He knew it would."

I swallowed hard. How did she reach such heights?

As if feeling my eyes on her, she turned, smiling. "You have a question, daughter?"

Embarrassed, I turned to watch Claybones' head jerking up and down in time with the wagon's rhythm. "How many people do you expect today?"

"How many? Let's see, how many families, Wilhelm?"[1] Rebecca slipped her bonnet back to better see and laid a questioning hand on her husband's knee.

"Families? Ach, there iss John Swishers who lif' east of the tracks; the Koiners lif' chust beyond the church; there are the Wengers and Faubers who come from further north than we do . . ."

"Old man Balland, right on the river."

"Yah, and the widow Lydia Peters. Of course, Jacob Hildebrand, our preacher. Probably several more. But not many. Maybe eight to ten families."

"I see."

"There is a larger settlement, maybe a dozen families that live south of Waynesborough. We call it the Kendig section, after their minister, Isaac Kendig. Our people sometimes attend their services when it is not our Sunday for church."

I shifted Susan's weight in my arms. "Tell me what the people are like."

Rebecca's lips held a trace of a smile. "You are nervous, my daughter. There is no need. We be a common people. And there have been others who have become a part of us since the war began."

"Really?" My eyes widened with interest. "You had not told me."

"Yes, back in October. Three families. It was whispered that Preacher Hildebrand promised the men he would keep them out of the war if they would join. I know not if that is true."[2]

I dropped my eyes. An easy escape to avoid hardship sounded sneaky. Is that what Rebecca thought we were doing? Even if she did, she would be too kind to say so.

Wilhelm lifted the reins to turn Claybones into the grassy churchyard. A few scattered buggies and wagons were tied to trees around the small weatherboarded church building. Several staggered rows of tombstones stood behind the church against the woods. Three older men stood talking by the front entrance. They looked up curiously when the wagon drove past.

I felt a knot in the pit of my stomach. I busied myself with Susan to hide my nervousness. Wilhelm's quiet voice stopped me short.

"I haf one thing yet to say." His look was understanding. "Your David, we do not feel he tried to run away from the war. He is a brave man, your David."

Rebecca nodded. "Wilhelm met the church brother that David talked to. He spoke highly of him. David's move was not made selfishly. His faithfulness in what he's facing now is proof." She laid a reassuring hand on my knee. "You have nothing to fear."

Both outside doors of the church opened into one large room. I followed Rebecca into the women's side, holding little Susan close for reassurance. I was glad to sink into a bench toward the back wall. Here I would not feel so conspicuous, and at the same time, I would have a good view of the service.

Wilhelm and the boys found a place across the aisle and several benches forward. Everyone sat quietly. Only Andy's swinging feet betrayed his nervousness.

293

The men's side was noticeably emptier than ours. Gray-haired men and young boys made up the bulk of the sparse male population.

My eyes ran slowly over the white-capped heads in front of me. Some were young, bordered on both sides with children of assorted sizes; some sat alone, as old as Rebecca. Were their husbands in hiding? Had they been captured as David was and forced into the army? There was no way of telling. The faces, with lowered eyes, betrayed no emotion.

When the service began, I forgot my shyness as everyone joined in singing the familiar hymns. I felt my shoulders relax, and my mind grow calm as I listened to the rich words from Scripture. Here was something to feed the soul.

And when the thin-haired minister stood up to preach, I drank in his mellow words. His grave eyes ran carefully up and down the benches, pausing a moment on each person as if placing a blessing upon them.

". . . a number of our people cannot be here. We miss them. Their empty places in our families leave a ragged gap we cannot escape.

"We are not alone in this. Everywhere I go across the country, I meet people struggling with bitterness, hatred, fear, revenge, with pride in victory, or despair in defeat.

"Everywhere, people are in emotional bondage. Are we also? Is there hope for those that love the Lord? Are we alone in the storm to wash with the tide, as helpless as driftwood?"

He leaned forward earnestly, and his voice intensified. "No, a thousand times, no. We are misunderstood, shunned and despised by those around us. We are persecuted, but not forsaken, cast down but not destroyed."

He straightened and his eyes turned toward the window. I held my breath to catch the quiet words that followed.

"While I was in Staunton yesterday, a minister from a local congregation stepped out of Armistead Mosby's Saddlery Shop and came my way. We have met before and had friendly discussions about different things. Seeing me, he raised his hand in greeting and crossed the street to lean against the wagon beside me.

" 'Why, Mr. Hildebrand,' he said. 'I haven't seen you in almost a year. How's your family?'

" 'We are well,' I answered. 'And trusting in the Lord to care for us.' " The minister's eyes grew sad. "Things were friendly till he began questioning me about our stand on war.

" 'Is it true, that your people are allowed off scot-free while my parishioners are giving sons, fathers, and husbands for the Southern cause? How can you face your congregation and not feel guilty?'

" 'We have not escaped scot-free, my friend,' I told him. 'Our men have paid the exemption fine as required by the state.'

" 'Ah, yes,' he answered, 'but I've heard you let others into your church that wish to escape the call to arms. Is that so?' "

I bowed my head. My hands felt clammy. It seemed I could feel the preacher's eyes on my face.

"I answered this way, 'Our church has always been open to those who wish to live their lives entirely according to the Scriptures. We close the door of the Gospel to no man.'

"And even though I said it as humbly as I knew how, it angered him. He took a step toward me and his shoulders stiffened.

" 'Do you mean to imply we do not live by the Scriptures? Mr. Hildebrand, I'm afraid you are blinded to your own error. My Bible tells me to honor and obey those in authority. I have heard from reliable sources that there are those of your . . . your group that have eluded their duty by hiding or escaping to the North. And you claim to be a law-abiding citizen, a minister of the Word, and sit back and let the rest of us fight for the blessings you enjoy?' "

I was caught up with what the minister was saying. Hadn't I experienced the same kind of ridicule and scorn?

"I did not have a ready answer, and he thought . . . ," a smile flickered over his face, ". . . he thought he had proven his point and turned to go. But I reached out a hand and laid it on his shoulder. 'My son,' I said, for he was young enough to be a son, 'don't let yourself be blinded by temporal issues and factions and things that will pass away. We are all— North and South—children created by God. His message for men is as fresh and real today as the day the Lord said, "Love thy neighbor as thyself; bless them that curse you, pray for them that despitefully use you."

" 'Our Lord loved those that hated him. He walked among them without a trace of bitterness in his heart. Do you? Do I? He lifted no hand in self defense. Have you? His whole life was lived to help men find inner peace. Can I do the same if I seek to kill and destroy?

296

" 'My Bible reads those are marks of a hireling—not a true Shepherd.'

"He stood with bowed head, and so I asked him, 'Would you say God's people are all in the Confederacy? Would you say no one in the Union calls upon God for mercy and guidance and blessing?'

"He agreed that wouldn't be true.

" 'Well then,' I said, 'How is it that those on opposite sides can kneel and ask the same God for victory for their army and expect Him to hear and answer their prayers? It cannot be. For anything to be truly His will, it must be possible for all men to kneel and pray together and all say "Amen" to what is asked. If not, there is something wrong with our prayer.'[3]

" 'You remember when the men came to Jesus and asked Him, "Is it lawful to pay tribute to Caesar or not?" '

"He said he did.

" 'Well, the answer He gave would be the same I must give. You, in essence are asking, "Is it lawful to fight for President Davis or not?" My answer would have to be, "Give unto President Davis the things that belong to him, and give unto God the things that belong to Him."

" 'We pay our dues; we suffer the consequences of our stand, through arrest or compulsion into the army, or if need be, flee to a place where we can conscientiously live out the principles we see in Scripture.

" 'We owe President Davis our honor and respect. But our hearts and lives belong to God. We have given these to Him and Him alone. When He says "love," then we take it for all men at all times. We

297

must be faithful in all situations.' "

I sat back against the hard bench. A shiver ran down my spine. This was right, this was the way of truth! There was no pride, no defiant shaking of the fist, but a humility and respect for all men.

Little Susan squirmed in my lap and began whimpering restlessly. I lifted her against my shoulder, patting her absentmindedly as I listened.

"And so, my friends, we must not give up; we must keep our courage. These sufferings cannot last, for war and men's devices are always doomed to failure. Those around us need now, more than ever before, to see Christian love displayed by our lives. May God help us is my prayer."

He turned to sit down. As the strains of a hymn rose and filled the small room, I could see I wasn't the only one deeply touched by the message. It was good to have been here today! I had found where I belonged.

DIARY—6/25/63

Greenwood, Pa. Am exhausted. Have covered several hundred miles since we left winter camp three weeks ago. A battle at Winchester, marching through Maryland and now into Pa. The tramping at night is spiced up at times by putting candles into musket barrels.

We passed the battlegrounds of Antietam where shallow graves have heaved up bleached ribcages and rotting cloth for all to see.

The call comes suddenly for all except ammunition wagons to be sent to the rear. We're also ordered to cook ahead three days' rations. Such a scramble.

Evening

I missed my baggage wagon. I was hitched up and in line when I was called off, because a lieutenant's prize mare had stepped into a stump hole and broken its leg. He wanted it saved if possible. While I was gone, the wagons pulled out. The mare was beyond help and had to be shot anyway. I know battle lies only days, maybe hours, away.

The hectic schedule is irritating my old leg injury. I don't know how much longer I can keep on.

Ellen's sweet face looms in front of me whenever I close my eyes. For her sake, may God help me stay true no matter what happens!

DIARY—6/26/63

Left our camp in a pouring rain. My oil-cloth is being used to keep ammunition dry, so I just had to hunker down on the wagon seat and let the rain run down my neck. Muddy roads make hard pulling for the horses.

Crossed the Blue Ridge mountains. Camping tonight at Mummasburg. Because of the rain, the men are allowed to burn fence rails for the first time since crossing the Potomac. It feels good. I'm trying to dry my clothes.

If only there were a way to send word to the family. I feel a heaviness that won't leave.

The long hours of carding and spinning the sheep wool ended at last. On the first Saturday in July, Wilhelm hitched up the mule and gathered up the skeins of carefully dyed yarn tied into a sheet. Several bags of corn leaned against the wheel.

We all came to the door as the wagon stopped in front of the house.

"Anyone wish to come along?" He stood holding the reins, hat in hand, eyes twinkling. "Before dinner I return."

I shifted the bucket of freshly picked beans to the other hand, watching the youngest boys press forward.

Rebecca smiled. "You may as well go too, Ellen. Tell Wilhelm to let you carry the pattern. We went over it together and you should be able to answer any questions Granny Bristlow has. Men do not always understand such things." She laughed under her breath. "Susan will probably sleep until you return. Go, my daughter. The beans can wait till this afternoon."

I hesitated, then almost against my better judgment, gathered my skirts and gave Wilhelm my hand for a boost onto the wagon seat. Was I being silly?

Irresponsible? Whatever it was, it made me feel like a young girl again.

Rebecca came closer, holding the sleeping Susan in her arms. "An old widow lady, Granny Bristlow is, Ellen. She has been weaving for many years. Beautiful patterns she has, cup and saucer, dogwood petal, and goose-eye. Ask to see the blue and white whig rose bedspread she made, and she'll show you all her treasures."

"Thank you, Rebecca. I will. You are so kind." I leaned over impulsively and touched the older woman's cheek. "But give me my baby. I can't go without her. I don't think Granny Bristlow would be offended if I brought her too."

Rebecca gave her up reluctantly. "You are right. She will love her. She used to be a midwife in her day. Now go and enjoy yourself. You don't get an outing like this very often." She waved us off with a smile.

I settled back onto the seat, hugging the sleeping bundle. I let my bonnet slide back against my neck. The slight breeze felt good across my face. Working in the bean patch in the warm sun had made my coarse cotton dress stick to my damp body.

I tucked back strands of loose hair on my forehead and turned toward the mountains lying massive and green to the east. The mountain laurel and azalea blossoms had faded by now. Bright poppies nodded among tall weeds and grasses in the meadows. Along the roadside delicate spring flowers had shriveled, giving way to wild daisy, fever few, orange clusters of butterfly weed, and an occasional red spire of Indian paintbrush.

Wilhelm was humming under his breath, his eyes

watching the road before us. He looked up with a smile as I shifted Susan's weight in my lap. "It iss fine if I drop you off while the boys and I go on to the mill?"

"Oh, yes. They will enjoy the experience." I felt a strange wistfulness. "I've been there before. Old Silas would take me along sometimes with the winter's load of corn and wheat to be ground. I was only five or six. We would have come from Bridgewater, following Dry River south to the mill. We had wonderful times together, Silas and I." I managed a lopsided grin.

Burkes Mill, just the name brought back a flood of memories.

"So you haf been there before. It must haf been new in those days."

"Yes, quite new. I can still remember that fresh smell of wood shavings and lumber."

It was a two-story mill, built tall on Naked Creek, surrounded by alder bushes and willows within sight of the Valley Railroad. I had loved to watch the massive waterwheel turning and the water gushing through the flume, coursing over the shining paddles, and frothing into the millpond.

My favorite spot had been under a willow next to the dam where I could watch the tons of water thundering over the dam, water so clear that if I crouched at just the right distance, the sun made a myriad of sparkling colors on the bubbling foam.

Once I had sat there, oblivious of time, not able to hear Silas calling until I was jerked out of my dreaming by his work-worn hands.

"Land sakes, chile. What you do'en heah?"

"Oh, Silas! It's so loud, and the dancing rainbows ... !" I groped for words to describe it. "The willow branches make a tiny room, and there are violets in the pockets."

But he had not understood. "Mercy, chile. We got to go. Don' you go down heah no mo.' You jus' as might fall in and dat would be de en' ob me."

Somehow, I had never gotten to go along after that, and so the memory of that spot's charm had never changed in my mind. Strange. I had not thought of it for twenty years.

Granny Bristlow's tiny house sat back from the road in a grove of locusts on a sloping draw. My knock was rewarded by a shrill, "Come on in, who-ever ye be!" I found myself drawn into a front room, one side almost filled with a large wooden loom, its pieces smooth from years of use. Two chairs and a small table completed the furnishings.

The humpbacked woman clasped my hand in both of her own. "A visitor, with a least one!" The bright brown eyes and wrinkled face lighted with pleasure. "Who be ye, chile?"

"I'm Ellen Shull . . . from Staunton. My family is staying with Wilhelm Gochenours for a time. Rebecca sent me with some wool for you to put into the loom. She said she had spoken with you last winter."

"Maybe she did, maybe she did. Can't recollect one way or the other. But I'm glad to do it. Jest fin-ished up my last piece yes-ti-day, worked late to get it out 'cause I said to myself, 'The only reason you getting done with one is 'cause the Lord is sending you another. Best you be gett'en it all the way out before tomorrow.' Now look what's come!"

She chuckled, still holding onto my arm. "But let's not stand here dilly-dallying. Come awhile and sit." She pushed a chair in my direction.

"I have only an hour or so until Mr. Gochenour comes back through, Mrs. Bristlow."

"Jest call me Granny. Everyone 'round here does it an' I'm not offended. Been a granny since back in the forties, I reckon. Be one as long as the Lord lends me a bit of breath."

I smiled. This frail-appearing little lady still had lots of pep. "Rebecca told me you were midwife to many of the women around here."

"Aye, 'tis so. Helped with over a hundred, I reckon." She reached out a blue-veined, callused hand with swollen knuckles. "Let me hold the least one." She cuddled Susan close. "Ain't it a wonder now, how the little ones are? I never knew when the call might come to go out, midnight, or any hour of the day. But I finally couldn't go anymore. My legs got too stiff and lame. Now I jest do my weaving and leave the birth'en to the young ones."

"Why, you would have been old when I was yet a girl!"

The brown eyes snapped. "I be eighty-six come autumn, near as I can tell."

"Eighty-six! And you live here by yourself?"

"No, lassie. The Lord's been with me for fifty years. The go'ens been rough, but He has been faithful. I'd a never made it without Him."

"You have family?"

Susan began to cry, and the old lady handed her back.

304

"That's a hunger cry, I reckon." She patted the blanket with a wistful hand. "Yes, I have family, six girls and five boys. All growed and gone now 'cept the two that died as babes.

" 'Twas a time when the sickness was heavy in the Valley. Didn't have no railroad in those days, no big towns, no doctor to run to.

"All but the oldest was down with it, and I was run nearly ragged docter'en on them. My man, he had to do all the chores and most of the housework till he was nigh gett'en sick hisself. Then the call came that a young girl needed birth'en on the other side the river. Her husband was scared to death, it being their first one and all."

She ran an unsteady hand over her thin hair. "There was no one else to go, so I saddled up. It was night and the river was high from the spring rains. Nearly got washed away, but we made it through, and got there in time to save the girl. She had a fine boy, as fine as you could see." Her voice was matter-of-fact.

" 'Twas morn'en by then. The young man followed me back to the river, made sure I made it 'crost, then turned back. We was both in a hurry, I guess. Me for my family, he for his.

"My man was pretty distressed when I got back. The two littlest were very low. In spite of all my efforts, they slipped away the next night."

I looked at the rumpled figure before me in amazement. "You . . . How could you bear it?"

"Oh, it was hard at first. I'd go to bed and toss and turn, an' when I'd finally drop off, I'd hear them calling me. I'd be riden' my horse, trying to get there in time. Then 'fore I'd remember, I'd get up and find their bed empty and cold.

"Some folks said with the size family I had, I shouldn't miss if two of them were gone, but I did, I did. Pined for them till I thought I was losing my mind.

"My man tried to comfort me, but by then he was down with it, and I 'bout lost him.

"One night he was so low, an' I was so hurten' like inside, I went out and jest walked up and down the dooryard. The moon was shin'en, and I jest cried till I couldn't cry no more. I went to the drop-off 'mongst the trees behind our house an' stood a long time looking down. I told the Lord I was so tired and sad, I felt a hankeren' to end it all unless He give me some hope.

"An' He did. It came to me from the Bible, and I felt the hurt jest melt away. I never been the same ever since."

I drew my breath sharply. "Tell me about it."

The old woman leaned back, closed her eyes, and smiled. Her voice was soft, almost caressing. "I was sittin' early the next morn'en readin' my Bible, desperately looking for something to lift my spirits. I came 'crost the story about King David's baby dyin'. How he loved that baby. But it died. Afterwards, King David said though the baby would never come back to him, he knew sometime he'd go to where his baby was. An' that," she said simply, "was God's comfort to me. And mighty comfortin' it's been recollecting it.

"The Lord's been mighty good to me." She pushed herself out of the chair. "But this doesn't get that yarn looked at. My sakes, chile, you should have stopped me when I got started like that. I forgot what

306

I was a'doing!"

"Oh, but I needed to hear this, Granny. My husband was taken with Lee's army last fall, and I don't know whether I'll ever see him again. Sometimes it hurts so deeply . . ." I cleared my throat, swallowing hard. "I feel I can't keep on."

"Aye, you will, chile." Granny nodded soberly. "Life is a meanness sometimes, and men can get downright cruel to each other. This war is a blight on the name of mankind. Should never have been. But it don't change the fact of His faithfulness. I've found that out."

The words were like a cool balm filling the room. I jiggled Susan's whimperings into silence again and stood up to follow the bent woman to the door.

"Ah, this be a beautiful color to weave together. A prettier brown I never saw. Into trousers you wish to make it?"

"Yes, Rebecca hopes to get enough to make a couple pair. And the other is for a new shawl. She used her old one for a blanket for the baby."

Granny fingered the dark skeins. " 'Tis soft as a raven's wing. That brings something to mind." She hobbled over to a sagging bedroom door. "Let me show you some things."

My smile widened. "I was to ask to see your bedspread, a blue and white one, and some other work you've done. They had such pretty names."

"Aye, chile. I've done all kinds, and some I've made up myself." She let the door swing on its hinges and opened the lid of a dusty trunk, darkened with age.

She lifted out a pure white tablecloth. "Dogwood petal, this one is. See the petals running this an' that

307

a way? An' this one . . ." She spread a small piece of creamy yellow across the bed. "This one I colored from broomsage and yellowroot."

"It's lovely!"

"An' *this* one I fashioned into a blanket. Looks mighty gay-like when it's cold and blowing outside." Her gnarled hands opened up a soft piece, woven into contrasting shades of burgundy and mauve and rose. "Too pretty to use though. I only get it out once in awhile." She chuckled.

I shook my head in wonder. "How do you get the colors? Why, it's beautiful!"

"Madder root. I dig a lot of them and pokeberry, most any kind of berry. Grapes work too. I like to mix and dye till I's satisfied. That's the pleasure in it."

"What is this pattern called?"

" 'Tis one I made up myself. I just call it my sunset pattern." She reached down to the bottom of the chest. "But this is my pride and joy. Spent nigh to eight months on this one. This is my moonrise coverlet. Made it ten, fifteen years ago. Was my last piece before my man died. He picked up my indigo dye special, as a surprise from town, and I kept dying and hanging out to dry till I had skeins of all colors of blue." She handed me a corner, and together we spread it out across the bed.

The beauty of it took my breath away. The whole cover was a symmetry of varied shades of blue, from the palest cornflower at the tips, to azure and beryl, growing deeper into turquoise and navy at the middle, before fading back to repeat itself again.

"I have never seen anything like it! Why, you could sell this for a large price."

"Don't want to sell. I reckon to keep it till I die.

308

'Tis my strengthening coverlet. Whenever I got so lonely I'd think I couldn't stand it anymore, I got up, night or day, and set to my loom there, and worked away. Oft as not, the moon be shin'en right in that winder, and I'd jest be copying the pattern it was making in the sky. Ain't never been no time that God is as near, as when ye be all by yourself, jest you and Him."

I could hear hoofs coming closer. I folded the blanket up over Susan's face and stepped toward the door. Suddenly I turned and put a hand on Granny's shoulder. "What you've said is true. I have found it so." I looked deep into her brown eyes. "You have been a blessing to me, Granny Bristlow. Perhaps we can meet again soon."

"Yes, yes, chile. A look at your young face has brought me sunshine. Don't wait so long to come. And bring the little lassie." She reached out for me, and I could feel the wrinkled cheek moist with tears.

The ride home seemed short. The boys were full of things to tell about the mill, old Mr. Ferguson the miller, and men who had come. I listened absent-mindedly, my mind on Granny's remarkable faith. She had trusted God and allowed Him to nurture and strengthen her faith till now, in her old age, she could live alone and find God was all she needed.

I didn't think about Wilhelm's silence as being significant until later that evening. When I stepped inside with the pail of the evening's milking, Wilhelm and Rebecca were standing together by the kitchen window. Wilhelm turned, and the look on his face frightened me. I set the tin bucket onto the table. My mouth opened but no sound came out.

Rebecca came and put a hand on my shoulder.

"Wilhelm heard news today."

"News of David?"

She shook her head, looking at her husband. His head dropped, his brow furrowed as if in pain. "At the mill . . . the men tell of a great battle two days ago, across the Potomac at Gettysburg, just inside Pennsylvania."

I felt myself freeze inside. David had been there; I was sure of it. I had to concentrate to hear what Whilhelm was saying.

"Thousands of men were killed and many taken prisoner."

Rebecca's voice came as through a fog. "Wilhelm will go after a paper tomorrow for the list of missing men. We must hope that David is okay. Ellen . . . Ellen?"

A sound of moaning mingled crazily with Susan's insistent crying. Only later did I recognize it as my own.

❧ Chapter XV ❧

There was a whimper in the darkness and a fretful sniffling that grew quickly to a wail. I awoke with a start. A heavy weariness pressed in around me, making it hard to breathe. I reached out and pulled Susan closer, feeling her sobs lessen. Her tiny fingers grasped hold of mine.

I held her tightly. It was hot tonight, and the air coming through the open window was muggy. In the distance a muffled growl of thunder echoed between the mountain peaks, then all was silent again.

I felt dreadfully alone. I hadn't shared Wilhelm's news with the boys. It would be unfair to place the burden of the unknown upon their already burdened shoulders.

In many ways the summer had been easier, certainly easier than being at home with my parents' disapproval hanging over us. And food was more plentiful. The garden was producing a good crop of vegetables. Wilhelm and the boys had been working long hours to gather the early field harvest. But there was still the ever-present fear of the future, and the continuous threat of armies again pressing their way through the Valley.

Amid my turbulent thoughts came a soft bird song from the holly tree brushing the corner of the house. A mockingbird. It had to be. No other bird cared to sing his song of love and trust in the dark hours before a storm.

I lay awake listening, scarcely breathing. The gentle chirring and trilling were continual and ever changing in intensity, as if he were coaxing his audience to ever greater depths of emotion.

I soaked it in, marveling at his endurance. I must have dozed off, for I found myself sitting under the trees beside the end of the lane with Susan in my arms and the boys crowded around me. Far down the dirt road, I saw someone coming toward us, following the outside edge of the wagon tracks. An officer? Was it an army officer? Without even turning I knew that John and Peter had seen him too and had vanished toward the barn.

My heart skipped a beat. The limping figure was now parallel with the gate. Suddenly a band of galloping cavalry appeared, bearing down upon him. I leaped up. In my dream the man looked so familiar; it was . . . it had to be . . . !

A cry of joy mingled with horror and alarm on my lips. "David!" His head lifted as if listening, his eyes remaining blank. Then all vanished, and I was awake again, heart pounding.

He had been almost within my grasp. Was God showing me David was in danger? Were dreadful forces out to destroy him? I began praying desperately. I didn't know for how long, one hour . . . two, I could not tell.

The first drops of rain smacked against the cabin with driving force as the storm moved in. Fiery, convulsing fingers of lightning curled and spit across the black sky, casting eerie shadows on the walls. Then the rain poured down in torrents.

A draft of air pushing through cracks in the rough log walls brought a refreshing coolness into the room that felt good to my hot cheeks. When the storm had run its course, the mockingbird began singing again, none the worse for its beating. For me, it had special meaning.

Two days later Wilhelm brought home a newspaper reporting on the battle. I waited as his workworns finger ran down the list of men's names. In spite of my apprehensions, I felt surprisingly calm. Wilehelm's hand stopped, and he straightened slowly as if suddenly old and tired. He turned toward me, groping for words.

I laid a trembling hand on his arm. "I know, Wilhelm. He is missing, but I . . . I know God is with him. I have a peace. The Lord encouraged me through a storm and a song. I can't explain it."

Wihelm looked at me for a long moment. I

couldn't tell what he was thinking. At last he said, "If it be so, Gott has been gracious to you, my daughter. And we know . . . we know for *sure* he iss in Gott's presence. Whether alive or no, he iss in the presence of the Lord."

My eyes fastened on him as I drank in his words. Yes, that much we knew beyond a shadow of a doubt. I took a deep breath.

"If you'll excuse me, I must find the boys. I'd . . . I'd like to be alone with them when I break the news."

I found them in the barn. As I opened the creaking door and stepped inside, slanting rays of sunshine filtered through the dusty windowpanes. The smell of hay and drying onions came from the loft overhead.

The boys were all bent over John, watching intently as he did something on the dirt-packed floor. "Boys . . ."

They all turned as one, Andy jumping in excitement. The delight in his eyes died away as he caught the seriousness on my face. John stepped protectively to my side. Peter and Davie stood motionless, heads bent.

"Boys, we have news, some good and some bad." I stopped, impulsively reaching out my arms toward them. "Here, let's sit down."

John led the way to the grain sacks piled against the back wall, shifting one so I would have a post to lean against.

"Remember Papa's last letter said his regiment was joining up with General Lee's army heading north?" I glanced at Andy crouched at my feet, wanting to make sure he understood. He nodded.

314

"And do you remember *why* Papa thought they were headed that way?"

Peter gave a quick nod. "They needed food and fresh horses."

"Yes, it's hard enough to support an army's vast needs in peacetime. It's nearly impossible during the destruction of war. Of course the soldiers from the north would not allow an army to enter unchallenged. Last week there was a terrible battle lasting several days. Thousands of men were killed. And boys . . . Papa is among those listed as missing."

The boys were shocked into silence. I took a deep breath and plunged on. "Several nights ago, I somehow felt Papa was in great danger. More than that I do not know. But I *do* know that no matter what happens, God is with him, watching over him, caring for him. It makes our lives seem terribly dark and uncertain, but God sees through the blackest darkness. And right now His hand is around us, even now!"

Twilight was falling as we gathered on the porch for the evening Scripture reading. Susan fell asleep halfway through, and after I laid her down and helped the boys to bed, I rejoined the old couple on the steps.

Rebecca's fingers were busy stringing leather britches beans, and I picked up my bucket again to help.

"I think I will hang them in the attic this year." The gray-haired woman draped another completed strand over the porch railing. "Last year I left them in the open air too long and some of them started to mold."

We worked in silence for the next half hour. At last Wilhelm stood up and pushed the remaining bucketful under the chair. "It gets late. We will finish another time. Come."

"If . . . if it's okay, I'd like to stay out a bit longer." I plucked at the ball of string in my lap.

"Why, of course." Rebecca's hand was warm against my shoulder. "Stay as long as you like."

A half moon hung suspended just above the tree line. A whippoorwill began his ritual song from behind the barn. The door opened, and John slipped out and sat on the steps beside me. "I . . . I couldn't sleep," he said lamely.

I squeezed his knee.

"When do you suppose we will find out more?"

I took a deep breath. "There's no way of knowing, son. The neighbor who talked to Wilhelm at the fence this afternoon came from near the Pike. He said wounded men are constantly coming past. There is always a possibility Papa could be among them. But he would surely come looking for us. I wrote him where we are. There is nothing else we can do but wait and trust God."

From along the creek, another whippoorwill began echoing the call of the one near the barn. I tilted my head listening. "Of course it may well be that he was captured and held prisoner."

"What if he's wounded and can't make it this far?" John asked soberly.

I smiled sadly. "There are hundreds of 'what if's' to torment us, John. I've struggled with them and panicked over them and exhausted myself in the process. I'm always brought right back to where I started." The shrill yapping of a fox came from across the field. I shivered. "I have nothing except the assurance God is watching over us. Can you trust God?"

He swallowed hard. "I want to."

I stared unseeing into the darkness. "We have something more stable than our feelings. Even when we are past feeling, we have His promises to hold to. Even through death He has vowed to never leave us. Never! And death is a real possibility, not only for Papa, but for all of us." I touched his arm. "Do you think we did right to commit ourselves to stand for peace?"

He leaned against the porch post. "People say we are radicals."

"I know. It is not easy to stand against such pressure."

I couldn't see his face in the moonlight. He kicked against the post several times, then sat down heavily. "When we were at Uncle Fred's, I wasn't sure you made the right choice. But when I compare the difference it makes in a person's life; in Grandfather's, or Uncle Fred's, or Grandpa Gochenour's; no one can deny who has found the greatest strength for living, or the greatest joy in hard times. And so," he paused, "I choose to stand with you."

In the days and weeks that followed, we watched the newspapers closely. There was no further word of David.

Even though my emotions often threatened to drown it, a touch of the assurance of God's goodness did not leave me. I clung to it, fearful even to talk about it lest my fragile faith would crumble. With multitudes of families mourning losses of husbands or sons, who was I to deserve more than they?

One afternoon I picked my way to the far end of the field where Wilhelm was bent over a wheat bundle. The late sun beat down against my sunbonnet. Grasshoppers sprang away in confusion as my skirts brushed the stubble.

John and Peter were gathering bundles into piles of three, and standing them upright. Sheaves dotted one corner of the field like golden sentries.

At my lifted bucket, they waved, grinning, and started out to meet me, cutting diagonally across the field.

"Chust what I've been wishing for." Wilhelm straightened slowly and pulled a cloth from his pocket, mopping his face.

My eyes ran the length of the field. "You're almost finished."

"Yah, hopefully we can finish tonight if we work late. The boys, they be goot helpers."

His voice sounded scratchy from the dirt and heat. His face was thin, and his eyes were hollow and tired. Last year army scouts passing through had taken a large part for themselves just as he was finishing the harvest.

He drank gratefully, then handed back the cup for more. I reached in my pocket for a piece of cold cornbread. "Here, eat this for strength. Do you think you can save the crop this year?"

"I know not. I will be glat when it iss put away. So

grateful I am for the goot stand. Every kernel is precious."

I waited until he finished eating. "Rebecca said you plan to take some wheat to be ground soon?"

"Perhaps in the morning. You wish to stop by the old mother's house?"

"I think maybe I should."

"When I picked up the woven wool she asked about you."

"I know. You told me." I reached for the bucket handle once more. "Yes, I think I may go along if that's okay."

The voice that welcomed me the next morning was not the one I remembered. I was alarmed to find the old woman in bed. In spite of the warm room, the covers were piled high and a shawl was tucked awkwardly around her shoulders. I bent over her, caressing the bony, clutching fingers. "Why, Granny, you're ill!"

"No, chile. Jest tired, tiredness jest all the way through. Seems I be too tired to even feed myself." Her brown eyes brightened as they ran eagerly over my face. "But you came again! I be praying that ye would. I have something for yer baby chile. Ye had a baby chile, didn't ye, Suella?"

Was the old lady rational? I wasn't sure. I patted her cheek. "You're a dear, Granny. Of course I'd like to see what you have." I held up the basket for her inspection. "Look what I brought along from Rebecca."

"Aye, chile, it be tea. I can smell it from here."

"I'm going to make you a cup right now. And there's some honey to sweeten it with. There's nothing you like better than Rebecca's sourwood honey."

"Mebbe so, mebbe so. But I'm not a hanker'in fer it right now." Her head sank back onto the pillow.

I grabbed the water bucket by the door and moved quickly out into the sunshine. How long had the poor woman been laid up like this? The bucket came up brimming full, and in my hurry I slopped water onto my skirts. I didn't hear footsteps until someone spoke behind me.

"Good morning, ma'am."

"Oh!" I let the bucket drop to the ground.

"I didn't mean to frighten you." He removed his hat, nervously tapping it against his leg. A week's growth of stubble covered his face, and one sleeve swung empty. "Would you be so kind as to let me have a drink? I've walked a long way this morning."

He was painfully thin, and his face held the unnatural whiteness that accompanies fever. His trousers hung loosely on his lanky frame, and his shoes were worn down at the heel.

"Certainly." I lifted out a dipper of cold water. He drank thirstily, the water trickling out the corners of his mouth and down his dusty chin. I watched him. Something about him reminded me painfully of James. At length I asked, "Where are you from?"

He did not meet my gaze, and his answer was guarded. "I'm on leave."

His accent sounded neither local nor from the deep south. Could he be from the north? In any case, he was some mother's son.

"Won't you come in? You should have a bite to eat

before going on."

The hunger in his eyes dispelled any fear on my part. I turned toward the house.

Granny Bristlow seemed asleep when I checked on her. I motioned the young man to a chair and filled the only pot I could find with water, swinging its hook over the fireplace. The fire was almost out, with only a few coals hidden under the mound of ashes.

I arranged the last pieces of kindling stacked against the hearth. What did I dare feed him? Granny's stores were pitifully low. I carefully ladled out some ground wheat to cook into a thin gruel, and mixed up a small batch of biscuits. Granny needed to eat too.

All the while, I could feel those wary, dark eyes upon me, the body rigid and ill at ease as if ready to leap at any moment.

When the food was prepared, I fixed a plate for the stranger, and carried a dipperful on a saucer to the bed. "Granny, I have a bite for you. Won't you let me fluff up your pillows so you can eat?" Not wanting to frighten her, I continued, "You have a visitor. A young man traveling through stopped by for lunch."

The brown eyes fluttered open, and the wrinkled face turned in his direction. "Aye, so I see. Well, 'tis okay. Feed the poor boy, lassie. I'm not so hungry, and he be a starv'en. Young boys always be." She leaned back against the cushions. "You say this be one of your boys?"

"No, Granny, just a friend." Although I dared not stare, I couldn't help noticing the pathetic eagerness with which our visitor mopped up the last bit of gruel on his plate. I held out a steaming cup of tea to

Granny. "Here, let me help you sit up. Have a sip of something good and hot." I lifted the drooping head from the pillow.

There was a sudden movement behind me, and before I could turn, the stranger's hand was grabbing my shoulder hard.

My eyes widened, the hot tea slopping onto the sheets. Then I heard it too. Hoofbeats!

"You've got to hide me, please!" His eyes were desperate.

Without waiting to think, I jerked up the bedspread and stepped aside. He scrambled underneath the bed, pulling his legs out of sight. I let the spread drop. My heart was pounding wildly. Horses were coming to a stop beside the door. It couldn't be Wilhelm. There had been no rattle of wagon wheels.

I bent over Granny once more, my hands trembling. What had prompted me to do such a thing? Was I crazy? How much had the old lady caught of what had happened? What would I say?

There was no time to think. Footsteps were striding across the porch and a tall uniformed figure filled the open doorway. The yard was full of milling horses and men.

The man's voice was crisp. "We are searching for an escaped prisoner-of-war, a valuable one. Have you seen a young man with a missing arm?"

My breath felt painful in my throat. I stared at him for a moment. What could I say? I ran my tongue over my dry lips. "Sir, I . . . I don't live here. I'm just visiting."

A second man's face appeared around the doorway. There was a sarcastic laugh. "She's doctoring the poor granny. Looks like the old crone needs it.

'Pears 'bout dead already. Come on, Lieutenant. We're wasting our time."

The officer's eyes narrowed angrily. "You stay out of this, Williams." He took a step toward me. "Have you had any visitors today?"

By now the porch was filled with men, overflowing into the yard and out onto the road.

Granny stirred and her eyes jerked open, her eyes widening at the heads crowding into the room. "Land sakes, lad. Have I had visitors? This is enough visitors to last me a month of Sundays. How many of you boys is it anyway? Don't know if I can feed all of ye. I'm not too pert today..." Her words trailed away and she sighed. "Mebbe..."

The second man turned away with a guffaw. "Come on, Evans."

The officer hesitated, opened his mouth to say more, then turned and joined the others. There was the clumping of boots, the squeaking of saddles, and hooves raising the dust.

I couldn't move until the last horse was out of sight, and the last hoofbeats faded into silence. Then my shoulders slumped, and I found myself trembling uncontrollably. I sank into a chair.

"Didn't any of them stay, lassie?" Granny Bristlow's creased face pulled into a frown. "Not even for a cup of tea?" She shook her head bewildered. "Folks jest ain't mannerly these days like they used to be. Give me a cup. I be aim'in fer a taste after all."

I pressed my fingers to my lips to steady them. "Of course. But let me dip you a fresh cup. This one is getting cold."

While I was helping her drink, the clatter of wagon wheels turned onto the grass. Not a sound

323

had come from under the bed since those long legs had disappeared from sight thirty minutes before. I sat the cup down and hurried outside. I must confess to Wilhelm what I had done.

He listened gravely, thoughtfully stroking his beard. "We know not whether this man iss guilty of a crime or not. But I hurt to gif a person up without a chance of a fair hearing." He climbed down over the side. "Right now our first worry iss the grandmother. We make a bed in the wagon to carry her along home. Then I talk to the man."

It took some maneuvering to get Granny situated. "You're coming to visit me, Granny." I carefully tucked the sheet up closer around the thin shoulders, and shoved more loose wheat straw underneath her head. "Does the sun bother you?"

"Hits ah shin'en awful bright." The old lady squinted her eyes more tightly closed. Her hands moved restlessly under the cover. "Where is it ye be taking me?"

I leaned closer. "You're coming home with me for a visit. Won't we surprise Rebecca?" I held up her shawl as a shield against the sun's rays.

Her mouth twisted in a frown. "Can't understand it. Not nary a' thing. But I reckon . . ." She coughed feebly. ". . . if you have something to do with it, 'tis alright." She turned her face aside with a sigh, eyes still closed.

I glanced impatiently toward the house, wishing to see and hear what was taking place inside, yet anxious to get Granny Bristlow settled into better quarters.

324

We kept the man three days, hiding him in the attic and allowing no one to take him food, or even see him, except John. Rebecca sent up her food concoctions to build up his strength and ease the fever.

I lived in fear the whole time someone would come along and ask us outright about him. And if they did, what would I say?

The young man had said little about himself, only that he was from Ohio and since joining the war, had fought in a number of major battles. He had been taken in a skirmish earlier in the summer. He hoped to make it west to the relatively safe Alleghenies, and from there find his way back to his own territory.

One night during new moon, Wilhelm took him, hidden under a load of straw, twelve miles northwest to a friend who knew secret and seldom traveled routes through the mountains.

Wilhelm was back at dawn, his eyes bloodshot and his shoulders slumped with fatigue. Dragging one foot after the other, he sat down with the rest of us to breakfast. His head sagged after only a dozen bites, and Rebecca and I helped him into their bedroom, sitting him down and taking off his shoes.

"Did you have any trouble?"

He shook his head. "Had to leef my straw there so no one be suspicious. If I would have been stopped, I be accused of keeping my harvest from army hands. But I saw no gray coats.

"He was not a mean boy, that fellow. We talked a goot bit of the way. Quite quietly, you can be sure. I asked him if he luffed Gott." He passed his hand over his face.

"He told me that though some turn to drink, many men read their Bible before going into battle. Hiss wife always sends her prayers in her letters.

" 'If it were not for her prayers,' he said, 'I would not be here. My whole body cries out to lif'. I wish to see my son—he iss my first, just born a month ago. My deepest desire iss to outlif' this war and be there to raise my son to manhood, to teach him a different way than slaughter and destruction.' "

Wilhelm looked up at his wife. "Yet he cout' not explain that two sides want Gott's help for victory. I asked him if it be safe to say Gott will gif' victory to those most deserving, most in the right, or to those who offer the most prayers. 'Can we move Gott to our side by out-praying your wife?' I asked. 'Or will the Almighty leef mankind to fight on their own to the bitter end?'

His mouth trembled. "He did not answer, and I said no more. Who can understand the mind of Gott? We cannot even understand this land's dilemma."

Wilhelm laid back with tears in the corners of his eyes. "I pray for him now, and for his wife and little son."

His eyes closed, and I tiptoed out of the room.

It was difficult to get Granny Bristlow to eat. In spite of all my efforts, she was sinking fast. One evening less than a week later, she turned her face aside even for a drink.

326

"Granny, you need to drink to give you strength."
I leaned closer, talking directly into her ear.

The old lady's eyes flew open. "I hear ye. I hear ye. Ye don't have to shout so." Then her voice sank back to a whisper. "But I'm ready to go, chile. Don't need . . . don't need anything no more." She kept on with effort. "I want you . . . you to have the chest with all my pretties."

"Why, Granny, you can't do that!"

There was a hint of fire in her eyes before they closed. She reached out claw-like fingers to grasp my hand. "Don't contrary me. I'm bulldog stubborn! I reckon I can do what I need to. Always was a giv'en person, always will be."

I thought she had gone to sleep, and I turned to go when her face lit up and she said joyfully, "Oh Lord, I do see them a'coming!"

Those were her last words. The rays of evening sun fell across the wrinkled face, lighting every crease and furrow, and I saw the color fade from her cheeks. Her chest heaved one last time and was still.

We buried her the next day on a little knoll behind her house in the shade of a spreading cherry tree. The bare mound would be protected from wind and sun, and in the wintertime the nearby pines would shed needles over the hillside.

When the brief service was over, I knelt to hunt for a handful of tiny black seed pods from under the surrounding violet clumps, scattering them over the fresh dirt, taking solace in the thought that in the spring, hundreds of lavender blossoms and the dropping cherry petals would cover the mound, forming patterns of color as beautiful as any cover the old lady had enjoyed.

The chest was loaded, and the rest of the house closed up and barred. Except for the ancient loom, there was very little of value among the old lady's possessions. But what wealth I had gleaned from her life!

Summer days faded into fall. After the terrible battle of Gettysburg, Lee's army retreated to Virginia, leaving behind thousands of men who would never come home to lighten the hearts of lonely wives and children. My mind recoiled at the growing list of dead: seventeen thousand, nineteen thousand, and finally an estimated twenty thousand. Was David, by this time, among them? I hardly dared hope otherwise.

The surviving troops set up camp seventy-five miles away in Orange County, and from there officers traveled all over the country rounding up deserters and new recruits, rebuilding their ranks for another desperate attempt to regain the upper hand in the war.

John's birthday came and went. He was now seventeen. I fixed a corner for him to sleep in the attic next to the chimney. Any time we saw men or horses appear on the road, he would silently disappear up the rope ladder.

An old blanket, a jug of water, some apples or dried corn—whatever we could spare—was always kept there. I was constantly listening, we all were, for the first sign of danger. Susan grew and gurgled and laughed, unaware of the constant tension from which there was no escape.

The attitude toward those against taking an active part in the war seemed to grow more vocal. Wilhelm brought home shocking word that some of the church leaders had been arrested.[1]

"They be charged with gif'ing help to those wanting to escape." Wilhelm pulled Rebecca close as he spoke.

"And if they find out what *you* did, Wilhelm!" His wife dabbed at her eyes and turned away to the window. She swung back with a gasp. "Where's John? They're coming!"

My hands flew to my mouth. "He's in the barn! Peter—run!"

Peter darted out the back door just as half a dozen men and horses trotted up the lane. I pulled the younger boys into the back bedroom where they crouched wild-eyed and trembling. Susan lay asleep, one chubby hand thrown back over her head, dark ringlets of hair circling her head, thumb in her mouth.

"Watch Susan. If you hear the door opening, pull the blanket over her face and crawl under the bed!"

They were too frightened to answer. I pulled the door shut and stood leaning against it. My knees refused to hold still. Oh, how I hoped John and Peter were safe!

"Hey, the house." The rough voices rose in a laugh. "We know who you are, you Union Mennoniters, helping out deserters, feeding runaway slaves and prisoners. Well, we're going to let you help the right side this time. We need money, and we know you Mennonites have it."

They caught sight of Wilhelm through the window. "We see you, old man. Come on out and talk to us."

I stared at Wilhelm. His head was bowed. Rebecca grabbed his arm. "Nay, you must not. Bolt the door and let them go away. They be filled with strong drink."

The outside voices grew more churlish. "Come on out or we'll come in and get all of you."

Wilhelm straightened his shoulders. "I must go. Gott be with you, dearest; and with you . . ." His sad eyes turned in my direction.

Arms around each other, Rebecca and I watched as the men pulled him away from the house, making a circle around him under the apple tree twenty yards away.

"Isn't there some money, Rebecca? Just enough so they'll go away?"

"Not enough to appease them. They be too drunk to listen to reason." She sucked in her breath sharply. A rope was being brought from a saddle horn, and one end thrown over a high limb. In an instant the other end was fastened around Wilhelm's neck and his body roughly jerked off the ground.[2]

"Oh God, oh God . . . !" Rebecca's voice was broken. "We must do something."

Suddenly the rope was lowered, the noose loosened, and Wilhelm was helped to his feet. The angry inquiries began all over. Then, to my horror, the rope was again tightened, again his body swung for a dreadful moment in mid-air.

I closed my eyes and turned away. My stomach churned. I could not bear to watch. How could men become so beastly? I heard Rebecca stumble across the room to the fireplace and check the mush cooling on the hearth.

Then before I could stop her, she stepped quickly to the door and out onto the porch. With determination she walked toward the men, who were jerking Wilhelm up for the third time.

Hearing her, they swung around. The one holding the rope let go, and Wilhelm's body dropped with a thud onto the ground. They stood staring at her, smirks on their callused faces.

Rebecca's soft voice carried clearly to the house. "I thought you be men. Is this conduct becoming to such men as you be? I think not.

"We have no large amount of money, but our house is open to anyone and everyone, no matter which side he claims."

The smirks had changed to a mixture of hatred and embarrassment. She stood looking over them for a long moment and gradually their eyes dropped or shifted to look elsewhere. "You are hungry. Won't you come in? Hot mush and my corn bread with honey are waiting to be served."

As they stood rooted to the spot, she darted between them and knelt by her husband's side. "Wilhelm, Wilhelm . . . !"

Her hands swiftly loosened the rope and massaged his neck and face. "Wilhelm, it is time to eat. Shall these men help you to the house?"

It was a silent group that shuffled in and sat with averted eyes around the table. Wilhelm was helped to the rocking chair and propped with pillows. Already his neck was swollen black and blue.

I dipped out the mush into plates and poured tea into ever-emptying glasses. There was no sound except noisy chewing and slurping of food and drink.

331

These men were famished, embarrassed, and in a hurry to get away.

Finally there was a scraping of chairs, and the men rose, heading for the door. Though not a word of thanks was heard, several of them tipped their hats toward us. Shortly they vanished out of sight down the road.

We stood motionless, watching, then collapsed weeping into each other's arms.

"Oh, daughter, God is good! He is merciful!"

"Yes . . . I must check on the boys."

"And I, on Wilhelm." Rebecca dipped out a pan of hot water from the kettle, and with a rag, began forming a packing to wrap around his neck. His breathing was labored. It took both of us to help him totter to bed.

⁓ Chapter XVI ⁓

The pain and swelling in Wilhelm's neck was slow to leave, stubbornly hanging on despite the massaging, the poultices, and the hot stones wrapped in wool cloths. His heart would not take heavy work anymore.

Wilhelm said very little about the experience. He seemed even more peaceful and aware of heavenly things, and less concerned about earthly things.

John spent most of his time in hiding. Almost daily, soldiers could be seen riding past. Already a number had stopped at the barn or the house. One of the first took Claybones, leaving a worn-out horse in its place. It died soon afterwards.

The sheep had also disappeared after one such

visit, and only by taking the goat into the cellar did we manage to keep our meager supply of milk.

All the outside work, the gathering of wood and harvest, fell to Rebecca and me. Peter's stretching form made me fear for his safety. Young boys his age were being forced into driving supply wagons at the whim of any soldier who happened by.

Davie and Andy helped as they could. Together we tried to spare Rebecca from the heaviest jobs. The extra work was making her old. There was a droop to her shoulders that had not been there before. Yet she never complained.

We had spent all of one day picking what corn had been left in the quarter acre patch Wilhelm had managed to plant in the spring. Much of it had been stripped already by foragers with provision wagons looking for food for their camps.

Even so, the cart held a nice little mound of corn. We were grateful. "Think of all the meals this will provide for us." Rebecca pulled herself up the steps, a smile lighting her tired face.

I dropped the last ears into a sack and dragged it onto the porch, leaning it against the wall. My hands were stiff and red from working in the cold. I scraped the dirt off my shoes with a sharp stick. "Yes, we are blessed. John and Peter will find grinding this a welcome change to carving, or mending shoes. A coffee grinder will be slow, but they have all the time they need."

I opened the door to the welcome warmth, and helped the older woman take off Wilhelm's boots which she had worn in place of her own shabby shoes. Susan waved her arms, squealing from her blanket on the floor. I dropped my wraps across the nearest chair and reached for her with hungry arms. It was then I saw the letter lying on the table.

It was torn and dirtied by many hands, but still intact. I picked it up eagerly, moving closer to the fireplace to read. My hands were almost too clumsy to open it.

The letter came from Staunton, so it was not David's. It must be word from home. Back in the summer I had first gathered my courage to send a note asking about the family's welfare. There had been no reply. I had written a second letter. And a third. Only silence.

Now I held the answer in my hands. The paper shook a little. Painstakingly done, the letters were scrawled across the page.

> Dear my liddle gerl,
>
> Dis be Tansy dat be talk to you. I fin yer ledders an ax de maddem why she not rite to you. She sass and fuss me out. So Willie be helpen me by riten dese wordz.
>
> Yer Fadder is gooder dan befo. He walk roun slow. James stop here in de summer, he lost won arm frm de war but God spar his lif. De farm been strped by all de men come by, but we stil kard fo by de Lawd.
>
> I mis yo and de boes all de tim an ax de Lawd to bring yo bac somday. Yo was my tru fren.
>
> I want to se yo baby chile, bles her sol. I hear nothng ob yo man. I prayz fo him an all de res ever nite.
>
> Dis be from Tansy an de riten from Willie

Tears of disappointment and joy mingled on my face. I read over it the second time, this time aloud. It was as though I was talking to the fuzzy-haired cook face to face once more. I could see the broad hands clasped tightly, the toothy smile, and the almond eyes.

Davie swallowed hard. "As long as we don't hear anything from Papa, we can still hope, can't we, Mother?"

"You know nothing more about David," Wilhelm shuffled over, putting an arm around his wife's shoulder, "but neither do you know less. We thank Gott that *He* knows all things."

Fall drifted into winter. With it came the blinding snow and numbing cold. For days on end, freezing rain fell, turning to ice and covering the ground, the trees, and the muddy, rutted road.

The fear of abduction did not lessen. Though the armies had pulled into camp and were concentrating on surviving the winter, we heard of frequent raids and skirmishes between Staunton and Harrisonburg and as far west as Buffalo Gap in the Alleghenies.

The infrequent Sunday services no longer took place at the church, but rather in members' homes behind shuttered windows.

The security and abundance before the war seemed like a dream. Flour was selling for the unheard-of prices of eighty dollars, then ninety-five dollars a barrel. I wondered how the Confederacy could continue in the face of such shortages. Sometimes I lay in bed, walking again in my mind the streets of town before this holocaust began.

Then it had only been necessary to decide which items, and how much, my small, but adequate amount of money could purchase.

Back then, piles of boxes stood beside every store entrance. Shelves and counters were loaded with goods: molasses, cones of sugar, coffee, tea, cheese, fish, hard biscuits, crackers, and hams. The confectioner's shop windows were heaped with cakes, candies, and fruit. Flour, potatoes, meat, and apples were abundant.

Now people were saying it took a larger basket to carry your money to the store then to carry home what you bought. A person was counted very fortunate who could raise vegetables for himself or could find someone willing to sell a barrel of flour or a couple bushels of corn.

We had little money to buy anything. I had doled out of the small amount I had, but now, just as with the Gochenours, it was gone.

The boys had spent hours and hours grinding corn in the coffee grinder, cranking the small handle. Now the sack was nearly empty. Dinner would consist of plain bread and tea sweetened with honey; supper, a thin soup from beans we had dried.

Twice we were awakened by cautious knocks on the door to find a Mennonite brother with some food to share. As much as we needed it, I felt guilty knowing someone else was doing without so we would have food.

The goat was religiously fed corncobs from the attic, armloads of grass pulled in the meadow, half-rotted cornstalks, even the tips and branches of bramble and vine. Every drop of milk she produced was given to Susan.

But now, even the beans were coming to an end. One morning I sat down in desperation beside Rebecca as she rocked beside the hearth, her Bible in hand. Her hair had turned from gray to a silvery white, and I ached at the hollowness in her face.

I kept my voice low, for I did not want the others to hear. "Rebecca, I do not know what we will eat. There are only enough beans and cornmeal for about three more meals. We cannot count on church people being able to keep on sharing with us. They are all in as bad a shape as we . . ."

She looked at me for a long moment, then her eyes dropped. "I know."

I touched her arm. "I have an idea. When Mr. McChesney stops in the next time on his way to town, let me see if he would try selling my roses clock. I know there are still *some* people in town with money enough to think of buying finery."

"Nay, child. You dare not part with your only memory of David. You have already used the last of your money. Let us talk to Wilhelm."

But he was equally firm. "Not your roses clock. Not as long as I haf means to keep us alif' some other way. I haf been thinking. The spinning wheel I haf fixed and polished as new. We will see if it can be sold or traded for food." He shook his head at my protests. "I can make another. *Arbeit macht das Leben süss.* 'Labor makes life sweet.' "

And so, by selling some of the few valuables we possessed, we managed to eke out an existence. While Rebecca patched and re-patched our worn-out clothing, I pulled threads from my only shawl, and using the bright colors, embroidered a ring of daisies around the edges of Granny Bristlow's dogwood petal tablecloth. I had misgivings about my plan. "Do you think she would resent me exchanging her gift for food?"

Rebecca was reassuring. "I don't think she would be more pleased."

When we had almost given up hope, spring arrived. Freezing cold again gave way to dripping eaves and dark-brown earth. There would be no need for Claybones this year. Even if we had him, there was little left for planting, for we had been forced to eat all we had gathered.

We decided against working up the ground very deeply. Some stray seeds might come up on their own. Other than that, we would have to depend on wild herbs and plant roots Rebecca knew where to find.

Susan's first birthday came and went. It seemed so long since she had been born, and yet I marveled that a year had already passed. I depended heavily on her. Her bright little face, happy smile, and loving eyes following me about were a constant source of courage and joy. And to think David did not know she existed! *Oh David! Did I do wrong to keep it from you?* I wished I knew.

The spring campaign opened with fighting near Richmond. We would not have found out about the desperate struggle between General Lee and the Union's new top commander, U. S. Grant, except for a freak accident.

About sundown I had stepped onto the porch and flung the dirty dishwater across the grass already turning wet with dew. Rebecca and the younger boys had finished hoeing the cabbage plants, for I could see them coming down the hill from the garden. Little blinking lights flickered around them and all across the yard and into the meadow—fireflies!

They were the first I had seen this year. I stood watching for a moment, then went back inside. After putting the dishpan away, I sat down across from Wilhelm. The never ending basket of mending was on the floor beside me. I reached for a pair of socks lying on top of the heap.

The bedroom door opened, and I looked up. John and Peter emerged, grinning sheepishly, each with one of my dresses pulled over his own clothing.

"What in the . . . What are you boys up to?"

Peter fingered his dress collar nervously. "We heard Wilhelm say the place he took the goat is still too risky. We want to find a better place for her."

I laid my sewing aside and stood up. "You'll do no such thing. Why, you know the danger. Your safety is more important than the goat's."

John pulled at the tightly fitting skirt, trying to adjust it more comfortably. "Mother, we're about going crazy stashed in that hot attic. Nobody will be out this time of evening. Please say we can go."

Wilhelm's eyes were twinkling. "What fine ladies you boys make. I haf to remember my manners and

340

offer you my seat." He stood up slowly and held out his hand. "*Wie geht's?* 'How is it with you?' "

"Do tell them it is too great a risk. No time is safe, even in the dark," I implored.

"We'll wear your bonnets, yours and Grandma's. Anyone seeing us will think it is you two going out for something." Peter took a step closer. "Come on, Mother."

Wilhelm's face was solemn. "It iss true, there iss always a risk. Yet the milk iss a goot thing to have. The mite of a lass would suffer if we had none. Perhaps . . ."

"We won't take any chances. We'll be okay. You'll see!"

When the others came inside, everything had to be explained all over again. Because of my foreboding, I couldn't smile with the others at the bonneted faces, the too square shoulders, and the manly builds that showed up so awkwardly under the faded cotton material. One would have to be quite some distance away to mistake them for feminine figures. I couldn't concentrate on my handwork after they disappeared through the lean-to door.

Andy came and hung over the arm of the chair, watching my hands. He glanced up quizzically. "You didn't mean to, did you?"

"Mean to what? Let them go?"

He shook his head, pointing to the sock in my hand. I held it up, looking closely.

"The hole. You've shut up the hole where Grandpa sticks in his foot!"

I gasped. "Why so I have! How could I . . ."

"You're worried, Mother."

I was ashamed. Leaving David in God's hands

341

was something I *had* to do, there was nothing else in my power. But my sons . . . How weak my faith!

I laughed nervously and handed the funny-shaped article to Andy. "Do you want to reopen the threads? I hear Susan crying."

Glad to escape to a place alone, I sat on the bed's edge in the darkness, patting Susan until she quieted. An hour had passed since the boys had gone. *Surely they should be back soon. I must keep my imagination from running wild,* I thought. *What was faith if it gave way as soon as it was tested?*

A sharp knock against the side of the house made my heart leap. I heard Wilhelm's tread going to the back door. I took one step to the window, drawing back the curtain. Three figures stood in the shadows. I felt sure of it. Two with dresses . . . yes, that would be the boys. But who else . . . ? A horror of possibilities held me motionless.

Everyone was standing just at the door when I slipped up behind them. A deep voice was talking rapidly. "I found them hiding only a few hundred yards up the hill from the creek. They said they were looking after a goat. Likely story, there wasn't any goat around. I don't know what you think of all this, Gochenour, but I am surprised you would endorse the hiding of young men in a time when every man with any sense of responsibility should be volunteering to protect his family and country."

The swarthy, dark-haired stranger turned as I stepped closer. His black eyes were hard. His eyebrows raised questioningly.

Wilhelm held out a hand. "Ellen, our neighbor Mr. Cochran. Mr. Cochran, this iss the boys' mother, Ellen Shull. Ellen has come to live with us for a time."

Cochran spoke earnestly. "Mrs. Shull, you would agree that there is no greater honor than to give two fine sons in such a time of need. For the last two weeks Lee and Grant have been fighting west of Fredericksburg. We've lost over twenty thousand men.

"Now I'm told Grant has surrounded Petersburg and more of those loathsome Federals are coming into the Valley from the north and the west. All we have is a skeleton crew under Imboden. We must round up all available men to bear arms and stand with us. There's already been a battle at New Market, and they're coming closer."

Mr. Cochran stopped to catch his breath, and Wilhelm started to speak, but the neighbor broke in again. "I respect you highly, Mr. Gochenour. You have treated me fairly and aboveboard all the years we've known each other. It was out of respect for you I brought the boys here before taking them on. I felt I should check out their story. I can hardly bring myself to believe that you would actually stand in the way of protecting your wife and friends."

My heart was in my throat, and I could hardly think. Because of the bonnets, I could not see the boys' expressions. Their eyes were glued to the floor.

Wilhelm sighed heavily. "I fear you cannot understand. We do not take part in violence uf any kind. A life is a life—in Gott's hands we must leef to sever it. Upon myself I dare not take that right, or I be guilty uf murder. *Ein gutes Gewissen ist ein sanftes Rukekissen,* 'A good conscience is a soft pillow' ."

Mr. Cochran smacked his fist in his palm in rising frustration. "You'd rather let your loved ones be tortured and maimed and killed? Do you know who the

Northern general *is*?" His voice rose to a hiss. "It's David Hunter, that's who it is. He's a devilish man, he is! Full of hate and destruction, burning and killing upon any whim of fancy." His eyes narrowed to angry slits.

"A life is a life, that is true. But some have forfeited their right to live. If you had any thought for your people at all . . ."

The older man shook his head. "I'm sorry, my friend. I must leef the future in Gott's hands. The fact that my Jesus rejected an earthly kingdom iss enough to convince me I cannot take part in the same. Hate makes no comforting bedfellow. Do you ask me to be no better than they, to be another David Hunter?"

The black-eyed man's face grew so red I thought he would strike Wilhelm, but he stepped back, his voice growing lower, and hard. "I've tried to understand your people. You have twisted what I said, Mr. Gochenour. And if I may be so blunt, your people are well practiced in that. You are forever taking your ideas and giving them out as though they were God's laws delivered directly to you; as though you are the only ones who have a word from the Lord. You're stubborn and immovable—not caring for the hundreds of defenseless godly women and children living all around you.

"You've withdrawn when your state needs you the most. I'd be ashamed to own your name! You hang your head? I'm not surprised. How can you say you love God when you are heartless and cruel?"

He stopped, waiting for a reply, his gaze sweeping Wilhelm from head to toe. I could see the blood pumping along his temple.

I could feel my ears burning with embarrassment, and I marveled at Wilhelm's silence. Why didn't he respond to this unjust charge? How could anyone say this godly man was anything less than kindness itself?

At last Wilhelm raised his head. His eyes were sad. "Iss that all you haf to say?"[1]

Mr. Cochran was caught off guard, and his mouth fell open. "I . . . I suppose so, but . . ."

"Let me tell you, my friend, you haf not told haf of my faults. But it iss only in those things that I differ from my Master, that I am ashamed. In all things I want to follow Him. I dare not take one step from His side. Surely, you would not ask me to do otherwise."

Mr. Cochran swallowed hard, struggling for an answer. He set his hat firmly on his head and turned toward the door. "I think you realize I have the law on my side. There are posters all around the countryside requiring all who can fire a gun to join up. All I need is an army official to give me the authority to take them by force. Good night, Mr. Gochenour. We shall meet again very soon." The door slammed behind him.

Wilhelm's shoulders sagged. I wondered if the rest of our faces looked as white as the boys'.

"Well, sons, we will haf to find you a better place, not? Best we be going there right away. Take off your extras, and we will be leefing within the hour." His eyes locked with mine for an instant. "Do not ask where we go."

I did not sleep at all that night. There was the smell of smoke in the air, and I thought of what Mr. Cochran had said, ". . . burning and killing upon any

345

whim or fancy . . ." My feeling of dread grew with each passing hour.

My ears strained constantly for any sound or movement, but not until daylight did Wilhelm return. There were dirt stains on his shirt and trousers, but he did not seem overly tired.

A faint drizzle created a low-lying fog that intensified the feeling of gloom pervading the room. We sat down to eat, but I found it hard to concentrate. The rest must have too, for the food, sparse as it was, was barely touched.

Wilhelm pushed back his chair and pulled his worn Bible onto his lap. "Perhaps we need *this* more than food for our bodies. This be the day of worship. Let us listen to what Gott would say to us."

He thumbed through the pages, then stopped and lifted the Bible closer to his eyes. His white beard moved slightly as he spoke. "This be what we worship Him for this morning, 'Who shall separate us from the luf of Christ? shall tribulation, or distress, or persecution, or famine . . .' "

The words were beautiful, and I clung to them.

" 'For I am persuaded that neither death, nor life, nor angels, nor principalities, nor things present, nor things to come, nor height, nor depth, nor any other creature shall be able to separate us from the luf of God which iss in Christ Jesus our Lord.' "

He closed the Book and looked around the circle, his eyes tender. "We can be no more secure than that. If there be bad times ahead, it iss enough that He knows about them. Let us bow for prayer."

As we rose to our feet, I sniffed. Smoke. Much stronger than last night. The others noticed it too. Wilhelm flung open the door.

346

A smoky haze hung above the newly leafed-out trees. Then we could hear it, the sharp crack of muskets from the west and a deeper boom of artillery.

I whirled, heading for the bedroom where Susan lay sleeping.

"Quick, to the springhouse, all uf you!" Wilhelm reached for his Bible and a bucket on his way out, the water sloshing over the edges in his haste. "Mother, take the rest of the food. We haf not a moment to spare!"

Andy was crying, the tears running silently down his face. I held Susan against my chest, snatching a couple blankets as I ran out the door.

The old man was already ushering Rebecca and the younger boys into the interior of the rock-walled building. How did he think we could all fit inside? And where were the older boys in this time of danger? In my panic I tripped over a trailing blanket and almost fell.

Rebecca almost pulled me in and shouldered me to one side, sliding the door shut. As my eyes adjusted to the dim light, I saw Wilhelm frantically pulling rocks away from under a large flap of ancient cowhide draped over the opposite wall and stacking them along the back of the water trough. He was panting with his efforts. I wondered wildly why he was wasting time at such a task. Through the gap along the eaves, the sound of galloping horses grew louder, then faded. The roaring of cannon was interspersed with crackling gunfire, the screams of horses, and the throaty yells of dozens of men.

Then Wilhelm was kneeling and pulling open a small trap door that bordered the floor. "All uf you—inside!"

Andy and Davie were first, Rebecca following. I handed Susan through, then crawled inside.

Susan's whimpering turned into loud wails, and I could feel Davie's silent sobs as he pressed up against me.

"I will light the oil wick for a moment so we can see our surroundings." In a moment Rebecca's steady hand lifted the crude oil lamp. Its flickering flame cast moving shadows over our faces.

"John! Peter!" Tears of relief coursed down my face, and I crawled closer to crouch next to them.

"Mother!" Peter was swallowing hard, wiping the back of his hand across his eyes.

"Are you all right? You've been here all night?" I rocked Susan back and forth in an effort to calm her hysteria.

"Yes, Grandpa brought us straight here and stayed with us till just a little while ago."

"Here . . . ," Rebecca thrust the last of the breakfast into their hands. "Eat this."

I spread the blankets down, and gradually we adjusted our seating until we all had space to settle onto.

"Tell us, Papa, what is happening out there." Rebecca held the lamp high. "While you talk, I will blow the lamp out. We must save our precious oil."

"I know not, except for what Mr. Cochran said last night. The two armies must haf met close by."

The muffled sounds of battle could be heard even through the thick dirt walls, and I shivered.

"Mommy . . ."

I leaned my head close to Davie's in the darkness.

"If they find us here . . . will they kill us all?"

I couldn't find it within me to answer. "Remember

348

what Grandpa read this morning, son? His love is the safest place we can be right now."

In the nightmare of that musty hole, the words of a psalm rose above Susan's wails. Rebecca's clear voice joined with Wilhelm's gruff one, and the rest of us took up the familiar phrases. They were reassuring in the blackness.

"The Lord is my shepherd; I shall not want. He maketh me to lie down in green pastures, he leadeth me beside the still waters . . ."

Nothing else was said as the hours crept past. The waiting pressed as heavily upon us as the bad air, the hunger, and the weariness of our bodies. Susan's sobs had diminished to hiccups, then sleep.

I reached to feel for Davie and Andy's hands, and was reassured by their answering squeeze. Pieces of dry cornbread were passed from hand to hand.

The sounds of fighting lessened, increased again, then finally faded to the south. There was little room to shift position, and my body felt stiff all over. John's elbow was against my left side, and Davie huddled over my legs.

"Can . . . can I open the door? I can hardly breathe anymore." Peter sounded hoarse.

"I will check. I be at the door." There was a grunt as Wilhelm turned to reach for the handle.

The rush of fresh air was glorious. We all took deep breaths, our eyes drawn to the light as if to a magnet. The steady trickle of water was tonic to my taut nerves.

Wilhelm crawled into the larger room and began to stand up. "Let me . . ."

Suddenly he dropped and lunged backward, pulling the door shut with a thud. "Men chust outside!"

Susan woke up and began to fuss. I hugged her close, caressing her face, her hair, rubbing her back. "Hush, darling, hush . . . hush . . . Mommy's here. Hush . . ."

There was a stamping of feet, then voices came clearly through the wooden door.

"Ah, a drink of water. Here, let me give you some. My tongue burns like powder."

Water was being splashed across dirty faces and slurped up from hand to mouth.

"That wound there, let me wrap your shirt tighter around it."

"Nothing but a flesh wound, lucky it didn't go any deeper, I'd have ended up where all those rebels deserve to go." There was a string of words and sarcastic laughter that made me cringe.

"This place wasn't made for horses, but mine is coming right in, see if she don't."

Their conversation became indistinct for a moment, then I heard the squeak of a saddle, hoofs upon cobblestone, the sucking of long draughts of water, and then snorts, blowing, and dripping water.

"Okay, let's go. Back up, back up. That a girl."

"The troops are almost out of sight. We'll push those yellow necks all the way to Staunton, if I have anything to do with it."

There were loud guffaws, then silence returned. My cheeks were wet. I hadn't known I was crying. My leg ached where Davie was clutching it.

At last, one by one, we crept out into the next room, almost too stiff to stand. My legs collapsed under me, and I sat down on the wall. There was mud and horse hair along the trough's edge and splattered blood.

350

Wilhelm's bucket was passed around, and we drank eagerly. Outside a cricket chirped hesitantly then fell silent. All was quiet except for an occasional drip of water from the roof. I blinked against the smoke's acrid burning.

"Mommy . . . I can hardly see!"

" 'Tis the smoke of war, Andy." Rebecca drew him close and with her apron, wiped the dirty tear streaks off his cheeks. "It will leave. Thank God we are safe."

"Ah, yes. Thank Gott we be safe. Before we go out, we bow our heads to offer our praise." Wilhelm held both hands outstretched.

As the door opened, I couldn't help exclaiming at the transformation before us. Through the smoldering haze, trees stood battered and splintered, big limbs hung jaggedly earthward. Twigs and branches, their baby-green leaves wilting and scorched, covered the ground.

The hayfield was trampled flat, mud ground into every square foot of earth. By the lane's edge, a horse sprawled, its eyes glazing over, and its legs stiffening in the position of its last thrashing agony. The ground around it showed dark with blood.

John and Peter returned to their hiding place in the spring house, and Wilhelm hurried the rest of us toward the house. He helped his wife up the steps and through the door. She sank gratefully into a rocking chair. Broken glass was scattered over the floor, and dishes lay where they had fallen.

" 'Tis a wreck. The glass, we must sweep it up before the children get hurt. But first, to eat."

"Here," I settled Susan into her arms, "you just stay put. I'll get something together right away."

While we ate, an occasional figure could be seen

351

limping toward Staunton after the departing army. It seemed the furious fighting had carried everything along in its wake. I shuddered as I thought of those next in their path. What would happen to my parents, to Tansy? What kind of destruction would this David Hunter deal out to the citizens in town?

What made David Hunter so hateful? Robert E. Lee was a respectful gentleman, religious, and regretfully doing what he saw as his duty rather than out of revenge and malice.

I picked up Susan from where she had fallen asleep over her plate and carried her to bed. Did God make a difference between the two? I wished I knew the answers.

I thought again of what Wilhelm had said many weeks before. "Can you show luf by dealing out hate? Is that what we learned of our Gott?"

How could killing, even done from a sense of duty, come from a heart of love, a heart true to the nature of the King it served?

I pulled a sheet over Susan's legs and tiptoed back to the front room. Perhaps I could not judge, but neither could I excuse that kind of activity. I must be true to the highest truth I had come to understand. The rest I must leave to God.

Wilhelm helped sweep the floor, then reached for his hat. "I think I go see if there be someone who needs help."

Rebecca placed her small body in front of his. "Wilhelm, you will get captured. You yourself said there are apt to be stragglers from either side still around. Any of them would be glad to use an old man like you."

He stood there, hat in hand, looking at her quietly. I could hear her sharp intake of breath.

"I am sorry, Papa." Her mouth opened to say more, then closed, and she looked away.

"I said my house iss always open to any who needs my help. Do I shrink from my duty at such a time as this? There may be stragglers, true, but either one, north or south, needs to see the luf of Jesus."

He put his arm around her, his eyes never leaving her face. "I go now, my little wife. Gott be with you."

The corners of her mouth trembled. "And with you."

We watched his shuffling step cross the muddy hayfield and onto the road. Rebecca stood, shoulders hunched, eyes fixed straight ahead for a long moment.

At last she turned with a sigh. "You see, Ellen, how weak I am. I be remembering how old he is and feeble."

She picked up the empty plates from the table. "But we must not disappoint him. We must be ready should he bring anyone back with him.

"Here, take this out to the boys. They be hungry for dinner."

It was almost dark when Wilhem returned. He came alone. "The next road had the worst of it, a whole field full of prisoners and wounded men."

His wife looked startled. "How far did you go?" She dipped out the thin gruel into his plate. We sat across from him at the table as he ate.

He shrugged. "I cut cross-country to the cross-road. You remember the McCues, the Walker brothers. Their houses be full of wounded. I helped bury the dead. So many uf them there were. The whole village of Piedmont iss wreckage."[2]

I wished the younger boys were already sleeping. Davie sat with eyes wide.

Rebecca pressed the knuckles of one hand against her teeth, a slight groan coming from her lips. "What of the rest of our people?"

"Their crops ruined just as ours. Corn and wheat . . . ," he swung his hand straight across, "*verschnipped,* 'cut to shreds'! Clover up to the knees, trampled in the mud. I know not that any got killed, Mennonite or Dunkard. But the houses be full of holes, the trees cut to pieces. We must share the little we haf with others less fortunate."

He pushed back his empty plate and stood. "They say David Hunter himself had his headquarters at the Shaver farm." He glanced at me. "They be Dunkards.

"And now, the goat I could not find this afternoon. You would go with me to search once more?"

It was so late. I wondered at the intensity of his look.

"Of course. Let me get a light."

"Let us go along. We can help look." Davie and Andy had already jumped up and headed for the door.

"Not tonight, *snicklefritz.** We must not leef

---

* an expression of endearment, literally playful prankster

354

Grandma here to clear away the dishes alone. Plenty of times there will be later when I need your help." He gave their arms a squeeze.

They had to be content with that. I followed his stooped figure down the steps and around the house. He reached for the shovel propped inside the lean-to door.

His mouth twisted at my look of confusion. "We are needed for more than a goat tonight. There iss some burying that needs to be done."

He gestured in the direction of the wood's edge, leading the way to a wild plum thicket along one side. A pair of shoes was sticking out into the grass. I gulped.

We rolled the body onto the buggy robe he brought to cover it with, and dragged it to the hill behind the barn.

"To the old lane . . ." He was panting, and I straightened up to catch my own breath.

At a place where the ruts were deep, we stopped and Wilhelm reached to pull the robe across the distorted face.

"Wait . . ." I gritted my teeth. "I . . . I must look, for his family's sake."

The pockets held two cartridges; a wallet, empty except for some folded papers; and a battered fork. I stuffed the wallet inside the folds of my dress, and together we lowered the body into the ditch. We took turns shoveling dirt, the falling soil sounding loud in the darkness.

The air still hung heavy with the smell of gunpowder and smoke, the smell of death. I shivered, my fingers closing around the worn wallet. My heart was heavy as I bowed my head. Wilhelm was kneeling, hands outstretched over the grave.

"It be true."

My eyes widened, and I started, almost losing my hold on the lantern. It swung crazily for a moment. "You what?"

Wilhelm reached out a steadying hand. "Careful, daughter. Yes, I knew him as soon as I saw his face. He was the one who tightened the noose."

I gaped at him before concentrating on the path again. "You prayed over him; helped bury him?"

"I haf no bitterness, Ellen. It be . . ." he grimaced, holding his hand over his heart. "It be strange that I be free, while he be in bondage to hate. Perhaps, if I could haf got to him in time . . ."

I felt a wonder inside of me I couldn't explain. Love like this . . . it could only come from something greater than oneself. How far superior to those who killed, even for duty's sake! I caught my breath. If only all men would live out this life of love!

I followed the old man's slow and steady footsteps, thinking. Hate and evil were always together. Hatred could only breed hatred . . . the absence of God . . . darkness . . . I felt goose bumps on my arms. "Breathing out threatenings . . ." Where was that verse found?

We were now within sight of the cabin, standing gray and solid in the moonlight. A lone candle glowed from somewhere within.

Conquered by hate? Not for an instant! The picture of Rebecca standing behind her husband's chair,

356

quiet and clear-eyed, feeding the men who had meant to kill; the dim lantern-lit face of Wilhelm, bent over the grave, his lips moving in prayer.

No, I had forever in my mind a living picture, a beautiful living out of love that conquered evil, a love that refused to die.

Perhaps those who lived by less had never seen such love in action. How could they embrace what they had never seen as possible?

If so, then what a rare privilege I had been granted tonight! Compassion and warmth welled up within me toward the saintly old man walking before me.

❦ Chapter XVII ❦

Several weeks later we learned more about the trail of destruction left behind the fast moving Federal army. After ravaging Staunton, David Hunter had directed his army toward Lexington, the home of Virginia Military Institute. Here, with chilling derision, he repeated the orgy of plundering and burning and killing.

Then with a large number of military and civilian prisoners and wagonloads of plunder, he crossed the Blue Ridge mountains at the Peaks of Otter, burning more homes on his way to Lynchburg. He was determined to cut railroad connections and further disable the South. But finding himself confronted with fierce fighting, he turned aside, and separating into three columns, began a hasty retreat.

With General Early's men following close behind, Hunter pushed night and day till he crossed the Alleghenies into West Virginia. The Valley was relieved at the news.

Once again mail resumed its three-times-a-week delivery from Charlottesville. Railroad repairs began as far south as Christians Creek. The Staunton newspaper began to be printed once again.

The many buildings burned and razed to the ground—depots, factories, steam mills, government workshops and warehouses—would take much longer to replace.

Now, more keenly than ever, we felt the vast gap between us and the rest of society. Had we helped during the emergency? Had we reached out to defend our family and neighbor's property?

The July 8 edition of the *Vindicator* bitterly put in print the feelings growing around us.

> . . . To the enemies of our country, the vile Yankees, we desire in closing to say that what they have done to us in common with our neighbors, has not varied the sense of our feelings toward them one iota. We have ALWAYS hated them, and what we have seen (or felt) of them in their late raid through our Valley could not possibly have lowered them in our estimation.[1]

Union sympathizers were threatened with violence, Wilhelm being no exception. Crime and

360

harassment went unpunished. Then word came of the murder of John Kline, the Dunkard elder of Rockbridge County.[2] Was anyone safe? Fear became our constant companion.

Fearful or not, the harvest had to be gotten in. I worked feverishly, praying always as my fingers flew, my back aching with weariness. My skin burned and peeled and burned again.

The army supply wagons came by often, sometimes several times a week, gathering up any food they could find.

Then something happened that was far more terrifying than the increased hostility and the scarcity of food.

John was taken.

I had needed him so desperately. The cartload of hay Davie and I tried to push up to the barn hit a rut and rolled backward. Suddenly I found myself in darkness, my back against the rough dirt of the lane, pinned fast by the crude heavy frame, the hay shutting out the sun.

I struggled for breath, turning my face sideways, fighting against the searing agony that flooded my body. I could hear Davie's feverish efforts to push aside the hay, and at last I looked up into his terrified face. "Mommy! Can you move?!"

I gasped for air. "I . . . I think so. Help . . . help me push it off."

Our combined efforts only lifted the cart a few inches before dropping again. The new burst of pain brought tears to my eyes. I couldn't keep from moaning.

Davie was crying now. I tried to speak calmly through clenched teeth. "We need help, Davie. Run to the house and get John."

He was gone before I finished speaking, bounding away like a scared rabbit.

I shut my eyes, groaning, biting my lips till I tasted blood. "Oh, God, let him hurry!"

And then I could hear running footsteps, and John's white face was leaning over me. "Take a deep breath, Mother. We'll have this off in an instant."

Suddenly the terrible pressure lifted, and I was panting with relief. Rebecca's hands were on my legs, brushing aside the remaining hay, probing.

"It is your right ankle, Ellen. But I think no bones be broken. Thank God for that. The boys will carry you to the house."

She heated water and brought a bucket to my bedside. "Can you stand to soak it, Ellen?"

I pinched my mouth in a straight line. "I believe so."

My foot turned red from the heat. The ankle swelled rapidly, becoming streaked with purple and black and blue. I held it in the water as long as I could bear, then let her wrap it tightly with strips of an old sheet. The throbbing inched up my leg, pushing upward into the rest of my body.

I grimaced. "I am so sorry about this. Now how shall the fall work get finished? I don't have time to be laid up right now."

Rebecca sniffed. "You'll be laid up for some little time, daughter, and you may as well submit to it. I am also sorry it happened, but don't you worry. Wilhelm and the boys will manage somehow. God always provides a way."

But before I recovered enough to hobble as far as the bedroom door, John was captured. As dangerous as it was, he had come out of hiding to help finish up the hay, to plant the fall turnips, and help gather the winter supply of honey.

One evening at twilight, they caught him and forced him to march ahead of them into the woods.

"I feel sure they be Jesse Scouts, for they know the shortcut to the East Road and the river." Wilhelm was pacing the floor. I had never seen him so distressed before. Even in my shocked numbness, his anguish touched me.

He was cupping both hands over his heart. "I watched them until they blended into the trees again. We haf searched for two hours and found nothing. I should haf been more careful . . . more careful."

He came to a sudden halt and knelt abruptly in the middle of the floor. "We must pray to our Father who knoweth all things."

He must have spent the whole night in prayer, for the next morning his eyes were bloodshot with dark circles underneath. He took no breakfast but left again, searching the hills and the woods. The only clue was John's hat, lying on the ground a quarter mile north of us.

Two tormenting weeks went by before I hobbled to answer a knock late one night, and found a man standing outside the door. For one wild moment I thought it was David, and then he spoke.

"Mother!"

"John!"

I pulled him inside, sobbing, and shoved the door shut behind him. "Are you all right?"

His voice was choked. "Yes, Mother, except I'm famished."

I held him at arm's length, my eyes sweeping him from head to foot. His appearance left me dizzy. No shoes, feet scratched and bleeding, and clothes grimy and torn almost beyond recognition. Across his left cheek was a large bruise, and his eye was still partially swollen.

"Here, sit down and let me feed you." I was already building up the fire and filling the large kettle with water. He would need a lot of cleaning up too, the poor lad.

I pulled out a plate and emptied the supper leftovers from the earthen jug on the hearth. "Have some. It's still warm."

He grabbed for it with shaking fingers, and while he ate I went to wake the boys. There were movements in the old couple's bedroom. They were already getting dressed.

John was almost tipped over backwards by the boys' welcome. We all had tears in our eyes. Wilhelm raised his arms in thanksgiving. "May the Lord be praised!" He gripped John's hand until the boy winced. "Tell us all, my son. Tell us what has happened to you."

John swallowed the last of the soup and rubbed his stomach appreciatively. "My, that feels better." He began rolling up his pants' legs as I set the bucket of hot water by his chair.

"There were only nine in the gang, plus the dozen or more of us prisoners. They headed west as fast as they could. For the first three days we traveled night and day. They made us take turns running alongside their horses for as long as we could keep up."

He whistled as he dipped his feet into the water. "Scalding fire! Could I have a bit of cold to put in with this?"

Davie and Andy both jumped up, and in their eagerness, what little was left in the water basin was dumped over John's pants legs and into his lap.

Andy stood stricken, mouth open.

Davie's ears reddened. "I'm sorry, John. I didn't mean to douse you first thing." He reached for the empty basin, clattering back and forth on the floor.

John laughed. "Don't you worry, Davie. There's plenty more where that came from, and I don't mind the wet. I've had enough drought to last me a long time." He stifled a yawn.

"We only stopped an hour or two a day to rest and eat. And we didn't get much, only a handful of meal and a slice of fatback. I was so tired I'd stuff it in my mouth and flop down and sleep where I landed.

"By the third night we had reached the Alleghenies. They must have felt safer, because that night they stopped to sleep at an old, dilapidated barn. I wanted so badly to escape. I was afraid if I didn't get away soon, I would never find my way back home. I took the chance to pull up a loose board in the floor and crawled underneath. I hung by both hands and feet to a floor joist.[3] I don't know how long I hung—it seemed like an hour, till they got everyone going the next morning."

He shrugged his shoulders. "They went about half a mile before coming back to find me. And were they angry! The leader held a pistol to my head and swore something frightful at me for delaying them."

I clutched his arm. "Oh, John!"

John glanced at Wilhelm. "I remembered how you told me if I was ever taken because I don't believe in war, to never be ashamed, for God is on our side. So I tried not to be scared, but just looked him steady in the eye. Finally he just smacked me good with the pistol barrel and told the others to make me run at gun point till we caught up with the rest."

"So that's what caused the bruise." Rebecca reached a gentle hand.

I dipped some steaming tea into a cup and set it before him. "Oh, son, the Lord was watching over you. Where were they heading?"

He took a sip, frowning. "I think they were trying to catch up with Hunter's army. At least that's what I figured from snatches I overheard.

"No matter how upset they were with me, I was determined to try again the next night. There was another boy about my age, and when we stopped at noon, we had a chance to make plans to try it together.

"I waited till dark, when we had almost made it to the next peak. We were climbing through heavy shadows and underbrush when I poked the other fellow. He didn't make any sign he had noticed, nor did he the second time. So when we passed a big boulder, I took my chance and jumped over the edge.

"I slid and rolled about one hundred feet before catching hold of a big root. Such shooting and shouting! I wasn't sure I'd live to tell the story, but I hugged the side of the mountain till they gave up and moved on."

Peter took a deep breath. "They were afraid to come down after you?"

"I guess. It was rough country, and they were in a hurry. I lay right there hanging on till morning. I even dozed a little. Then I waited till the sun rose enough to see which way was east and started walking. It took a long time to get home again, but here I am."

We all sat motionless. How close we had come to losing him—forever!

Was there no hope of normal living? Would this go on forever? God had spared us so many times thus far! How much longer dared we stay here, presuming on His mercy, knowing we were exposing this dear old couple to a great risk of punishment if any of the boys were found again? I was desperate for an answer.

The next day Widow Wright came over. "I hope you don't mind me stopping . . ." Her voice was highstrung and nervous.

"Of course not. Do come in. Rebecca is out in the smokehouse." I pulled the rocker up close, and the angular woman collapsed into it. "Rest yourself for a moment. I'll go call her."

The pallid fingers picked at my sleeve. "Oh, no, don't bother please. You don't have any meat yet, do you?" She sighed. "It's been so long since I've tasted meat."

"No. The hooks have been hanging empty for a long time. She's trying to get some salt."

"Salt?"

"From the floor. We try to clean out the dirt."

"Ah yes, we must do what we must to survive. I've eaten things I didn't think would ever pass my lips. Necessity is the mother of invention my father always used to say." Her dim eyes squinted in my direction. "Now who did you say you are again?"

"I . . . I didn't say. I'm Ellen Shull from Staunton. My husband . . ."

"Oh yes, yes. I remember now. There's been talk. I often wondered what happened to you. Haven't been able to have church for so long, you know."

I nodded. It had been too dangerous. Most families huddled close to home, almost completely cut off from fellowship with other believers.

The lady dabbed at her eyes. "I miss my Levi so dreadfully, but 'tis merciful God took him last winter when the diphtheria passed through. At least I know he's safe. You'uns have it?"

I dropped the last young turnip into the kettle and swung the crane hook around over the fire. "No, no, thankfully we didn't."

She came to lean against the corner of the window ledge. The geraniums, so full of blossoms several months ago had largely faded, the stems turning yellow.

I forced myself not to stare at her gauntness. "Do you have other family?"

As soon as I said it, I wished I could take back my words. The homely woman burst into tears, throwing her apron over her head.

Aghast, I stood awkwardly by, rubbing her arm, fumbling for words. I was relieved to hear Rebecca come through the lean-to door, her platter heaped with a mound of dirty whiteness.

"Sarah, dear!"

"Oh, Rebecca!"

The older woman pulled her close. "Sarah, Sarah . . . How good to see you." She took a handkerchief from her apron pocket. "Here, tell us all about it."

The pitiful story was soon told. Their livestock had been taken over a year ago, and her husband's death left her with only one son.

"My Michael strapped himself to the plow last spring, and we plowed the garden that way." She sniffed convulsively. "He a-pulling, me holding onto the handles. And now my only way of making money is gone." She took a long shuddering breath. "I swept out the meetinghouse every week you know."[4]

Rebecca nodded soberly. "No meetings mean no cleaning for you."

"But that's not the worst of it. Three weeks ago my Michael was taken . . . taken, and I'm left alone in the world." Fresh sobs racked her body.

John had slipped silently down the ladder to listen. I saw him straighten suddenly. "Ma'am." At her startled look he hurried on. "I'm . . . I'm John, and I think I saw your son."

Her hands flew to her throat. "You . . . you what?"

"I was also taken not long back, but got away. There was a boy . . . a blond boy with hair the color of . . ." His eyes narrowed, remembering, ". . . of risen cream."

"That's him, that had to be him! My Michael! God be praised . . . you've seen him! Please tell me more."

"I escaped when we reached the mountains. And as far as I know, I was the only one of the prisoners that tried it. I jumped off the trail during the night, and they were in too much of a hurry to wait till light to come after me."

"Oh, if he would have only come too! He didn't even try?"

John hesitated. "You have to understand, ma'am, it was a risky thing I did."

She nodded. "Ah, yes. He was only fifteen, but big for his age, I tell you. Broad across his shoulders as my Levi. He would have been afraid to take the chance."

A fresh burst of tears muffled her words. "And now, even the ransom money doesn't help any more. They done crossed out that law they made for folks like us."[5]

"The exemption law?" There was disbelief in Rebecca's words.

"That's what they say. All our men are in danger. A lot of them are going north to safety. I wish my Michael had been able to go with them."

My mind was racing. If this was true, then John was in worse danger than he had ever been. Peter too. And Wilhelm, surely they wouldn't press him into service, or would they? I forced my mind back to the present. Rebecca was speaking.

"Do you have food?"

The widow was embarrassed. "Well, I'm . . . that is . . . I've been digging cattail roots for the last week. They make tolerable pancakes."

Rebecca put her arms around the thin shoulders. "Be that all? You will come and live with us. We will share what we have together." She raised her hand. "No. No protests. Wilhelm would say the same."

At the supper table it was agreed; Sarah would come and join the household, at least for the time being.

That night I couldn't sleep. Besides sharing the crowded bed with Mrs. Wright, I couldn't shake the feeling of dread that once again it was time for a change. But would it be everyone, or just the older boys? I tried to think it through from every angle, as David would do.

If we separated, what was the likelihood of

370

reuniting? What if something happened on the way, could I ever forgive myself for taking the risk? No, I couldn't take that chance. It would be all of us, or none at all.

I slipped out the next morning as soon as I heard the old couple stirring, and despite their objections, held firm to my decision.

"You are in no position to feed this large a family over winter. The fall work is done now. There's fighting going on as close as Harrisonburg. You yourself said the Yankees are wiping out every bit of food they can find."

Rebecca's hands were on her throat. "But how? How could you ever hope to make it through?"

I didn't look up. My fingers kept smoothing the chair cushion. "Perhaps you remember the name of the man who escorted that escaped prisoner to the mountains? He would help us, don't you think?"

"But little Susan . . ." Rebecca protested. Her face turned haggard. When I did not answer, she moaned. "Ah, this be a time of misery."

Wilhelm's shoulders sagged. "You are aware uf the dangers for your boys, daughter? You haf thought this through?"

My cheeks felt hot. I raised my head, begging with my eyes for them to understand. "We must go, all of us. I cannot divide the family even for a day."

The time came quicker than I dreamed.

The burnings began, the time that everyone in the Valley would remember for years to come.[6] There was terrible destruction of crops and buildings. It was one last, desperate effort by the Federals to crush the Confederacy. Through the haze of smoke and terror came the message, the short,

371

swarthy Federal general, Philip Sheridan, would furnish wagon and team for any family wishing to follow his army north out of Virignia.[7]

This was our answer, I was sure of it. Though I would never have guessed it to be this way.

"We will go to David's folks. Somehow. Perhaps we can even find out word of . . ." I couldn't say the rest. It had been long, so long since any word had come of David.

There was the rush of packing. We would take only what we could carry. Sheridan's army was camped near Harrisonburg, twelve miles away. It would take at least two days to get there.

"We will save Granny's trunk for you, Ellen. And the clock."

I felt Rebecca's tears on my cheek. I buried my face in the older woman's shoulder until I could gain control of myself.

She lifted my face and held it between her hands. "My daughter, the Lord be with you. Perhaps when the war be over, you will be back. You will find it waiting for you."

Wilhelm cleared his throat. "It cannot go on much longer. My Gott iss bringing it soon to a close. We will pray for you always."

Andy threw his arms around the old man's waist. His thin body shook with sobs. "I don't want to go! Mother, do we have to leave?"

I pulled myself away and took Andy by the hand. My steps felt like lead. There was no need to answer.

372

Susan glanced from Peter's arms to the old couple on the steps. Suddenly it dawned on her that they were not coming along. "Gran! Gran and Pap Pap!" She burst into a wail.

Wilhelm put his arm around his wife. Raising his hand in benediction, his trembling voice began the words: " 'Whither shall I go from thy spirit, or whither shall I flee from thy presence? If I take the wings of the morning and dwell in the uttermost parts of the sea; even there shall thy hand lead me, and thy right hand shall hold me. . . .' "

He faltered, then continued, "Go, my daughter, go into the darkness of the unknown. But if you put your hand into the hand uf Gott, that shall be to you better than a light, and safer than a known way."[8]

❧ Chapter XVIII ❧

The silvery wet grass became purple and blue-green in the half light of the coming day. All around us the wagon train began coming to life. A gray squirrel's chatter in the grove of oaks behind us was soon drowned out by the bawling of cattle and rattle of harness being fastened into place. Mid the shouting and whip-cracking came the shrill cry of children.

"Forward! Easy now. Keep your place. Let's go!" The man on horseback came along the line at a trot, his eyes checking each wagon in turn.

Susan was sobbing piteously. I held her close on the rough wooden seat, fumbling for a hard biscuit from the bag at my feet. "Here, deary, chew on this."

I gave a quick glance behind me to make sure the boys were settled into place before handing the bag in their direction. There had been no time for breakfast.

John snapped the lines. The lurch almost unbalanced me. The wagon creaked in protest and then started to move. Behind and before as far as I could see, wagons loaded with people and possessions were jolting into action.[1]

My shoulders slumped. We had made it. We were actually on our way!

Yesterday it had taken all my willpower to keep pushing ahead. Fresh billowing smoke and leaping red glares in a dozen places on both sides of the pike were a sure sign the Yankees were still on the rampage.

By late afternoon, low clouds had moved in off the mountains, bringing a steady drizzle. Our backs grew wet, and the smoke and dampness of earth reeked in our nostrils. Had it not been for the courteous, young soldier with the empty wagon who caught up with us in the last miles, I don't know how we would have gotten to Sheridan's camp in time.

When we finally arrived about dark, I was dismayed at the wagons, horses, and hundreds of milling strangers. I could tell by their dress that some of them were Mennonites, but I knew none of them. Rugged-faced men in rumpled army clothes were everywhere. A group of cavalry dodged in and out among the crowd, herding people through the mud toward the line of wagons on the far side of the camp. Their loud oaths and rough orders left me shaken. These men were prepared to kill. They seemed to have lost all sense of decency and common courtesy to ladies.

It was dark before it was our turn to be questioned, and a wagon finally assigned to us. I laid a blanket underneath and kept the boys close. It would never do to become separated in this multitude.

As the morning progressed, the mud gradually turned to swirls of dust which rose and thickened until it became difficult to see any distance. The wagons were two and three abreast, spilling over into the grassy fields, the horses' hooves trampling wild aster and goldenrod.

Just ahead, crashing across the slope and up the knoll toward us, swarmed a group of men in blue, driving before them several dozen head of horses and cattle. They plunged through a patch of dead, wild sunflowers, crushing their stalks and churning them into the earth. The smoke rising to the west behind them told of the destruction they were leaving.

What of the owners? Were they killed? What of their children, their terror and screaming? Had anything been left to survive the coming winter?

I felt sick.

I forced my eyes to follow the swaying body of the sorrel horse in front of me. I must steel my mind to think of nothing but the horses' hooves moving up and down, up and down . . .

There was a half-an-hour stop at noon. John looped the reins over one arm and reached out a hand to help me down. My legs were stiff, almost numb, from the long hours of sitting.

We sat close to the back of the wagon, and I brought out the meager portion of food I dared allow us. As I divided it out, a pair of boots came to a stop amid the steady stream of footsteps passing us. Unconsciously my grip on Susan tightened, my eyes traveling up the ragged blue pants, belt pulled tight across lean hips, one arm bound in a sling.

Then I was scrambling to my feet. "James! Oh, James, is it you?" Even with the deep scar across one cheek and the unkempt beard and mustache, I could tell it was him. A light leaped into his blue eyes as he pulled me to him.

"Ellen!"

"James! What are you doing here?"

He pushed my question aside. "More important than that; what are *you* doing here? And the boys . . ." He reached a callused hand toward them. "My, you have grown. John . . . Peter . . ."

He touseled Andy's hair. "So have you. And Davie." He turned to Susan who was pressed against me, her eyes wide. "And who is this little lady?"

"This is our Susan. Susan, say hello to your Uncle James." She dug her face into my shoulder and would not turn her head even with my coaxing.

His eyes softened for a moment. "Let her go. Maybe later. May I join you?" He squatted by the younger boys. "I have only a few minutes. This is quite a train, isn't it? Over five hundred wagons, or I miss my guess."

My gaze lingered on the unconscious hardness of his face. "You have aged, James."

He shrugged.

"Tell me, *how* does it happen that you are with

Sheridan's army?"

A wary look came into his eyes, and he smiled dryly. "Don't know if that's worth using our precious time to tell. Some folks believe I'm a turn-coat." He turned away and spat into the grass.

Some folks . . . What did he mean? Was he a spy? The hardness in his eyes dared me to pursue it further. I coughed awkwardly.

"Have you heard lately from the folks?"

"Stopped in for a couple hours back in the summer."

"How is Father?"

"Bedfast."

"Bedfast?"

"Another stroke. Mother is a bitter, irrational woman. The farm is grown up in weeds, and the slaves all ran off except Tansy. She is still faithfully doing what she can." He shook his head as if to shake off the memory. "But what about you?"

I took a deep breath. "A lot has happened, James. God has been good to us. Although it's not been easy."

"David . . . ?"

"Taken soon after you left. We received a couple letters from him, but haven't heard anything since July a year ago."

"July?"

"The battle of Gettysburg."

"Oh." His eyes narrowed. Whatever he was thinking, he was not saying.

"We don't know if he's dead or alive, but it doesn't look good."

The word James spat under his breath made me wince. I hesitated, then went on. "We are heading to

379

Pennsylvania."

"So I gathered. To David's folks?"

"I suppose, or to friends."

"Friends?"

"We have become a part of a new 'family,' James. Mother turned us out—we had no other place to go."

His eyes took in my dress and covering. His lips pressed together.

"We stayed with Uncle Freds for several months until they couldn't support us anymore. Then we moved on. The kind people who took us in treated us as family. You couldn't help but love them."

"Some of those idle pacifists, I suppose!"

"Not so loud, James. No, not pacifists. The Mennonites hold no group of people above another. All they want is to love and respect all men and live in peace as best they can."

There was almost a smirk on his face. "Peace? Who knows what peace is anymore?" He stood up. "I must go. Until next time . . ."

He took quick steps around the wagon bed and was gone. We watched till he was swallowed up by the crowd.

I sighed. "Poor boy."

Davie's eyes were sober. "He's not the same."

I pulled them out of the way of a horse and wagon going past to a new position further up the line. "I'm afraid he's not the happy, carefree youth he was a year ago."

He had laughed at the thought of peace. How could I have explained how precious peace had become? The peace of God that reached deeper than grief and uncertainty and kept a person going when there was nothing else. I must have an answer for

380

him when we met again. We all had a lot to think about as the train began to move.

At twilight the dark clouds again moved in and a gentle rain began to fall. We shoved our belongings under the wagon bed with us and tried to sleep. But it was almost impossible.

Susan's crying was echoed from other wagons on either side. Mingled with children's sobbing came the occasional lowing of cattle and shouts of men in the darkness. And only inches above our heads was the steady drumming of rain that then dripped through cracks onto our damp covers.

The next day promised to be another hot one. I lifted my bonnet off my ears for a moment. The sun was already beating down. The rain which had tapered off an hour ago, left the air still and muggy. Peter had arranged the packs and blankets in the back of the wagon so that they could dry, and threw a piece of canvas across the corner post to make a little shade. There Andy and Davie entertained Susan with a corncob doll Rebecca had given her.

I reached for John's sunburned arm stretched across his knees grasping the reins. "I must grease your arms again tonight. Perhaps you should go back under the blanket. I can call Peter."

He shook his head. "Let him go. I'm just soft from being indoors all summer. Besides, that lady he's helping needs a driver worse than I need the shade."

"She talked to you?"

"A little." He swung his battered hat at a horsefly circling above the horse's rump. "Her man was sent home to die after the second battle of Bull Run. Her oldest girl died of typhoid last winter, and her baby is only a month old.

"The Yankees burnt the farm buildings two weeks back. All she has is in that big burlap sack."

"The poor woman!" My heart went out to the pale, haggard lady bent over her little bundle two wagons behind us. "I must talk to her when the wagons stop at noon."

"May I hold the baby?" I smiled up through the heat. My face, my dress, my whole body was sticky with sweat and dust. The tight feeling on my neck warned me that John would not be the only one needing greasing tonight.

The rounded shoulders beneath the faded linsey sagged with relief, and the careworn face brightened for a moment. "Oh, would you? I can't find any way to please him." She handed the whimpering bundle past the wagon's edge and reached to help the two crying children over the side. "I don't know how I'm going to manage. They are so thirsty, and we haven't much food." She stepped down beside me.

I swayed gently back and forth, crooning into the pinched feverish face.

"He's hungry, and I don't have much for him, poor least one. He's had nothing but hardship from the day he was born." She grabbed at the wagon wheel for support, and I reached to steady her.

"Come sit with us for a bit. We would be glad for your company. The boys can take care of your horses. But I didn't ask your name."

"Hilda . . . Hilda Wilson. And you . . . ?"

"Ellen Shull. My husband was reported missing

last year. We haven't heard from him since." I paused, trying to keep my composure.

Hilda nodded, her head bowed. She reached blindly for her baby and cuddled him close. Her brown hair held glints of copper in the sunlight.

I swallowed hard. "You must eat with us." I turned toward the others. "Davie, Andy, spread the blanket out here. We will share what we have."

The two older boys were standing at the horses' heads, gazing at something I couldn't see to the east. Peter pointed to a dip in the field a quarter mile ahead. "I think there is a pond over there. People are unhitching horses. If we hurry, I think we may have time to water both teams before they start up again."

They were already unhooking the traces. I lifted a bucket tied onto the tail gate. "Oh, I hope so. They need it so badly." I put an arm on Davie's shoulder. "Do you think you could fill this? We are almost out of drinking water."

The lead wagons had already started out till the boys got back and swung the horses into position. Davie wrinkled his nose as he held the full bucket out for me to see. "The pond is so low, there's hardly any water left. Everything is stomped up and muddy."

I made a face. "It's no wonder, with so many people and animals. But we must save it. Maybe some of the mud will sink to the bottom."

The afternoon was long and hot. I took Hilda and the three children in with us, leaving Peter to bring along the wagon behind us.

"They say Sheridan is only furnishing transportation to Martinsburg. What are your plans after that?"

Hilda looked down at the boys sleeping at her

feet, their tousled hair straggling over their dirty faces. "I guess I'm not sure. My husband was a teacher. We were planning to move to Ohio three summers ago. His brothers moved out in fifty-eight, but then he was asked to serve as principal of the Rockingham Male Academy in Harrisonburg."

"Why! That's where my brother was supposed to go."

The younger lady forced a smile. "I see. Well, it seemed too good an offer to turn down. We rented out our farm in Dayton until the school was forced to close because of the war.

"We had only moved back five weeks when he was mustered into service." She flinched. "They sent my Lewis home to cough his life away on that farm. His leg had been amputated. The stump oozed pus and swelled to twice its normal size."

The fresh horror of it showed in her dark eyes wincing in disbelief. She fumbled with the blanket on her lap.

"Toward the end, I sat up with him night after night. For two weeks I hardly had a bit of sleep. And when he died, it was in the middle of a terrible snow-storm. There was no one around to help me bury him. I rolled him up in the softest piece of cowhide we had left and pulled him out to the woodshed till the weather broke. A neighbor man brought a preacher out a week later, and they dug a grave in the only ground that wasn't frozen . . . under the manure pile beside the barn."

Lord help us, what all had she gone through! I thought. My eyes dropped from her bent face to the small hands, rough from unaccustomed labor, twisting a fold in her dress.

384

"Before spring, our Margaret died. It . . . it was hard to see her go. She had hair the color of amber, and was my constant cheerful helper. I miss her dreadfully.

"The boys and I managed to survive the winter drinking tea and eating biscuits made from cow feed. I had no midwife the night the little one was born. It hasn't been easy." She gave a long shuddering sigh.

I wet my lips. There must be a point when the heart can bear no more sadness. And yet, here was this young woman bravely telling her story.

"Have you learned to trust in God?"

She looked at me dully. "I don't know. I don't know. For the children's sake I keep on. Lewis and I, we prayed at times, but it was not a very personal thing. You feel God close to you? How could He be involved in my life? If He was God at all, He would step in and stop this misery."

I opened my mouth to speak, then closed it again. How could I say anything? Yes, we had suffered, but God had always given us someone to support and care for us. Her husband had died before her own eyes, gone forever. There was still a faint hope mine was still alive.

The silence was awkward. I fumbled through my mind for something meaningful to say. The slow plodding of the horses' hooves beat an unchanging rhythm in my brain. I brushed at the dust settling over the wagon seat. The hours dragged by.

A sudden burst of gunfire from behind made me cringe. I jerked around, feeling my heart stop cold. Soldiers! A long row of them, mounted, with rifles ready were pouring out of the trees at a gallop.

I had known Confederate cavalry were nipping at

Sheridan's heels. There had been occasional skirmishes ever since we left Harrisonburg. But nothing this close![2]

At the first whine of bullets, John yelled, yanking at the reins and bringing the horses to an instant trot. The wagons before and behind also jerked into action, their horses snorting wildly, their wheels jolting and rattling over ruts crisscrossing the road. I clung to the seat to keep from bouncing off.

Dust rose and enveloped us, making it impossible to see the group of Yankee cavalry until they were rushing past toward the rear with drawn guns, leaning forward in their saddles.

There was a whine and a whack as a bullet ripped through the piece of flapping canvas erected at the back of the wagon. "Down! Down! All of you, down!" I shrieked.

The blood pounded in my ears, and the rushing wind brought tears to my eyes, streaking them across my grimy face. I pulled screaming Susan against me, bending low over her body.

With his jaw clenched, John was crouching over the reins. His narrowed eyes were fixed straight ahead, his arms and body rigid.

The gunfire was steadily increasing. I shoved the heads of Hilda's boys under the wagon seat. Were we destined to be picked off by a stray bullet only two days from safety?

Hilda's face was ashen beside me. The horses had broken into clumsy gallops, the wagons all around us fanning out in a wide racing band across the field, all heading for the gap in the hills a quarter mile away.

I heard the shrill neigh of a horse close by and realized with a shock that the wagon floundering to a halt was Peter's. I just got a glimpse of him leaping over the side before the rest of the train went sweeping past, leaving it in the dust. "Oh, Peter!" I cried. My breath was coming in gasps.

Then as suddenly as it had begun, it was over. Bluffs on either side of us shut out the fighting. The horses began to slow, flecks of foam flinging back from their muzzles, their bodies lathered with sweat. Before us the wagon train was converging on a row of trees twisting off to the south.

But where was Peter? I half stood, facing the back of the wagon. With one hand gripping the seat and the other holding on to Susan, my blurred eyes scanned the throng of wagons for any sign of Peter. The sight of him coming up behind us in the rear of another wagon brought a feeling of relief so great it left me weak.

I sat down and hushed Susan's crying. Hilda's eyes were filled with terror. We clung to each other as John brought the wagon to a stop near the edge of the milling mass of horses and wagons.

When my head cleared, it came to me with a jolt where our conversation had left off. I turned to the shaken woman beside me. "If you had stayed in your own wagon, you would all have been left behind!"

Her wide-eyed stare told me she had thought the same thing. I hugged her close. "See, Hilda, my God is merciful. He does care."

"All luggage off please! Hand over the reins." The short, lanky man stepped up to our wagon, one hand drumming impatiently on the sideboard, the other fingering his drooping mustache.

I handed down the last bundle and took Susan into my arms. She wrapped her arms around my neck with a whimper. "Not let him get me, Mommy."

"No, sweethearts. Come, let's go this way."

We had reached our destination, Martinsburg. Sheridan had ordered the wagons to circle on a slope on the outskirts of town.

As far as eye could see there was noise and confusion. Some people were gathering up their children and belongings to walk into town, hoping to find something to eat. Others were heading straight for the railway station, planning to catch a train for as far as their money would take them. Many were aimlessly wandering about, uncertain what to do.

Hilda had already left. The day before, while helping her search for a wet nurse for her emaciated son, we had found a Dunkard family with their own wagon who were heading to Ohio. She would ride along, and maybe with relatives she could attempt to reassemble her life.

I was glad for her. The Hemp family had experienced a number of tragedies themselves. They would be able to point the young widow to the One she needed.

I pushed through the crowd to where the boys had found seats on the ledge of a large outcropping of boulders at the edge of the field. Several others had already found these rocks a good gathering point. I nodded briefly at the tall man with a gray beard, his hair long under a wide-brimmed black hat. He sat on his spurs, a saddle and saddle bags lying beside him. He held an empty pipe in his hand.

"Mother, can we eat now?" Davie sat on his bundles, his elbows on his knees. "I'm starved as a half-grown cougar."

The sober face of our neighbor cracked into a smile. "I'm hungry as two cougars." His teeth flashed as he stuck out a hand in my direction. "Arnie Banks, ma'am. Pleased to meet ya."

I withdrew my hand quickly from his grasp, nodded at his introduction but not volunteering any information of my own.

His eyes ran slowly over the boys and me. "You alone?"

I opened my mouth to answer, I didn't know what, but John came to my rescue. "We came with friends."

Mr. Banks raised his eyebrows but did not block our way as I pushed the boys ahead of me toward a group of strangers.

"Look, boys," I hissed, "we must stay together and keep an eye on each other at all times. John, your answer wasn't actually . . ."

"It was true, Mother. We had friends among this crowd." He glanced back at the tall stranger still looking in our direction. "What are we going to do now?"

"I'm not sure, son." I shifted Susan to a better position. "But I'm not staying here for the night. I don't feel safe. The town is too full of travelers. I think we will start north until we reach a place far enough away to camp. For right now, let's see if we can get something to eat."

The meager amount of Federal money saved up from before David had left home was already gone, but I had hidden inside my skirts a small bag of coins

James had given me the last time he had stopped by to talk.

"I don't have any paper money, but this will come in handy for you. It's worth more than dollar bills anyway."

I had hugged him then, and begged him to be careful. "What are your plans?"

He had looked at me queerly. "I don't suppose I can answer that, Sis. I'll take care of myself as best I can. I'm heading back to my own infantry soon. I've found out what I need to know. Hopefully we'll see each other again before this is over."

But I had seen him no more. Every day since then, I had been constantly on the lookout for him in the continual movement of men in and around the wagon train, but without success.

Now, as we started out walking, I couldn't keep back the tears wondering if I would ever hear how things turned out for my stubborn younger brother! He was too stubborn to admit he needed help and too proud to ask.

We were fortunate to find a farm four miles out of town where we could trade work for a night's lodging. The lady of the house begrudged our addition to her table, but I tried not to feel too guilty. The work the boys did for the farmer well paid for what we were fed. Though simple fare, it was still better than what we had had while traveling.

We started again at daybreak, following the road through open land, then into woods which cut through the hills. The abrupt slopes in this part of Virginia were sometimes so steep they blotted out the sun, casting a gloomy chill across our path. The brilliance of fall had faded to golds and browns, and the trees were rapidly growing bare.

A stone's throw away we could hear a mountain stream, its clear water icy cold, spilling over rocks, tumbling around leaf-cluttered curves and miniature waterfalls. In spite of the dull brown of leaf and soil, there was still the rich green of moss and fern. Tall gray boulders were scattered along its length.

"Wouldn't Rebecca love this place." Peter readjusted his backpack and stopped to follow with his eyes the tall poplars thrusting their many branches into the scope of blue overhead.

I set Susan down, pulling the blanket closer around her neck as we all stopped to catch our breath. "I just know what she would say, 'Sit down! Sit down and soak in this part of God's garden. Of what worth is this bit of beauty unless one enjoys it?' "

"I wish we *could* stop."

The weariness in Andy's eyes cut like a knife. The poor child had not properly rested for so long. Yet, we really had no choice. The Indian summer days were rapidly growing shorter and could not last much longer. We needed to move along as swiftly as we sensibly could.

I smiled encouragingly. "If we make good time, Andy, we should come to the Potomac sometime today."

Davie followed a fish hawk's circling flight until it vanished among the treetops, then frowned. "Jumping junipers! If we'd have wings like that we'd

391

have it made. How are we going to get across?"

"Davie! I will not have you using unnecessary words."

He looked at me in disbelief, then stammered, "Sorry." He grinned sheepishly. "But I heard a heap worse words last week."

"I'm sure you did. But we will not degrade ourselves to the level of every soldier, teamster, and roughneck we hear around us. We were in their company because we had to be, and we were grateful for it. But I must say, it's good to have some quiet once again."

I thought of James. These months of association—what effect would they have on him? The change that had already taken place had been startling.

I reached for Susan. "Come, Susie girl. We must get moving again. I guess we'll figure out how to cross the river when we get there. I don't know how wide it is at this point. Maybe someone will come along. We aren't the only ones traveling today."

"Here, Mother, let me take a turn." John gave his sister a swing onto his shoulders, and we walked on for some time in silence.

We had just gotten a glimpse of the distant shimmer of moving water when I heard something overtaking us.

"Whatever could that be?" John shaded his eyes in its direction. "A horse and wagon, I believe."

Peter grinned. "Someone needs to grease his wheels. Sounds worse than a mad woman."

Shortly, a weathered surrey pulled up alongside. With a shock I found myself looking at the same curious eyes and gray beard I had seen the evening before.

The man pulled the wagon to a shrieking halt. "So, we meet again." He grinned and raised his eyebrows. "You told me you were with friends. No longer? Well, how providential that I came along just now."

He shoved his black hat back on his forehead. "The crossing ahead is pretty rough if I remember right. You'll need a ride across."

I felt Susan's arms tighten around my neck, and my heart was beating erratically. "Sir, I thank you for your offer, but we'd rather go on at our own pace."

He laughed dryly. "Won't be much of any pace unless you can get across the Potomac. Don't be a'feared of Arnie Banks. I've got kin just five miles the other side. I'd be a'pleasured to take you all over."

I looked helplessly at John. He shrugged his shoulders. This fellow *seemed* harmless enough. A little too friendly perhaps, but . . .

We ended up reluctantly climbing in. John took the front seat, pulling Andy beside him, and the rest of us squeezed onto the seat behind.

"We are obliged to you for your kindness, sir." I forced a smile. "I really didn't know how we would manage."

"No need to mention it, ma'am. Glad to be of service to someone. Traded my belongings back in Martinsburg for this contraption. Not many miles left on it, but it will do."

Within half an hour we began the descent to the

river. The horse slowed to a walk, picking its way carefully down the steep slope, bracing itself against the surrey's weight.

As we crossed a sandy wash, the rushing sound of water just ahead made it hard to hear anything else. Along the opposite bank the trees hung over the edges, screening out most of the slanting rays of evening sun.

Our driver clucked to the horse and shook the reins. The wheels of the surrey sucked at the mud along the river's edge, then gave a lurch and water began to splash against the spokes. I held one arm around Susan and the other across Davie's shoulders.

"Not long before cold settles in to stay. No lady should be out traveling this time of year, walking like you are." He spoke over his shoulder. "You come north with Sheridan's army out of the Valley?"

I kept my eyes on the water climbing the wooden wheels. I hope he showed the same concern for his driving as he did for his passengers. "Yes, sir."

"Don't 'sir' me. Just call me by my name. Run out of your home by the Yankees, I reckon? What are you planning to do now?"

I hesitated before answering. "We're going to live with relatives."

He nodded. "Lots'a folks have to do that these days. Fact is, I'm doing that myself. A man has no business trying to live by himself. Ain't meant to be. But what did you say your name was?"

I pinched my mouth together. I hadn't said.

His nosiness made me feel stubborn. He was looking back, waiting for an answer, so I said carefully, "My father is Mr. Bernard Palmer of Staunton."

394

He frowned as if trying to place what I had told him. He began to say more when the current caught the surrey. It swayed, shuddered, and was almost lifted off balance. The gray-haired man sprang to his feet, gripping the reins, his eyes sharply scanning the water ahead.

Suddenly the surrey was tipping violently, and water was slapping at the floorboards. The horse floundered and fought for firmer footing. I grabbed for Peter's arm. Mr. Banks was leaning forward over the dashboard, shouting over the rush of water. I hid Susan's head to my shoulder, my head down against hers. Fear knotted my stomach, and I couldn't bring myself to watch.

After a terrifying moment, the front wheels struck and grated against the bottom, and the horse scrambled out of the current and onto the far bank. Water streamed from its back and legs.

Our driver pulled the surrey to a stop, lifted off his hat, and wiped his brow. "That's the worst I've seen it yet." He looked apologetically at John and whistled. "Thought we might have a mite of trouble there for a bit. But I reckon we made it. I clean forgot about that drop-off hole halfway across."

He turned to face me, embarrassed. "Land sakes, lady; I didn't mean to give you such a scare. I'll just take you on to where I'm heading for the night. Mrs. Blair would take you in, I know she would. Don't want to leave you and your young'uns here in the dark."

I fumbled for an answer, but he was already speaking again. "My children have long left home, but I had a wife till two years ago. I've been plenty lonesome since then. You lost your husband?"

I felt crimson creep up my neck and over my face. Peter's eyes met mine, his expression a mixture of exasperation and amusement.

"I . . . I have a husband in the war. It's been a while since we've heard from him, but we're hoping to get word of him soon."

The man's eyes were still on my face, and I dared not look up.

"Well, I just thought, it be a shame that two lonely people can't help each other. Reckon you could tell me where you're going, and your name and all. You've got a nice family. Too nice to raise without a man about."

I felt hot all over, then cold. I was glad for Peter's reassuring squeeze on my elbow.

❧ Chapter XIX ❧

J ust as Mr. Banks had said, we were soon nearing a small cluster of houses, their windows spilling lamplight into the growing twilight. He pulled up in front of a low, dark building and began helping us unload. "Now, if this ain't suiten' you, just say so, and I'll take you on to my kinfolk. They'll find a place for you, I'm sure."

I was greatly relieved when a tall thin woman with stooped shoulders finally heard our knocking and invited us in. In exchange for helping with cooking and the endless job of washing dishes, the postman's wife accommodatingly unlocked the spare room in the back of their tavern and eating hall. She hustled off to bring fresh linens for the two beds. The room was plain, but it was clean and tidy.

Although not my preference, staying here was much better than going further with Mr. Banks. I was very thankful for the tavern keepers' kindness.

Mr. Banks set off to go the last half-mile to his destination, his wheels' shrill monotone gradually fading into the darkness. "Land sakes! That's enough to make a deaf person weep." Mrs. Blair wiped her hands on her apron and reached to help carry the last of our luggage inside. "You can stay as long as you care to. Just get yourselves situated, then come out front again, and I'll feed you. I know I can round up something. I'll bet you haven't eaten well for who knows how long."

The second day I looked up from wiping tables to see a cart stop next to the row of hitching posts out front. A middle-aged Dunkard couple with two robust children were leaning up against the cart's side. Curious, I slipped to the door. Susan tagged along, hanging onto my skirts.

"Good afternoon." The husband stepped up to the group of men who had just finished eating and were watering their mounts at the watering trough. The loud talking stopped, and the men turned.

"Do any of you know of a horse for sale around these parts?"

Several men looked at each other, but no one answered.

The broad-shouldered man cleared his throat. "My family and I are heading for the Cumberland

Valley to live, and had the misfortune to lose our horse to some army officers several days ago." He motioned towards his wife and children. "As you see, we've made it a ways just by ourselves, but I don't care to be a beast of burden for the rest of the trip." He grinned, passing one hand over his face.

A chuckle ran through the group. One of the men set down the water bucket and stepped forward. "You got means to pay for it?"

"Not much money, but we have several things that may be worth bargaining over." He held out his hand. "Hiram Shaver, sir. Glad to meet you. If there's nothing available, we'll just push on to the next settlement."

"Alfred Thomas, my name." The farmer scratched his head. "I don't know of any right here. Do you, fellows?" He rubbed his neck thoughtfully. "Come to think of it though, old Elmer McConnell might sell his Mabel. She's 'bout too old to do much farmin' anymore, but I suppose she could pull that." He lifted his thumb toward the cart. "That is, if you're not in any big hurry. Elmer's no further out of town than a hen can spit."

"Thank you. Thank you. We'll check into this. Appreciate your help. Now I'll just step inside to see if we can get a bite to eat."

My heart skipped a beat. Would there be a chance . . . ? I moved back out of the doorway. As he came inside, I summoned the courage to speak.

"Sir, I heard what you said, and . . ."

He stopped in mid-stride, surprised. "Who are you? Do you live here?"

"Oh, no, sir. We were with the Mennonites close to Piedmont in the Valley. I and my children came north with Sheridan's army."

"Ah, yes, we were along too, until we got left behind. But where are you going?"

"I fear my husband is dead, we have not heard from him for over a year. We are going to my father-in-law's place at the edge of the Alleghenies. Would it be at all possible for us to travel with you until we turn west?"

He slid his hand across the table top. "I'll ask my wife. But I'm sure she will say it's okay."

"My sons will be glad to help pull your cart."

"We'll see about that later. But right now we need food. Would you be able to help us?"

While our new friends ate, I rounded up the boys, gathered up our luggage and thanked Mrs. Blair for caring for us. Within an hour we were on our way. I took one last glance behind, afraid I would yet see a faded surrey coming into sight, with a hunched figure in the driver's seat. But there was no sign of our benevolent driver, poor fellow. I hoped he would find someone to ease his loneliness.

After stopping several places to ask about a horse without success, Mr. Shaver set a brisk pace for us to follow. We crossed into Pennsylvania the next morning, and the family was delighted when Hiram successfully bartered for a homely old cow. We named her Hipbones on the spot.

The man who sold her seemed equally pleased with the trade. "She's nary any good to me. No calf she has given for so long." He stood in the barn door, rubbing his hands together for as long as we could see.

We made slow but steady progress. Several days later we topped a ridge and started down a long hill bordered by a deep ravine. At the bottom was a wooden bridge just clearing the wide waters of a shallow creek.

Although the bridge was new, something about this place prodded my memory. I turned to the others, "Is this Licking Creek? If it is, the road splits just a couple miles from here."

Mr. Shaver's eyebrows lifted in surprise, and he leaned harder against the cart's wooden brake, trying to keep it from bumping into the cow's hind legs. "You've been this way before?"

"Yes, if I'm not confused. It was years ago, right after we were married. I remember crossing Licking Creek. My husband told me it got its name from the salt lick found just south of the roadbed."

The scene came clearly to my mind. The stage-coach had come to the creek at twilight. We had been the only passengers for the last three hours, traveling at a slow and endless pace. The snow crunched and squeaked under the horses' hooves. In spite of the constant jostling I couldn't keep my eyes from drooping.

Then David had nudged me. "Ellen, Ellen . . ."

I jumped.

"Were you asleep?" His hand was warm on mine. "I'm sorry, but look over there."

My eyes followed to where he pointed. There, only ten yards up the creek's edge stood a doe, head lifted, water still dripping from her nostrils. Behind her in the shadows of a giant hemlock, stood the buck, his body braced for flight. In an instant they were gone. I caught only a glimpse of their white tails above the snow before they were out of sight, but I never forgot the serenity of that scene.

I had been anything but serene, knowing we were nearing David's homeplace and never having met his folks. The mixed feelings of fear and excitement were as forceful in me now as they had been then. I swallowed hard.

Mrs. Shaver's voice brought me back to the present. "What town did you say you are heading for?"

"Buffalo Mills."

She put her arm through mine. "You sure you don't want to keep on with us? From what you've said, you're not sure you will be well received."

I looked up to where the boys were skipping ahead with the Shaver children. They had become good friends in these few short days together.

Then, thrusting aside the temptation, I shook my head. "It is so kind of you to offer. We are indebted to you so much already. No, we must go to my husband's place. There may still be a chance we would receive news from him. I'm sure you understand."

She gave me a quick squeeze. "Of course. We wouldn't expect anything else of you."

All too soon the parting of ways came for us and our new friends. "Thank you for your kindness. We will never forget it." I lifted my hand in farewell.

"And you. We'll be praying you get to your destination safely."

I smiled up at John and Peter standing tall beside me. "I'm sure we will."

We stood waving until the cart had at last rambled over the crest of the next hill.

"Well, boys," I spoke more briskly than I felt, "we must go on. It's only twelve more miles."

This had to be the place. There could be no mistaking the large orchard behind the house, the picket fence around the garden plot, the hip-roof barn built into the hillside.

I felt a sudden weakness. As glad as I was to finally see our journey's end, I feared, even dreaded, this meeting. We looked far from presentable: wrinkled, dirty clothes; straggly hair; and begrimed faces. Would David's folks understand?

But surely, surely they wouldn't turn us away. Not their own son's family. I smiled for reassurance and wiped Susan's tear-streaked face. She had been sobbing with weariness for the last half mile.

And then, inside the picket fence, I saw her. Hoe in hand, she stood with her back toward us. The garden was bare except for corn stubble and withered pumpkin vines.

Hearing our footsteps, the frail woman turned from the heaping bucket of freshly dug carrots at her feet. Her eyes grew wide at seeing us, a group of strangers turning in the driveway. She brushed her dirty hands onto her apron as she stepped toward the gate.

Then her mouth fell open, a look of confusion crossing her face. "Ellen! It has to be David's Ellen!" She hobbled toward us, and I felt the shock of seeing the whitened hair, the thin, hollow-cheeked face, the work-worn hands. But her eyes . . . her gray eyes were identical to David's. And the erect way she held herself as she walked, it was David all over.

I handed Susan to John and hurried to meet her, taking her outstretched hands in mine.

"It *is* Ellen! But how? How did you come?"

I moistened my lips carefully. "The Federal army provided transportation north to the border. And we walked the rest of the way."

"Walked?" She brushed her hand across her face as if unable to believe her eyes. "Your boys," she sobbed. "I see David as a youth again." She held out a trembling hand to greet each one. "You brought your children, your fine young men . . ." Then she stepped back and peered into our faces. "But why are you alone? Where is David?"

I shook my head. "We don't know. I had hoped . . ."

"Don't know? Was he killed?" His mother clutched at her throat.

"No . . . that is . . . we hope not. He was wounded at Gettysburg over a year ago. We have learned nothing more."

Susannah's shoulders sagged and her face puckered up. "Clarence gone; Edward gone; Thomas, . . . and now David . . ." She turned her face away.

"Clarence?"

"He died of a heart attack back in the summer. I've been alone ever since." She looked off past the orchard toward the barn. "Found him in the loft. He had been putting up hay all day." She bowed her head. "David . . . oh, David . . ."

I held her close, fighting back my own tears.

Then she shook herself. "But here I stand holding you here. My son isn't here, but his family is! Please come inside."

Once in the house, she seated us in the kitchen

404

and bustled about stirring up the fire and getting food on the table. "It won't be a fancy meal, but there's plenty of what we have. I'll just fry up some side meat and stick a passel of potatoes in the coals to bake. We've got plenty of butter and . . . ," she clasped her hands together, "I'll make a batch of biscuits. I've still got a bit of wild strawberry preserves in the pantry.

"No, don't you get up. You look worn out. All of you do. Just stay right where you are and tell me all you know. We've heard so little from elsewhere since the war broke out, Clarence and I. And now it's lonelier than ever, being by myself."

It was a meal to remember. When I reprimanded the younger boys for dishing out such generous portions from the platters of food, Susannah waved me aside. "Let them be. It does me good to see them eat so. You must have suffered dreadfully with all you've gone through." She dabbed at her eyes with her apron.

"Mommy, pretty!" Susan's eyes lighted upon the crystal dish of red preserves in the middle of the table. "What?"

There was nothing in her short memory of the sparkling treat before her. I pulled the dish closer, giving her a kiss on the forehead. "It's jelly, sweetheart. Something to go on your biscuit. Here . . ." I handed her one.

Her mouth widened with delight, her eyes shining. Not waiting to finish swallowing, she giggled. "Not hot!" I realized she remembered the glowing coal she had burned her finger on several nights before.

Before Grandma Shull brought out the stewed

pumpkin dessert, Susan had gone to sleep, her head leaning onto the table, the last bite of biscuit in her hand.

As soon as the dishes were done, David's mother showed the boys upstairs. "I know you are tired as can be. Here's a kettle of hot water. Pour it into the basin in the corner, and you can wash up if you care to. Take the larger room." She handed the boys each a load of bedding. "We'll let your mother have the smaller one. One of you, maybe two, will have to sleep on the floor."

I laid Susan down in a corner nest and followed them up the steps. After Susannah had gone back down, John and Peter dropped onto the floor mats. "Isn't this glorious." I sank down on the bed built into the corner. "She is tremendously kind."

"Just think, a safe place to be; no war to be afraid of . . ." Davie laid back against the pillow and sighed.

"And food to eat." Andy rubbed his stomach. "I never was so full before."

"Me too." Davie smiled up at me. "Now all we need is Papa."

I hugged him fiercely. "Let's have a special prayer for Papa tonight."

At the bottom of the stairs, I pushed open the door. Across the room sat David's mother holding Susan's drowsy little form close with her twisted hands.

"Mother Shull! You . . . I'm sorry. Let me take her. Something must have awakened her."

Susannah's thin cheeks creased in a smile. "You just let me hold her. It doesn't hurt these fingers at all. Since Clarence passed away, and the boys have gone, I've been hankering for a hand to hold, yes, I have. Sit down and tell me the whole story. The evenings get awful lonely here."

I first told of the conflict with my parents over our marriage, the happiness David and I had found together, then of his experience in the army, his wounding and recovery, and our decision to change churches.

Susannah rocked quietly, not saying a word, but listening intently. She didn't bother wiping the tears glistening on her cheeks. Only one part I softened, the stark horror of David's encounter with Edward on the battlefield. I said only that they met and were wounded in the same awful battle. The rest would be David's to tell, if he cared to. Only a son should bear that kind of message to his mother.

"The Valley is a place of destruction. We had to leave. I thought it would be best to come here, at least for now."

The crippled hands dug for a handkerchief from the folds of her skirt. "You may make this your home for as long as you wish. As far as your beliefs, I don't have any bones to pick with anyone. Clarence and I always said we wouldn't interfere in our children's decisions. I don't know too much about this group of people, though I've heard the name."

She blew her nose. "We didn't like the war either, though the boys felt duty-bound to serve. Clarence didn't feel we should stand in their way." She moaned. "But all the suffering it brings."

She swallowed hard and her voice dropped.

"Edward was the youngest, yet he was the first to go. It 'bout killed Clarence and me when we got word. Then it was Thomas, and then Clarence himself. Only the two oldest left, Wilferd and Allen. And David . . . maybe David.

"Folks told us how proud we should be, to give five sons to fight for our country, and I don't want to begrudge the giving, it's just that . . ." She dropped her head and the firelight played over her thin hair. "You have a mother's heart, *you* know . . ."

Two months went by. Christmas was almost upon us when something happened that erupted all the emotion I had held under control for so long. My feet felt strangely light climbing the narrow staircase to the room where Susan lay sleeping, yet the hand I cupped around the flickering candle flame was trembling. It was late, but there was a letter I must write. I wouldn't be able to sleep until I did.

Just this morning the boys and I had walked into the village to barter some butter and eggs. At the corner of an alleyway, a farm wagon lay tipped on its side, the lathered horse still pitching and kicking at the traces. Six sacks, now trampled and dirty, had been thrown out. One bag burst and cornmeal lay scattered in the gutter and up across the wooden sidewalk.

A short rawboned man, with a full red-blond beard extending over his mackinaw, stalked just out of reach of the horse's hooves, shouting and raining lashes on its head.

John was in the street before I could say a word. Dodging the flashing whip, he grabbed for the horse's bridle. I gasped as the horse reared almost lifting him off his feet. Then he was stroking the horse's sweaty neck, talking softly.

The man's mouth sagged open, and his hands dropped in surprise. "What are you doin' with my horse? Get back I say!"

John, ignoring the angry words, kept up a constant murmur, holding tightly to the bridle. He began wiping the horse's neck and head with his handkerchief.

The owner took a step closer. "I say, what do you think you're doing? Get out 'fore I send you hopping with this whip o' mine." He let it pop dangerously close to John's ear. The horse snorted and jerked his head, wrenching John's arm sideways.

John refused to look his way until he had quieted the horse again, then turned to the fuming man and let go of the bridle. "My brother and I will be glad to load up your wagon again." His voice was clipped.

"Why, I . . . why you, ah, . . . I . . ." His sputtering voice trailed away.

The boys had already righted the wagon and were scooping up meal and tying bags shut, lifting them carefully into the wagon bed. Thrown out of sorts by their swiftness, he could only grab the harness and hang on, keeping the horse's nervous stamping from breaking into a walk.

When they were done, he cleared his throat, uncertain how to respond. The smile looked pasted on. "Much obliged to ya. Didn't mean no harm." He lifted his hand in a clumsy salute. Then clamping his hat on his head, he clambered onto the wagon seat and started the horse off at a trot. The crowd which had slowed to pick their way around the edge of the confusion began to clear away. I sighed.

"Oh, John! I was frightened for you."

"Ah, it was nothing." He grinned.

"Yahoo!" Someone hailed us from across the street. A tall dark-bearded man with coattails flapping made a quick dash in front of a buggy and came to a panting halt in front of us.

He bowed courteously and held out his hand. "Mr. Stevenson, ma'am. I couldn't help seeing your son's courage. I want to personally thank you for what you did." His brown eyes smiled at John, and his fingers tugged at his beard.

"Glad to be of help, sir."

"Yes, of course. Now, perhaps I can explain why Mr. Dunberry was out of sorts this morning. He stopped at my office an hour ago . . ." He motioned to a small clapboard building squeezed between two stores on the opposite side of the street. ". . . to see if I had made any progress on the exchange of his youngest son. In the war, you understand."

The creases above his eyes deepened. "I had the unpleasant duty of informing him his son had died in a southern prison, Andersonville." He shook his head. "He was to be released next week."

I stood riveted on the spot, my mind racing. "Oh, sir . . ."

"Ma'am, are you all right?" Mr. Stevenson stepped closer. "You look pale."

I gasped. "Yes . . . But, sir, I . . . Perhaps you would be able to help me."

He bowed slightly. "By all means."

I swallowed hard. "My husband was with the

Confederate army. He was reported missing after the Battle of Gettysburg. I haven't heard from him since. Oh, sir, would you . . ." I could feel John's hand on my elbow. "Do you suppose you could find word of him?"

"Why most certainly. I should be able to help you find some clue to his whereabouts. No word since Gettysburg, you say?" He frowned. "Why, that's a year and a half ago. That's too long to be left in the dark. Would you have a moment?" He nodded toward his office, and I found myself following him across the street.

One small window looked out of the gray weathered building we were approaching. The panes were dusty from passing traffic. As Mr. Stevenson reached for the doorknob, I noticed the sagging window shade, faded to a nondescript beige, had a rip along its side as if some child had gotten too close with a pair of shears.

Inside, the back wall was filled with shelves stacked high with papers and books, several ledgers, and a portfolio of maps curled by much use. A large desk with a kerosene lamp was squeezed into the left side of the room. A row of high-back chairs lined the other.

"Have a seat, Mrs . . . ?"

"Shull." I took off my gloves and sank into the chair nearest the door.

"You have four fine sons, Mrs. Shull. No wonder you are most anxious to hear from your husband. This is all your family?"

"A baby daughter—at my mother-in-law's. My husband hasn't even seen her."

"You haven't tried contacting him before?"

I nodded slightly. "Once, sir. But I must explain. We moved north along with Sheridan's wagon train a couple months ago. We are originally from Staunton.

"I sent a letter to his regiment headquarters last year, but other than missing-in-action, there has been no further word. I'm not sure if . . ."

The clerk shot a look my way I could not decipher. He shuffled through the papers on his desk and pulled out a form, writing rapidly across the top of the page.

"First, I'll need some information, and then we'll see what we can do. I'm going to give you two addresses to try, Fort McHenry and Point Lookout. Both of them are in Maryland. It is most likely that if he lived, he would be in one of these two places."

He pursed his lips, watching me, as he continued, "Things are really tightening up for the South. You've heard about Lincoln's reelection? Yes? Well, I just found out by telegraph that General Sherman has left Atlanta in flames and is marching south with sixty thousand men.

"Lee's been cornered in Petersburg for almost six months. There's going to be a lot of bloodshed before this thing is all over." His lips tightened. "Let us pray Providence will bring it to a close soon."

I made no reply, and the subject was dropped. After the interview was over, he handed the papers across the desk and rose to his feet. "I don't want to embarrass you, ma'am, but you've made me awful curious about something."

My eyes faltered under his direct look. "I'll . . . I'll try to answer any question you have, sir."

Abruptly he sat back down and crossed his legs in front of him. "You are a Quaker, perhaps?"

"Mennonite."

"I see." He was still puzzled.

"Actually, sir, I grew up with the Episcopalian church. My husband's folks are Lutheran. We only joined the Mennonites a couple years ago."

His eyebrows bunched together. I could hear the nervous swinging of one of the boys' legs against his chair rung. My fingers clasped tightly the papers in my lap.

Mr. Stevenson cleared his throat. "I've had a little contact with Mennonites, not much. I understand they, along with the Quakers, are opposed to war. Not that I agree with them, quite the contrary. But I couldn't help wondering how your husband . . ." He was searching for the best way to finish his sentence.

I smiled cautiously. "I'll try to explain, sir. My husband joined the army while we lived at Staunton. Not because he wanted to, but because he had no other choice. No one wants to fight against his own family, sir.

"He was badly wounded in the Battle of Port Republic, that was in May of sixty-two." I glanced at John for confirmation. "And during his recovery, we decided to join a group that held the same convictions we had come to. Shortly after this, he was forced back into the army. We stayed with a Mennonite family till coming north last October.

"Most Southerners protest Northern interference in their affairs by fighting back, by wounding and mutilating, by trying to destroy the very thing this country desperately needs—her men.

"I do not know what this past year has held for my husband, if he is even still alive. But I know one thing, sir, he has committed himself to a higher way.

He protests hatred by showing love; he protests war by aiding the wounded; he protests destruction by helping rebuild."

I folded and refolded the gloves in my lap. "People look on and misinterpret his stand for cowardice, an escape route for fools. But I feel you can see it otherwise. Surely you can, sir."

I leaned forward. "And the peace, the inner assurance that we made the right decision, has never left me." I took a deep breath. "It's a wonderful thing to be at peace in your own soul, Mr. Stevenson."

His face was immobile, and I hesitated before going on. "I don't know if you can understand, sir. It's something you have to experience." I sat back self-consciously.

He blinked, his mouth twitching. When he abruptly rose to his feet, I herded the boys to the door, feeling sure I had offended him.

But his parting words were courteous. "Little lady, anything that gives you that kind of confidence is bound to be worth staking your life on."

With the form letter and addressed envelope in hand, I leaned over the makeshift table. The pen in my hand insisted on trembling. The chill of the damp quarters was not the reason, I knew.

I bent closer.

Dear Sir:

This is to inquire into the whereabouts of one David Shull, a private in Company

414

F of the 52nd Infantry originating from Staunton, Virginia.

He has been reported missing since July of 1863 when his regiment took part in the Battle of Gettysburg.

Should you have any record of him, please notify his family at the address enclosed.

> Respectfully,
> His wife, Mrs. Ellen Shull

After making a second copy, I addressed the envelope to Fort McHenry and another to Point Lookout, and sealed them carefully. I would send them with the next person going into town.

The first answer came six weeks later. It had no information. The next came near the end of February.

Dear Madam,

I apologize for the delay in answering your letter. After inquiring about your husband, I can only inform you he came here from the Letterman Hospital at Gettysburg in the fall of '63, and is on record as prisoner here for only three months. He was then moved to De Camp Hospital; David's Hospital, New York. Please use this address to inquire further.

> Sincerely,
> Thomas A. Conkley, Prison Warden
> Fort McHenry Prison
> Fort Henry, Maryland

"Can you understand it?"

I looked up at Susannah with dismay. "I . . . I don't know. It's not what I expected. He was alive . . . at least till last fall, but he's been sent elsewhere. Here, you read it."

David's mother read carefully aloud.

At last John spoke. "New York! That's several days journey north. If they planned to exchange him, they wouldn't have sent him that far away."

Susannah pressed her knuckles lightly against her clenched teeth, whimpering a little as she got to her feet. "Surely they know more about my son. If only Clarence were here. He could go up there and find him. But he's finished his work forever, may he rest in peace . . ."

Peter scanned the paper grimly. "Why don't you write to the New York address too, the Letterman Hospital. Ask for more information."

Andy's dark, solemn eyes sought mine. "At least Papa wasn't killed."

Susan patted my cheek with a chubby hand. "Papa? I not know Papa." She shook her head.

I squeezed her hand, breathing deeply. "I'll write to every address again today. And hopefully someday you will, Susie girl." I buried my face in her dark hair.

I remembered the assurance I had felt of David's well-being the summer before. It seemed like a long time ago, almost too far back to remember. At the time, it had been the only thing I had to cling to, but I knew now God doesn't always give His people assurance about the future. Sometimes He let them step into it with only a thread of hope . . . and the assurance of His presence.

416

❧ Chapter XX ❧

March came with a vengeance upon the broad Cumberland Valley and surrounding mountains. Snow piled upon snow. The boys watched in wonder as bushes, springhouse, and even fence posts disappeared, covered by the heavy expanse of whiteness.

How grateful I was for the plentiful supply of food laid aside. It would see us through the remainder of the winter.

"I filled my days with work," Susannah said, "planting, picking, and putting away. I did it to keep from going stark, raving crazy, here all by myself. Why I was doing it, I didn't know. I couldn't use it all myself. Now I understand." Susannah shook her head in wonder. We were gathered around the large cast-iron stove, listening to the latest storm pelting icy flakes against the walls.

I smiled, taking Susan in my lap and settling myself into the rocker nearest the stove. "That reminds me of Tansy's work song—

> Watch de sun, see how she run,
> Neber let her ketch yo
> With yer wurk undun . . .[1]

Susan rubbed her head against my arm, whimpering, and I fitted her up against my body. She had been fighting earache and its misery for the last two days.

John brought a steaming wet towel that I laid over her ear. "This will make it better. That's right, lay back. Let's see if Grandma would have a story to tell us."

The boys looked up expectantly. Susannah smiled.

"I was thinking, matter-of-fact, of something that happened to me as a child right after a hard snow just as we are having now." She dropped her knitting into her lap. "Let's see, I couldn't have been more than four, because it was before my baby brother died." She pursed her lips thoughtfully. "That would make it in eighteen-hundred-four or five. Back in those days there were a lot more wild animals about than there are now. Occasionally we would see a bobcat or mountain lion. Sometimes even a wolf.

"One afternoon my brothers and I were playing fox and goose, a tag game, in the snow. We heard dogs barking furiously, bounding across the snow in the pasture, chasing something before them. The snow was deep enough that their backs disappeared each time they leaped.

"We stopped our game to watch, and suddenly a

great, shaggy wolf leaped over the fence almost into our midst. We all screamed and fled for the house, except me. I was so frightened, I fainted.[2]

"They say Mommy was running from the kitchen almost before I fell to the snow. She thought sure the wolf had bitten me, but I was all right.

"My oldest brother tracked it to a ravine back of our place, where he found it backed into a small cave. My brother got up close enough to shoot it between the eyes."

Peter whistled. "Did he skin it?"

"Yes, and for quite a few weeks that hide was fastened to the corncrib. I was too scared to go close to it."

"What happened to it?"

David's mother massaged her stiff fingers. "He used it for a rug beside his bed till it got to losing too much hair." Her eyes twinkled. "I remember how glad I was when my mother said it had to go. I stayed by the trash pile, watching it go up in smoke and waited till it was all burned down to ashes. I wanted to be sure it could never torment me again."

John chuckled.

Susan began crying again, and I stopped rocking to fit the wet pack closer around the side of her face. "Poor little girlie. I must give you another dose of mullen salve." I stroked her flushed face, brushing the ringlets of hair off her forehead.

Her eyes began to droop. "Hold me, Mommy."

"Sing for her, Mommy. Like you did that time I burned my hand and couldn't go to sleep."

"You remember *that* long ago, Davie?"

He nodded, smiling. "I picked up a horseshoe Daddy was working on, didn't I?" His smile was triumphant. "I remember it slipped off the bench, and I grabbed for it before Daddy could holler at me."

Peter turned over on his side, propping his head up in one hand. "I nearly forgot about that. I was standing right there when it happened. You were squalling something terrible. Daddy swooped you up and ducked you in the watering trough, hand and all. He sent me tearing to the house for Mother. You were squealing worse than a newborn pig." He grinned, ducking Davie's punch.

Andy flipped his book aside and pounced on Peter from behind. "I got him, Davie. Now grab him!"

There was a wild scramble on the rug and flailing feet.

"Boys! Save your rowdiness till later. How can I . . ."

But Susan's eyes had already opened, and her mouth formed a pout. "Pe-dah, don't be naw-nee!"

Peter rolled over onto his knees and bowed low, taking her foot in his hand and bringing it to his lips. "I beg your pardon, my lady. Peter be a good boy now."

Her white teeth showed as she smiled and gave her foot a kick. "Mommy, sing now." She squeezed her eyes tight shut again.

I breathed deeply, thinking. A haunting minor tune began to tug at my mind, and I began humming, searching for the words. "Here's one I sang as a child . . ."

> Quiet is the night, soft is the breeze,
> Dim is the moon over the trees,
> Sleep, children, sleep; be not alarmed,
> Angels on guard shall keep you unharmed.[3]

There was no sound except the squeak of the rocking chair and the occasional pop of the hickory fire. The wind was dying to an occasional moan at the eaves.

Susan's earache was much improved when the snow finally ended. The clear day set the boys to feverishly scraping and re-scraping paths between house and outbuildings, digging hay from the stacks along the west barn wall, and replenishing the large pile of wood in the cramped shed outside the back door.

Andy and Peter soon had a fire built underneath the large vat filled with ice cold water to heat for washing clothes. Even Susan was bundled up and set in the woodshed's sheltered doorway to watch while Susannah and I bent over the steaming tub, our hands red and sudsy from scrubbing.

It was Davie who first saw Mr. Wagner turn his horse into our lane. The retired harness maker never forced his horse faster than a walk, and I, with an inward smile, thought it good he didn't. The short-legged mare, humorously named Crossfire, was already sway-backed. With Mr. Wagner's added weight, which was considerable, it was a wonder the animal made any progress at all.

Harness Jake stopped by often to buy eggs for himself and his ailing wife. He usually ended up taking as many pats of butter as Susannah could spare.

"So, ye wanna know why she got sech a name?"

he had begun the first time we met. He settled back with satisfaction in a chair and popped a stick of licorice into Andy's gaping mouth, snorting with amusement at Andy's gulp of surprise. "Wael, years back I got into a tad of trouble, fighting trouble. Nothun' serious, ya know. And weren't none of my own do-uns neither."

He jerked his head toward the dozing mare, her head hanging low and her resting hoof propped sideways. "She never got ahead of the crossfire'n between the ones afore me and the ones behind. Ever after, I made it my business to keep out ah trouble.

"Course that was long ago." His portly stomach began to shake. "Yes, suh, life was differt back in those days. This was wilderness back then. The cats we knew were those big monsters from the mountains. None of these fancy little house cats, mind ye.

"Back then there was sometimes *need* for hurry. But now . . ." he flicked some bits of mud from his faded trousers, "now, ye might as well enjoy yerself while yer goin' somewheres."

This morning, in spite of the snow spread crazy-quilted across the lane, he prompted his old mare into a semblance of a trot as he rounded the last corner post, and his rasping voice was panting. "Hey, you'uns! Yoo hoo! I got somepin 'portant, I tell ye. Lookee here!" And he waved a white envelope in a circle above the horse's head. "I done rode in sech a hurry from town, that I'm nigh plumb tuckered out."

He handed the envelope to the first eager hand that reached him and waggled a finger in John's direction. "Here, lad, help me get off and set awhile. My Crossfire is about fired cross at me. She . . ." He caught hold of the saddle horn and dragged his leg across. There was a grunt as he reached for the ground and sank gratefully onto the stump John pushed his way. "She can't understand what's done got into me."

He winked at John. "Thank ye, son. And now, while your mammie's busy . . ." His eyes twinkled, noting the interest Andy showed in one bulging pocket of his coat. He took off his hat, scratching his balding head with unconcerned thoroughness. "I'll jest sit here quiet-like, and let you boys visit wid me." He glanced to the far side of the yard where I was wiping my hands on the nearest piece of wash. My face felt hot and my heart was thumping wildly.

Andy cast a look our way, torn between the news sure to have an important bearing on his life, and the obvious treat that lay in store for him. But it was Susan who trotted up to the old man's ample waist and patted the coat with her mittened fist. "Want it, Har-nee Jake! Want it!"

Mr. Wagner guffawed with laughter and slapped his thigh. "Can't trick a woman, even a tiny bitty one! No, sir." He chortled again. "Come here, chile . . ." And he lifted her up on the small bit of knee that extended past his coat. "Reach yer hand in here, lassie. And get enough fer all yer brothers."

The letter was short and looked hastily written.

To whom it may concern:
This is to report that one David Shull, wounded in the Battle of Gettysburg, was taken prisoner and kept in the Letterman Hospital under my care from July of '63 through October of that same year.

After several months, his side wound closed up, healing in a remarkable way. His head injuries had caused temporary blindness, and memory loss from which he suffered while under my care. I have no record of him after leaving Letterman Hospital.

> Signed, Milford Aikens
> M.D. Letterman Hospital
> Gettysburg, Pa.

Underneath was a brief addition:
This is all I could find concerning Mr. Shull of whom you had inquired about in an earlier letter. I hope it may be of help to you.

> Thomas Conkley, Prison Warden
> Fort McHenry Prison
> Fort Henry, Maryland

It was the last day of March before a doubled and stained letter came from the New York address. I read it in a rare moment alone.

Dear Mrs. Shull,

Regarding your request for information about your husband, David Shull, accept my deepest apologies for not sending word before now. I feel certain a notice was sent to his regiment, as is always the policy, but their attempts to reach you were most certainly sent to a different address than the one you have now.

Mr. Shull was brought to our prison on April of last year in fair health, though subject to sudden severe headaches and blackouts.

By the time he was detailed for exchange last November, except for an occasional migraine, he seemed almost back to normal. He was most anxious to make contact with his family and was, as I recall, making arrangements to see you after reporting to his regiment headquarters in Staunton.

Signed: J. W. Cooper, 2nd N.Y. Cavalry Attending Steward Federal Military Prison David's Island, New York

Detailed for exchange in November. That was four months ago. Had David been returned to the Confederate army? I wondered. It was almost impossible to sleep that night. Harness Jake had said recently a large portion of the Northern army was being pulled to Petersburg where General Grant had cornered General Lee and his dwindling forces. The local newspapers were full of hope for a final defeat of the Confederacy. Had David been freed merely to be snatched into a certain massacre?

"Mother," Davie stood squarely before me searching my face. "Mother, why do you look so sober?"

"Do I?" I tried to smile, stroking his mop of dark hair. "You need a haircut, Davie. You all do."

He pushed his forelock impatiently to one side. "That letter, the one you got last night. It was about Papa, wasn't it?"

"Yes . . . yes, it was. When the other boys come in, I need to read it to all of you."

It was a sober group that absorbed this latest piece of news.

"Does it mean Papa went to find us, and we weren't there?" Andy jumped up, upsetting his chair in his distress. He grabbed for the paper in my lap.

I didn't answer right away. I finished washing Susan's face and set her down on the floor. "Comb, Susan, can you get Mommy a comb? Mommy didn't fix your hair yet this morning."

John jammed his hands into his pockets. "He might have gotten waylaid and sent to Petersburg."

"True." I looked at him strangely. "There's too much we don't know, that we have no way of knowing."

Then I shook myself. "But what am I doing? We should be having a special thank-you prayer. For a whole year-and-a-half, while we knew nothing, God was watching over him and helping him regain his health. That was . . . up till four months ago."

❧

Knowing my hunger for news from the front, David's mother asked Harness Jake to bring a second-hand newspaper whenever possible on his trips out to the farm.

The gruesome details of General Sherman's rampage of destruction across the South were soon replaced with news of the suffering of Northern troops entrenched around Petersburg.

The day Susannah and I stopped at the meat shop on a rare visit to the village, the butcher's wife thrust into my face a crumpled letter she had just received from her son. I glanced at the paragraph her finger jabbed at.

> There are a good many of us who believe this shooting match has been going on long enough. An army out of rations cannot expect to do much more fighting. Our rations are somewhere near a pint of cornmeal a day, and once in a while, a piece of bacon which, if you're lucky, is big enough to grease your plate. I can only guess what it must be like *inside* the city defenses. It is just a matter of us being able to tighten our belts a notch tighter and hold on a mite longer . . .[4]

The swarthy woman wiped her greasy hands on her stained apron. "It beats all I ever heard. My boy suffering like that, and here I stand in the midst of all this." She swung her wide palm toward the shelves of meat, coming dangerously close to swiping Susannah in the face. "I'd say it's time they rush those stubborn Rebels and put them in their place. Don't they see they can't hold out any longer? Why, we have them whipped already." She smacked her lips and looked triumphantly on the small group of customers who had stepped in behind us. "You'll agree, lady, I'm sure."

There was a murmur of approval from the others

and my eyes faltered under the plump woman's gaze "Well . . ."

"Why! Do you or do you not? You're not a sympathizer, are you? Think of all the suffering those no-goods have caused everybody. I . . . I hope they starve to death—every one of them!" Her face was growing red. "They're making my boy nigh well starve. Serve them right, it would."

I picked up the package of meat from the wooden counter and turned to leave. A hand was grasping my arm. It was David's mother. Her touch was trembling, her voice tense. "Let's go, Ellen."

But I couldn't. I couldn't walk out that door without giving an answer. I reached up and took off my bonnet, exposing the white covering on my head. The lady facing me almost choked, her eyes growing hard.

"So . . . so that's who you are. I . . ."

I laid a hand on her arm. She recoiled as if I had struck her. I forced a timid smile. "Ma'am, you must love your son a lot."

Her answer was terse. "Course I do." Her eyes were still narrow, fastened on my face.

I retied my bonnet strings and reached for my package once more. "Every man on the field is equally important in God's sight, ma'am. Would you rather hold to a law that does not approve of forgiveness, peace, and goodwill during time of war? Surely if your son were captured, you would wish for him to be entitled to these graces.

"God will not force man to turn from hate, but it's not His way, ma'am. His ways are ways of peace. Thank you, and goodbye."

Indignant voices followed us onto the street. I felt

428

as if the belligerent stares were burning holes in my back.

The boys fell into step beside us. When we reached the edge of the village Susannah spoke. "You . . . if I may say so, you were quite blunt, Ellen."

I looked into her gray eyes soberly. I kept my reply low. "It was only the truth, Mother."

The older lady reached for Susan's hand and her lips tightened. "Perhaps. But was it necessary to say anything? Best leave be when it causes trouble."

"I respect your feelings, Mother, and I wouldn't want to offend you for the world, but I dare not compromise with truth."

No more was said, but there was a barrier that hadn't been. I could feel it. My heart sank.

Nothing unkind was ever mentioned about what had happened. No, David's mother would never be rude, but the difference in conviction had been brought to the surface.

Susannah called it radical.

To me, it was following Jesus Christ.

Chapter XXI

It couldn't be true! And yet there it was in black and white. The newspaper trembled in my hands.

THE WAR IS OVER! LEE SURRENDERS after final desperate effort to escape Grant's pursuing army.

The words swam before my eyes, and the cheers and excited laughter of the children was punctuated by Harness Jake's bellowing, "I told ye it had to come! It had to be, I tell ye." He slapped his thigh, his face flushed and his eyes watering. He looped the lines of his mare around the porch post and heaved himself down onto the bottom step.

He pulled a rag from his pocket and blew his nose lustily. From where I was standing, I heard his voice soften as if speaking to himself. "I'll be blustered. Ain't we been praying this a'way for the last four years? Ah, thankey, Lord, ain't it good!"

John took the newspaper from my hands. We listened as he read aloud the surrender terms and the orders for a two-hundred gun salute to be fired at every army headquarters, post, and arsenal. Every article held tone of jubilant victory. They told of dancing in the streets, of parties and celebration.

In spite of the overwhelming sense of relief and gladness, I couldn't help wondering what emotion the other half of America was feeling, left with nothing but the bitterness of defeat.

It wasn't until the next day that I began to think ahead. What now? Should we wait here till we received word of David, or should we be heading south to try to find him?

Peter was anxious to go. He pulled up a chair to the table, watching as Susannah and I carefully separated her collection of garden seeds into different piles.

"Papa may be waiting for us right now at Uncle Fred's or Grandpa Gochenour's. I think we should start right away."

The younger ones eagerly echoed his suggestion. I waved them all to silence. "Careful—don't shake the table. You'll disturb our piles. I'd like to hear what John thinks. And we mustn't forget Grandma. She should have something to say about this."

Susannah's thin face creased in a slight smile, and her fingers plucked nervously at the empty bag in her lap. "It is your decision, Ellen. You know that. But . . ." She stopped herself, then went on cautiously, "I wonder if you are carrying this too far. Going to join 'your people.' Why don't you stay here? The war is over. There's no need to be so different now. Let David, if he is still alive, come back to the place he loved for so many years."

No one said a word for a while, then John cleared his throat. "I think we need to remember there are going to be a lot of strange men on the roads for the next weeks, maybe months. Many of them may be more than happy to find someone willing—or unwilling—to 'share' their possessions. I think we should wait, at least for a while."

I nodded thoughtfully. There was wisdom in what he said. As for my mother-in-law's advice, I must talk with her again, sometime when we were alone.

John spoke again. "The mail should begin going through before long. Why don't we write a few letters first to see if anyone has seen or heard of him."

I slid the last few seeds onto the center pile and rose to my feet. "You are right. I know you are, John. In fact, that's what I'm going to do tonight." I dusted my hands together. "Just as soon as I shoo all of you off to bed."

I shook my head at the boys' objections. "No fussing, Andy and Davie. Tomorrow is going to be a big day, and Grandma will need all the help she can get. Without a horse, we'll have to work up the garden plot by hand."

In the end, I wrote three letters: to the Gochenours, to my own family, and to Uncle Freds on Naked Creek. If David *was* alive, and able to travel, surely he would head for one of these places.

Days went by. Every week Harness Jake would bring word of more young men and fathers who had trickled home, and of others who would never return.

I pushed myself hard. From first light until the sun sank over the Cumberland Mountains, I labored in the warming sunshine, working up the garden, making strawberry preserves, pruning fruit trees, and helping the boys cut and haul wood.

"You must slow down, Ellen." Susannah put her rheumatic hands around my sweaty waist. "You're going to wear yourself thin. You're doing too much." Her eyebrows were creased above her troubled eyes.

I laughed lightly. "You worry too much, Grandma. I'm feeling stronger than I have for a long time, and younger."

Susannah turned away, a catch in her voice. "There was a time when I too was young and supple. David's father used to lift me high and swing me in a circle around the room. He said my hair was as thick and brown as a horse's mane. My arms were quick and strong, used to carrying babies or swinging a scythe.

"But that is all in the past now." She straightened her weary back, folding her arms tight against her chest.

"But we are reaping those years, Mother. All the hours you put into David's life, we are merely paying back a small portion. Don't worry about us. We want to leave you in good shape in case we leave."

"Must you?" she flared, then hung her head. When I did not answer right away, she glanced at my face, then hurried toward the house.

I watched her go before bending over my hoe.

She rarely brought up the subject of our differences again, even though now with the war over, neighbors raised their eyebrows and said harsh words about the queer white-capped lady who wouldn't take part in the town's victory celebrations.

I sighed. I tried not to pay any mind to other's disdain, but it was painful to stand opposite those you loved, those who needed you. It left a wedge of guilt that wore and tormented.

After the planting was done, the two older boys began working away from home. It did not take long for word to get around that Susannah Shull's two young grandsons could do more than their share of a job. Families still missing sons or fathers were glad for help they could trust. And I was glad for the bit of income it brought in.

For so long we had been obligated to live off of others. It felt good to know that at last we were able to help support ourselves.

One evening the boys came home streaked with dust. Only their eyes and weary grins contrasted with the dark brown that coated their clothing.

"Stop! Stop right where you are!" I called. Grabbing a tea towel to wipe my hands, I stepped to the open door. "Let me bring the washbasin outside. Whatever were you doing today?"

John bent sideways, smacking puffs of dust from his trousers. "Bertum Price had us harrowing his ten acres along Clover Hill. It hasn't rained for a while, and I do believe that hill catches all the wind from here to the mountains."

Peter reached for the block of soap and began sudsing up his arms in the steaming water. "I never saw a man as particular as he. If the ground isn't worked just a certain way, he said the rain will wash all his topsoil away. The wind is going to blow it away if you ask me." He snorted through the lather over his face.

"I hope you were respectful, Peter."

"Oh, we were, Mother. It wasn't quite that bad, although Mr. Price *is* finicky." John explained as he unbuttoned his shirt. "It doesn't hurt us to work for that kind of man."

"Didn't help us either," Peter said, his head buried in a towel.

"What do you mean?" I moved closer to them, conscious of Susannah's figure just inside. "Did anything else happen?"

John's eyes clearly signaled, "Wait." I turned back to the kitchen. "Well, I'm glad you're home. We have fresh cooked greens and custard pie for supper."

The next morning I cornered the boys as they stepped out of the barn with their pails of milk. "John, Peter, now tell me what happened."

Peter kept his head down, and I couldn't see his expression. I used to easily lift his chin with my hand and make him look me in the eye, but I dared not treat him as a child anymore. He was too close to manhood. Both of them were.

"Well, Mother, I guess we had . . . what you might

call a discussion of sorts."

Peter shot a stabbing look at his older brother. "Discussion! I'd say an argument. And too much a one-sided one too. If John wouldn't have been so meek, I could have told Mr. Price enough to make his ears tingle."

"Peter! You're upset." I reached for his arm. I could feel his muscles tighten. "John, maybe you can explain."

John coughed awkwardly. "I guess it all started when he asked us whether we'd be available for hiring out all summer. We told him we may be going back to Virginia."

" 'You mean you want to go back to where those yellownecks live?' " Peter mimicked the older man's accent so exactly my mouth twitched. " 'You ought to know better than to associate with folks that turn against their country, and kill the president too. I'm sure those rebels had something to do with it.' "

John picked up a stem of hay that had fallen out of the manger. "I told him we didn't know who was responsible for Mr. Lincoln's death, but we don't approve of taking anyone's life, no matter which side they are on.

"Then Mr. Price started a long lecture that didn't give us a chance to get a word in edgewise. He said we were too young to see ahead to where this whole thing was leading to, that America was facing treason and anarchy."

Peter coughed. "Then John asked him if there shouldn't be a better way to work out differences than pointing guns at each others' heads?"

John grinned wryly. "He didn't appreciate that too much."

"I'd say not." Peter's voice rose. "He said the Union tried every way they knew to bring about unity again, but when nothing else worked, they had no choice but to fight to avoid tyranny and barbarism, as he put it. Then he said, 'We were fighting for a holy cause. None of the rebel camp can say that.' "

John winced and colored slightly. "I didn't know what to say."

Peter's eyes smoldered. "We stood there like dummies, letting him talk us into a corner. Finally we just turned and left." Peter laughed harshly. "What's a person supposed to say? I felt like socking my fist right between his conceited eyes!"

Tears welled up in my eyes. "Peter, . . . Peter, anger and retaliation is not the way of peace. The way of peace begins with love in our hearts, even toward those who are against us."

Peter sighed deeply. "I'm sorry, Mother. I know what's right. It's just not always easy to do."

"You are learning, boys, that regardless whether it's between men or nations, anger and conflict have the same origin—selfishness. It is not within us to give in, to show humility, or let another get the best of us. We have to deal with that selfishness first of all. If you would have retaliated against Mr. Price, you would have been no better than those who use war to gain their end." I gave Peter's shoulders a squeeze before letting go.

"And we'll likely face more of this. Let's encourage each other and pray for God's help. Have other people treated you this way?"

John reached for the milk pail. "Not often. There have been some sarcastic remarks by a few folks when we go through town. But the ones who hire us

438

generally aren't interested in our differences as long as we're quiet and do a man's work."

"I feel sure some went to war out of an honest heart of duty," I said. "But even so, there remains a higher way. The way of love is needed now more than ever."

I straightened myself, leaning on the hoe handle to catch my breath. The dry ground was hot to my bare feet, and I felt a trickle of sweat slide down my neck. "Yes?"

"About leaving . . ."

I gave John my full attention. "Have you learned something new?"

John waited till Andy, with Susan trotting behind, came up toting a bucket of water. The water slopped deliciously over my dusty feet as he set it down and held out the drinking gourd to John.

"Here, let Mother have the first drink." John dipped out a cupful and handed it to me. I drank gratefully.

"Oh, this is wonderful. Thank you. We ought to have the whole field of corn done by sundown if we hurry. Is Grandma making out okay?"

Susan's head bobbed. "Davie helping Grandma."

"We were too, until she sent us out with this. She won't let us get close 'cause she says the soap stuff burns terrible." Andy shifted the bucket to his other arm. "Here, Susan, you help carry on the other side. Got it okay?" He grinned down at her water-streaked toes. "We're a big engine again. Now, let's carry it to

Peter."

I smiled, watching them go, then turned to John again. "What were you going to say?"

"Tom McAllister stopped by this morning right after you left for the field."

My eyes widened. "The farmer with the crippled feet? He's interested in the place?"

"I think so. He heard talk, I guess, that it might be available. He has a son home from the war who is getting married next month. He'd pay Grandma extra for the corn crop put in, and she could still have right to harvest the garden come fall."

My forehead creased as I bent over my hoe again. "What did Grandma tell him?"

"She didn't say much, just that she needed time to think it over." John spoke matter-of-factly. "I think she's beginning to see we are serious about trying to find Papa, and that the farm is too big for her to keep."

He wiped his brow with a handkerchief. "That cottage in town would be a nice place for her. I wouldn't blame Grandma for wanting to be settled into a small, manageable place before next winter."

There was no other sound for awhile except the dull thud of metal striking earth.

If only we would hear from David! My mind was in a whirl. I dreaded yet another move with the children. I rubbed my damp hands against my skirt.

"Here, let me finish your row." John began hoeing again. "I'm done with mine. You go on in and wash up. It's almost time for supper."

I looked up into his tanned face, and he grinned, giving me a gentle push toward the house. "Run along. The biggest is boss now-a-days."

440

"You'll quit soon?"

"As soon as this row is finished. Shouldn't be more than five minutes. And Peter will be in too."

"Thank you, son. I don't know how we would manage without you."

I clung to the warmth of his smile as I retraced the narrow cow path that wound through the neck of woods leading to the front pasture. John was eighteen now. I shouldn't fear to let him help make decisions for the family, and yet I did. Something would have to be decided—and soon.

Wilhelm and Rebecca's reply gave no clue to David's whereabouts. Neither had Uncle Fred's. There had been no answer from my folks. I was not surprised.

I took a deep breath. Twilight was bringing cooler air. The neighbor must have begun his first cutting of hay. I could smell its fresh sweetness.

I thought of the chores. Maybe if I hurried, I could milk the cows before the boys came in. They would fuss, but that wouldn't hurt. They were no less tired than I.

I stood in the barn door, my eyes adjusting to the musty dimness. A breath of air fluttered the cobwebs along the ceiling and swirled loose bits of bedding at my feet.

"Surprise! The chores are all done. All except milking old Fern." The two smaller boys jumped out from the other side of the hayrack.

I stopped short. "Are you sure? Who milked Daisy? Davie?" I reached to tousle his hair. "Not my little Davie!"

"I'm not little, Mother. I'm almost twelve now."

"I know it, son." My eyes glowed. "This is wonderful. Let's go see what you have been up to all afternoon. I'm sure Grandma is tired."

"Hept good, Mommy." Susan reached for my hand, swinging it back and forth happily.

"I stirred soap till I thought my arm would break off. Phew! How it smelled." Andy pointed to the large overturned kettle tilted against a big stump. Blackened remnants of wood and ash still smoldered beside it. The strong odor of lye hung over the metal tubs lined up by the barn wall.

I peered at the gray cooling mass. "It made a lot, didn't it?" The ugly mess was precious stuff. How many piles of dirty clothes would be scrubbed with the blocks of soap until it was gone? It had been a long time since I had helped with soap making.

"Grandma make yummies. Let's eat!" Susan tugged at my skirt.

"You run along with the boys, little girlie. Mommy wants to milk Fern before John and Peter come. We'll be at the house in a little bit." I sent her on her way, waiting till she and the boys were out of sight before working at the kinks in my aching back and shoulders.

I was stripping the last drops of milk from Fern when I heard the older boys coming in the far end of the building. There was a clink of tools being propped in a corner, and Davie's voice calling out that the chores were done. Then their voices faded in the direction of the house.

I leaned into Fern's brown flank. John thought it was time to move. I could tell he did. But was it? And where would we live if we did leave? If only I could know for sure.

I frowned. How had Rebecca said in their letter?

People around here are disillusioned with life. It is as if suddenly their whole purpose in life has been taken away from them, and to pick up the broken remnants and begin anew is almost too much to undertake.

There has been a rush to post war damage claims with the government, even among our own people. That may not be wrong, except it appears often to be prompted by selfishness. When a people are bereft, they tend to grasp for any means to regain material possessions.[1]

We as Mennonites need to show the way by being willing to share and help each other.

As much as we long to see you, we must be honest and say it would not be easy to set up housekeeping in this community any time soon. But then, you were never one to shrink from hardship.

Widow Wright moved in with her younger sister's family several weeks ago. You are welcome in our home at any moment and for any length of time. I hope you always know that.

We are skimping along, but spring is here, and we've had good rains. The garden should do well.

Give the children our love. Pray for us, as we have been for you.

Wilhelm and Rebecca

Across the bottom of the page, she had carefully penned, "And if I take the wings of the morning and dwell in the uttermost part of the sea, even there shall thy hand hold me and thy right hand shall guide me."

The lifting and holding arms of the Lord, how could I doubt them? The tightness in my chest began to relax and I stood. Somehow He would show us what we should do.

"Soo, Bossy. Move on out." I pushed the stool aside and slapped the cow's rump. Tying the gate behind her and shifting the bucket to my other hand, I rubbed my feet on a thick clump of grass. I must remember to stop at the pump and wash them properly. It would never do to go into Grandma's house with dirty feet.

The purple and turquoise sunset had rapidly faded into gray, darkening into the blackness of a summer night. Even while I stood there, the stars began to appear. Millions of them.

I quickened my step. They were calling for me. I didn't catch the sound of footsteps behind me until a voice spoke only a few feet away.

"Ellen!"

I screamed.

My heart leaped into my throat and I swung around, stumbling backward. The bucket tilted precariously, sloshing milk across my skirts. That voice! It couldn't be! My heart raced wildly.

The man took a step closer. "Ellen! Don't you know me?"

Then I was crushed against him, my arms around his neck, and I was sobbing. "David, David! Is it you? Can it be? Oh, God; oh, God!"

444

My cheek felt the roughness of his shirt, and I felt his tears on my hair.

"It's me, darling." His voice was choked with emotion. "How did you get here? I dreamed of this day. I dreamed, but I feared it would never happen."

"Oh, David, are you all right?" My fingers caressed his face, his hair. I felt the roughness of a jagged scar under his beard and caught my breath.

"It's just a scar, darling." He pulled my head onto his shoulder, and took my hand in his.

Then I noticed. One shirt sleeve was pinned shut at the wrist. I gasped. "Your hand."

He pulled me close again. "I've been pretty torn up, Ellen, but thank God, I'm okay."

"Mother . . . !" came a call from the house.

I lifted my head toward the light from the open doorway. Footsteps sounded across the porch, then stopped suddenly at the sight of the two of us.

The door filled with wide-eyed faces, speechless with surprise. Then Andy's impatient voice chimed out from behind. "What's going on? Who's out there anyway? Let me see, will you!" And his head thrust out past Peter's arm.

"It's Papa!" With a leap that carried him over the porch railing, he was racing across the grass and threw himself against David, almost taking him off his feet. The others were close behind.

"Papa! Papa! Papa!" There was hugging and laughing and crying all intermingled, and I, laughing through my tears, suddenly noticed Grandma attempting to come down the steps, with Susan burying her head into her skirts, sobbing as if her heart would break.

She didn't understand! I berated myself for not

realizing sooner. I hurried across the yard.

"Susan . . . Susan dear. Come to Mommy." I swept her into my arms and held her into the light for David to see. "It's Papa, Susan. Your papa."

Abruptly the commotion stopped. David's mouth opened but no sound came. He took a step closer. "Ours? You never told me."

I blinked back tears. "I . . . I couldn't."

He reached out and tenderly gathered Susan close. "Can it be?" He ran his hand over her dark curls, patting her back, trying to gain control of his emotions enough to talk. "What you must have gone through! My family . . ."

Susan, eyelashes still wet, a hiccup now and then breaking the silence, gravely observed the man who held her. Then her lips parted in a smile, and she patted his cheek. "My papa!" She gave a delighted chuckle.

David laughed. He reached out his good arm toward the rest. "I came here to rest before going further, and God has brought my family to me."

He took a stumbling step toward his mother. "Mother!"

They wept on each other's shoulders.

"Where's Father?"

"He's gone, son."

"Gone?" David pulled back.

"Last summer. Heart attack."

I could see his shoulders sag, and I touched his sleeve. "Come in, darling. You can hardly walk anymore." I could feel him trembling.

"Tired? Yes, but happy too. Happier than I've been in years."

I reached for Susan, and with the other arm

around his waist, drew him up the steps and into the kitchen. The forgotten food was still waiting on the stove.

Grandma Shull hobbled about getting another place set at the table. "Imagine that! David being here with us on this special evening." She dabbed at her eyes. "I do believe I am not as tired as I thought."

We sat around the table long after the meal was over, drinking in David's story. His brow furrowed. "It's much too long to tell in one sitting. And much of it is foggy to me. After this last injury, I was in a hospital for quite a while, then in different prisons."

Peter leaned forward. "Was one of them Fort McHenry?"

David looked startled. "Yes."

I stroked his hair. "A man from town showed me where to inquire about you. But the letter said you had been moved."

"I was on the exchange list for the last six months of the war, but was unable to be sent because of my condition. They wanted healthy soldiers for exchange."

He gazed into the fire glowing on the hearth. "Then I'd think of you all and nearly lose my mind. I tried getting letters out through others who left before me, but evidently they never reached you."

We were oblivious to time until finally a pained expression on David's face made me jump guiltily to my feet. "Here, we are wearing you out with talking. You need a bed."

He passed his hand over his face. "It would feel mighty good, I must admit. But I don't know if I can bear to let any of you out of my sight. I've dreamed of this for months on end. Except for little Susan."

He reached out and touched her face. "I didn't know about her."

John and Peter helped him to his feet.

"You'll sleep right in here." His mother shuffled across the room to the door of her own bedroom. "No going upstairs for you, son." She held her finger to her lips. "Not a word of disagreement from you either."

I filled a basin with hot sudsy water and followed, closing the door after me. "Let me take off your shoes." I sank down on the floor beside him. "How do you manage with only one hand?"

"You soon learn." He grimaced as I gave a tug. The shoes literally came to pieces in my hands.

"I don't think I've taken them off for the last two days. I was afraid I couldn't get them to stay together anymore."

There were blisters on both heels and another one, festering and red, where he had fastened his shoe on with wire.

"How long have you been walking?"

He spoke through clenched teeth. "I've about lost track. A couple weeks, I suppose."

I pressed my lips together and grimly went to work. I smeared a liberal coating of Susannah's mutton tallow salve over both feet and wrapped them in strips of old sheeting.

He was settled comfortably in bed before I spoke again. "Is the pain pretty bad? I'll brew a pot of your mom's goldenseal root tea."

He roused himself with effort. "Might help . . . but I'm about too tired to care. Why don't you just sit down here for a little, would you?" He patted the bed beside him.

"Yes?"

"Tell me more about what happened to you all while I was gone. You stayed at Gochenours' till last fall?" He reached for my hand.

"Yes. They treated us like family, David. Susan was born there. They couldn't have been kinder had we been blood kin."

I smoothed the pillow under his head. "But let's talk about yourself. We prayed for you night and day. I tried to get word of you a number of times."

He shaded his eyes with his sleeve. "I was hurt at Gettysburg by a shell exploding right in the middle of our group of teamsters. I remember seeing horses flying through the air, and then everything went black. I can't recall much until a few weeks later when I woke up in a makeshift hospital. I couldn't see for a while, but that came back gradually." He dropped his hand to finger the long jagged scar along his side. "This took longer to heal, but my head wound gave me the most trouble. I was afraid I'd never be able to remember or think clearly again. Sometimes I felt like beating my head against the walls."

I stroked his arm.

He smiled. "You recollect I said you were a brave woman, Ellen? You've proved it to be true."

I looked him full in the face. "I can't agree with you, David." My lips quivered. "Many women suffered a great deal more. I've just learned a lot more about the goodness of God."

Over the next several weeks, David rested, took short walks, and tried to do justice to the bowls of food set before him. He did not talk much about his experiences, and I did not prod. His fragile composure could not handle the painful memories as yet. It was enough for now to rejoice in the healthier glow of his countenance and the healing of his body.

One evening we sat alone on the porch steps. The half moon was already climbing the sky. A cooling breeze fanned our faces and rustled the corn in the garden plot.

Gradually the rest of the family joined us until we were all there except David's mother, who had gone to bed shortly before. I leaned against the warmth of David's arm. "David, what are we to do?"

"About what?"

"You know—leaving or staying."

He coughed uneasily. "I don't know. I can hardly bring myself to leave Mother. I need to make the trip to Johnstown and talk to my brothers, Allen and Wilfred. Mother said she wrote to each of them a couple weeks ago."

He looked up at John standing behind us. "What do you say, son? Any suggestions?"

John dropped down beside us. "I like it here. If Mr. McAllister wouldn't have already asked about the place, I think I'd be for staying."

"There may be something else close by." Peter spoke up from where he lay on the grass. "Maybe someone needs help on a farm. We know quite a few farmers by now. Now that we're all together, why do we need to look for another place?"

I stirred restlessly. "But a church, David, do you know of any Mennonites near here?"

David's jaw set. "Not close enough to be a part of really."

I fumbled with a loose thread in my sleeve. "Sometimes I get so lonely for Wilhelm and Rebecca. And yet it frightens me. The valley was so completely destroyed."

David ran his tongue painfully over his lips. "I really don't know. I really do not know what to say." His eyes took on such a tormented look I regretted bringing up the subject.

I forced a smile. "Well, it's bedtime. We could discuss this till morning, but we can't do that." I brushed off my skirt as I moved up onto the porch.

"Why couldn't we? I'm not tired in the least." There was an ominous ripping sound as Andy slid off his perch on the railing.

"Oh, son, there go your second-best pair of pants." My exasperation melted at the comical look of surprise and embarrassment on his face.

"Mother said it was time to get ready for bed, but she didn't mean to start right here, Andy." Peter couldn't resist teasing a little. Davie snickered.

I caught the quivering chin and misty eyes, and pulled a hairpin from my hair. I backed him up against my dress, fastening the flap of material back up in makeshift fashion. "Don't you worry, son. Peter just forgot when he had to show James how well he could 'skin the cat' on that old crab apple tree."

David gave a loud guffaw, and Peter grinned sheepishly. "Yeah, I guess I do."

"What, Mommy?" Susan yanked on my skirts until I sat down again, pulling Andy down beside me. "Let Papa tell it. He saw it happen. I didn't."

David chuckled. "Yes, that was right comical, but

I didn't dare laugh at the time.

"James had come over about something—I don't remember what. We were standing in the door of the blacksmith shop talking, when we heard Peter come whistling up past the barn to the crab apple tree.

"Peter climbed to a low-lying limb, swung himself up, and holding tightly, flipped himself backwards. A snag hooked his britches, and when he came around, they stayed caught. He couldn't keep going, and he couldn't go backwards without tearing his pants.

"They tore anyway. And by the time we got there, he had dropped to the ground and took off for the house as fast as a scared rabbit. All he left behind was his ripped pants leg still swinging from the branch."

I laughed along with the others but my mind was still mulling over our future. *Security—or a church family? Must one be chosen without the other?*

❧ Chapter XXII ❧

The long days and heat of summer were upon us. The boys spent long hours in the fields. Susannah kept putting off Mr. McAllister's inquiries about the farm. Outwardly we were settling into a routine, and I began to relax. True, there was not a church group close by, but we had provisions, and we were all together. Maybe God wanted us here after all. David hinted as much. Yet underneath I sensed a restlessness. But we didn't talk about it. It was as if he were waiting, waiting for . . . I wasn't sure what.

And then the letter came.

Susannah tried to read the scratchy scrawl on its creased front. "I do believe it's for you, Ellen. I declare, my eyes are either getting worse or this handwriting is awful. Can you read it?"

She handed it to me as I came down the stairs with an armload of dirty clothes.

I frowned. "It is from Uncle Freds, I'm almost sure. It looks like Malinda's writing." I dropped my laundry and sat down on the wooden bench next to the door.

> My dear Ellen,
> I wonder if you are still with Susannah. A great sadness has touched our home. Fred was kicked in the head by the horse one evening several weeks ago. I found him at dark, and I managed to get him to the house, but he didn't live through the night.
> It seems I can hardly live anymore. My health has gone backward so much. Fred had been doing most of the housework since last winter.
> What are your plans? I don't suppose you would have any interest in coming back to the farm? It has gotten so run-down, and life is so hard. Some are trying to . . .

I couldn't make out the next word. I held the paper closer. Was it "take"? I puzzled over it awhile, then glanced down to the last paragraph.

> I don't understand all the legal work that needs to be taken care of. And I don't know who to trust to help me. I wish

David was here. I know he wouldn't let
me down. We Shulls stick together.

Malinda

Malinda was offering us the farm? I backtracked
again to the sentence I couldn't decipher. No, it
would have to wait for David. It sounded as though
someone was trying to place some claim on her land.
When David came home from town, I told him
about it.

"Perhaps." He frowned, holding the letter to the
lamplight. "But I have a feeling their will hasn't been
changed since Michael died. It would be pretty easy
for someone to take advantage of the poor widow."
He leaned against the wall thinking.

I broke the silence. "Who could we ask to help
her? Gochenours? One of the other Mennonites
close by? They would be trustworthy."

David didn't answer.

"Even Father; Father would be fair with her. Or
James. James is home from the war, remember?"

He was looking at me strangely and with rising
dismay I could already guess what he was going to
say. I cringed.

"You think you should go?" I took a step backward. "David, no. You are not strong enough to
handle that right now."

He pulled me close. "Please, Ellen, let me think.
This is so new."

"She wouldn't be expecting you, David. She
doesn't even know you are here." I wrapped my arms
tightly together. "You couldn't leave us and go.
Please!"

I grew weak with the very thought. There had

455

been too many partings, too long a time in uncertainty and dying hope.

David's mouth twisted painfully. "No, Ellen. We won't separate the family. It would have to be all of us, or none at all." He let out his breath. "Think of the poor woman, and no one to help."

He turned to face me. "I didn't get to tell you yet. Allen sent another telegram today. He is serious about buying Gilberson's tailor shop and moving close by. If so, he would be only down the street from Mother."

He touched my chin. "He knows we are unsettled about what to do." He cleared his throat. "Is God trying to give us direction, Ellen?"

I didn't reply.

He shook my shoulder. "There is no easy answer. But would we be willing to follow if He opens the way? Would we, Ellen? Ellen?"

I turned away, pinching my lips against the questions welling up, pressing to be asked.

David squeezed my elbow, waiting, but I could not respond. The Lord had always proved Himself faithful, that I knew. Yet right now I could think of nothing else but my dread of the unknown.

The next weeks were hard. David's eyes grew haggard, and I woke up more than once to find him on his knees. Finally one night I slipped down beside him.

"David, I'm sorry. I've lost my hold on God. I can't seem to get above the fear of what may happen to us."

He grabbed my hand. "I don't want to torture you, Ellen. I don't want to disturb the peace we've begun to build." He fumbled with the oil lamp. "Is it worth it to keep the way we have chosen to live? Is it worth the hardship it will bring the family? God will not force us to do anything. If we feel the risk is too great, we can choose to stay."

I buried my head in my hands. For some reason I thought of the bunting story Rebecca had shared and shame flooded my face. "He needs to be more real to us than all the darkness around us . . . Faith needs to be fed to grow . . . I took a long shuddering breath. "Forgive me, David. If God would lead us elsewhere, we dare not turn our back on Him. We have no one else."

The lamplight flickered over his strained face. His eyes held mine for a long moment before he spoke. "Are you sure, Ellen?"

I wrapped trembling fingers around the stump of his arm. "The signs to go . . . they would have to be very clear."

He took a deep breath. "And if they are?"

"Then we must take the risk."

Our willingness was tested almost immediately. David brought home news the next day that Allen was definitely moving to Buffalo Mills. Less than a week later, Mr. McAllister and his son came by to talk business. I heard the news with amazement. It was too direct a confirmation of God's leading to ignore.

Mr. McAllister was anxious to come to agreement on the price, and the purchase was completed on the spot. The newlyweds, temporarily boarding at the homeplace, were delighted to begin housekeeping so near by.

We went ahead with preparations to move Susannah into the cottage at the edge of town. I threw myself into a fever of cleaning and packing, feeling ridiculous to do so when we had no way of going elsewhere.

One afternoon Susannah came looking for me. She found me upstairs. "Please, Ellen. You're working too hard. Tomorrow is soon enough to finish whitewashing these walls." She shook her head. "You'll be too tired to be of any good when you *are* ready to . . ." She stopped short.

I swiveled to face her. She was leaning against the doorjamb, her face twisted to one side. Feeling suddenly stricken, I slipped my arm around her waist. "Oh, Mother, how can we do this to you?"

Her body went rigid, and a muffled gasp escaped her lips. Then she crumpled into my arms, and we wept together.

"It's all right, Ellen. It is for the best, I know. It's just that you've become like family, you and Susan and the boys. But David and I have talked it over. This is meant to be. I'll have Allen and his family. Malinda has no one."

I choked. "I know you think this is irrational to continue getting ready like this when we have no means to travel."

Susannah took a deep breath. She straightened up painfully and ushered me into a chair. "Ellen, listen to me. I've watched you from the moment you turned in our gate last fall. I watched what you did with the scorn of others, with loneliness, and now with uncertainty. You've shown me something, Ellen. You've shown me that what you believe is real, and that you'll follow it, no matter where it leads you. If God can bring you to that place, surely He won't let you sit before He's taken you all the way. I wish I had that faith, Ellen. I wish I had learned how."

One afternoon before the month was up, a horse
and wagon turned in the lane. I was in the attic getting a few boxes when the boys' shouts made me set
down my load and scurry down the stairs.

It was John! But where was David, and what was
John doing with a wagon? I ran to the door and
jerked it open.

John's eyes found mine above the noise and confusion.

"Papa's okay." I could read his mouth even from
the porch and the tightness in my chest relaxed.

He looped the reins over the hitching post and
came to stand beside me. "Papa's found a way for us
to travel south. Can we get Grandma moved by
tomorrow evening?"

By tomorrow evening? Yes, we could make it
somehow. "But why isn't Papa with you, son?"

He gave my hand a squeeze then released it gently. "A Mr. Simms from Staunton came north to stock
up on supplies for his store. Allen met him in
Bedford last evening and mentioned our wish to go
back to the Valley. The man jumped at the chance to
get extra drivers. But we can't take along anything
except what we can carry on our laps. Papa went by
the cottage to get things finished there. We are to
pick up Mr. Simms two days from now, on our way
out."

So the way was clear at last. I took a deep breath.
David looked very serious as we sat around the

supper table for the last time that evening. "I thought it quite coincidental to meet up with Mr. Simms. I have thought this over as carefully as I know how. What do you think, Ellen?"

"It does seem a direct answer. We had asked for an unmistakable sign, hadn't we, David?"

"Yes, we did." He nodded. "But it will be far from easy. Mr. Simms says food and clothing are hard to find. There are no newspapers and hardly any mail is going. Staunton is still under Federal military occupation."

"It may be hard—very hard. So many heads of households are gone and families torn apart." Then he smiled, and reached for another biscuit. "This is good bread, Mother. You're the best biscuit maker this side of the Potomac."

She flushed with pleasure. "Then take some more. A recuperating man needs all he can get into him."

David ate his biscuit in three bites and grinned. "There's nothing like a compliment to win a lady's heart. Isn't that right, Andy?"

"What's a compliment?" Andy asked.

"What you give ladies to make them generous." David smiled at me and laughed.

I understood. To concentrate only on the hardships ahead would discourage everyone. I refilled his glass. "Is Grandma's house ready?"

David put his arm on the back of Susannah's chair. "I think so. I finished repairing the roof, and dug a ditch to drain the water away from the door when it rains. The inside is all cleaned, and the hollyhocks are blooming at the doorstep." His arm tightened on the chair back. "This is one of the hardest things I've done, Mother. I want you to know that."

Susannah pushed to her feet. "You are doing it for my good, son. I know I am in good hands." She swallowed hard, then turned businesslike again. "Now we best hurry with the dishes. You wished to load the table yet tonight."

It was harder than I had imagined to leave David's mother standing bent and thin on the cottage doorstep the next morning. Wisps of white hair played across her cheek in the early air, and her hands were folded in her apron.

I put my arm around her. "You've been so kind. If it hadn't been for you, I don't know what we would have done." I could feel her shoulder blades protruding against the faded dress as I gave her one last squeeze. I took the twisted fingers in mine. "God is calling us elsewhere, or I would never leave you."

"You've been good to me. I'll be okay. Allens will be moving yet this week, and Mertie, the grocer's daughter, plans to come by every day. She's a good housekeeper."

"I know she is. She's a sweet lass." I swallowed hard. "Perhaps after we are settled in we can fetch you south if you care to come."

Grandma Shull bent over Susan, and her lips brushed her forehead. "You might convince me yet. Now, child, don't forget your old grandma. Just because you'll live so far away, don't forget to write to her time and again."

There was no time for lingering good-byes. I climbed blindly into the wagon, waving my handkerchief to the small figure in the distance until it faded out of sight.

David reached for my hand. Susan's sobbing

drowned out what he tried to say. I pulled Susan onto my lap and bent over her rocking back and forth. Andy leaned over my shoulder. "I'm bawling on the inside."

I nodded. I did not trust myself to speak.

It took a day to pick up Mr. Simms and his merchandise. Mr. Simms was a sober man with a dark, gray-streaked beard that hugged his thick chest. As we pulled to a stop beside the boarding house door, he laid his suit coat carefully over the buckboard's side. After nodding gravely in my direction, he spoke only as necessary while directing the loading of the pyramid of boxes and crates.

His hands, uncalloused and clean-nailed, for some reason made me think of my father's hands, the same short fingers, the same wide palm, except these hands looked as if they had never held a plow handle or fought a battle. He must have held a government job. He was a man of culture, and all business.

For much of the trip he sat hunched beside whoever was driving, meticulously figuring in a small notebook, his lips mouthing numbers, brow furrowed in concentration.

As soon as the horses were set in motion, he would draw out a pistol and place it on his lap. I was almost certain I had seen the bulge of another hidden under his waistcoat. He seemed relieved to let John or David do all the driving, while the rest of us didn't seem to exist.

Yet I knew he was conscious of all we did, because we couldn't change positions without his bloodshot eyes sweeping over his load of valuables. His nights probably held little sleep for him, and stripped as we were returning to the Valley, I sensed a blessing of being poor.

We pushed the horses hard, going until the light had faded to complete darkness, stopping during the day only long enough now and then to let the horses blow. Only once did we have trouble.

It was just after sunset the third night, when two men jumped out of the underbrush, grabbing for the horses' bridle. David shouted and slapped the reins hard, breaking the horses into a trot. Before I was barely aware of what was happening, there was a sharp crack, and a bandit fell to the road.

Mr. Simms stood, looking back over his shoulder, a pistol smoking in his hand. His mouth twitched. "Sorry to disturb you, ma'am."

He took over the reins, and forced the horses on until long after midnight. As tired as I was, I only wanted the wagon to go faster. His lack of emotion shook me even more than the robbery attempt. I felt very uncomfortable with someone who had so little respect for human life.

The farther we traveled into the Valley, the more destruction we saw. The landscape lay stripped and idle. Fences were down, trees shattered, and barns empty or reduced to ashes. Houses held gaunt-eyed children staring at our passing. I looked away, unable to face the misery in their drooping shoulders and pinched faces.

The morning of the fourth day found us at Harrisonburg, and by that evening the horses were turning off the Valley Pike onto the dirt road that

463

wound beside Naked Creek. I pulled Susan's sleeping body closer. My hands, my face, my whole body felt stiff and cold. When the buckboard came to a halt before the darkened house, I sat as frozen to the wagon bed.

David mounted the back steps as John reached out a hand to help me to the ground. When I made no move, he took hold of my arm. "Mother . . ."

Mr. Simms stepped to the ground and stretched his short frame. He leaned closer, his shaggy whiskers brushing my arm. "Mrs. Shull?" He cleared his throat. "Mrs. Shull, pardon me, ma'am, were you sleeping?"

"No . . . no. I just . . ." I shook myself.

"Here, hand me the lassie. Your son says this is the place?" His words were gruff.

"Yes, sir." I stood for a moment trying to get my balance, then handed Susan over the side and stepped down.

A light flickered and grew inside, moving out of the kitchen to the back door. Then David, with Malinda hanging onto his arm, was standing in the doorway.

David's aunt was overjoyed to see us. I pushed my fears aside and embraced her. "Oh, Malinda!" I backed up to look her in the face. I was shocked by her thin bent form.

"You came."

"Yes, Malinda, we came."

Her shaking hands reached for support. "I didn't know. I didn't know . . . "

"We're here to help, Malinda." I put my hands under her arms and helped her to her room. "But you're tired. Let me help you back to bed. We'll talk more in the morning."

464

She gave in easily. I lifted her feet into the bed and drew the worn cover around her. "You've been through a lot, Malinda, all by yourself." I bent to kiss her. "We'll stay as long as you need us. Don't worry anymore."

Tears stood in the corners of her eyes as her lips formed a faint smile. "Maybe so . . . maybe so."

As I blew out the light I heard her mumbling in the darkness.

We set up housekeeping in a home reduced to poverty. With our coming, Malinda seemed to fade into a world all her own. David's efforts to talk to her about the farm didn't seem to register in her mind. It took too much effort to stay part of a reality that did not include Fred and their life together.

The younger boys and I scoured the barnyard and adjoining fields in daily desperation to keep food on the table. David scouted around for work but found nothing. People were too poor to pay wages, and there was a limit to what a crippled man could do. It was depressing.

The older boys began cutting and splitting firewood, then fanning out in different directions, trying to sell it for a few pennies a bundle. David took his turn as well. They weren't always met cordially. After discovering who we were, some people were not sympathetic of our stand during their struggle for independence.

We had been expecting hardship. We were not afraid of hard work. And skimping with the barest sustenance had become a way of life for us. But the ill will and open hostility jolted us.

The day David returned with a half dozen welts across his back, I could bear no more. "You won't go

465

out again, please."

"Ellen, I must."

My chest rose and fell. "We can't have you killed by those who have lost all sense of human dignity. We will manage somehow."

He took my chin in his hand. "Ellen, you don't understand. I have to, for us to be able to survive the coming winter.

"A rider overtook me on the way home and liked the looks of the half peck of potatoes I had been given. He accused me of stealing. I couldn't convince him otherwise."

He winced. "As you see, he put up a good argument."

I opened my mouth, but he held up his hand and shook his head. "Ellen, I have to do what I can do, and so do you. We know God wouldn't expect less of us."

His words were tender, but there was a desperation in his eyes that made me unable to reply. I looked away.

When we had collected enough food to last several days, David took off two days to go to Staunton and check into the legal status of the farm. He may as well have spent his time otherwise. What he found was not encouraging. He returned shaking his head. "I shouldn't have gone. There are so many people pushing to get things worked out. The records are in a bad state, many of them destroyed. The town is in shambles. Some rebuilding is going on, but only a paltry amount. Federal sentinels are everywhere. People hardly have the barest necessities."

My heart slumped. "Oh, David!"

He stepped closer. "Don't despair, Ellen. I'll wait

awhile and try again." Then he brightened. "Guess who I met on my way home."

"Who?"

"James."

"James? He's safe?"

"Yes, but he had sad news." He put his hands on my shoulders. "Your father passed away a week ago."

"Father!" I began trembling.

"Another heart attack. He seems to have passed away very peacefully."

I could not hold back the tears. I took David's hand in mine. "What will Mother do?"

"She was there."

"She was?"

He cleared his throat. "James was the perfect gentleman, of course. He insisted on taking me to the house and finding something to eat." He paused. "But guess what else he told me. He has a lady friend now."

I looked at him in astonishment. "James! But he's not old enough . . ."

"He's older than you were when you got married, little lady." David's face crinkled in a half grin. "Or don't you remember? Why John isn't far from that himself."

I sucked in my breath. "Why yes . . . I suppose so, but I can hardly believe it. Do I know her?"

"Um . . . perhaps. She is the hat maker's daughter who lost her husband in the war."

"You mean the hat maker that lived above her shop next to the market? Her daughter?"

"You knew her?"

"Yes . . . yes! She was helping at the hospital the same time you were there. We talked together a number of times. Agnes . . . Agnes Whittington was her name."

"That sounds right."

"But she must be older than James by several years."

"Three, I think James said."

"She's a very sweet person," I said, trying to let it all soak in. "How does Mother feel about it?"

"Oh, she's pretty happy, I believe. Mrs. Cartwell is a right high-class lady in town, you know.

"I think it is taking some of the edge off the trauma of Bernard's death. She at least has something to fall back on; something with promise of better days ahead."

"Did she talk to you?" I asked.

"Not more than she had to. I was acknowledged, that was about all. But actually, Ellen, I don't struggle with bitterness toward her . . . and I don't think you would have either. She's not the powerful lady of society she used to be. She's just a shriveled, gray woman who's about at the end of life and facing the future pretty much alone. She wasn't sharp to me, in fact, she actually seemed embarrassed at my presence. I wondered if she wishes she could take back some of the things she has done in the past, but doesn't know how."

"Poor Mother." I stood for a moment, thinking. "Does James seem hardened from his . . . from all he's gone through?"

David's eyes narrowed. "We didn't talk much about things in the past. I asked him about the time you met up with him in Sheridan's army. He just left me hanging. 'Some things are better left unknown,' was his answer.

468

"I think he is trying to block out the past by thinking ahead—Agnes, taking over the homeplace, farm responsibilities."

"That won't bring him peace."

"No, no, Ellen, it won't. I told him so, but it made him angry. 'It's hard enough to remember how to be a gentleman without reliving it all over again. Lee should never have surrendered. We hadn't given up, and he shouldn't have either. I'm proud of having been a part of the struggle; and I'm not done fighting—not yet. But for now, I'm trying to forget the whole affair.' That was what he said, and I've thought about it all the way home."

There was no dealing with sin and hate, just stuffing it away, hoping to hide it under life's present pursuits. My heart ached. How could a society teach its men to hate, to destroy, to take revenge without mercy, and then expect those same men to file quietly back to their former lives and meekly take up where they left off?

"There will be reaping from this," I said.

"Much reaping. More than I care to think about. It would have been easier to stay in the North." David rubbed his brow. "I don't wish to frighten you, but James says lawlessness is rampant, men living off the land, looting, living by force. No better than war days, maybe worse."

He hesitated. "I guess I should tell you . . . Twice now I have gone out early and brushed away fresh horse tracks that crossed the barnyard. They always follow the same route. I can only guess what they are after."

His face darkened as he looked down at me. I knew he was waiting for a reply, but I could find none. Suddenly the safety we had had in the North seemed a tantalizing dream.

The days grew cooler, and the nights were nipped with frost. Along with the falling leaves, my hopes continued to crumble. Measuring time from one meal to the next and watching the boys at the table with only enough to whet the appetite pained deeply.

Then one day the unexpected happened. Through a wood customer, David got wind of a teamster job hauling wood ties through Waynesborough and Rockfish Gap to repair railroad tracks east to Charlottesville. It was only a slim chance, but he prepared to leave immediately.

We saw him off the next morning. I was frightened to let him go, yet we all knew how close we were to beggary.

"Stay in after dark. And be careful." He looked at us tenderly. "I'll be back."

By now John and Peter needed to go further than ever to find wood. They put in long hours chopping and splitting enough to keep our own fire going besides some to sell.

I was fixing supper the third afternoon when I heard footsteps pounding across the yard. I straightened up in time to see John and Peter leap the porch rail. They burst inside, slamming the door. John leaned against it panting and pulled home the bolt. Peter lunged toward the window, his gaze sweeping the yard.

I grabbed his arm. "What is it?!"

He pulled me back against the wall. "They might have guns."

"Who? What is going on?"

"Squatters," Peter hissed. "Papa hasn't returned?"

"No."

"Then pray he's not close by."

For over an hour we remained quiet. Peter held Susan on the stairway, and John kept his eye on the window. The gruel bubbled up over the pot and down into the fire. No one moved. *God, protect us all*, I prayed. Daylight faded into twilight and the room darkened.

Suddenly we heard footsteps mount the steps and a fumbling and tugging at the door. We were petrified. "What's going on?" a voice called.

It was David. I collapsed with Susan into a chair as John unbolted the door and swung it open.

David walked inside and slid a small bag of flour off his shoulder onto the chair. "What's going on here?"

"They were after us," John found his voice.

"We stumbled onto their camp," explained Peter. "They chased us on foot all the way from the ridge."

"How many?"

"Three."

"Guns?"

"I'm not sure. At least they didn't use them."

"No mounts?"

"Tethered too far away, I guess."

David's mouth was tight as he paced the floor. Then he crouched in the darkness by the open window, listening intently for a long time.

"That settles it," David said later, long after the children had gone to sleep. I picked at the mending in my lap.

"Settles what, David?"

"We're leaving. We can't exist here over winter with so little food and no job. That job is over, just as

I thought. They could have included my name in the group that will be hauling from near Cross Keys, but they didn't. I overheard one of them say they didn't want a galvanized Yankee taking a job from their own people."

"David! A what?"

His jaw tightened. "A Northerner who tries to appear a genuine Southerner."

"How did they know . . ."

"They torture with words until they find out what they want."

I tried to thread the darning needle with trembling fingers. Panic threatened to rise within me.

David's voice was harsh. "I asked for work all the way home. Nothing."

"I don't understand," I bit my lip. "The direction to come seemed so clear. And Malinda would have starved if we hadn't."

He ran his hands roughly through his hair. "We'll leave and take her along."

"David, the woman can hardly get out of bed, much less walk out the lane."

He stared at me. "Do you realize how close to starvation we are? And one of us could get picked off each time we step outside the door."

"You said we had to do what we had to do."

"I know. But does God expect us to sit here with no regard for the family's safety?"

I forced my voice to stay calm. "The Lord knew all that before He opened the way to come . . . didn't He? Why, David? Did we do something wrong?" I clasped and unclasped my hands.

His face twisted painfully. "I don't know, but I'm going to pray until I do know." He eased out of his chair, rubbing his stiff leg. "Someone rode by the house while you were upstairs putting Susan to bed. There's trouble brewing, Ellen.

"I don't see how we can get the land scrap straight anytime soon. Anyone doing legal business has to swear allegiance to the Union again. And those who consider themselves 'true Virginians' are angry toward anyone that does. Anyone from north of the Mason-Dixon line is despised. Bitterness is everywhere. I think we would do well to clear out."

"When? How, David?"

"I don't know. But as soon as I can figure out a way. We have to think of the family."

I took a deep shuddering breath. "Where, David?"

He shrugged. "North."

I closed my eyes. *Again?* I thought. *Again without a home? Are we following God or slinking off on our own?*

℞ Chapter XXIII ℞

"Mommy." It was Susan at the door, her face still groggy from sleep.

I gathered up my load of kindling from the woodpile and moved toward the house. "Hi, little girlie. I'm coming."

"Mommy, Grandma Linda fall down."

"What?" In my haste I dropped the wood and rushed past her into the bedroom.

"Malinda!"

She lay where she had fallen, her right leg twisted under her. I knelt and turned her head toward me. Her eyes were blank and staring.

"Malinda?" I felt for her pulse. There was a slight

flutter of movement, and then she moaned, and her mouth opened and closed.

"Malinda, what happened? Here, let me help you." I bent closer, then stood up uncertainly. Though Malinda wasn't heavy, I dared not risk moving her alone.

I found Andy outside, and we carefully lifted her back into bed. I ran my fingertips over her legs and arms, probing for broken bones.

"Is she okay?"

I looked up. It was Peter. Andy had found him somewhere.

"I'm not sure, son. She's not breathing well."

Malinda groaned every time I tried to straighten her right leg, so I wrapped it well with warm cloths and let it be. I knew nothing about setting broken bones.

Swabbing her face, I stroked her arm and talked to her. It was distressing to know she was suffering, and I had nothing to offer.

David came home after dark, and together we sat by her bedside. By now David's aunt was grasping at her heart; and her eyes, still unfocused, were wild and frightened.

David stroked her forehead. "Malinda, can you hear me? We're here, Ellen and I. Will you take some tea? No? I'm sorry, so sorry. Shall I pray, Malinda? Would you like me to pray?"

There was no indication she had heard, but he lifted his head. "Oh, Father, you see the suffering. Would you bestow your mercy upon her body and soul . . ."

Tears ran down my cheeks. I tried to soothe the old lady's restless hands in mine but the trembling

476

only increased. As the night wore on, her breathing began coming in short gasps, and her arms and legs pulled up stiffly. With one last desperate gasp, it was over. She was gone.

I sank back in my chair, unable to move. After such a struggle, the silence was almost more than I could bear. At last David pulled the sheet over the limp form and straightened up. His eyes found mine. "Let's wash her up then go to bed. The night is almost gone."

We laid down but couldn't really sleep. In the morning David pulled some boards off the barn and fastened them together into a semblance of a coffin. I laid out the body in the only decent dress Malinda had left, then stood by the window as David and the boys dug a shallow grave in the cold drizzle.

After Scripture and prayer at the grave, David and the boys gently lowered the coffin and filled the grave with the rain-dampened earth. I stood, holding Susan, my cheek pressed against hers.

When we returned to the house, David followed me into the next room. "We will leave tomorrow."

Even though I had been expecting it, I couldn't help staring.

"I've been thinking about Allen and his tailoring business. A one-handed man could help tend a store, I think." He coughed. "What do you think?"

My shoulders sagged. "I don't know how I feel anymore, David. We've been homeless for so long."

I went on hoarsely. "Father's gone, and I didn't even get to say goodbye. I watched Malinda suffer, and I couldn't do a thing. I feel so guilty, David. I let her down. How can we leave so soon? We haven't even gotten to meet any of the Mennonite people."

He blinked. "I have, Ellen. I've gone up that way with wood a time or so. They've paid no more mind to me than anyone else, not a sale to any of them."

I couldn't believe what I was hearing. "You didn't tell me, David. Did you tell them who you were? Did you ask for work?"

He cleared his throat. "No . . . no, I didn't. It's no use."

I stared at him. Was this my husband who had endured war, hatred, and prison? The one who had vowed to stand for peace no matter the cost? I touched his arm. "David, have . . . have you given up?"

He did not reply, and I crumpled into his arms. He kept his face averted and his breath came sharply. "I am sorry, Ellen. I've failed. I'm a failure! I've not accomplished anything I had hoped since we moved down." His voice was harsh. "But what choice do we have? How destitute does a person have to get before concluding God doesn't want us here?"

My head throbbed. I felt confused, alone, forsaken. Had God led us here just to leave us hanging?

Before dawn, we were on the road. As we came to the bottom of the hill, I looked back. The pain was more than I could bear, and I turned away. I kept swallowing hard, breathing deeply. I remembered what David had said before we left. "Only God knows where we will end up. I don't know if what we are doing is right or wrong, but God knows we tried."

Did God understand? My mind felt numb. I gathered Susan closer, forcing my feet to keep moving ahead. A verse slowly came to my troubled mind, "He that followeth me shall not walk in darkness but shall have the light of life." I took a deep breath.

We kept moving all day, stopping only for David to rest his bad hip. By evening we were at Burke's Mill.

One glance showed what we had not seen coming through in the darkness back in the summer. Naked Creek now ran over blackened timbers and warped pieces of gearing. The mill had not survived the time of burning.

But the miller's house had been spared. It still stood half hidden back of the clearing. David led the way off the pike and down to the creek.

He knocked repeatedly before the door finally cracked open. After a few words which we could not hear, David turned and motioned us to come.

Not only did the old couple insist we come in to sleep, but they sat us around the table to share their thin cabbage broth.

"We don't mean to be hard-hearted. God knows we need friends this day and time." Mrs. Ferguson hobbled over to the door and bolted it again. "But we've had so many come through. They all want food and what'ere else they can see. We scarcely have enough like 'tis."

Her husband was as quiet as she was talkative. He merely nodded and let her go on with the conversation.

"I always said if the good Lord weren't kind to us we'd uh been gone long ago. I never thought I'd see the day when I'd turn anybody away from our door, but I've had to the last while." She lowered her voice as if embarrassed. "Why jest yers-dey we cut the light and pulled the shutters and let a man knock till he finally went on 'bout his business. Turner here, he didn't like it none, but a body has to do some'thun."

Her husband cleared his throat. "We're not out to make enemies."

Effie snorted. "Why, as much as you like to eat, you ought to be glad I treated him thataway. You'd give away the last crumb in the house." The sharpness in her voice softened, and she stroked his back. "But neither of us can turn away a young'un. How old is she?"

I smiled into the wrinkled face and pulled Susan close. "She was two last summer."

The old woman nodded. "Small for her age. Puny like. But who of us ain't. Got perdy eyes though, and sech dark hair. Purdy chile."

She stood up again. "You'll tell us 'bout yourself, I reckon. We aim to let you stay the night, 'ere you care to. Ain't so, Pop?"

Turner pushed himself to the edge of the chair. "Most certainly."

They both listened to David's story with great interest. When he was finished Effie turned to her husband. "We know some of the Mennonite people. Though I don't know what's happened to them with all the fight'en goin' on. But they stick together, so I've heard. Like family."

Before I could stop myself I found myself asking, "Do you know of anyone needing a hired hand?" I swallowed hard. I felt color rise in my cheeks, and I could not bring myself to look at David.

I heard his chair scrape, and he cleared his throat. The old man and his wife glanced at each other.

"Can't say that we do. But let us study on it till morning. We may recollect somethun'."

We all spread out across the wooden floor for the night. I found it hard to relax. I was afraid I had offended David with my impulsiveness. He had not said anything. I strained my eyes to see him in the dark, then gave up and watched the gray outline of the small window on the opposite wall.

Oh, David. The Gochenours. It would be so encouraging to see them again. You couldn't help but love them. The roses clock is there, David . . . They wouldn't turn us away, not my Wilhelm and Rebecca.

The sounds of light breathing were the only sounds around me, then Susan whimpered, and I pulled her close, stroking her back and staring unseeingly into the blackness of the night.

Much to my surprise, in the morning David turned east instead of following the pike. He passed Susan to the boys to carry and came to walk beside me.

"We'll give it one last chance, Ellen. We'll stop by those you know and ask about work." His mouth tightened. "Then we'll head out of the Valley, the farther the better."

My heart leaped, and I caught his hand. "Oh, David!"

He frowned. "Don't get your hopes up, Ellen. It's a waste of time. The land is as bare here as it was around Staunton."

I caught my breath. "I know, David, I know. But at least we are giving God a chance. We're not leaving without giving God a chance."

Suddenly my feet had purpose, and I found myself hurrying, gazing ahead as if I could pull us

481

along by mental force. It was late afternoon till we came up the long draw and around the hill where Wilhelm's cabin stood. We stopped to rest. I looked eagerly over the landscape, trying to tell whether things had changed.

There was a slender wisp of smoke, hardly enough to see, rising from the chimney. Several trees were gone from around the house, and the fields were tall with weeds.

Then from the corner of the woods, I saw them coming. A few steps at a time, their arms full of twigs, helping each other along. My breath caught in my throat, then we were moving forward. Andy broke the silence, "Grandpa! Grandpa and Grandma!"

Both heads raised to look, then they dropped their loads and hobbled hurriedly in our direction. I swept Rebecca in my arms and held her close, giving support to her trembling legs.

Wilhelm was shaking David's hand and reaching for the children, wiping tears and patting Susan on the head. "I cout' not haf guessed, nefer guessed! Gott bless you all! Come in, you will, and rest.

"Haf you hat' food?" he asked. "I thought not. Come in, come in. Stay as long as you wish. We will share together."

We followed him up the steps and into the familiar room. I helped Rebecca to a chair, unable to ignore her thinness and ragged clothes. Her cheekbones stood out under paper-thin skin, and her hands had a constant tremor.

But the smile was the same, and her blue eyes held the same measure of peace I had marveled at months ago. Her voice quavered. "May God be praised! I prayed for you day and night ever since

482

you left." She turned to Susan. "And this is my Susan. Come to Grandma, my dear." She pulled her close. "And your boys, they've grown so!"

Then she held her hand in David's direction. "And this is your David." She shook hands, then leaned back and closed her eyes. "What a miracle of God! How weak was my faith."

Our meal hardly sufficed to go around, yet I had never felt the presence of God so near! The afternoon was not long enough to share all that had happened since we had parted from each other.

Finally I turned to Wilhelm. "But tell us how you managed to survive during these times of famine?"

He passed his hand over his face. "Only by the mercy of Gott. As you can see, the hardship has taken its toll. We were able to stay alif', that iss all. But we had the Lord."

He opened his eyes. "But for you. You are leefing again? He takes you elsewhere?"

David looked at the floor. "We have perhaps grown weak, Wilhelm. Weak in faith or weak through affliction. I felt the way was clear to come back, yet we cannot stay where there are not provisions to live. Now that Malinda passed away, there is nothing to hold us there." He cleared his throat. "To be honest, you were our last stop on our way out of the Valley."

The old man's eyes narrowed and he nodded. "It seems impossible, I know." He pressed his heart. "You feel how, in here?"

David rubbed his stiff leg for a long moment. "We've felt rejection and hostility since we're returned. There is neither enough food nor work to stay alive over winter. We were in constant danger. We stuck it out as long as we could."

483

Wilhelm sat silently looking through the window. I wondered if he had heard. When he spoke it was as if he were talking to someone we could not see. "Nefer undo in doubt what you did in faith." He leaned forward. "A servant doess not choose where he serves—only *who* he serves. But . . . it is goot that you haf come. We will pray with you."

His expression softened, and he raised himself to his feet. "You would wish to help me bring in the wood we dropped in the meadow?" He stopped by the table. "Here, we found it to our advantage to skip the last meal uf the day, so haf a piece uf cornmeal."

David and the boys followed him as he shuffled out the door, and I turned to Rebecca, still settled in the corner rocking chair. "Let me bring you a bite before you lie down."

She waved my offer aside. "I am not so hungry tonight, my daughter. Save it for your boys."

"But, Rebecca . . ."

"There comes a time when food does not mean so much anymore. I'm just tired." She smiled up at me. "We packed your roses clock in the attic for safe-keeping. Now we can return it again. And Granny Bristlow's trunk. God is good, Ellen, God is good."

I helped her to her feet, and we started to the bedroom. I pulled the coverlet down, and she lay back gratefully into the pillow. "Even in the worst of events, His goodness does not dim. It is only our weakness that causes us to not see it clearly."

I bent to kiss her cheek. "You can say that even after all you've gone through?"

Her face registered surprise. "What else could give as much comfort as that? 'Tis the one thing to keep one's sanity in a time of turbulence. All who

484

love Him will find it so." She smiled again, then closed her eyes. "God bless you, my daughter."

Susan had already fallen asleep on the rug when I again entered the front room. I fixed her a nest in the side room then washed up the few dishes. It was almost sunset when I picked up the water bucket in a corner and headed to the springhouse.

The continual gurgle inside the dark walls brought back vivid memories. Suddenly I was in a hurry. I lifted the brimming bucket and carried it through the doorway. Wilhelm was approaching, his own container in hand. He paused. "How iss it with you, daughter? You haf an urge from the Lord?"

His fatherly manner toppled my carefully held-in emotions. I broke down and wept. "I am so afraid we may step outside of God's leading. I don't know what to do. I just can't tell."

He set his bucket down. "You haf gone through much and haf been shaken to the core. The Lord knows your desire—and your weakness. Do you not think He can speak His answer so you can see to follow?"

I wrapped my apron around my arms. "It's just been so hard. Like crossing an ocean with no destination in mind." I took a shuddering breath. "What should we do?"

He pointed into the twilight. "Do not fear the darkness, Ellen. When the sun goes down, Gott lights a star. Gott would not be Gott if he did not gif you a prod in the right direction." He cupped his chin in his hand. "I would say to wait for a token from Gott—a token that iss followed by His peace."

"Please help us."

He nodded. "I haf been thinking. And we will

pray together. Come, we will talk to your David."

And he did. Although it was growing late, he gathered the family around the table. "This is what I think as I pick up wood outside. We haf a morning service at the church this Lord's day. It iss too far for the old father and mother to walk. But you should go. Ask our people. See vat they say. Perhaps there will be a place you can be used among us."

David did not look up. I kept my eyes on his fingers, pulling at the frayed edges of his sleeve. I could hear embarrassment in his answer.

"At Buffalo Mills I feel almost certain we could get work. People know us there." He cleared his throat. "We are a large family. It seems impossible that anyone here would be able to offer us a place to live, or work for pay, even if they would wish to."

Wilhelm nodded. "So it seems. But if Gott wants you here, He has provisions already prepared for you. If not, then you are free to go. It iss for you to decide.

"Iss there a church group there to feed your soul? A wise man looks far ahead and sets his course to where he wishes to be at in the end no matter the shoals and rapids he must go through."

I held my breath. David bit his lip, drumming his fingers on the table leg. He looked at me thoughtfully, weighing his decision in the balance.

He smiled into my eyes. "I guess that's fair enough. Would you say so?"

I did not have to say a word. His smile widened for a moment. "And you boys?" They nodded. He turned back to Wilhelm. "Then I guess we will go."

The old man beamed. "It iss goot. Now we pray."

In the end we took only John with us, leaving just

after sunrise. The half-light soon brightened. The most vivid colors were now fading into bronze and gold. The maples and birches had already dropped their leaves.

In spite of feeling nervous, I felt more hopeful than I had for many weeks. I held onto David's sleeve and matched my steps to his. "Do you remember the verse I wrote to you while we were apart?"

His lips tightened. "Which one?"

"The one, 'O that I had wings like a dove, then would I fly away and be at rest.' "

David hunched his shoulders under his thin coat. "Yes, Ellen, who wouldn't wish for such a thing? Why?"

"Well, we can't, can we, David? We have to take the 'rest' along with us or we will never have it at all." I squeezed his hand. "If I could take the wings of the morning, even there shall thy right hand lead me . . ."

He did not reply, but I thought the creases around his eyes eased a bit. An hour went by.

John, now a bit ahead of us, stopped under a tree to wait. He shaded his eyes toward the south. "There are some people at the foot of the hill. I think I see the church."

We came to stand beside him. There was a nervous twitching around David's mouth. "I hope we don't regret what we're doing. I don't know a soul." He held his breath, then let it out forcefully. "May His will be done." He led the way down the hill.

By the time we reached the field's edge, two men at the door had seen us and were coming in our direction. My heart leaped. Wasn't one of them the man who had taken us in over a year ago?

The tallest one stepped forward, meeting us with

outstretched hand. "Welcome to our gathering. I'm Isaac Grove, a minister here. Do we know each other?"

"I don't suppose so. I'm David Shull. This is my wife Ellen, and our oldest son, John."

The minister shook hands all around.

"I know you," I said eagerly. "You may not remember me, but my children and I found shelter in your home last year before going to live with Wilhelm and Rebecca Gochenour."

His eyes brightened. "Yes, I remember. The young mother and children, homeless and seeking the Lord. I'm sorry Jacob Hildebrand, our head minister, cannot be here today. He would remember you too, I feel sure.

"So, you found your husband." He clasped David's hand again.

I could sense David relaxing. "Yes, after the war this past spring."

"At Gochenours?"

"No, in Pennsylvania. At my parents' place."

There was a look of surprise on the man's face.

"My wife fled north when Sheridan's wagon train left the Valley; I was released from a federal prison in New York."

"May God be praised! That is a miracle. It would be refreshing to hear more. Come in and worship with us." He led the way inside, introducing us to the small but friendly group clustered around the tin heater in the back of the room.

An old man perched on a stool in the corner pushed himself to his feet and shuffled over to peer into John's face. *"Wie gehts?* You strangers?"

The minister laid his hand on the thin shoulder.

"This is Pete Balland. Pete, this is David and Ellen Shull and their son John.

"Peter lives alone down by the river. And you . . ." He raised his eyebrows.

David wavered. "I'm not . . . until recently we lived with my aunt across the pike. She died a week ago."

Isaac Grove's eyes were kind. "You have suffered much in the war. Thank God, He has reunited you."

Old man Balland clasped David's hand and his chin wobbled. *"An Gottes Segen ist alles gelegen."*

"Yes, everything depends on God's blessing." The minister's eyes grew bright and he turned away. "Pete lost his wife the first winter of the war. This has been a time of hardship for all of us." After a moment's hesitation, he gestured toward the benches in front of us. "Find seats. It is time to begin the service."

We watched as the others filed in and took their places, the women on one side of the room and the men on the other. We seated ourselves near the back across the aisle from each other and concentrated on the service. The opening songs were followed by a German sermon, liberally sprinkled with English, for our benefit I felt sure.

At the end of the service, the minister stepped off the raised platform "Does God always answer the prayer of a person in need?" His eyes furrowed as he looked out over his small audience. No one spoke. They seemed as caught off guard as we were.

Mr. Grove took a step forward. "I know this is rather unusual, but before I close the service I would like to ask our visitor to share. Mr. Shull, would you care to tell us of your experience?"

489

I was stunned. I glanced at David. I could see his legs tense and his jaw grow tight. His mouth worked a moment, then he stood up slowly, his hand gripping the bench in front of him.

"I've never done this before. I don't know if I can share this with a group of strangers or not." He grimaced apologetically. "It's pretty personal at times. I hope you can understand if I keep it brief."

He coughed and looked down. "I am from the North, but came south to find work. I met and married my wife, Ellen, and we made our home near her family at Staunton. We have five children.

"Perhaps you can imagine the quandary we were swept into because of the war; my family on one side, her family on the other. I never felt comfortable with either side but had no choice but to enlist with a local regiment."

He rubbed his hand along the bench back. "War is terrible. I met my youngest brother from Pennsylvania on the battlefield, and we both were shot, both badly wounded. I held him . . ." he cleared his throat, ". . . as he died."

He shook his head as if to clear his mind. "My injuries took months to heal, and all the while my mind fought for a way to ease the guilt." He lifted his head and looked the minister full in the face. "And beyond all my personal agony, the thought kept coming back to me, aren't all men flesh and blood? Aren't we all brothers? Why should men cause such suffering for one another?

"Once I was able to talk to one of your people, and as I recovered, my wife and I determined we wanted to become a part of a group that practiced peace toward all men.

490

"We suffered for it, just as all of you have. I was taken prisoner-of-war and held for over a year. We were only reunited back in the summer.

"A couple months ago we came back to the Valley to live. But the impossibility of supporting a family, along with prejudice against our beliefs, has forced us to start back to the North." He began to sit down, then straightened up again. "May God give you the strength to endure."

Silence hung thick in the room. I dared not look up. Then an older man rose to his feet. "I think you would find it different if you dwelt among our people. My potatoes did well this summer. And I could use help rebuilding my barn. Come stay with us a few weeks."

There was a suppressed cough. A man whom we'd met before the service stood up. "Our house is too small to offer, but I could spare a bag of wheat to be ground for their use."

An elderly lady spoke next. "My husband is ill. The man and his sons can take our share time on road maintenance. We can pay them a little for whatever time they can give."

My amazement grew as one by one, each grownup rose to offer some of his meager means for our behalf. With each commitment David's head hung lower until he looked close to tears.

The minister looked as moved as we were. "The way of sacrifice is the way of love. How can we say we love God whom we have not seen, and not prove our love to one who stands among us?" His eyes rested on each of the audience. "I am thinking of the tenant house vacated on Pete Balland's place. It has only one room, but I have a feeling Pete would be glad for someone close by."

He spoke in a quick undertone to the old man leaning on his cane on the corner bench, then straightened up and smiled at David as a light sprang up on Pete's wrinkled face.

"He says, by all means, you are welcome."

The old man spoke again and motioned rapidly with his hands. A titter of laughter crossed the audience and someone next to us explained.

"He says the roof and walls are tight and should be quite adequate if you can get rid of the skunks who have tunneled under the floor. They could make life unpleasant."

I smothered a gasp in my hand, and David grinned weakly. He cautiously rose to his feet and braved the eyes focused expectantly on him. "Your . . ." he stopped to compose himself, "your openness to strangers has touched us deeply. Wilhelm told me living out God's way in its purity calls for the highest level of sacrifice. Now I am seeing the fruit that kind of living produces. Although we are not worthy, we would feel honored to become a part of your group."

He motioned towards John and me, "Without the encouragement and steadfastness of my wife and our five children, I would have given up many times in these last weeks.

"Now with your openness to share, the Lord is giving overwhelming evidence that He wants us to continue in the path we have chosen, and to trust His provisions to meet His calling here." He lifted his hand in an awkward salute. "You have my deepest gratitude and respect. You have strengthened my hold on God once more. May God bless you, each one."

492

It was nearly two hours after the service before we could pull ourselves away to leave. Although I knew there were countless hardships before us, yet I felt a joy I had never known. I could sense David felt the same. He set a brisk pace for us.

When we passed the poplar tree where we had first seen the church, he pulled us to a stop. "It would only seem fitting to offer our thanks for the mercy of the Lord. John, will you lead us?"

The color heightened on John's face but he bowed his head. "Lord, we thank Thee for Thy love and for Thy people to share it with us. Help us to show that love to those who do not know Thee. Amen."

"Amen." David raised his head and took a deep breath as we resumed walking. "What acceptance! I can hardly soak it in. How enriching it is to talk with people free from hatred and bitterness."

He looked back in the direction we had come. "We have a life to live before them, and we must not let them down."

I held up the stump of his left arm and pressed it to my lips. "God was good to lead us here."

He leaned his head back, chuckling. "You were the one who had enough courage to listen, Ellen. I had given up." His eyes, his mouth, his whole face was smiling. "Who deserves to forge our path? Lead on, little lady!"

I pulled back. "Oh, no, I couldn't. There are still the skunks to deal with."

His laughter was hearty. "We'll go over and check them out tomorrow."

John grinned then grew serious. "I suppose varmints will be the least of our worries."

David looked John in the eyes. "Do you feel it's

too great a risk to take, son? Tell me honestly."

John ran his fingers through his hair and straightened his shoulders. "Haven't you said, where God leads His provisions follow? It seems He is showing us where to chart our course. I'd say, unfurl the sail."

David gripped his hand firmly. "Thank you, son. It's going to be tough. We'll need all the fortitude we'll be able to muster. Our lives are still in danger, but at least we are not alone, no longer alone." He shook his head as if to clear his mind. "But what are we waiting for? We're almost home. Look up on the hill. Who's poking their heads out the door?"

The bent form of Wilhelm in the cabin doorway suddenly disappeared behind the boys' lanky figures jumping off the porch steps. Susan, with Rebecca's shawl wrapped around her, came trotting after them.

"Wait fuh me . . . !" Susan's voice piped out from behind. Peter stopped to swing her up onto his shoulders, then followed the others with long swinging steps down the hill to meet us.

Notes

CHAPTER I

1. Brice, Marshall M., *Conquest of a Valley*, p. 4. During the last decades preceding the Civil War, the town of Staunton progressed from a frontier village to a thriving county seat of almost 4,000 people. Miles of telegraph wire and railroad linked the Valley to the outside world. Five stage lines radiated out in all directions. Factories and schools for higher learning drew male and female students from a distance. Its public institutions for the handicapped were known far and wide. It was no surprise, then, that Staunton was named, along with Gordonsville and Wheeling, as a Virginia mobilization center.

2. Driver, Robert Jr., *52nd Virginia Infantry*, pp. 1, 2; Waddel, Josh. A., *Annals of Augusta County*, p. 461. The 52nd was organized in August, 1861, and made up of men from Augusta and Rockbridge counties. Its growing number of enlistees set up camp on the grounds of the Deaf, Dumb, and Blind Asylum whose inmates were moved to the smaller Staunton Female Academy.

3. Major snowstorms were a common experience as cited in Waddel, *Annals*, p. 448. In 1857 the people of Staunton endured a storm with blizzard conditions for 24 hours with temperatures dipping to 0 or below. No trains ran for 10 days.

CHAPTER II

1. Waddel, *Annals*, pp. 454-458.

2. Ibid., p. 463. The Southern Army stationed in the West Virginia mountains depended almost entirely upon supplies sent by wagon from Staunton. Many of the wagons were hired or pressed into service, the owners being paid $2.50 for a two-horse team; $4.00 for a four.

3. Ibid., p. 465. The Virginia Hotel was one of three hotels in the city. Its stables were destroyed by fire on Dec. 13, 1861 with a loss of close to 50 horses, most of them privately owned. The rest belonged to the government.

4. Driver, *52nd Infantry*, p. 4. The 52nd's first orders were to march to Greenbrier River to join other Confederate units as a stationary front against Federal attack. They went into camp in the Alleghenies, were briefly involved in two skirmishes with Union forces, and spent the rest of the fall preparing winter quarters.

5. Waddel, *Annals*, pp. 463-464. Confederate election day wasn't held until November 6, 1861. Baldwin had been a member of the State Convention before being elected to Congress.

CHAPTER III

1. Gordon, George, *Poems of Byron*, p. 207. This worn little classic came to me with this inscription on the flyleaf, "L. Crowder, University of Virginia, July 25, 1925." There are numerous notations scattered throughout its pages. Among them is this one, "Only in civilization did man fail. State of man in savagery is happier than civilized man."

A warped philosophy also comes through in Byron s actual poetry. It is not written from a Christian perspective, but Ellen, at this time, was not sure what her outlook on life was.

2. Irvin Bell's book, *They Who Fought Here*, tells us that 2½ times as many men died from sickness as in battle.

CHAPTER IV

1. Waddel, *Annals*, p. 464. There seemed to be a constant rush of wagon traffic coming and going during the winter months. Nearly every day large groups of worn-out horses were being brought in to be replaced by any that could be found.

2. *Ibid.*, p. 418. James Buryhill, the bachelor, who kept a liquor store, was also the self-appointed policeman of the well at the street corner. He lived in Staunton in the 1830s.

3. "Walking Tours of Historic Staunton." A pamphlet printed by the Historic Staunton Foundation.

4. Waddel, *Annals*, p. 478. A diary entry dated December 23, 1862 tells of a local milliner and female companion making a trip to Baltimore to purchase goods not available in town. The two women came back wearing several layers of dresses and cloaks, along with a large number of bonnet frames hidden under their hoods.

5. Driver, *52nd Infantry*, p. 7. This battle occurred on December 13, 1861. The two men killed made the 52nd's first fatalities.

CHAPTER V

1. Harris, J. C., *Uncle Remus, His Songs and His Sayings*, p. 183.

2. Miller, F. T., *Poetry and Eloquence of the Civil War*, p. 349.

3. Tapert, A., *The Brother's War*, p. 37. General Alpheus Williams writes home from the winter mountains of West Virginia expressing the hardships of camp:

> If you will . . . figure up how much provisions it takes to feed a few thousand, daily; hear the cries not of men only but of half-frozen mules and horses of which I have upwards of 800 . . . , witness the effort it takes to get forage . . . and you will be satisfied that in winter months a stationary front has about all it can do to subsist itself.

4. Horst, S., *Mennonites in the Confederacy*, p. 53. This group of 74 were kept in Castle Thunder, a large prison in Richmond for about a month before being released. Twenty-seven of them signed a paper saying they were "willing" to enlist, but these were non-church members, and not eligible to request exemption.

Waddel, *Annals*, p. 466. The diary author of this chapter calls them "simple-hearted, inoffensive people," and expresses this opinion about their capture:

> There is something pitiful in the case of these people, flying as they were to escape conscription, and being taken like partridges on the mountains. The whole crowd had a pocket pistol between them and no other arms.

CHAPTER VI

1. Waddel, *Annals*, p. 469. This occurred April 19, 1862.

2. Driver, *52nd Infantry*, p. 120. There were a number of Mennonite men whose names are given as being part of this division. Manassas Heatwole joined the 52nd, Co. F.

3. Waddel, *Annals*, pp. 469-470. This took place May 4, 5, '62.

4. Driver, *52nd Infantry*, p. 13. The Battle of McDowell was fought on the 8th of May. The incident of the bullet passing through a man's pocket occurred to Marion Coiner of Company B of their regiment.

5. *Ibid.*, p. 143. Richard Phillips, former president of the Female Institute of Staunton, was Chaplain of the 52nd for the first two years of the war.

6. Waddel, *Annals*, p. 471. All wagons in Augusta and adjoining counties were ordered sent to Winchester and other towns near the Maryland line. The townsfolk of Staunton were expecting 275 wagons to return on June 3 with captured store from Martinsburg.

7. *Ibid.*, p. 472. The first news of the battle of Port Republic was brought into town on Sunday evening (June 8).

CHAPTER VII

1. This account is based on an incident from Phoebe Pember's book, *A Southern Woman's Story*, pp. 66-68. As a prominent nurse in the Chimborazo

Hospital in Richmond, Phoebe had many haunting experiences with death. One such as this was especially sad. This young fellow had been brought into the hospital almost dead and over ten months' time, slowly brought back to health. His sudden death was devastating.

2. There are numerous accounts such as this, families divided by state lines or conflicting loyalties, to be ironically brought face to face on the field of battle. One such example is given in Poe's *True Tales of the South at War,* p. 170. This quotes the diary of Mrs. Judith McGuire, a refugee in Richmond. Her story was first published as *The Diary of a Southern Refugee,* E. J. Hale and Son, 1867.

CHAPTER VIII

1. With Jackson's army joining Lee's, they pushed their combined forces against General George McClellan, who was bringing his men up the coast toward Richmond. A series of fierce battles occurred over a week's time, resulting in neither side gaining a great advantage. McClellan, believing his forces to be outnumbered, finally retreated.

2. Waddel, *Annals,* p. 477. October 13 was cited as a public salt distribution day.

CHAPTER IX

1. Horst, S., *Mennonites in the Confederacy,* p. 62.

CHAPTER X

1. The comparison of worth ($500, $900, or "nuthun") was gleaned from and elaborated on from an incident

recorded in *True Tales of the South at War,* p. 108, under the chapter, "Diary of a Soldier's Wife on Looking Glass Plantation." Mrs. Catharine Edmondston of Halifax County, N.C.; first printed by Mrs. Stephen H. Millender, edited in part by Margaret M. Jones.

CHAPTER XI

1. James White, a promising young man of the 52nd, deserted in February of 1862.

2. The *Farmer and Housekeeper's Cyclopedia* of 1888 gives this recipe:

Potato Pie

Bake till done: 1 potato, 1 lemon, 1 beaten egg white, 1 cup sugar, 1 cup water

Topping: 3 egg whites, ½ cup powdered sugar, lemon flavor.
(Spread on, and bake.)

3. Poe, *True Tales of the South at War,* pp. 72-73. This technique was used successfully by a grandmother in Georgia to ward off Federal soldiers.

4. Waddel, *Annals,* p. 479. Used for light during the war's times of impoverishment, these candle substitutes were called Confederate candles. They burned quickly, gave poor illumination, and needed constant trimming to keep the whole taper from going up in flames.

CHAPTER XII

1. Brunk, H., *History of Mennonites in Va.,* Vol. 1, p. 155 (map).

2. The reader may question David's judgment in this, feeling he did not stay true to principle. The war caught the plain people mostly unprepared for a united stand. Responses varied among Mennonite and Dunkard men. Some gave in to the pressure of society and enlisted. Others, forced to enter the army, chose to be teamsters or have some other noncombatant duty.

It is interesting to note the responses of several Quaker men from the New England states who were arrested. When asked to do fatigue duty about camp, they at first complied. But then, ". . . the more we discussed in our minds the subject, the more clearly the right way seemed open to us; and we separately came to the judgment that we must not conform to this requirement."

They held true to their convictions, and after several months of ridicule and physical punishment, were paroled and sent home.

CHAPTER XIII

1. Horst, *Mennonites in the Confederacy*, p. 62. William Coffman was tried for "assisting deserters and communicating information to the enemy" in Dec. of 1862.

2. Gustavus Vassa, a Virginia slave who purchased his freedom and moved to England in the late 1700s, wrote in his autobiography, "Oh ye nominal Christians! Might not an African ask you, learned you this of your God . . . ?" Quoted in *Before Freedom Came*, by Edward Campbell, ed. Published in 1991.

3. This is told with pathos in any number of stories. A few examples I ran across:

a. *Green Mont.* The diary of a teenage boy from the tidewater of a North Carolinian plantation. His older brother is in the war; his mother's letters of prayer and loneliness are included in the book.

b. *The Children of Bladensfield.* Evelyn Ward's recollections of her childhood during the war years. Her mother's faith loomed large in her memories. She witnessed her mother's distress one night as the Yankees swept into the house and captured Evelyn's older brother, Charles. She awakened several nights later by her mother's cries at the news of Charles' death. She watched her mother's agony as she sat beside the deathbed of a second soldier son. The young man, upon seeing the suffering on her face said these words: "Mother, you have taught us all the faith we have, but you haven't faith enough to see me die" (p. 72).

c. *A Diary With Reminiscences of the War and Refugee's Life in the Shenandoah Valley* by Cornelia McDonald. Her husband a prisoner-of-war, Cornelia flees with her family from Federal takeover at Winchester. She makes her home in Lexington and suffers the brutality of David Hunter's army sweeping through. Although her husband dies before he can be released, she is comforted by the change of heart he betrays through his letters as he reaches out to God. Her faith is the one thing she clings to as she seeks to provide for her children.

4. Tapert, *The Brother's War*, p. 131. Quoting a letter by R. B. Goodyear, a private in the 27th Conn. Voluntary Infantry, written 2-14-1863:

> We have in the army a host of unprincipled men who do not care which way the wind blows. They would like the name of being

victorious, but they are not engaged heart and soul in putting down the rebellion. They talk "secession" and their sympathies are just about as strong for one side or the other. In reality they are our enemies.

5. *Ibid.*, p. 204. Quoting M. Gleichmann, a private in Company A of the 136th Ind. Volunteer Infantry:

... Oh the temptation is great. The character is tested here. My daily prayer is, "Lord, don't lead me into temptation but protect me from all sin . . ." My firm decision is to be true to my Savior to the end only by the grace of God. This morning I left the turmoil and sought out privacy. There I read a chapter and came close to my God, and the Lord richly blessed me, but of love to my God and Savior I had to cry. I am not afraid because I know the Lord is with me.

Quoting Frederick Pettit's letter to his parents (p. 203).

Company C, 100th Penn. Volunteer Infantry

Let us . . . put our trust in God. As long as we live right . . . we can do our duty without fear. War is a sober thing, and a soldier needs something more than mere courage to support him. Reading the Bible never seemed to afford me as much comfort as it does now . . .

(Frederick was killed July 1864 at Petersburg.)

6. Wayland, John, *History of Rockingham County*, p. 126. The author quotes a letter by Joseph Funk, writ-

ten Oct. 2, 1842:

> . . . We abound in the provisions of life. But with regret I mention, that I fear there is too little of true and unfeigned religion among us, which in a great measure may be owing to the clergy. If, in the room of a pious life . . . the preachers read their sermons and live in conformity to the world . . . I think the church . . . cannot grow and thrive.

CHAPTER XIV

1. Brunk, H., *History of Mennonites in Va.*, pp. 395, 403-405. These names were gathered from a map of the Southern District of Mennonites in the Valley during the late 1860s, in addition to several lists of church members.

2. *Ibid.*, p. 166.

3. Kinnear, Angus, *Against the Tide, The Story of Watchman Nee*, pp. 196, 197. Watchman Nee, the great Chinese evangelist, gave this thought while in prison during wartime.

CHAPTER XV

1. Horst, S., *Mennonites in the Confederacy*, p. 91. There were arrests made in August and October of 1863.

2. Poe, C., *True Tales of the South at War*, pp. 71-72. This is based on an incident told in the above book, related by Mrs. Troy L. Moran (Collensville, Va.) about her great-great-grandparents.

CHAPTER XVI

1. My grandmother's bishop, Daniel Mast, gave this response to an accusation given by a fellow-church member.

2. Marshall M. Brice gives a detailed account of the Battle of Piedmont in his book, *Conquest of a Valley*.

CHAPTER XVII

1. Brice, M., *Conquest of a Valley*, p. 129. Quote from *The Vindicator*, a Staunton newspaper, article by editor W. H. H. Lynn, written during the summer of 1864.

2. Horst, *Mennonites in the Confederacy*, p. 92. This occurred on June 15, 1864.

3. Based on an account of Cornelia McDonald's son captured during David Hunter's raid on Lexington and told in her book, *A Diary With Reminiscences . . .*

4. Brunk, H., *History of Mennonites in Va.*, p. 405. In the list of church members in the 1860s Sarah Wright is mentioned as the one who swept the meetinghouse.

5. Horst, *Mennonites in the Confederacy*, pp. 88, 92, 94.

6. Young, T. A., ed., Time-Life book, *The Shenandoah in Flames*, p. 137. Sheridan reported the razing of 2,000 barns, 120 mills, and the destruction of ½ million bushels of wheat. Fifty thousand head of animals were estimated taken. One official commented that many families were left without any means to live, not even firewood.

7. Horst, *Mennonites* . . . , p. 104. The same day Sheridan gave out his message, a number of families whose houses had been burned, loaded up and traveled as far as Harrisonburg. Of the more than 400 refugee wagons, most were Dunkard, some Mennonite, and a large number of 16-17-year-old boys.

8. This blessing, by M. Louise Haskins, was found on a New Year's card. (Quoted with slight variation.)

CHAPTER XVIII

1. Horst, *Mennonites* . . . , p. 106. The immense wagon train of over 1,600 wagons included army conveyances and Federal troops driving livestock rounded up during the burnings. Starting out on October 6, it stretched out for 16 miles.

2. Young, ed., *The Shenandoah in Flames*, pp. 137-9; 158. Angered by the vast destruction wreaked by the Federal army, Confederate General Jubal Early followed hard on their heels. Two days after the main train of refugees reached Martinsburg, a battle occurred at Cedar Creek. An early Confederate victory was overridden by a strong Federal comeback, and by the next evening (October 20), Early's army was completely defeated. The Valley Campaign was over.

CHAPTER XX

1. Campbell, E., *Before Freedom Came*, p. 52. Quoting George P. Rawick, Jan Hillegas and Ken

Lawrence, *The American Slave: A Composite Autobiography,* Supplement Series I (Westport, Conn., 1977). Mississippi, Vol. 6: part 1, p. 243.

2. Based on Martha Gay Masterson's experience as a young girl in her book, *One Woman's West.*

3. Pitts, L. B.; Glenn, M.; Walters, L.; eds., *Singing Our Way,* p. 60. "Quiet Is the Night" is an old rhyme set to music by Henry M. Halvorson.

4. The ironic truth (noted by N. C.'s governor in 1865) was, that while many soldiers suffered by want of hunger, hundreds of thousands of bushels of grain sat rotting at Southern railroad depots because of poor transportation.

CHAPTER XXI

1. Brunk, *History of Mennonites in Va.,* pp. 173-175. Includes a list of 20 war claims posted in the "Rockingham Register" on March 24, 1865 for a portion of District 8 of Rockingham County. Total claims came to $33,725.

Bibliography

Bacon, Margaret H., *The Quiet Rebels—The Story of the Quakers in America*, New Society Publishers, 1985.

Barrick, Mac E. (ed.), *German and American Folklore*, August House/Little Rock Publishers, Arkansas, 1987.

Bell, Irvin Wiley, *They Who Fought Here*, Bonanza Books, New York, 1959.

Bradburn, John, *An English Combatant, Battlefields of the South*, reprint edition, Time-Life Books, New York, 1984.

Brice, Marshall M., *Conquest of a Valley*, University Press of Virginia, Charlottesville, Va., 1965.

Brunk, Harry A., *History of Mennonites in Virginia*, Vol. 1, McClure Printing Co. Inc., Staunton, Va., 1972.

Campbell, Edward D.C. Jr. (ed.), *Before Freedom Came*, Museum of the Confederacy, Richmond, Va., 1991.

Catton, Bruce, *Gettysburg: The Final Fury*, Doubleday Co. Inc., New York, 1974.

Cooper, Alonzo, *In and Out of Rebel Prisons*, reprint edition, Time-Life Books, Oswego, N.Y., 1983.

Coulling, Mary, *The Lee Girls*, John F. Blair Pub., Winston-Salem, N.C., 1987.

Craighill, E.A., *Confederate Surgeon*, reprint edition, H.E. Howard, Inc., Lynchburg, Va., 1989.

Davis, Julia, *The Shenandoah*, Farrar & Rinehart, Inc., New York, 1945.

Davis, William C. (ed.), *Touched by Fire, Vol. 1, A Photographic Portrait of the Civil War*, Little, Brown, & Co., Boston, 1985.

Driver, Robert Jr., *52nd Virginia Infantry*, H.E. Howard, Inc., Lynchburg, Va., 1986.

————, *The Staunton Artillery*, H.E. Howard, Inc., Lynchburg, Va., 1988.

Editors of Time-Life Books, *Decoying the Yanks*, Time-Life Books, Alexandria, Va.,1984.

————, *The Shenandoah in Flames*, Time-Life Books, Alexandria, Va., 1987.

Fleet, Betsy, and John Fuller (eds.), *Green Mont*, reprint edition, University of Virginia, Charlottesville, Va., 1962.

Gordon, George (Lord Byron), *Poems of Byron*, reprint edition, Oxford University Press, England, 1923.

Griess, Thomas E. (series ed.), *Atlas for the American Civil War*, Avery Publishing Group, Inc., N.J., 1986.

Harris, Joel Chandler, *Uncle Remus, His Songs and His Sayings*, reprint edition, Esther LaRose Harris, New York, 1921.

Hess, Nancy B., *The Heartland, Rockingham County*, Park View Press, Harrisonburg, Va., 1976.

Hitchcock, Susan T., *Gather Ye Wild Things*, Harper and Row Publishing, N.Y., 1980.

Horst, Samuel, *Mennonites in the Confederacy*, Herald Press, Scottdale, Pennsylvania, 1967.

Houck, Peter W., *A Prototype of a Confederate Hospital Center in Lynchburg, Va.*, Marwick House Publishers, 1986.

Johnson, Jerry M., *Down Home Ways*, Greenwich House, New York, 1978.

Kercheval, Samuel, *History of the Valley of Va.*, 4th edition, Shenandoah Publishing House, Strausburg, Va., 1925.

Kinnear, Angus, *Against the Tide, the Story of Watchman Nee*, Tyndale House Publishers, Wheaton, Ill., 1978.

Kless, Fredric, *The Pennsylvania Dutch*, The MacMillan Co, New York, 1950.

Masterson, Martha Gay, *One Woman's West*, reprint edition, Butte Press, 1986.

McDonald, Cornelia and Hunter McDonald (eds.), *A Diary with Reminiscences of the War and Refugees Life in the Shenandoah Valley*, reprint edition, Cullen & Ghatner, Nashville, Tn., 1935.

Miller, Francis T., *Poetry and Eloquence of the Civil War*, Castle Books, N.Y., 1957.

Moore, Edward, *The Story of a Cannoneer under Stonewall Jackson*, reprint edition, Time-Life Books, 1983.

Pember, Phoebe Y., *A Southern Woman's Story, Life in Confederate Richmond*, reprint edition, McCowat Mercer Press, Inc., Jackson, Tn. 1959.

Pittenger, William, *Daring and Suffering*, reprint edition, Time-Life Books, 1982.

Pitts, Lilla B, Mabelle Glenn, and Lorrain Watters, *Singing Our Way*, Ginn and Company, Boston, 1949.

Poe, Clarence, *True Tales of the South at War*, University of North Carolina Press, 1961.

Reinbaugh, Lowell, *33rd Virginia Infantry*, H.E. Howard, Inc. Lynchburg, Va., 1987.

Schultz, Kathleen, *Create Your Own Natural Dyes*, Sterling Publishing Company, Inc., N.Y., 1975.

Straubing, Harold E., *Civil War Eyewitness Reports*, Archon Books, Hamden, Conn., 1985.

Tapert, Annette (ed.), *The Brother's War, Civil War Letters*, Time-Life Books, 1988.

Waddel, Joshua A., *Annals of Augusta County 1726-1871*, reprint edition, C.J. Carrier Co., Harrisonburg, Va., 1972.

Ward, Evelyn D., *The Children of Bladensfield*, Viking Press, N.Y., 1978.

Washington, Booker T., *Up From Slavery*, reprint edition, Doubleday, Garden City, N.Y., 1963.

Wayland, John W., *Art Folio of the Shenandoah Valley*, The McClure Co. Inc., Staunton, Va., 1924.

——, *History of Rockingham County*, Ruebush-Elkins Co., Dayton, Va., 1912.

Wigginton, Eliot (ed.), *The Foxfire Book*, Doubleday, Garden City, N.Y., 1972.

——, *Foxfire II*, Anchor Press/Doubleday, Garden City, N.Y., 1973.

————, *Foxfire III*, Anchor Press/Doubleday, Garden City, N.Y., 1975.

Williamson, James J., *Mosby's Rangers*, reprint edition, James J. Williamson, N.Y., 1895.

Wilson, Howard, *The Tinkling Spring—Headwater of Freedom, A study of the church and her people 1732-1952*, Garret and Massie, Richmond, Va., 1954.

Wintz, William D. (ed.), *Civil War Memoirs of Two Rebel Sisters*, Pictorial Histories Publishing Co., Charleston, West Virginia, 1989.

Young, Agatha, *The Women and the Crisis*, Am. Book-Stratford Press, Inc., N.Y., 1959.

Other Sources

"Civil War," *The World Book Encyclopedia*, 1984, vol. 4, pp. 472-493.

"Food From the 1880's" *Farmers and Housekeepers Cyclopedia*, New York, published 1888, reprint edition, 1977.

Hartman, Peter, "A Stand was Taken," *Family Life*, (April, 1970), pp. 26-28.

————, "A Stand was Taken, part 2," *Family Life*, (May, 1970), p. 26.

Lester, Janice K., "The Woman Who Would Not Tell," *Reader's Digest*, (December, 1968), pp. 95-99.

"The Surrender of Lee," *The New York Herald*, (April 3-10, 1865), reprint edition, A compilation

of excerpts and maps from the week of Lee's surrender.

Walking Tours of Historic Staunton, Va. (Brochure)
Historic Staunton Foundation, 1986.

Yoder, Mary E., "Amish Settlers and the Civil War,"
Christian Living, (Jan. 1962), pp. 28, 29, 39-40.

Christian Light Publications, Inc., is a nonprofit, conservative Mennonite publishing company providing Christ-centered, Biblical literature including books, Gospel tracts, Sunday school materials, summer Bible school materials, and a full curriculum for Christian day schools and home-schools.

For more information about the ministry of CLP or its publications, or for spiritual help, please contact us at:

Christian Light Publications, Inc.
P. O. Box 1212
Harrisonburg, VA 22803-1212

Telephone—540-434-0768
Fax—540-433-8896
E-mail—info@clp.org